Praise for *THE SIXTH FLEET* novels
by Captain David E. Meadows

"Rip-snorting, realistic action-adventure from a man who has been there. David Meadows is the real thing."
—Stephen Coonts, *New York Times* bestselling author of *Flight of the Intruder*

"An absorbing, compelling look at America's future place in the world. It's visionary, and scary. Great battle scenes, believable heroes, plus villains you'll love to hate."
—Joe Buff, author of *Deep Sound Channel*, *Thunder in the Deep*, and *Crush Depth*

"If you enjoy a well-told tale of action and adventure, you will love David Meadows's series, *The Sixth Fleet*. Not only does the author know his subject but [his] fiction could readily become fact. These books should be read by every senator and congressman in our government so that the scenarios therein do not become history."
—John Tegler, syndicated talk show host of *Capital Conversation*

"Easily on a par with Tom Clancy, *The Sixth Fleet* provides an awesomely prescient picture of the U.S. Navy at war with terrorism and those who support it. It has the unmistakable ring of truth and accuracy, which only an insider can provide. In the aftermath of September 11, this is not just a good read, but an essential one."
—Milos Stankovic, author of *Trusted Mole*

"Meadows will have you turning pages and thinking new thoughts."
—Newt Gingrich, Former Speaker of the House

JOINT TASK FORCE
FORCE
FRANCE

DAVID E. MEADOWS

BERKLEY BOOKS, NEW YORK

JOINT TASK FORCE: FRANCE

A Berkley Book / published by arrangement with the author

PRINTING HISTORY
Berkley edition / September 2004

ISBN: 0-425-19799-9

BERKLEY®
Berkley Books are published by The Berkley Publishing Group, a division of Penguin Group (USA) Inc., 375 Hudson Street, New York, New York 10014.
BERKLEY and the "B" design are trademarks belonging to Penguin Group (USA) Inc.

PRINTED IN THE UNITED STATES OF AMERICA

10 9 8 7 6 5 4 3 2 1

To my United States Navy Seabees

ACKNOWLEDGMENTS

It is impossible to thank everyone who provided technical advice on and support of this and other novels. My thanks for those who visited http://www.sixthfleet.com and provided comments. I do read each email personally, and my goal is to respond to each of them.

I do appreciate the encouragement from the authors and readers who honor me by reading and providing reviews on my books—such as Stephen Coonts, W.E.B. Griffin, Joe Buff, Robert Gandt, Victoria Taylor-Murray, and other fellow authors. I wish I could express my personal thanks to each one of you. Many of you offered good advice, all of which I considered. Many were kind enough to encourage, provide technical guidance, or many times just answer questions unique to their professional skills and qualifications. If I have inadvertently missed some of you, I apologize, but my individual thanks to LtCol Scott Heckert-USMC, 'Storming' Normand; retired reservist Seabee chief, Ms. Sharon Reinke, Mr. Art Horn, LtCol Randy Coats-USAF, LCDR Nancy Mendonca, CDR Scott Fish (helicopter warrior), Mr. Ed Brumit, Maj Howard Walton-USMC, and a Royal Navy supporter-Stephen Barnett. My continued thanks to Mr. Tom Colgan for his editorial support and to his able right-hand person, Ms. Samantha Mandor.

While I have named a few for their technical advice, rest assured that any and all technical errors or mistakes in this novel are strictly those of the author who many times wanders in his own world.

David E. Meadows

CHAPTER 1

"I KNOW WHAT YOU'RE DOING," BILL HAMPSHIRE WHIS-
pered into Kurt Vernigan's ear.

Kurt tried to push his chair away from the desk, but
Hampshire had his leg against it, wedging him against the
gray metal government desk. A bead of sweat broke out on
his forehead. "What do—"

"What do I mean?" Hampshire laughed and pushed his
leg hard against the chair. "You know what I mean. You
don't think I haven't been watching you, you fat, ugly piece
of shit?"

Kurt placed both hands on the edge of the desk and
pushed. It was hard to breathe. The desk edge had caught
under the bulk of his stomach and pushed it upward into his
diaphragm, obstructing Kurt's ability to take full breaths.

Hampshire laughed. "I wouldn't make too much noise,
asshole," he purred into Kurt's ear. "These cubicles don't
hide noise too well, and you just might cause others to come
over to see what in the hell is going on. When that happens,
I'm going to be one hell of a hero, and you, my fine smelly,
ugly, sweaty pig of a friend, are going to be hauled off in
handcuffs. Even your mother will disown you."

Kurt felt the pressure against the chair ease, but his stomach was still pressing against his lungs. Little white spots danced around his vision.

"What do you want?" he asked, thinking, *How could he know? How could anyone know? I've been too careful. I've done everything I was told to do. What if I pass out—*

"What does any nice-looking, underpaid bachelor in Washington, D.C. want? I want money, and I don't mean a check. I want cold hard cash, and I want it now."

Kurt started to turn his head. A slight slap against the back of his head stopped him. The number of lights dancing in front of his eyes increased.

"Don't turn around. Just hand me the cash."

"I can't breathe."

"I don't care."

"And, I don't have any money."

Hampshire laughed and kicked the chair, pushing it tighter against the desk. "I was in the credit union in the basement today, asshole. I overheard the teller talking to her supervisor. I bet it surprised the shit out of you when you discovered the credit union has a cash limit of five thousand dollars a day. I was surprised. I was even more surprised when I heard the supervisor say some bullshit thing about you buying a house and that today was the last day you planned on withdrawing five thousand because you had withdrawn the same amount for four days in a row."

"I *am* buying a house," Kurt said through clenched teeth. He put his hands against the desk and pushed. It moved an inch before Hampshire put his full weight against the back and pushed.

"I'd quit that, my asshole friend, unless you want to find your body chopped in half."

"But, I can't breathe."

"You may be buying a house, Kurt, but you and I both know it won't be in the good old United States. I guess the question I have is, in how many banks or credit unions do you have access to such money? You know what I think, Kurt, and I've laid awake at night for two weeks thinking about it ever since—"

"What do you want, Bill?"

Smoker's breath rolled across Kurt's nostrils as Hampshire, close to his ear, breathed softly, "I want the five grand you took today and the five grand you'll withdraw tomorrow." The stale smoky breath of someone with years of the habit enveloped Kurt's head. He thought, *How can he know?* He shook his head, trying to draw fresh air through his mouth, his breath coming in short, quick draughts.

"Tomorrow's Saturday," Kurt gasped out.

"Keep your voice down," Hampshire ordered. He slapped Kurt lightly across the back of his neck and laughed. "Tomorrow, Vernigan, I want ten thousand more on top of the five you're going to give me now. When I get that, you'll have no more problems with me. I will *toddle* back down to my dark little hole in System Administration, pull a chair out, and ignore the snoopers on the servers while I count this money. Ignore them when they beep to tell me that someone is downloading classified data. Ignore the flashing red light when someone has downloaded the same classified data to an unclassified disc several times. I may even do you a favor and erase the historical file over the weekend. That way you'd have no digital evidence of what you're doing or what you've done. Just think of this small token payment as insurance."

The pressure against his chair back relaxed completely. He pushed away from the desk, opening up a few inches. Kurt took several deep breaths. His stomach settled back over his beltline, freeing his lungs. Air had never tasted better. Only a few seconds passed and the white lights dancing across his vision disappeared.

The smoky envelope rolled across his nostrils again. His stomach turned at the horrid air he knew was filling his lungs. Kurt wanted to wash his hands, wash his face.

"So, give me the money before your teammates up here on the third floor return from lunch or pounding the pavement or snatching a little fuck in some out-of-the-way closet."

Hampshire's arm hit Kurt's shoulder and his hand extended in front of Kurt, palm up and opened. "Just slap that money right there, my friend, and you've got a service you never expected to have."

His handler had warned Kurt something like this might happen. He had discounted it. Kurt was smart. Smart to the point of arrogance, and arrogance was the worse kind of stupidity. It never occurred to Kurt that someone as technogeek as this Hampshire fellow would figure out what he was doing. If anything was good about this, it was the fact that by tonight Kurt would be on an aircraft for the Caribbean where he would pick up the retainer they had been stashing in a marked bank account only he knew about. But, he wasn't going to leave his own money—money he had slaved and saved for over twenty years of faithful— *well, maybe faithful was too strong a word*—service to his country.

"I'm waiting," Hampshire said, wiggling his fingers several times and then snapping them once. "Give it up, Vernigan."

"Why are you doing this here? Don't you think it's a little dangerous to both of us?"

The breath rolled down from above. *This must be what hell is like,* Kurt thought. Millions and millions of hardcore smokers blowing their breath in your face.

"Yeah, I thought about following you home and doing this there, but this is my turf; at home you might feel a tinge of braveness that would usually be completely out of character for a milk-toast asshole such as yourself."

Think, Kurt told himself. If he handed over the five thousand he had on him, he could still take the forty-seven thousand he had drawn out. Think of it as a fee for a job well done. But, decades of scrimping and saving overrode the logic of giving the man the money, agreeing to meet him tomorrow with more, and forgetting about it. That other money waiting for him in Aruba was different from the money he had saved over the years. Maybe deep down inside of Kurt Vernigan, a moral dilemma was surfacing between the honest money earned through years of hard work and the easy tainted money given for betraying one's country.

"Kurt! I'm waiting."

"I can't give it to you here."

"Why not?"

"It's in a money belt around my waist, and to get to it, I have to unbuckle my pants."

"Unbuckle them here and get the money," Hampshire snarled.

"It's not that simple. The zipper is against my skin, under my t-shirt," he lied, his mind searching for a way out. Kurt had no intention to give the man money. His handler had also told him what he would have to do if someone discovered what was going on. It was another thing Kurt had dismissed, but here it was, wrapping its evil breath around his head.

"Then, I think we'll have to go somewhere more discreet."

Kurt licked his lips. They were awfully dry.

Hampshire pulled the chair back. Kurt's hands rested on the desk drawer, unintentionally opening it a few inches when Hampshire had pulled. Without thinking, he grabbed the letter opener in his pudgy hand.

"Get up," Hampshire said.

Kurt turned his head. The man had moved a couple of feet back. He glanced down at the letter opener, grabbed it with two fingers, and slid the silver instrument up his sleeve. Then he stood.

Vernigan was a foot shorter than the information professional who stood in front of him, but he easily outweighed the man. The arms emerging from the short-sleeve shirt were wiry, and a lone tattoo on the upper left arm was faded such that Kurt couldn't make out what it was. In that instant, Kurt knew Hampshire saw him as a cash cow to be milked forever. If he knew Kurt had no intention of being around after tonight, there was no telling what he would do. Like men did all the time when they saw a rainbow they had slip away into the clouds, Hampshire would rant and rave and then turn him in because there were always fame and glory for those who ratted out a traitor. The feel of the letter opener pressed against the naked skin of his wrist gave Kurt a confidence he lacked while trapped against his desk.

"There's no one left on the floor above," Hampshire said. "They're done for today. The contractor sends them home before noon on Friday—part of his cost-saving measures."

"Okay," Kurt said, nodding his head. "Lead the way."

Hampshire grinned. "No, I don't think so. We'll walk together with you slightly ahead. While I know you're a coward and a fat slob, I'd hate for you to try something stupid." He leaned down slightly, his face only a couple of inches from Kurt's. It was almost as if Kurt could see the roiling gases of age-old smoke shooting out from the man's lips as he said, "And, with your good luck, my friend, you'll be back at your desk in minutes."

KURT HATED STAIRS. GOING DOWN WASN'T SO BAD, BUT going up brought shortness of breath, causing him to rest after each floor. Of course, the first two floors he could always make, but the third brought aching muscles screaming from his legs, and by the fourth, between the leg pain and shortness of breath, Kurt always had to stop for a few minutes. Thankfully, the cleaning closet where this Hampshire fellow was taking him was only one floor above. The fourth floor was nearly empty in the old Navy Annex of Arlington. There were no permanent people assigned to the floor. The only ones who moved through the empty corridors of this floor were the cleaning people and the small cadre of contractors who had been working for years to remove asbestos from the World War II walls and ceilings.

If the man's breath didn't kill him, the small fibers floating in the air would. Kurt covered his mouth with his left hand as he opened the door to the unoccupied floor. Faint muscle pain from hurrying up the stairs throbbed slightly, but he had more important things on which to focus his attention.

Kurt stopped inside the corridor. Hampshire walked up beside him, the man's head turning back and forth, looking up and down the corridor, making sure they were alone. He had a long neck with a sharp Adam's apple a couple of inches beneath an even sharper chin. *I'm being robbed by the Ichabod Crane of techno-geeks,* Kurt thought. Hampshire pulled a handkerchief from his back pocket. Kurt noticed the green and brown stains on the rumpled piece of cloth and cringed when the man wiped his face with it. *Yes, I'm in hell.*

The handkerchief still in his hand, Hampshire grabbed Kurt's arm. "Come on, you flabby piece of shit."

Kurt jerked his arm away, not in a fit of bravery, but in a heightened state of dread at the thought of the handkerchief touching the sleeve of his shirt.

Hampshire's mouth dropped and his eyes narrowed. "What the—"

"I'm coming," Kurt said quickly. He glanced at his shirt, imagining month-old stains from the man's filthy rag of a handkerchief jumping onto his clean shirt. He washed and pressed his shirts daily. There was no cause for any person to be dirty, to be untidy.

Hampshire relaxed. He motioned to Kurt. "Then, come on. I want to get this over with as much as you."

Halfway down the corridor, Hampshire stopped in front of a solid door, green flakes of old paint warped along the sides, and near the bottom of the door a small hole had been chewed, probably by the multitudes of mice that inherited the building when the lights went out each night. Here on the fourth floor, they had more time for their destruction.

Hampshire twisted the doorknob. The door swung open easily. A set of three glazed windows on the far side provided light to the room. A set of unshielded fluorescent lights hung in the center of the room by a single chain, the electric cord weaved in and out through each link. Kurt reached for the light switch on the wall.

"Don't touch that!" Hampshire demanded.

Kurt quickly removed his hand.

"I don't want to see any more of your body than I have to."

Kurt shuffled toward the man.

"And no need to get too close either."

I need to get closer, my evil friend.

"Unbutton those pants and get me my money."

Your money! It's my money. Money I've earned and I intend to keep, Kurt thought. Anger welled up inside of him. He reached for his belt and pulled the end out from the buckle. He placed his right foot forward. Hampshire was two feet from him. Kurt nearly smiled as the man shifted several inches to the right—Kurt's movement hid the belt buckle, and Hampshire didn't want to miss a thing.

Kurt's stomach rolled when he saw Hampshire lick his lips.

Kurt pulled the belt back, letting the latch clear the hole. Hampshire leaned closer.

The letter opener slid down, the tip touching the end of Kurt's middle finger. His handler had spent a few minutes with Kurt teaching him how do this with a knife. The knife had already been firmly clasped in his hand at the time, and Kurt had only done the exercise because the man was paying him mega bucks for the information he was providing.

He dropped his right hand, his left hand pushed his stomach up away from the waistline, and he unbuttoned the top of his dark trousers. Hampshire was watching Kurt's waistline. Kurt had numerous sets of work trousers, as he called them, but they were all either dark blue or black. Dark blue and black were the colors of a successful government employee, he had always thought.

Hampshire watched Kurt's waistline, waiting for the

sight of a money belt that didn't exist, licking his lips lightly like an expectant grammar school kid waiting for candy to be pushed across the counter to him.

The letter opener slid further down until it was in his palm. Kurt gripped the handle, taking a deep breath at the same time.

Hampshire looked up at his face. "What's the matter, asshole. Scared? Don't be. I'm not interested in killing someone who's going to meet me tomorrow with another fifteen thousand dollars."

"You said ten," Kurt blurted, his eyes wide.

Hampshire laughed, tilting his head back.

Kurt shoved the letter opener up, toward the exposed neck of the laughing devil. He shifted his entire two hundred and eighty pounds onto his right leg, putting every bit of energy that fear could produce behind the flashing letter opener.

The silver tip entered Hampshire's neck just above his Adam's apple. It traveled through the skin and into the throat, stopping a half-inch shy of the spine.

Kurt dropped his hand. The flat end, with a small hole for hanging it up in your cubicle that only Mary Smith ever used, protruded from Hampshire's neck, blood spurting around it. Kurt took a few steps back as Hampshire stumbled around the small office, his hands flailing at the letter opener, a gurgling sound—*probably blood filling his throat,* thought Kurt, surprised at his own lack of emotion and impressed with his ability to observe scientifically the man drowning in his own blood.

Hampshire fell to his knees. At that moment, he looked up, his eyes pleading with Kurt. Hampshire's right hand slapped a couple of times on the letter opener.

Kurt shifted closer to the door.

Hampshire gurgled toward Kurt.

"Hampshire," Kurt said softly. He reached up, quickly unbuttoned his shirt, and pulled it apart. "Fat boy doesn't have a money belt." He laughed, staring at Hampshire's eyes. He had never killed anyone. A year ago if someone had told him he was capable of killing someone he would have laughed. He wasn't one of those military types who wandered the halls of the Navy Annex and the Pentagon, showing their notches to each other, scoring the number of kills against their ranks.

Hampshire's eyes were losing their sparkle. Kurt had read of this and now he was going to see it. Hampshire's hand fell by his side and his torso started a slow fall forward. Kurt watched, disappointed that he didn't see the last of the light disappear from the eyes.

The body thudded when it hit the floor, dust swirls rising around the head and chest. *For a cleaning room, it sure is dirty.* Kurt bit his lower lip, mentally patting himself on the back for being so calm. He took a deep breath and waited. He didn't move forward to check the body and make sure Hampshire was dead. Kurt watched the chest, satisfied it wasn't moving up and down, satisfied the man wasn't still breathing. He was curiously proud of his actions. He could stand in the center courtyard of the Pentagon now and when the senior officer Ground Zero Cigar Club made their parade every few days with their halo of smoke, he could hold up one finger. They wouldn't know what it was about, but it didn't matter, because it wasn't going to happen. He was going to be sunning himself on some beach with a couple of paid-for escorts taking care of his every whim.

The dust settled around Hampshire, providing a skin over the pool of blood that had spread around the dead man's head. Kurt worried for a fraction of a second what would happen if the blood soaked through the floor and dripped on some unsuspecting young woman working intently on the floor below. Then, he quit worrying. Even if it did, it would take more time than was remaining in the day for the blood to work its way through the tile, the insulation, and whatever else existed between floors.

Kurt opened the door, stepped into the silent hallway, and pulled the door shut behind him. It'll be Monday before they find the body.

* * *

"KURT!"

He nearly dropped the CD teetering on the edge of his classified computer. Kurt glanced over the top of the cubicle wall at the clock, his lower lip pushed against the upper. He would have jumped regardless of the fact that a dead body, which he created, lay lifeless less than a hundred yards from where he sat.

The shout came from the direction of the exit door. Four-thirty, the clock read. *Time really flies when you're having fun,* he thought sarcastically. He laughed. *What a bunch of fools.*

Kurt placed the CD alongside the keyboard, covering it with his left hand while his right searched the drawer for a plastic sleeve.

Leave it to his fellow government workers to beat the door down in a mad rush to climb into cars so they could idle in gridlock on the Washington, D.C. beltways. At least, even on his last day of government service, he was sensible enough to use public transportation.

Kurt started to stand to glance over the six-foot cubicle wall to see if the colonel was in his office, but his hips caught on the arms of the chair. Rather than exhaust energy wiggling free, he told himself, *What the hell. Why should I worry about someone who I will never see again? Someone who will never know that thanks to his encouragement, I've made a fortune that will keep me happy for the rest of my life.*

Kurt had seen military officers come and go in the Missile Research Defense Agency—Mister DA, as the yuppie assholes coming into government service liked to call it. Mister DA. It was enough to make him throw up every time he heard it used.

He tried to listen to any noise coming from the direction of the colonel's office. He thought about looking again. It wouldn't be hard to see if the man was still here, but he knew that he was without verifying it. This military leader had a sharper edge on his "A-type" personality than most. It was probably titanium-tipped, fueled by a growing ego and tenacious ambition to have so many stars on his shoulders that he'd need helpers to hold him up from the weight.

This colonel was so hell-bent on the Air Force recognizing his dedication with a one-star rank, he rode those beneath him relentlessly. *"Team, I'm disappointed. Where are those statistics I asked for earlier? It's been nearly thirty minutes, so get the lead out of your asses and get them to me. We don't want to disappoint the boss."* What a crock of sh—well, it was a crock full. The only team was me, myself, and I. Everyone else was a cog in the man's ambition for stardom. Kurt laughed. *Stardom—I've made a pun and didn't even know it.*

No, Colonel Darnell—*of the Darnells of Calvert County, home of the jumping frogs*—wouldn't be heading out the door, Kurt thought. He wondered for a moment where the colonel really came from. If he knew, he'd send the town a condolence note when he got to Aruba.

Kurt knew Darnell would stay in the office until the summer sun set. The only time the man wasn't at his desk or having his nose halfway up some superior's mile-wide sphincter canyon was when he was taking his two-hour PT/lunch break, which was very fortuitous today.

No, Darnell never left early on Friday. Friday was a chance to excel for his superiors. While his peers were turning off their computers and gathering up their stuff for a weekend home with their families, Darnell would be sending out a bunch of email updates to his superiors and to their superiors. Make yourself look good by making others look bad—another chapter in the bestselling Washington management book.

Kurt pulled the protective sleeve from the back of his desk drawer, smiled when he noticed the empty spot where he kept his letter opener, and wondered how long it would take authorities to match that thing in Hampshire's neck with his fingerprints. He'd give them until Tuesday, if they were really good.

He shut the drawer. Monday was going to be a golden day for him.

Kurt heard a door open from the direction of Colonel Darnell's office. That proved it for him. Darnell was the only one in this maze of cubicles who had a door to the glass-walled office located in the middle of the maze. If you wandered through the maze from one end to the other, eventually you'd stumble into the walled kingdom of Darnell, a dark place of evil for those pure of heart to avoid.

Yeah, Monday, when those wearing the golden rings Darnell worshipped and desired read the Colonel's emails, they would see the time on them and realize how late Darnell had worked on Friday. They'd respond with praise disguised as concern over him working so late. Kurt had nearly gagged from the number of times general officers had mentioned their concern over Darnell's late hours, never asking how many people were forced to ignore their own work to make him look good.

No, for Kurt, give him an old-timer who had been around the block a few times with no illusions about making flag—about chasing those stars. They understood. They knew the game and they appreciated the government service personnel who slaved daily in the service of their country. But, those military "A-type" personalities and their "holier than thou" attitude pissed him off. The military people could leave anytime they wanted. They didn't have to stay late. They didn't need to come in early, but not Darnell. He did both and he expected those serving him—you were never working *with* Darnell, you worked *for* Darnell—to do the same, except Fridays. Friday was the man's day for his career, not that the other days weren't either. However, Friday was his chance to stand out. And it looked better if he was by himself when he worked, in the event one of those flag officers dropped by unexpectedly.

Kurt saw the folder in his inbox. Any other day he would have signed it earlier and hand-carried it to the office manager—a fancy name given to secretaries today. Kurt pulled the folder stamped with the words "Time Card" on it, opened it, saw the familiar document, and without scrutinizing it closely as he normally would to make sure they weren't screwing him out of his pay, he signed it and slid it into the outbox. He did this knowing that no one ever picked up things from your outbox. They'd throw things into your inbox, but the outbox was your responsibility.

The time card folder in the outbox would lay undisturbed until the Criminal Investigation Division—the notorious CID—showed up to crawl over his stuff. Military personnel didn't have to put in time documents. You might call them salaried employees. So whether they were doing one-upmanship on number of kills or jogging umpteen thousand miles, they never documented their hours.

The Department of Defense even had career plans for military brethren and sisters, though civilians were like serfs of the Middle Ages. Didn't need a career plan for serfs. They're fodder to do menial labor while political appointees and military members dance to ever-changing agendas reverberating through the halls of the Pentagon. He taped closed the plastic sleeve over the CD and laid it on top of the first one. His last delivery and upstairs his departing gift to his fellow loyal citizens whose sense of patriotism kept them at their monotonous tasks day-in and day-out.

Kurt should have been a Senior Executive Service. And he would have, too, under the Navy captain that preceded Darnell. But Darnell took an instant dislike to him. Kurt knew what it was. He'd seen it too many times in the eyes of others. He grabbed his love handles and jingled them. More like group-sex handles, he told himself. Darnell hated him because he was fat. But Kurt knew his professional capabilities. He hadn't been placed in charge of the Air Force laser weapons program because he was incompetent.

Like rough weather, captains came and went, but he and other government employees stoically remained to carry on the work of the Department. He could wait Darnell out, but his last government appraisal had damned his professionalism. Called him incompetent. Not in those words—supervisors never wrote anything concrete. What they did was praise your work and in the little-used section of the appraisal where the supervisor identified areas for improvement—that's where you found the dirt.

"Kurt! You coming?"

You still here, Thomas? he asked of himself. Kurt ignored the question shouted from near the exit door of their work area. Friday afternoon drink-a-thons at the Pentagon City complex across the beltway weren't his thing. He glanced over his shoulder at the beam that ran the length of the huge room at the Navy Annex. Black blocked letters identified the room as belonging to the Missile Research Defense Agency. You could still read the title, Ballistic Missile Defense Office, where the workers had partially removed the letters when BMDO moved to new quarters.

His computer beeped, drawing his attention. The words "download complete" blinked on the screen. He ejected the third CD and quickly replaced it with a fourth.

Kurt raised the CD to his lips and kissed it. He turned it side to side, smiling at the markings that showed this to be an unclassified CD. This was it. This was his passport to getting the hell out of here and enjoying the remaining years of his life. *Let's see,* he said to himself, *I'm fifty-four now; my father died when he was seventy-four. My grandmother at seventy-five. I still have another twenty years of life, if genetics are any indication.*

The CRT showed his download nearly complete. This fourth one would be quick. It only held the decoding sequences for the first two CDs. He waved the CD in his hand and glanced at the third CD. The third CD held supplemental database material, but this fourth CD held the programmatic key. You could play all day with this data, but without the programmatic key it wouldn't make a lick of sense to the viewer. This fourth CD opened the first two CDs, and, once opened, the data on the third CD could easily be retrieved.

Kurt pulled his handkerchief out and wiped the sweat from his forehead. He looked at the handkerchief. Nice, white, and clear. Put into his trousers this morning freshly folded from the dryer. He shuddered a couple of times, thinking of the dead man's handkerchief. Couldn't really call it a handkerchief—more a rag. Probably used it to check the oil in his car between blowing his nose in it or stuffing it in his ear to screw the wax out.

He wiped his forehead again. He shouldn't be sweating. If he was going to be nervous, shoving that letter opener through the man's neck would have been cause for sweating. *It did go in easily for such a blunt instrument. The air conditioning must be broken,* he thought.

He grinned for a moment, but only for a moment. Tonight was the night. He lifted the roll of fat—*group-sex handles*—hanging over his beltline, felt the sweaty ring around his waist. Cool air rolled across the wet line. A personal trainer! That's what he would get when—

By Monday, his co-workers would be shouting his name, but it would be shouts wondering where in the hell he had disappeared. No one suspects anyone of anything in Washington until it's too late. Then, that old index finger swings a 360, pointing at anyone or anything to shift the focus away. *Heat on you is heat off me.*

He knew how the serfs in the fields would react. He was one. One of those government employees who arrived on time every day—did their jobs—filled out their time cards so everyone looking over everyone else's shoulder could make sure no one was cheating—and then around four-thirty dragged their sorry asses from the buildings to head home to the average American family of two and a half children. What ever happened to the other half a child? Some were like the asshole shouting his name, searching for something to do until the beltway cleared. Nope; the government servants were truly the hidden masses among the self-proclaimed heroes of the nation's capital.

"Hey!"

Kurt jumped.

"You hear me shouting your name, Kurt? You going to stay late again?" Tom Brass asked, leaning around the opening to Kurt Vernigan's cubicle.

Kurt dropped the CD. Like a dropped coin, the CD rolled across the tight carpet, curving in its trajectory to wobble a few inches before falling at the feet of Brass.

Brass laughed, bent over, and scooped it up. "Boy, you're sure jumpy lately." He stepped fully into the cubicle and tossed Kurt the CD, laughing at Kurt's clumsy attempt to catch it. The CD bounced off Kurt's knuckles and landed on the desk behind him.

"Thanks," Kurt said with a tinge of anger. He picked up the CD and slipped it into a protective plastic sleeve. Then he laid it on top of the other three.

Brass slapped him lightly a couple of times on the back and in a quiet voice asked, "Kurt, why do you do it? You're here before the rest of us every morning and you're still here when we leave at night. Don't you ever go home?"

"I know, but—"

"Kurt, you're a GS-15 government employee like the rest of us." Kurt waved his hands. "Scratch that. You're not exactly like us. You've been with the Department of Defense . . . how long?"

"About—"

"Twenty-five years, if I recall correctly, and I think I do. You should be knocking on the door for Senior Executive Service status years ago. You know. I know. Everyone knows that if anyone deserves it, it's you."

"That's all well and good—"

Brass slapped him on the back again. *You're one lucky*

bastard, Thomas. If only I had an extra letter opener, Kurt thought.

Kurt wondered if he could grab him and break that hand before Brass realized what—

"But, it isn't going to happen. Like I told you last week; the colonel has it in for you. For that matter, he has it in for all of us, but you, he takes great delight in torturing."

Kurt looked up at the face of his middle-aged cohort from the cubicle several doors down. The man's lips were moving, but Kurt's attention was on the large white-faced clock behind Brass. Ten minutes to five! Near the steel combination door leading into the Missile Research Defense Agency someone shouted another "bye." The whine of the heavy door opening as unseen government employees and military officers hurried through them, heading home after a long week stuffed in the bowels of the Navy Annex in Arlington, drowned more of Brass's words. Kurt reached up and absent-mindedly pushed long strands of disarrayed hair up and across the bald spot that had conquered a once-mighty bush that had forested the top.

Brass laughed, reached forward, and playfully poked Kurt on the arm.

Kurt wished he could break that arm. The finger would be fine. He grinned as he envisioned the expression on Brass's face if he jumped up and, with one quick twist and flick, broke the man's arm. Of course, until he lost weight, quick twists and flicks were purely imaginary. He smiled.

"See, I knew you wanted to come. Besides, it's time to get over this 'all work, no play' syndrome. What're you going to do? Sit here until six or seven and then go home to that empty apartment of yours. Why don't you come with me to Old Town Alexandria. Tonight's Pet Night in one of the local pubs. You bring your pet, look like a concerned lover of animals, and meet enchanting one-night-standers who'll share their body with anyone who 'ohs and ahs' their pets."

Kurt laughed. In his mind, he could see the arm dangling from the elbow and Brass mumbling, "Why, why,

why?" *Why? Because you're an asshole.* Did he really think that word?

Brass, tall and lanky, was a much-divorced perennial bachelor who loved women until the moment of orgasm and then Redskin football took precedence.

"Sure, I'd come with you, Thomas. I'll be up there dancing on the tables with you and having the women look up, whistle—"

"Just what I'm saying. They'd whistle."

"—and ask me if I need help back to whatever home I escaped from." Brass laughed loudly. The computer beeped. Kurt turned around and closed the MS-DOS program screen. He was finished copying the information he needed. He was finished with the computer and he was finished with this place.

Unconsciously, he placed his hand over the stack of CDs, his fingers lightly playing a tattoo on the protective cover. Thought, *Well, Tom, time to skedaddle. And Monday, when you come in, you can tell everyone here how you were the last person to speak to me before—*.

Kurt looked up and saw that Brass was staring at the CDs.

"What're you copying, Kurt? You afraid the system is going to eat your hard drive by Monday?"

Kurt saw Brass's eyes widen. He knew the nosey bastard had noticed the CDs were marked unclassified, but the last CD ejected had come from the classified computer. It was one of the deadly security sins to mix CDs between classified and unclassified computers. He lifted the CDs and bounced them on edge for a second before taking a pair of scissors out of the top drawer and dropping the CDs in it before closing it.

Tom Brass leaned down. "What are you doing, Kurt?" he asked in a concerned whisper. "If the colonel saw you doing this he'd have your nuts for breakfast."

Kurt shrugged. "I didn't have time to run out for classified CDs," he offered, knowing as he said it that Brass's eyes had shifted to the box of classified CDs near the edge of his desk. "The system administrators are upgrading the system this weekend. You remember what happened last time."

Brass licked his lips. "Kurt, I don't know . . . you know I'm going to have to turn you—"

Kurt surprised himself. His right hand drove the scissors up through the soft tissue below Brass's chest cage, ripping into his heart. The look on the man's face. Sweat poured down his face as he grunted several times, his mouth opening and closing like a dying fish out of water. Kurt grinned. Brass's eyes stared directly into Kurt's. Kurt forced himself to meet the stare; not knowing what he expected to see. *I'm getting quite good at this for a novice.*

Brass mouthed, "Why?"

"I don't like Old Town," Kurt whispered in reply. He twisted the scissors as he pushed Brass away. The body fell backwards. Kurt released his grip on the scissors, leaving them embedded in the man. He looked at the eyes. The light was gone. He'd missed it again.

"Amazing how good government scissors are, aren't they, Thomas?"

He looked around the area. "I'm surprised," Kurt said, looking at the small amount of blood that flowed across the man's chest onto the floor. "You didn't have much blood at all. Nope, not at all," he said quietly to himself. He touched two fingers to his right wrist. His eyes widened. His heart was beating normally. He had expected it to be surging upward. Even his breathing was normal. *No turning back now. Not that I ever had that opportunity, after that first meeting.*

He hadn't been this calm in the past six months. He had come a long way. He had nearly passed out when he made the first delivery, leaving it under a flattened QVC box along Jeff Davis Highway. This second delivery should fix the problems his contact told him they were having with the data from the first. This delivery was to be a face-to-face meeting, because his handler wanted to assess the information before Kurt arrived in Aruba. Kurt was no fool. He knew if the information proved false, the money in the bank would disappear. But he didn't worry. Either way, he could handle the drop this time. And the information was good; it always had been. What they didn't know and he did was that the laser weapon didn't work. Sure you could point the thing at a target and, as long as the target didn't move for several minutes, you could even burn a hole in it. A hole in tempered steel was even possible. Kurt believed he was selling the buyers unusable data. But it never occurred to him that even unsuccessful gambits saved money and time by identifying avenues that didn't work.

He forced himself carefully onto his knees to avoid the blood on the floor. He pushed Brass across the floor toward the desk along the wall, a smear of blood marking the path across the green tiled floor. He'd take care of that later. Kurt pulled the boxes out from under the desk and ten minutes later had Brass's body shoved against the flimsy wall of the cubicle with the boxes blocking any casual view.

Ripping linen cloth from a roll, Kurt wiped the blood from the floor and then with fresh linen he wiped his hands. He'd have to stop and wash his hands. With soap. The idea of blood on them was too much to bear along with everything else good that had happened today. *Does this make me a serial killer?* He'd stop at the bathroom on the ground floor on the way out and soap them up good. He looked down at his clothes and thought the stains at the bottom of his pants were probably blood from the killing. Which killing, he wasn't sure; but probably Thomas's since he'd stayed well clear of the system administrator's body.

He had never killed a man before today—or a woman or child. This day was quite the revelation to Kurt. Confidence that was always quickly crushed by his military superiors over the years rose considerably. He felt a rapport with those same military superiors, believing that they experience the same rush he had experienced twice today. Kurt believed he understood why some military types opted for the dangerous, bloodletting missions.

Kurt grabbed a bottle of water and chugged the cool

liquid. He glanced a couple of times to where the body was hidden. He could see Brass's shoes sticking out, but he was going to be discovered anyway come Monday. The first person in his cubicle who looked around half-heartedly would find the body. He imagined the fright rolling across this office like a tidal wave.

Kurt straightened his desk, filing papers in the small cabinet to the side and tidying the stack of folders awaiting his attention in the incoming tray. This time Monday, he'd be on some beach in Aruba, sipping one of those drinks with paper umbrellas in it. And, yeah, maybe even with a blue-eyed blond rubbing sun block on his chest and telling him how great in bed he was. He shrugged. It would be a lie, but he didn't care if it was a lie.

He reached down and grabbed two handfuls of fat. *Look at this honey. These are group-sex handles made for three, so where's your sister?* He laughed to himself.

The other thing he was going to do was hire a professional trainer and get these excess pounds off. "Yeah, Tom," he said softly. "This time Monday they'll find you and I'll be with her." *Whoever "her" is.*

He shut his eyes for a moment and fantasized about himself a hundred pounds lighter, jogging on some white-sanded beach to the admiration of onlookers. With the right amount of money, you could buy anything, and Kurt had earned enough in the past six months to retire comfortably under a new name. A new name supplied by his handlers along with a new passport from their country and a false biography. Of course, he didn't have much faith in them, but the papers would serve his purposes until he found the right people to build him another. The next thing on his agenda was to drop out of the sight of his handlers. You never knew in the world of espionage or politics when you became the expendable element.

He patted the briefcase as he picked it up. He glanced at his watch. Two hours to the drop at the Washington Mall, then *Voila!* Tomorrow he'd be just one more American at the bank in Aruba changing money from one account to another. He had no intention of leaving the money in an account his handlers had access to.

Sure, he had enough in his off-shore banking account to live on, but everyone should have a separate retirement account. No need to go yet. There was time yet to relax. To dream. He pulled the chair away from where the body lay hidden, sat down in it, and basked in the fantasies his future held, watching the clock on the wall until it was time to go.

HE COULD EVEN INVEST IN U.S. FUNDS—STOCKS AND bonds—under his new identity. He sighed. Seven o'clock. Time.

He opened the briefcase, checking for the third or maybe fourth time that the CDs were still there. Kurt wasn't concerned anyone would stop him when he left the complex. They seldom inspected bags, and the few times they did, all you had to do was tell them they were unclassified and they waved you on. They never checked. The key was to make sure you had no classification markings on anything you took out of the office. With his new confidence, Kurt had no doubt of his ability to appear calm, cool, and collected, even if they did stop him.

He stood, his eye line slightly above the top edge of the cubicle walls. Fluorescent lights illuminated the office of the head of the MDA Project Phoenix. Kurt could see Colonel Darnell bent over his desk, writing something—probably screwing over another government servant. The slight bald spot on the back of his head made Kurt wonder why an officer so hell-bent on promotion wouldn't cover the baldness. Kurt shaped his hand like a gun, pointed it at Darnell, and said, "Bang! Your career is dead."

He reached up and brushed a few strands of loose hair over his own bald top. Darnell was probably editing his proposed emails for tonight so they'd look better, more professional, have some quotable sound bites in them.

Don't forget to mention the dead man in cubicle forty-nine, Kurt said silently. *Or, the screams from the floor above you.*

He imagined the Air Force generals talking now.

"Apparently the man was killed within forty feet of where Darnell was writing emails."

"Too bad. Thought Darnell was on the ball. Knew what was going on around him."

"Well, you must not know what's going on around you if this traitor kills a man within feet of you and you don't hear anything."

"Maybe he did hear something, but—"

"No, I think if he'd heard, he'd have done something."

"Well, we'll never know. Too bad. He was a great officer."

Kurt undid his tie, pulled it from around his neck, and stuffed it in his briefcase alongside the CDs. Thought, *Yeap, Colonel Darnell, you were a great officer. Until they realize what I've done anyway. But with good ole Tom Brass resting in his own blood right over there, you're on your way to wherever the Air Force sends officers who have no future. Probably a base without a golf course.*

Kurt reached for his coat, stopped and dropped his hands, staring at the blue dress coat. He didn't have to take it. He could leave it here. It'd be just one more thing Monday for them to figure out. Maybe he should drive his car over to one of the parks, cut himself and drip some blood around so they'd have some DNA, leave the keys in it for some unsuspecting young juvenile delinquent to steal, and laugh when the man was caught and charged with his murder. Be just his luck to do all of that and then actually get mugged and murdered for his briefcase while he walked away. What a waste. Besides, it may confuse things while they're trying to figure out what happened, but it wouldn't confuse them for long. And he didn't know if he had time to do it. The security lines at Dulles were notorious for being endless before an international flight, and what if he went to all that trouble and missed his flight?

Kurt had an immediate urge to urinate. *Don't even think about missing the flight.* He looked at the body one last time. A pool of blood lined the edges of the boxes. *Does that mean Brass is still alive, or is it just blood from earlier still spreading?* he wondered curiously. Kurt shrugged. *Well, I'll just wait until the papers come out and see whether or not Brass was dead when I stuffed him there.*

He reached up, took his coat, and draped it over his arm. Carrying his briefcase in his right hand he walked toward the door, glancing at Darnell's office. He didn't see the man, but he was in there somewhere. For a second, he thought about killing Darnell, but just as quickly dismissed the idea. Darnell would beat the hell out of him. He wasn't some little nondescript coworker with no combat experience.

A sense of freedom enveloped him for a fraction of a second as he neared the exit. Then a second idea swelled forward clouding the first: he might miss his flight tonight. But he said to himself, *Nothing bad is going to happen.* After all, who else could kill men with office instruments— twice in one day—within the nation's most super-secret technology development agency with work going on around him, and have no one notice? Probably put him in *Ripley's Believe It or Not*—most office workers killed by office instruments in one day by one man.

He punched the red button at the door. The gears whined. As he waited the few seconds for the door to open, Kurt glanced at the office where Colonel Darnell worked. He was there the whole time. He was looking at Kurt through the glass wall that surrounded his office. Kurt smiled and raised a couple of fingers to his head in a mock salute and, without waiting to see Darnell's reaction, stepped over the threshold, heading toward freedom. By the time he walked down the marble steps to the executive parking area in front of the Navy Annex, he was humming. He felt clean now. It had only taken a few minutes to wash his hands and use the urinal.

He raised his right hand and then his left, shifting the

briefcase so he could look at them. The soap had done the job. Then he spotted blood on the right sleeve of his white shirt. He hadn't noticed it inside the building. Kurt looked around, saw no one, so he put the briefcase down long enough to slip his coat on. In doing so, he noticed the time on his wristwatch. Another hour and he'd be done. Then, when the sun was rising over Washington tomorrow morning, this boy would be stepping off the aircraft to Aruba. "Aruba, Aruba, Aruba," he said aloud—never to return.

He was still humming when he reached the guard gate, nodding to the Defense Protective Service officers manning the turnstiles. The computer-generated database recognized his badge swipe, a green arrow appeared, and Kurt Vernigan was outside the compound. God, if he wasn't afraid of passing out from the exhaustion, he would've danced down to the bus stop.

He was still humming when four black sedans sped up and flipped on their sirens. Men wearing shirts with the large black letters "FBI" across the front leapt out. He had barely ceased humming when one of them tackled him from behind, knocking the briefcase out of his hand. As Kurt fell, he saw the black briefcase and his future spinning over and over toward the grass on the other side of a chain that paralleled the sidewalk.

Dampness soaked his leg, and he realized that he had wet himself. The crying clouding his ears was his also. *This cannot be happening. So close. So unfair.* And the crying rose in intensity. "Unfair, unfair, unfair," he mumbled through tears, the mumbling continuing even when they jerked him to his feet, twisting the arms handcuffed behind him. He cried from the pain.

When he glanced around, standing at the edge of the FBI agents surrounding him stood Darnell, alongside an Air Force general.

A red haze of rage broke across him, adrenaline surging free from places he never knew existed. Kurt managed to free himself from the two men holding him on each arm, and, screaming at the top of his lungs, he ran toward Darnell, who calmly turned toward him and laughed. Kurt screamed louder, ignoring the shouts and cries around him. He ignored the agent who ran forward with his club raised and slammed it against Kurt's temple. Darnell's laughing face was the last thing Kurt saw. The knowledge that he would make general because of Kurt was the thought he had as darkness slammed across his mind as his body fell toward the pavement where his face cushioned the fall.

CHAPTER 2

"SKIPPER, THE F-16S ARE ON RADAR," PETTY OFFICER Schultz said. Without waiting for acknowledgement, the former high school tight end adjusted his headset over his ears and returned to monitoring his screen. The broad-shouldered Operations Specialist's right hand rested on a baseball-size roller mounted on the desk in front of him. His fingers rolled the ball slightly. On the integrated radar screen, the cursor shifted off the forward video speck to another radar return directly behind it. His right thumb pressed a flush panel alongside the mouse and immediately a circle encompassed the small speck generated by the radar return. Information appeared in a small box below the upside down half-circle that identified the hooked radar return as a friendly aircraft. Course, speed, call sign, and altitude were illuminated in the box for any viewer in the Combat Information Center and the bridge of the USS *Winston S. Churchill*—United States Arleigh Burke–class destroyer, hull number DDG-81.

Commander Troy Harrison slid to the seat edge of the captain's Chair in Combat and, with a quick shove of both hands on the chair arms, jumped to the deck. Harrison leaned over Schultz's shoulder, watched the radar track of the approaching aircraft, and read the information on the Naval Tactical Data System as the OS petty officer worked the mouse around the radar returns.

Schultz shifted slightly in his seat, forcing the skipper to take a half-step to the left to see over the former *'I love football, y'all'* hometown high school hero from Concord, North Carolina. Harrison was used to adjusting to a Navy that seemed hell-bent on keeping his head level with everyone else's shoulders. At five foot seven he was shorter than the average male naval officer—if he stretched his neck, at that. What irked him more than this self-generated statistic was a belief that most women officers also matched or exceeded his height.

He never mentioned the height thing. He didn't have to. His classmates at the Academy, fellow officers—and enlisted men—he had served with during his career, and now his fellow commanding officers made sure he knew. There wasn't a short joke he hadn't heard. *'Hey, Troy, stand up! Oh, sorry—you are standing!'*

Image was everything in the military. The image he projected when he hopped down from the captain's chair was like a young child leaping petulantly off a highchair. On the other hand, he was the *gawldamn* skipper of this floating bucket of bolts, and the officers and crew could think what they pleased as long as they kept it to themselves—*and no short jokes, by God.*

On the Naval Tactical Data System console, short generated lines ran from the half-moon icons overlaying the four Air Force F-16s, revealing to the viewer the direction the aircraft were flying. The length of the line told him or her the relative contact speeds to other objects.

Operations Specialist Second Class Schultz sequence-hooked the radar returns into the computer, and, when he clicked the left button, the computer hopped from one contact to the other. New data, indicating type of aircraft, appeared in the boxes during sequencing, blinking. When the computer sequenced the first time to new data, it would blink until the user sequenced off.

NTDS was a fleet icon—one of the few information legacies to survive and transform in the fast pace of the information age. A fleet sailor from three decades ago would never recognize what was NTDS then and what sailors today called NTDS. NTDS was the all-powerful home for a variety of data links—the all-seeing eye of Navy "Oz"—interconnected through the Joint Staff's Global Information Grid, generating, delivering information instantaneously to the farthest reaches of the tactical battlefield, if the NTDS on the *Churchill* had been externally connected. As an Assistant Secretary for Defense (National Information Infrastructure) once termed it: Power to the edge. Today was an exercise, and you never sent exercise data over the real-world Global Information Grid. What if someone interpreted a war at sea training exercise as the real thing?

Each NTDS upgrade brought more information and better interoperability with other new sophisticated and digitized information systems such as the Air Force's RC-135 Rivet Joint aircraft and the Navy's venerable EP-3E Aries. The key to winning battles was sharing vital information so quickly that the commander could make combat decisions faster than the adversary could. The military term for doing that was 'Information Superiority.' Operation Iraqi Freedom continued to be the role model for future wars, with speed and information exponentially pushing the lethality of U.S. forces across every domain.

"Where's the tanker?" Troy asked, his Vermont accent drawing out the word tanker. Catching his reflection in a nearby turned-off CRT, Troy turned his head slightly. He needed a haircut. His hair was touching the top of his ears; time for another trip down to the ship's servicemen and have the former lawn mower men 'lower his ears.' He twisted his head the other way. Yes, the right side was his better half. You couldn't see the mole alongside his left ear nor the slight skin discoloration on the left cheek; a discoloration so slight that only he noticed it, but it was enough that he knew it was there. When he was a junior officer, he experimented with a mustache for a few months until he noticed that few Navy admirals had facial hair. Few had any hair. When he realized he knew no admirals with mustaches, *he shaved his off so fast he nearly set his cheeks on fire from the razor speed.* At least that's what his stateroom mate at the time, a tall gangly boy from Georgia, said about him shaving it off.

Lieutenant Albert Kincaid, the Tactical Action Officer for this exercise, interrupted Troy's drifting attention. "Sir, the anchor is about fifteen miles from the aircraft."

For a moment, the vision of the secured anchors near the bullnose of the ship came to mind before Troy nodded, realizing that this 'anchor' identified the orbit area of the Air Force KC-135 four-engine jet tanker.

Operations Specialist Second Class Schultz leaned left toward the center of the long console used by him and the Combat Information Center Watch Officer. Rolling the mouse, the cursor settled on another friendly aircraft icon. "Here it is, Skipper."

"Long trip for them."

"Yes, sir." Lieutenant Kincaid glanced at the digital clock on the console. "Those Air Force jocks been airborne for over eight hours from Langley and this will be their third refueling evolution."

"Long time for an Air Force officer to be away from a golf course," Troy said with a chuckle.

"Yes, sir," Kincaid agreed with a nod before continuing. "Once the fighters have finished their drink, they'll reposition and we can begin phase three of the exercise."

"They're turning, sir," OS2 Shultz said. "Approaching tanker operating area. Estimate twenty minutes to rendezvous."

"Very well," Troy said. The F-16s were to top off their fuel. The huge KC-135 could refuel two at a time. He

shuddered slightly and regretted the involuntary response
as soon as it happened. He had self-analyzed this habit
years ago and attributed it to a superior intellect that placed
his emotional self within the context of his thoughts. The
idea of flying along at three, or was it four, hundred knots
tethered with only tens of feet separating you from a bigger
aircraft in front, above, and flying at the same speed and
course was too much for him. What if you sneezed at the
wrong time? Three aircraft would be heading toward the
deep sea because of a pilot's cold. Like most non-aviators,
Troy had a mixed concept of the rigors and safety of
flight. To him, aviators were the cowboys of the sky
and the playboys of the beach. Work was a four-letter
word for aviators as far as he was concerned, whether they
were Navy, Air Force, Marines, or even Army. Show him
an aviator and he'd show you someone who sometime in
the past had done something he or she needed prose-
cuting.

A new air contact appeared on the radar repeater along
the bottom right side. The NTDS system automatically
hooked the new contact, slapping a top-half of a box icon
over the radar return, identifying it as an unknown air contact. A similar line highlighting the course and relative
speed of the contact emerged a second later.

*Just what I need. Why can't they stay away while I'm out
here?* he asked himself. Troy watched as Shultz spoke into
his microphone, reporting the contact to the Tactical Action Officer standing to Troy's left and to the Electronic
Warfare operator sitting at the AN/SLQ-32(V)6 on the
other side of the Combat Information Center.

"Looks as if our visitor has returned, Skipper," Kincaid
said in his dry, monotone voice. The TAO pointed to the
new contact. "Why do you think the French keep sending
their reconnaissance aircraft out to keep track of us, Skipper? It isn't as if we keep our Blue-Force locations secret
to them."

"They're a nosy lot," Troy said, scratching his chin.

This irked him. Captain Bennett, the senior officer of the Expeditionary Strike Group of which he had the misfortune of being a member, ought to do something about it. Then again, Bennett was an amphibious sailor, and, commanding the USS *Mesa Verde*—Amphibious Transport Dock, hull number 19—had probably lost any at-sea warfighting edge by being in the amphibious Navy. *It's people like me who command cruisers and destroyers. We're the ones with whom the burden of maintaining the keen edge needed to win a war at sea rests,* he thought.

Ought to be something he could do to make the French go away and stay away. As Harrison watched the NTDS icons close the Air Force tankers northwest of them to 'top-off' their fuel tanks, an idea burst into his thoughts. He smiled to himself. Great ideas such as this are always epiphanies to the person who thought them. It is only later in retrospect they realize not all epiphanies are great ideas— some stupid ones have bubbled to the top more times than history likes to reveal.

The USS *Winston S. Churchill* was located in the center of the screen. Northwest were the Air Force fighter aircraft preparing for the exercise with the ship, and to the southeast of the screen was the French reconnaissance aircraft boring holes in the sky, loafing around in a figure-eight pattern as it watched the Americans.

The grin grew, and a slight sparkle came to his eyes as he imagined the turmoil and fright aboard the French aircraft as it dove for wave height. The Frenchies would skedaddle back to the Ivory Coast with their tails between their legs.

He opened his mouth to tell the TAO what he wanted, but thought better about it. This wasn't something to share with everyone. He'd do it, but it had to be done in such a way so it seemed to be an accident. It wasn't as if he was going to kill anyone. *The* Washington Post *test*, he thought. The *Washington Post* test was a euphemism that grew in popularity in the early 2000s. Anything being done, any actions contemplated, and anything being said were bounced against how you'd feel if you read about it in the headlines of the *Washington Post*. Troy attributed his early selection to Lieutenant Commander and then to Commander to such skills as avoiding things which failed the *Washington Post* test. Rising to top ranks was a lot like sailing a ship at flank speed through shoal waters littered with sunken vessels. It wasn't the smartest way to reach the other side of the waters, but the prize went to those who navigated it the best. The good part about the Navy was that the majority of the time you were out to sea and the chance of failing the *Washington Post* test was minimal. You had to really screw up.

Out of the corner of his eye Troy watched the TAO. He had eighteen officers in his wardroom—sixteen men, including his executive officer, and two women. The gangly TAO running this exercise for him was also his Combat Systems division officer—Lieutenant Albert Kincaid. Al was a Navy aristocrat. The other three services had their legacy lineages. Kincaid was the son, grandson, great-grandson, and great-great-grandson of a Navy family that boasted a couple of admirals in its lineage—all of whom had graduated from *Boat-U* in Annapolis. Kincaid never mentioned this, but Troy knew.

He prided himself on finding out everything he could about the men and women who served under him. A good Navy officer knew the men and women who served under and with him. Besides, you never knew who could help you in your career or what little dirt you could discover to encourage loyalty. His eyebrows bunched into a sharp V. Kincaid could have become one of Troy's "golden boys." The Lieutenant had contacts. Troy wasn't sure just who and where those contacts were, but he knew the young officer had them even if Kincaid never discussed some of the facts Troy had personally researched and added to the Lieutenant's file. Naval Academy bachelor degree in engineering; picked for a prestigious Massachusetts Institute of Technology education grant directly out of the Naval

Academy, only to discover a month before he received a Master's degree in advanced engineering that he was going to be a surface warfare officer. According to the inside scoop Troy learned from one of Kincaid's classmates, his Combat Systems officer bounced off ceilings, screaming over the idea of a *Kincaid* being a surface warfare officer. The last three generations of Kincaids had been aviators—brown shoes and all that. Even the best of a new generation can't be a pilot if his eyesight doesn't pass the grade. Kincaid refused to fly as a naval flight officer. NFOs were back-enders who never saw the controls of an aircraft unless they tripped and fell onto them. The young Academy ensign, in a petulant fit, applied for the SEALs, only to discover that he had to pass a strenuous physical test. On the same day the Navy special forces turned him down, he applied to everything from Intelligence to Meteorology to Cryptology before "Big Navy," tired of his whining, hoisted its beltline and informed the young upstart that Academy graduates' first choices had to be one of the three warfighting designators: Aviation, Submarines, or Surface Warfare. Kincaid apparently started writing everyone he knew, and his father joined in. His grandfather told him to "quit this shit" and do what he was trained to do: go to sea. Before Kincaid's letter-writing campaign bore fruit, the Bureau of Naval Personnel sent a nice letter congratulating the ensign on his assignment to the Surface Warfare Navy, where "work" was the mantra of every day. The aviation community's loss was Troy's gain, if only he could break through that mask of indifference. If only he could gently knock that huge chip off the Lieutenant's shoulder. It wasn't as if Kincaid had done badly as an SWO. The man was a tenacious professional. He qualified as a surface warfare officer during his first two years on his first ship, the . . . Troy couldn't recall its name. Kincaid was an expert ship handler and one of Troy's three qualified officers-of-the-deck for battle group steaming. By God, the man had everything going for him, except an attitude that seemed to throw a fence around him when dealing with superiors. Overly proper, aloof, but professionally competent.

"Let's review the exercise plan," Troy said to Kincaid.

"Yes, sir," Lieutenant Kincaid said, reaching forward and grabbing a clipboard off the top of the main console. "Simple air warfare exercise, Skipper, from the Fleet Exercise Manual. The F-16s will complete refueling." Kincaid nodded toward the other side of the long console to another sailor manning a radar repeater. Then he continued, "Petty Officer Schultz has contact with the F-16s and is monitoring their refueling communications. Once they finish with the tanker, they'll check in with us and we'll commence the exercise, Captain. First phase will satisfy our basic fleet hostile-air exercise requirement. The fighters will fly straight and level. It will give our fire control operators training on illuminating them with our radars and tracking them with the narrow radar beams of the fire control radars as they close our position. Twenty miles out, one of the F-16s will act as a simulated air-to-surface missile, dropping rapidly in altitude and going full bore toward us with afterburners blazing. Five miles out, the Falcon will do a classic anti-ship missile pop-up maneuver before leveling off and passing overhead. The last five miles will allow us to test our close-in weapons systems—the Vulcan Phalanx."

"Thank you, Lieutenant." Troy knew all of this, of course. He was the captain. Even so, the key to perfection was never taking something for granted. A Navy heuristic is that ten percent of everyone involved in an evolution never seem to get the word—they never seem to understand what is going on around them. If repeated often enough, that ten percent who never seemed to know what in the hell was happening sometimes had their own epiphany of the world around them.

Troy looked at the huge Navy analog clock mounted on the bulkhead over the top of the consoles. A few minutes before ten. Even in the throes of the information and digital age, this inexpensive Navy supply clock with its two black hands and red second hand continued to decorate nearly every Navy compartment.

"And the other F-16s?"

"Sir?"

"The remaining three Falcons; what will they be doing while this one is simulating a cruise missile?"

"Sorry, sir. They will maintain altitude, course, and speed as they pass overhead while the fighter simulating the cruise missile flies a profile directly at us."

"I know we've told everyone the exercise plan, Lieutenant Kincaid. I'm satisfied you have a handle on it. Let's remind everyone then once again the order of events." Troy glanced over his shoulder, saw the lieutenant standing in the shadows of the blue-lighted combat information center, and motioned him forward. "The *Mesa Verde* has graciously provided an observer to grade us on this exercise." The observer stepped forward and Troy shook the young man's hand. "I hope you're ship's company and not part of the Seabee battalion embarked."

"Oh, no, sir," the lieutenant stuttered out. "I'm a qualified surface warfare officer, Skipper," the man said, pulling the edge of his blue jacket aside to reveal the gold SWO insignia over the left pocket of his khakis.

"Sir," Kincaid interrupted. "I finished reminding everyone of—"

Troy turned to him, his hands clasped behind his back. "Then do it again. Humor me, Lieutenant. It makes me feel as if I'm in charge."

"Aye aye, sir."

Troy waited while Lieutenant Kincaid passed around, via the internal communications systems of the ship, a recap of the exercise order of events. Surface ships—*and their commanding officers*—readiness was measured on how well they performed mandatory exercises. This would be the first of three progressively harder anti-air warfare exercises the *Winston Churchill* would do in the next three hours with the

Air Force fighters. Troy reached forward and shoved a couple of printouts off the top of a Navy publication he recognized—FXP-3.

The Navy had an entire set of instructions called the Fleet Exercise Publication series—referred to as FXPs—that showed exactly how an exercise was to be performed, when it was to be performed, what sensors and equipment on a ship were to participate, and finally why it was important to do the exercise well. Navy exercises were like programmed texts starting at the basic levels, building on each level of experience until the operator, the team, and the ship could respond quickly and effectively in a combat situation. The difference between combat and exercises was the adrenaline and pucker factor. When engaged in combat, the sphincter tightens, the heartbeat soars, and adrenaline races through your body, everything screaming to the normal human being to flee. You fight like you train, and if you train enough then fighting the ship in combat increases the chance of survival, and the side with more survivals when the battle ends usually wins the game.

The intermediate exercise would pit the four fighters in an air attack against the two ships. This intermediate exercise would test each ship's team in its ability to fight the ship. The final advanced exercise tested the two ships' ability to fight as one. FXPs were a lot like doing routine maintenance on a car. Every 3,000 miles it needed an oil change. For a ship, every so many months, certain scheduled exercises were needed to maintain its readiness.

All the AAW exercises today would be non-live-fire designed to test and train the ship's crew in detecting and tracking the F-16 that would be simulating a cruise missile. When the F-16 reached fire control radar range, the ship would illuminate it and simulate engagement. It was this engagement phase where Troy knew he could scare the bejesus out of the Atlantique and rid the Expeditionary Strike Group—hauling Seabees instead of Marines to Liberia—of the daily French reconnaissance missions. The good thing about being at sea was that what occurs is seldom what's reported.

"After the first pass, sir, the Falcons will reform southwest of us for the intermediate phase of the exercise, sir," Kincaid began. "They will orbit until we give the word, and then the four Air Force fighters will simulate a multiple air attack."

"Lieutenant, I want our fire control radar, once they've locked on to the aircraft, to maintain that lock on as long as possible."

"Sir," Kincaid said while allowing his headset to drop around his neck, "I told the fire control technicians to drop lock once the aircraft passed overhead."

"I know," Troy said, "but I want them to train on maintaining a fire control picture even when the target is opening up distance from us—good opportunity to get as much training as possible." He turned and smiled at the young *Mesa Verde* lieutenant who was concentrating on the grading sheet on his clipboard.

"Yes, sir," Kincaid responded. He put the headset back on, pressed the red button on the ICS system, and passed the new orders to the AAW team.

Petty Officer Schultz dropped his headset. "Lieutenant Kincaid, sir?"

Kincaid leaned forward around Troy and lifted his headset. "Yes, Petty Officer Schultz, what is it?"

"Sir, if we keep our fire control radar locked on to the Air Force fighters as they fly southeast, there's a chance we'll illuminate the French reconnaissance aircraft."

"Well, they shouldn't be in the area," Troy said.

Shultz nodded, "Yes, sir. Sorry, sir." The second class petty officer lifted his headset and readjusted it on his head, thinking, *Then you officers sort out that shit. Lord knows I tried to warn you, but I'm just a poor enlisted fool, so what in the hell do I know?*

Troy turned back to Kincaid, whose eyes met his. While Troy met his stare eyeball to eyeball, Kincaid slipped the right earpiece back in place and slowly turned back to the consoles in front of him.

When the fighters reformed southeast of them, Troy would have the technicians tweak the fire control radar for a few seconds—tweak it in such a way that it locked onto the French reconnaissance aircraft. He'd have time to maintain the lock-on for a few minutes while the Air Force fighters orbited, waiting for *Churchill* and *Mesa Verde* to assess performance. During that time, attention would be focused on him and the *Mesa Verde* observer, who would be providing an initial debrief of their performance along with his indepth professional opinion on areas to improve. Grades were either satisfactory or unsatisfactory. It would be after the eight o'clock reports tonight before Troy would receive the formal report. While the observer debriefed him, his fire control radar would be painting the French reconnaissance aircraft. All he had to do was look surprised when the French aircraft dove for sea level and turned toward the Ivory Coast, flying as fast as any two-engine turbo-prop aircraft could fly.

No, the F-16s would orbit long enough for him to include the Atlantique in the exercise. Long enough to scare the French out of the air. He shouldn't do this, and he wouldn't if he were where newspapers and television reporters were within reporting distance, but this was off the coast of Africa. Nothing was ever here. Plus, distance makes the facts grow fainter; and in basic FXP exercises, mistakes happen. He laughed quietly to himself. *Yeah, mistakes happen. So sorry. Won't do that again, sir!*

"What's the holdup, Lieutenant Kincaid? We going to start this exercise or not?"

"Yes, sir," Kincaid replied. "A few more minutes and they'll start their run."

"You've already said that. A minute here, a minute there, and the next thing you know we're talking hours. Let's get this show on the road, okay?"

"Yes, sir."

Always the same level tone of voice. *Can't tell what you're thinking, but I'll break through that façade one of these days. Yes, I will.*

Troy watched the CIC team for several moments. The murmur of lips speaking into mouthpieces as they exchanged information or relayed instructions to each other. Young sailors wearing sound-powered headsets moved within the limits of the lines connecting their huge headsets to the sound-power system.

Troy turned his head slowly, taking in the CIC team as they did their work in the shadows of blue light. Darkness breeds quiet. An intrinsic primal instinct, enduring through the eons from when mankind huddled around fire, whispering for fear of what lurked outside its meager light. He zipped up his jacket halfway against the extraordinary air conditioning that cooled and protected the sensitive electronics in CIC. The Electronic Warfare operator rested both elbows on the small table under her polar scope. A thumbed paperback book lay on the deck near her feet. Sailors were notorious readers, and none more so than on his ship. The AN/SLQ-32(V)6 EW systems she manned were flush against the forward bulkhead. Her blond hair, bunched up by the headset she wore, fluttered out both sides like misshapen wings, blocking from sight most of the EW display.

Troy looked at the bulkhead with its yards of electrical runnings and pipes carrying water to the cooling systems on the ship. On the other side of the thin half-inch forward aluminum bulkhead behind the EW suite were the vertical missile launchers, the bulk of the ship's firepower. A shifting pattern of light caught his attention, drawing him closer to where the fire control operators sat.

Someone had updated the Tactical Holograph Display. The holograph display was the greatest piece of visual technology yet to come out of the Navy's systems command. It provided commanders a pictorial profile of the battle space that surrounded their ships—air, surface, and subsurface.

From any altitude to any depth. You programmed and it provided. The Navy leapt ahead in technology with the installation of holograph displays, leaving behind every navy in the world as it jumped from manual tracking where operators used pencils, trace paper, and calipers to three-dimensional, digital-quality holographic projections hovering over a lighted table. When the system was secured—turned off—it became a table. Still, it was a sensitive information system, and it drove Troy up the wall when he saw a cup of coffee or some other drink or food sitting on it. It was worse when the holograph was functioning and you looked at the bottom of the technology sea being displayed to discover little items of trash.

Kincaid glanced from his clipboard to the clock. "Ten minutes, sir. Might be—"

"Ten minutes!"

"—slightly longer because one of them is having a slight problem with his connection. He's broken off twice and this is his third time reconnecting. The others are orbiting, waiting for him to finish."

Troy looked at the clock. In a way, this delay was good, even if it went against his grain to start things on time and finish them on time. If God didn't want you to do things on time, he wouldn't have made clocks. He nodded, reached forward, and pushed the "talk" handle on the 22MC sound-powered speaker. "Bridge," he said into the metal grill. "This is the skipper. Ask the XO to join me in Combat." If anyone would do what he wanted, it would be his fawning, useless executive officer. *When in doubt, bring in the 'yes' men.* He ran his hand through his hair. No doubt, he knew what he was doing.

A sailor apologized as he walked between Troy and the vacated operations console, drawing Troy's attention to his reflection on the inactive screen of the console. Troy was a true professional, and it bugged the shit out of him when people questioned his orders. Plus, this wasn't something he wanted to argue or discuss with his officers, and definitely not with the observer from the USS *Mesa Verde*. You couldn't trust officers and sailors who weren't part of your command to have any loyalty to you.

"Roger, sir," the metallic voice of the OOD responded.

"Captain," Kincaid continued. "For the second part of the training, the Intermediate Anti-Air Warfare exercise, the Falcons will simulate an attack from the southeast, sir. We'll separate them ten or fifteen miles apart before they start the multiple air attack run."

Troy's eyebrows bunched into a V. "I know that, Lieutenant," he snapped. *Did I ask him and forget?* he wondered.

"Yes, sir. I know you do, sir," Kincaid replied in his monotone voice. "I was following your earlier order to repeat the exercise requirements to ensure everyone was aware of what to do. I wanted to show the captain that I knew it. With your permission, sir, I will wait until after the basic exercise before I remind the crew of our duties for the intermediate exercise. This would help avoid any confusion of the chronology of the exercises."

Chronology of the exercises! What crap! Oh, he was smooth, that one. He may have the contacts Troy could use, but he also had a smart-ass mouth that would get the fine career, Navy-family Lieutenant into trouble. Troy was no one's fool; he wanted to befriend Kincaid, but he also knew that the young officer didn't care for him too much. He sucked in his lower lip. Regardless of the pull and clout a junior officer thinks he or she has, the commanding officer of anything in which they serve could squash them like a bug. *And, don't think I don't know that.*

"The radar return is starting to break apart, Skipper," Petty Officer Schultz offered. Troy stepped over to the air traffic controller's suite. On the panoramic screen, the large radar return created when the United States Air Force F-16/Falcons flew under the huge wings of the KC-135, combining the individual returns into one huge one, was beginning to break apart as the Falcons finished their refueling. A trained operations specialist such as Schultz could tell with a glance when he was seeing multiple contacts just from the size of the radar return.

"They're finishing their drink," Troy said to no one in particular. "What about the Atlantique?"

Schultz's head tilted back as he looked down at the right hand quadrant of his scope. "The French reconnaissance aircraft remains in orbit southeast of us, Skipper," Schultz said. "Figure-eight racetrack pattern from the track history trail on NTDS."

"Probably knows we're going to do a cruise missile exercise, Skipper," Kincaid added. "We've been in clear communication with the *Mesa Verde* during the morning, moving her position to off our starboard quarter so the metal mass of the Amphibious Transport Dock ship won't create havoc with our electronics."

Troy turned as his Command Master Chief, Boatswain Mate Master Chief Timothy Watson, walked up. "Yes, sir, Skipper. As much as I love the Amphib Navy, every one of those huge ships is just a sailing jumble of antennae, disrupting everything and anything in the air waves."

"Thanks, Master Chief. And to what do we owe the pleasure of your company?"

Watson put his hands behind his back and slowly rocked on his heels, his legs spread slightly in the event the ship rolled suddenly. "Done with my paperwork, Skipper, and just did my 'management through walking' tour of the ship. Morale remains high, the food is good, coffee is hot, and the ship is clean. Life don't get much better than this, sir."

Troy felt a tremble coming. He crossed his arms and fought to relax the muscles in them so it would go away. He only had these trembles when he tightened his muscles. The doctor at Portsmouth Regional Naval Hospital said it was caused by stress, but Troy discounted the diagnosis. Surface Warfare commanders didn't get stressed. He looked up at the smiling master chief and sighed. He thought, *What the hell! Why do glad-handling, cheerful shits surround me?* "Thanks, Master Chief. Don't know what I'd do without you."

Troy looked forward and caught Lieutenant Kincaid's eyes sliding off him and back onto the scopes in front.

Master Chief Watson leaned over, tapped Kincaid on the shoulder, and winked when the Lieutenant turned. "Lieutenant, how are you, sir?"

"He's fine," Troy interrupted. "We're in the middle of an exercise, Master Chief." Being at sea was where you made your bones, as an old Navy captain had once told him, but Troy also knew that being at sea meant being out of sight of seniors who ranked you against your peers. You could be the best damn sailor in the world, but if you were out of sight, you were definitely out of mind.

"Master Chief, why don't you go up and observe the exercise from the signal bridge." The signal bridge was directly above the ship's bridge. "Take one of our photographers with you and get some photos we can use."

"Sounds like a great idea, Skipper," Watson replied. Troy saw the forced smile. "Should be fun. How often do four single-seat fighter aircraft fly completely across the ocean to conduct a simulated attack on Navy warships! Sir, if you need me, I'll be topside enjoying some of this west African sunshine. And, if we're lucky, the Air Force will complete their mission before they exceed their air time and have to stop to take crew's rest."

Troy watched for a moment until the Master Chief, standing in the stairwell leading to the bridge, pulled the watertight door shut behind him. The less distractions the better. Master Chiefs were the top one percent of the Navy. No other promotion opportunities remained, so not much you could do to them and all of them seemed to believe in truth, honor, and the American way. Lord, protect him from people who had no chance for promotion. They could afford to be above the rabble of competition. He didn't want anyone not associated with this exercise mucking around in Combat while they did their exercise and while he rid them of the French.

The watertight hatch leading from the aft passageway opened and Troy's lanky XO stepped into the Combat

Information Center—Lieutenant Commander Joe Richman, a great American and patriot, strong like a rock; swift
like a tree. Richman would be coming from Engineering.
That was where Troy sent him this morning, and, unlike
when Troy was an XO, Richman would have stayed in Engineering until summoned. All Troy wanted was for the
man to review the engineering logs, check the fresh water
and fuel supply, and do a courtesy inspection of the fresh
water plants. His XO was a true example of work expand-
ing to fit the time allotted. If he told Richman to turn out
the lights in Engineering, the man would do it, do it gladly,
and stay there motionless in the dark until someone told
him he could leave.

Troy watched as the man from Iowa, that silly grin on
his face, weaved his way between the consoles, and leaned
down to say a few words to the operators who all greeted
him as he passed. Troy's left arm trembled, forcing him to
close his eyes and mentally relax his muscles. At night, he
would lay on his back in his rack, concentrating on his
breathing while his thoughts moved from one part of his
body to another, relaxing the muscles one by one until
eventually he fell asleep.

He was the commanding officer and, when he asked—
no, *told*—someone to come, they should be heading toward him as if their hair were on fire. Not meandering
along as if out for a Sunday stroll. The XO and Master
Chief acted most times as if they were on equal terms with
his command of the *Winston Churchill*. The Master Chief
found pleasure in telling him things he didn't want to know
about. Oh, no, he'd act as if he hated to do it, but deep
down, Troy knew the man was dancing with glee whenever
anything happened that was bad for the ship.

The XO never told him anything he didn't ask. The tall
potato boy from Iowa would grin and agree with anything
Troy said. *Or is it Idaho where potatoes come from?* Richman expected him to recommend the junior commander for
command, but how could he—a dedicated Surface Warfare
Officer—recommend an officer who showed no initiative

for command? Richman was so lax and laid back that Troy doubted he would argue with the adverse Fitness Report sitting in the safe in Troy's inport cabin. It would also show the board that Troy Harrison was not above identifying those unfit for leadership. It would be an oblique feather in his cap for Captain, and with enough small examples of objective leadership, the scrambled eggs of an admiral's hat weren't far away.

"Captain, you call, sir?" Richman said, saluting smartly.

Troy thought, *Can't you speak to me without whining?* Without returning the salute, Troy replied, keeping his eyes on the consoles arrayed in front of him. "Yes, I did, XO." Then, he turned and looked Richman in the eyes for a moment. Reaching out, he took Richman by the arm. "Step over here near my chair, Joe. There's something I want you to personally oversee and do. Something to help us do our best in the exercise."

Richman allowed Troy to pull him the ten feet or so away from Kincaid, Schultz, and the thin observer from the USS *Mesa Verde*. When Troy reached his chair, he dropped his grip and looked around the compartment, making sure they could talk without anyone overhearing their conversation. The captain's chair in the center of the compartment blocked the view of anyone watching them. People always watched the CO and XO when they talked. They were the two whose decisions affected each and every life on board the *Winston Churchill*.

He went over in detail what he wanted the XO to do, then did it again. Richman's head bopped like those heads on figurines bought and stuck in the rear window of cars. Troy never knew when the XO truly understood what he was to do or not until the man either screwed it up, which was often, or returned to report it being accomplished. Iowa, Idaho, the southern states in toto—nothing but country bumpkins, rednecks. *Christ! Glad I've never been stationed down there with their 'y'alls,' 'yonders,' and 'yokels,'* he thought.

He was going to go over it one more time with Richman,

when Lieutenant Kincaid interrupted them to report the basic AAW exercise had commenced. The Air Force fighters were making their approach.

"Why didn't you tell me?" Troy snapped. "I wanted to know when the exercise was ready to begin, not after it was already underway."

"Aye, my fault, sir. I thought I had mentioned it was going to begin in ten minutes, about ten minutes ago."

There it was again—the tremble. His eyes narrowed as he looked at Kincaid. "Thank you, Lieutenant. You may return to your station."

Kincaid was putting his headset on when Troy turned to Richman one last time. "You understand what you're to do?"

"Yes, sir, I do. And it will be done as you directed, sir."

"Good," Troy acknowledged. One thing about his sycophant XO, he knew the man would do just what he was told, when he was told, and how he was told. Of that, Troy had great confidence. What Troy lacked was confidence that his XO understood what he was being told most of the time. If only the man had better comprehension skills, they'd have less mishaps and misunderstandings. It never occurred to Troy that fault may lie in his direction. For some unknown reason to him, he had more than his share of officers and sailors on board his ship with whom he interfaced daily who seemed confused over what he wanted, when he wanted, and how he wanted something.

"Okay, XO, go make it happen."

"Yes, sir. You can trust me."

"I have never lost my trust in you, XO." *But then again, I've never had any to lose*. He smiled at his silent joke.

Troy moved back up to his position near the TAO and the exercise observer.

"Captain, with your permission, sir, I'll have the Air Force fighter comms piped through the speaker."

"Make it so, Lieutenant," Troy said. He glanced toward his chair. He really should be sitting in it and having his officers and crew approach him with their information. A slight muscle spasm vibrated his left leg. Sure, he was nervous, but navy heroes through history had been nervous when they were doing something for their nation.

Troy briefly had second thoughts about having the XO assume control of the fire control operator and directing the sailor to switch off the fighters for a moment and lock onto the French reconnaissance aircraft.

If he didn't do it, there were no lost opportunities; but if he did it and the French stayed away, the slight hiccup in the exercise report could be exploited as a future covert method to rid themselves of unwanted company. The lawyers wouldn't be happy, but when has anyone ever seen a lawyer with a smile?

What was the worst that could happen? he asked himself. Well, worst case was that the French would complain to the U.S.; but in today's Navy, having a 'French whine' was slang for doing something right.

"Skipper," Lieutenant Kincaid said. "They've returned to the staging point, regrouped—"

"Regrouped? Why in the hell did they turn back, Lieutenant Kincaid?"

"Sir, you wanted to watch the exercise from beginning to end, and they were only about a minute inbound, so actually we hadn't started the exercise. It only took a few minutes to return them to the starting point. They're now in position and we're ready to commence when you are, sir."

"Very well, Lieutenant. Pipe their communications over the speaker so we can hear them. Is the *Mesa Verde* in position?"

"Yes, sir. The amphib has completed its shift and is off our port quarter, four thousand yards—two nautical miles. She'll be able to watch and enjoy the spectacle while our fire control radars and guns revolve with the inbound aircraft."

Troy ran his hands through his sandy brown hair. "Not the same thing as it was when I first came in the Navy eighteen years ago. Back then we had missile batteries above deck and you could track the target from topside by watching the batteries turn in unison with the fire control radar. Now, with the missiles below deck in a vertical launch position and hidden by covers from prying eyes of the enemy, you can only watch the fire control radars and you never know if they're on target or not. Not the same, but technologically superior."

"Yes, sir. Not the same as when you came in," Lieutenant Kincaid said.

Troy cut his eyes to the left, trying to tell if Kincaid was serious or being sarcastic. Of course, eighteen years in the Navy was a long time, and with the exception of Master Chief Watson, who had twenty-six, and a couple of the senior chiefs and one chief petty officer, Troy had the most years of Navy service. Kind of a badge of honor to be brought up when he knew he led the pack.

"Alpha Whiskey, this is Falcon leader," came the broadcast from the speaker directly overhead. "We are ready to commence. Be advised that after the final exercise we need to be freed to continue to final destination— Monrovia."

"Probably crew's rest," Troy mumbled.

"Roger, Falcon Leader, understand. First exercise is basic anti-air warfare AAW-1-1. We will have Aegis fire control radar operating in lock-on mode. Missiles are disconnected and disarmed. Rules of engagement are one Falcon simulating cruise missile while three remaining aircraft fly same path at current altitude. Our challenge is to track inbound F-16 with air radar, switch to fire control radar, simulate engagement, and maintain lock-on as aircraft departs area. As F-16 nears five-nautical-mile range, we will activate Close-In Weapons System—CIWS. This should provide us with tracking, long-range engagement/shootdown, and close-in engagement shootdown training."

"Roger. Understand. Air Force standing by to provide United States Navy training it needs."

"Tell him I send my compliments and appreciation for

them taking time out of their transit to help us in this exercise," Troy said to Lieutenant Kincaid.

Kincaid passed the compliments as Troy listened. Kincaid went through the engagement checklist, which took a minute longer than Troy wanted—he looked at his wristwatch, ensuring the young Lieutenant saw him do it—before Kincaid asked the skipper for permission to commence the exercise. Troy was thinking more of the expression on the French faces aboard that reconnaissance aircraft when they found themselves lit up and locked on by the *Winston Churchill*'s fire control radar. What he wouldn't give for photographs of the event! Unfortunately, although the French aircraft was within visual range because of its altitude, it was too far away for easy eyeball contact.

The low murmur common to the Combat Information Center rose slightly as everyone prepared for the exercise. Speckled throughout CIC—a compartment that stretched the entire width of this Arleigh Burke–class guided-missile destroyer—the sound-powered telephone talkers relayed information to the watches topside, the bridge sound-powered talker, and to Engineering. Huge black helmets with headphones inside of them worn by the young sailors manning this critical information link reminded Troy of giant insect-like mandibles. Sound-powered telephones had been a staple of Navy warships since World War I. Regardless of the condition of the ship—it could be burning, powerless, and drifting with the current—as long as the sound-powered lines remained intact, the crew had internal communications. Sound-powered telephones were manned constantly when a ship was underway, with topside watches checking in with the bridge and combat whenever a visual contact was made. Within combat, a sound-powered telephone talker was always present, and at each console was the capability to join a sound-powered circuit. When a ship went to General Quarters, as the *Winston Churchill* was at this minute, additional sound-powered positions were manned to include Engineering and the damage-control stations.

Troy moved to the holograph display to watch the exercise. He listened to Lieutenant Kincaid give the Air Force fighters directions for their approach. To his right, standing over the shoulder of the fire control technician who manned the venerable AN/SPY-1 Aegis radar system, stood his executive officer, whose head rotated between Troy and the presentation on the Aegis fire control polar screen.

Troy had spent two weeks in Commanding Officer School relearning the specifics of the Aegis radar. People called it a radar system, but since its entry into the fleet in 1977 aboard the test platform USS *Norton Sound,* Aegis had blossomed into the workhorse combat system of the fleet. It wasn't just a radar. It was four megawatts of advanced combat weapons control system that was continuously searching, tracking, engaging, and controlling multiple missiles in flight against over a hundred targets. No modern warships, excluding warships like that damn amphib he was escorting to Liberia, sailed without Aegis, to his way of thinking. Ships like the aged Spruance-class destroyer ought to have been mothballed or sold for razor blades decades ago. If he went through *Jane's Fighting Ships* and 'X'ed' out every warship that had obsolete information systems, the U.S. Navy would be half its present size. People like his Command Master Chief were another anachronism. If you can't keep pace with technology and its impact on warfighting, then—by God—put your papers in and walk the sideboy gauntlet. Let those like Troy who prided themselves on keeping up with the information world keep the Navy moving forward.

"Skipper," Richman said, catching his attention. About ten feet separated them.

Troy nodded.

"Sir, how long you want to illuminate the French Atlantique?"

He shut his eyes. He opened them to see the surprised

expression on Lieutenant Kincaid's face. He eased around Kincaid and moved to where the XO stood.

"Long enough to get his attention, XO, and keep quiet. I don't want every Tom, Dick, and Harry to know what you're doing. Now, listen to me, when the Frenchie turns away toward land or takes evasive action, drop the lock-on. But," he warned, "you're going to have keep your lock on the four fighter aircraft simultaneously as they fly away from our position." His smile was intentionally tight. "Don't want them saying we specifically targeted the French."

"Skipper," Lieutenant Kincaid interrupted.

Troy looked over his shoulder to see the TAO standing there. Kincaid held his headset in his right hand, the cord trailing along the deck to where it was connected ten feet away.

"What is it, Lieutenant?"

"Sir, if you're about to do what I think you are, I respect-fully recommend you reconsider. Sir, if we intentionally lock on to an aircraft—or even a ship—of another nation in international waters, then, sir, we invite them to take appro-priate action to defend themselves." Kincaid's voice seemed almost pleading.

Troy thought, *Well, where's your monotone voice now, young man?*

"I know," Troy snapped. "This is not an intentional lock-on. It's just serendipitous that the Atlantique hap-pened to be in the fire control radar cross-section of Aegis when our fighters fly off in that direction."

"Sir—"

"That's enough, Lieutenant. I don't wish to discuss it. This is my decision. Your job is to focus on the exercise. My job is to take whatever actions I deem appropriate to enhance the security of our small naval force. We don't want another USS *Cole* incident—"

"Sir, the USS *Cole* was in port and—"

"Lieutenant, go do what you've been ordered to do. Thanks for your advice. If I want more, I'll ask for it.

Meanwhile, you make sure we pass this basic exercise."

"Aye aye, sir," Kincaid said. He turned away, lifting his headset and readjusting it on his head.

Troy looked past Kincaid. The *Mesa Verde* observer had been watching them. For a moment, he wondered if the visiting officer had heard their conversation, but then he relaxed as much as he could—the muscles in both thighs were trembling. He couldn't have heard enough to figure out what they were talking about, if he had heard them at all.

"Captain, you think Lieutenant Kincaid is right, and we should, maybe, not do this?"

"XO, don't be an ass at this time. Riches go to those who reach for them. Besides, what possible action could an unarmed French reconnaissance aircraft take against us? Fly overhead and flush its honey bucket across the ship?" He stopped abruptly. His voice had been louder than normal. "You do what you've been ordered to do. Okay?"

"Yes, sir," Richman said.

Troy turned away and returned to his previous position. *What if Kincaid is right?* he thought. *What if this backfires?* A ship's crew needed confidence in the man— and sometimes woman—who led them. Sure, he'd been the commanding officer for ten months, but this was the crew's first time deployed with him. This was an opportunity for him to show that the "old man" wasn't adverse to taking actions against forces that threatened the USS *Winston S. Churchill*—Arleigh Burke–class guided-missile destroyer, hull number DDG-81. Others in CIC pulled their headsets back onto their ears. He thought, *Had they been listening?*

As he walked behind Lieutenant Kincaid, the man turned. "Captain, I really do believe it would be in our— *your* best interest not to do this," he said in a soft voice.

"It doesn't hurt for us to flex our muscle every now and again, Lieutenant. I thought a brief flash of the fire control radar, just enough to light up their early warning devices, might cause them to abort their mission. But, you may be right. I've told the XO not to do it," he lied.

"Yes, sir. I think it's the right decision, sir. They're operating in international waters, conducting a peaceful mission much like our own reconnaissance missions. If we did this—"

"If we did it, Lieutenant, we wouldn't see them conducting hostile reconnaissance missions against U.S. Navy forces in this area for a long time to come," Troy scolded, each word spoken clearly and firmly in his best leadership voice. He mentally patted himself on the back. Even on the best-run ships, such as his, the crew needed to be reminded periodically who the commanding officer was. "So, I don't want to hear anymore. Your objection was noted and acted upon."

Kincaid nodded. "Thank you, sir."

There it was, back again—the monotone voice. Troy smiled. This was the first time he could recall when Kincaid had stepped out of character, when his voice actually took on some life. There may be hope for the man after all.

Kincaid turned his back to Troy and leaned down over the air intercept operator's shoulder. Troy stared at Kincaid's back for a moment and then stepped to the right where Petty Officer Schultz watched the air picture as the assigned air traffic controller.

From the speaker overhead came the voice of one of the F-16 pilots. "Alpha Whiskey, this is Falcon four; I am your missile for this afternoon's event. I am descending past angels two-zero heading for angels three. My range to you is thirty miles."

"Roger, Falcon four; we have you on radar. Falcon leader," broadcast Petty Officer Schultz, "we have you on radar, sir, at angels two-seven, heading one-five-zero at four hundred knots. Request confirm."

"Alpha Whiskey, Falcon leader; confirm altitude, heading, and speed. Request instructions."

"Alpha Whiskey, Falcon four; passing angels ten, descending angels three."

"Roger, Falcon four; continue descent. Continue reporting, Falcon leader. Continue current heading and speed. Maintain current altitude unless told elsewise."

The sound of a microphone being clicked twice acknowledged the ATC's instructions.

Troy glanced at the small fighter aircraft icon on the holographic display as it entered the outer range. He moved to the display to watch events unfold. Everyone had his or her assigned duties. Wasn't much he could do to change events now. They either performed well—which they would—or would face his wrath in training and training and more training.

Thirty miles wasn't much. Aegis could cut through radar and environmental clutter up to a hundred miles away, and with the right conditions could bend its signals to the curvature of the earth for another fifty to hundred miles. This AAW exercise also taught the crew how to use the ship's weapons to fight a close-in air attack, so the rules of engagement tying their hands to fully use the Aegis weapons systems was limited to exercise restrictions.

He remained quiet as the air tracker reported an inbound missile. With a critical eye, he watched Lieutenant Kincaid direct the fire control technician to switch on the fire control radar function of Aegis. A few seconds later, the FTG manning the console reported lock-on. Five minutes later, the fighter aircraft simulating an inbound cruise missile reached five nautical miles from the ship. Its altitude continued to drop, passing a thousand feet and continuing to descend. Lieutenant Kincaid ordered the Close-in Weapons System to take control.

TOPSIDE, MASTER CHIEF WATSON RUSHED FROM ONE SIDE to the other; the young third class petty officer operating the 35mm camera ran to keep up with him. They took photographs of the CIWS mount as it twisted and turned, its gatling gun protruding from the slit in its white dome. The gears whirled, and a faint metal-on-metal screech rode over the constant noise of a working warship as the guns tracked the inbound aircraft in unison with the CIWS fire control radar. The ship maneuvered right to left and then took sharp turns back to the right as it shifted its heading to increase the firing zones for the weapons. These moves also created a zigzagging in hopes of fooling a modern cruise missile. The CIWS turned nearly vertical as the aircraft flew directly over the ship.

"How about that, sailor!" Master Chief Watson shouted, pointing at the CIWS mount. "Make a mark of it, because you won't get to see that often."

The sailor raised the camera and clicked off a shot at the CIWS.

"Now, don't take photographs of everything I point out to you. I don't want to run out of film before the exercises are over."

The sailor shrugged. "I got loads of film, Master Chief," he said, patting the pouch strapped to his waist. "Loads of film."

Over head, contrails marked the presence and course of the three other Air Force F-16s as they flew by the Surface Action Group. Master Chief Watson shielded his eyes as they followed the low-level fly-by and as he watched the fighters pass overhead. Beside him, the clicking of the sailor's camera accompanied the young man's constant murmurings of awe: "Oh, God. Oh, God!" Watson smiled. Nothing new under the sun, except to a young man or woman who had never seen it.

The fire control radar of the starboard-side Vulcan Phalanx took over from the port-side CIWS and tracked the simulated cruise missile outboard from the USS *Winston S. Churchill* as the fighter aircraft began to ascend to rejoin the F-16 formation. The Aegis radar was integrated into the hull of the ship along the forward forecastle. Aegis did its job digitally, so no noise or indication of a change of radar tracking and fire control lock-on was visible or audible to those topside or below decks. Boy, he missed the old fire control radars with their quick, sharp jolts as they tracked aircraft along their narrow beams.

TROY GRINNED. HE WATCHED THE RADAR REPEATER AS THE Air Force fighters passed over the *Churchill* and continued on their southeasterly course. As the Arleigh Burke–class guided-missile destroyer continued on its course at twelve knots, it caused the F-16s to initiate a left-bearing drift to track the ship. Was he great or what! He glanced at the clock on the bulkhead. Two minutes—max—he estimated, and you'd be able to run a straight line from the *Churchill* through the F-16 formation directly to the French Atlantique reconnaissance aircraft.

Troy's grin widened. *Oh, God, they are right when they say there is no job better in the Navy than commanding officer of a Navy vessel.* The power was almost aphrodisiac. "That's good, Lieutenant. You keep providing me your advice and recommendations, but understand that once I discard them, or elect to follow another route, then I expect you to fall in line and carry out my orders."

"Ready, Skipper?" Joe Richman asked. He was still standing behind the fire control technician.

Troy looked at the display. The profile of the Air Force fighters and the French Atlantique reconnaissance aircraft were aligned with his ship. "Update the holographic display!" he ordered, hurrying the few steps from where he had been standing alongside Lieutenant Kincaid to the table located nearly center of Combat. Even as he moved, he saw the green shimmer of the holograph updating the display. "Add water depth," he said as he reached the display unit. *Best damn thing the Navy ever did,* he thought. Having a holographic display took everything around the ship and turned it into a smaller version, allowing a captain to see his or her ship and the surrounding vessels. Aircraft zoomed through the miniature virtual world while below the virtual seas submarines would cruise up and down to their changing depths. What his oldest son, Sean, wouldn't give for a computer game that could do this.

The display jumped a few inches as the operator added an artificial sea beneath the images. Troy didn't like ships maneuvering across the top of the table. Put some sea beneath them—made it realistic even if it was just a projection. He moved left so he was standing in line with the French reconnaissance aircraft as it continued to spin a figure-eight pattern along a predetermined track for its mission.

"Okay, XO. Let the fun begin," he murmured, turning to look at the XO, who was staring at him. The XO nodded, then quickly turned back to the display. "Show me the fire control beams," he said to the First-Class Operations Specialist who was operating the holograph display controls.

A yellow beam of light shot out from the image of the *Winston Churchill* to the image of the Air Force fighter. Troy reached down and put his hand on the roller ball that controlled the pointer. Clicking the left button beside the pool-ball-size controller, he placed the virtual pointer on the F-16. Immediately, beside the aircraft icon, identification and information data appeared showing the image as an Air Force F-16 Falcon fighter flying at five hundred knots. The image reflected an aircraft with its nose pointed upward. The altitude on the data display increased as the aircraft continued to gain angels.

The yellow line, showing the actions of the Aegis fire control radar, simmered and then shifted off the fighter aircraft to point directly at the image of the French Atlantique. He smiled. On board the French reconnaissance aircraft, the electronic intelligence operator would be shouting and screaming into his microphone that the Americans have locked their fire control radar onto them. How many minutes would it take before they departed orbit and headed home?

The French Atlantique image moved away from its racetrack orbit, its nose turning toward the *Churchill*. *Heading to shore,* he thought. Between the French reconnaissance aircraft and the USS *Winston S. Churchill,* pride of Commander Amphibious Group Two, flew the four fighter aircraft on a southeasterly course that, if maintained, would take them into the vicinity of the Atlantique. *I love it when a plan comes together,* Troy thought. Not only did he have a surface-to-air missile profile locked on the nuisance aircraft, but onboard the Atlantique, they must think they were under multiple attack. His missiles and his unsuspecting accomplices—the F-16 formation—should be causing all kinds of butt-tightening actions onboard that aircraft.

"XO!" Lieutenant Kincaid shouted, ripping off his headset, tossing it to the deck, and dashing to the fire control radar. "Break lock! Break lock!" he screamed at the fire control technician. "Break lock! Now!"

"What's going on, Lieutenant?" Troy asked, stepping toward the console.

The fire control technician was making the adjustments. Sweat ran down his forehead. Richman, his XO, had stepped away, not saying anything.

"Sir, we locked onto the French aircraft. I thought you said we weren't going to do that, sir!"

"Calm down, Lieutenant." He turned to Richman. "XO, didn't you hear me say to scrub the lock-on against the Frenchie?"

"No, sir . . . sir," Richman stuttered. "I thought you wanted it done. You were very precise."

"I may have discussed it, XO, but the last words to you were *not* to do it. You must not have heard it with your headset down."

"Alpha Whiskey, Falcon leader; we have reformed and are awaiting commencement of second exercise run," emerged from the speaker near Lieutenant Kincaid. "We are angels ten ascending, remaining on outbound course one-sixty."

"Sir, they're ready to do the intermediate exercise when we are," Petty Officer Schultz said aloud from his position.

Troy turned. "Lieutenant, keep them on current course for a few minutes while we get ourselves reorganized and ready for the exercise. Let me know when you're ready and I'll tell you when to start."

"Falcon leader, Alpha Whiskey; maintain course, speed, and continue climbing to angels twenty. Await instructions."

"Okay, we're waiting, but these F-16s are gas-hogs and we would like to land at Monrovia without refueling again. Would appreciate expedite remaining two exercises."

"Roger, sir."

"He doesn't look as if he's running, Captain," Richman said, one hand resting on the seat of the fire control technician while he turned toward Troy.

"Oh, shut up, XO." Troy walked back to the holograph. *Damn! Wasn't worth the effort. Didn't do a damn thing except make the XO look like a fool. At least it got Kincaid out of his papier-mâché character.* He watched the display for a couple of seconds before putting his hand on the mouse. He rolled the pointer onto the Atlantique, clicked on the track history file, and saw the French reconnaissance aircraft had steadied up on a course that would take it directly to the *Churchill*.

"Alpha Whiskey, Falcon leader; leveling off at angels eighteen. Cloud cover at angels twenty. Thought we'd stay below it."

"Roger."

What in the hell . . . Troy clicked on the image of the French Atlantique. The data display appeared. The altitude indicator showed the slow-moving reconnaissance aircraft ascending. It was still a couple of thousand feet below the Falcons, but if he didn't know better he'd swear the French were trying to intercept the F-16s. Maybe the French pilot figured if he put his aircraft near the fighters the ship couldn't fire on it. By now, the electronic intelligence experts on the Atlantique would have told the pilot

the ship's fire control was no longer locked on them. The
French weren't doing what he expected. Land was due
east, not northwest. This sinking feeling in the pit of his
stomach hit him at the same time his thighs started trembling again.

"Alpha Whiskey, we're showing a single air contact
dead ahead," came the voice of Falcon leader over the
speaker.

"Roger, Falcon leader. Contact is French Atlantique reconnaissance aircraft. It's been operating in the area for the
past two days," Petty Officer Schultz broadcast.

"Well, if you don't change our course and commence
this exercise soon, we're going to find ourselves . . . Light!
Light! God d—" The broadcast stopped, replaced by the
constant static of an empty airwave.

Chill bumps erupted all over Troy's body and his arms
started shaking. If he didn't sit down soon, he'd pass out or
fall.

"Skipper!" Lieutenant Kincaid shouted. "They're gone.
We've lost the Air Force fighters from our scope."

Troy didn't answer. He raised his head and looked at the
holographic display. Where four computer-generated icons
of the four fighter aircraft had been flying, the display reflected an empty sky.

"Sir, what should we do?" Joe Richman asked.

He hadn't heard his XO approach. He was too busy trying to figure out what could have happened.

Behind him, the speakers had carried the continued calls of
Petty Officer Schultz trying to raise the aircraft on the circuit.

On the holographic display, the Atlantique did a sharp
right-hand turn and steadied up on a course to take it back
to shore. What could have happened? For a brief second
he wondered if the French reconnaissance aircraft could
have had anything to do with the aircraft disappearance,
but he quickly discarded the idea. The Atlantique, like the
Navy's EP-3E Aries II aircraft, was unarmed.

He ignored the XO's continuing query for directions as he rolled the mouse around the display, believing somehow that this would bring the fighter aircraft icons back. The French reconnaissance aircraft was descending rapidly, heading for sea level. Something had gone wrong. The aircraft couldn't have run into each other. The French aircraft would have disappeared with them.

"Falcon leader, Alpha Whiskey; request acknowledge," Schultz continued.

Lieutenant Kincaid pulled up the black cord with the red push-to-talk button on it. "Fire control, this is the TAO. Cease operations and secure the history data." He reached down and pressed the 12MC to the bridge. "Bridge, this is TAO; please make the following log entry." He passed the location, time of disappearance, and other information he knew to the officer of the deck.

Troy took several deep breaths before he turned and faced Lieutenant Kincaid. "Lieutenant, I'll be on the bridge. Request stand-down from exercise, and rig for search and survival. Get the radio sweeps up and see if we can detect a beeper."

Master Chief Watson burst through the hatch leading up to the bridge. "Christ almighty, Captain! You should have seen it. The entire eastern sky lit up for a fraction of a second. Lit up like a camera flash going off. Me and the photographer had to rub our eyes to get our eyesight back."

"What are you talking about, Master Chief?" Troy asked.

Watson shrugged. "I don't know, sir, but for a second there, I thought we were in the Bermuda Triangle."

"Lieutenant," Troy said, continuing to stare at the master chief. "I'll be on the bridge."

With two steps he was through the door, taking the steps two at a time toward the bridge. Something had happened. Something had screwed up. And, although he couldn't see how it could have anything to do with him, he couldn't shake this feeling that somehow him locking the fire control radar on the French aircraft had something to do with the disappearance of the Air Force fighters. He needed air. He needed the bridge wing to go over events and make sure he had his story straight. Meanwhile, get the *Churchill* in the vicinity where the American aircraft were last seen.

On the USS *Mesa Verde,* LPD-19, one of the Navy's most modern amphibious warships and classified as a Landing Platform Dock, Captain Xavier Bennett rested one foot on the deck of the bridge with the other on the small metal step of the bridge captain's chair. He folded his sunglasses, stood up, and left the bridge. Minutes later he stood in the blue-lighted spaces of Combat, listening to a quick briefing by his Combat Information Center Watch Officer, referred to as the CICWO (pronounced sick-woe), on what had occurred less than fifteen minutes before.

The CICWO told Xavier that he had already ordered two CH-53 Sea Stallion helicopters to prepare to launch for a search and rescue mission. Xavier thanked him. On some ships, the decision to prepare for launch would have been held in abeyance pending the skipper's approval. Xavier believed common sense dictated most actions, and why wait for approval when your officers and chiefs knew what they could and couldn't authorize? Plus, it helped morale to know that your captain stood by decisions made by those serving under him. Confidence in leadership was second to respect of leadership, but Xavier learned years ago that the two traits were inescapably linked. How could you train future Navy warriors if you spent all your time micro-managing common sense decisions? He preferred the less stressful leadership style of letting his wardroom and chiefs manage the day-to-day operations. Within reason, of course. He had allowed the hotshot skipper of the *Winston Churchill* to run the show most of the way across. Xavier liked to see young, junior commanders who still had a sharp, pointy edge on their "A-type" personality leaping forward to test the bounds of their capability. This time, he needed to reassert his command as the Officer in Tactical Charge. He was sure the *Churchill* skipper could handle the search and rescue, but when life was endangered, it was better to err on the side of experience. Xavier had over sixteen of his twenty-eight years at sea as a surface warfare officer. His only regret was that he wished he could do it all over again.

"Get me the *Churchill*'s Charlie Oscar, Lieutenant," Xavier said.

A few minutes later, the CICWO put his hand over the mouthpiece and said softly, "He's on the bridge, Captain. I have his TAO on the other end."

Xavier nodded. "Pass him my compliments, and here's what I want you to tell him." He continued relaying his instructions verbally as the CICWO nodded comprehension. When Xavier finished, he ordered the CICWO to set the search and rescue details throughout the ship. He glanced at the clock. Five minutes at the most before the Seabee commander would appear wanting to know what was going on; not that the Seabees could do much in an at-sea SAR.

Some would have asked for a subordinate skipper to leave whatever he or she was doing to take a person-to-person call such as he had had his CICWO make. Wasn't in Xavier's grain. He patted the metal platform beside the combat captain's chair. He would never request that a skipper leave what he or she was doing to talk with him. The ship was always first. It was there when a skipper woke in the morning, it vibrated beneath his soles throughout the day, and it was the last thing on a skipper's mind when he shut his eyes for the night. Every square inch of that sleek, gray man-made animal that sliced through the surface of the ocean was his responsibility. The lives of those who sailed within her were his responsibility, too. The decisions a skipper made impacted everyone on board. No, it was a great responsibility to command a Navy warship and one that must always be respected.

"Let's lay out a search grid, Lieutenant, and get those helicopters airborne ASAP."

"IS CAPTAIN HARRISON ON THE BRIDGE?" THE VOICE OF Lieutenant Kincaid asked, the 12MC speaker broadcasting it throughout the bridge area.

The Officer of the Deck pushed the lever down on the sound-powered speaker. Captain Harrison nodded at him. "He's listening."

"Captain, Lieutenant Kincaid here, sir. Captain Bennett sends his regards and passes on that he has resumed tactical command. He would like our latest situation report and any further information we may have on the disappearance of the Air Force fighters."

Troy's teeth clenched and his eyes narrowed. He turned away so the bridge crew wouldn't see his right cheek, which had begun twitching. "Very well," he said after a few seconds. This Expeditionary Strike Group concept where cruisers and destroyers were assigned to an amphibious group was demeaning in his eyes. The USS *Winston S. Churchill* was an Arleigh Burke–class guided-missile destroyer. Sure, amphibious ships needed air and submarine defense while they transited and did their missions, but cruisers and destroyers could be deployed when necessary from the Cruiser-Destroyer Groups. Leave them with their own classes, was his philosophy. Transformation shouldn't mean giving up Navy tradition. He walked back out on the bridge wing, the temperature of the hot sun baking down on him as he stood hatless, looking out to sea.

The Air Force fighters had flown across the Atlantic in formation and had refueled two—or was it three?—times. They had to have been tired. He let out a deep breath. That was it. One or all of those fighters had collided with each other. Had nothing to do with his fire control event, though he wished he hadn't done it now. It would be one more thing to cloud the investigation. There was always an investigation when a human life was taken. Thankfully, it wasn't his fault. He told himself this as he stared out at the endless sea.

CHAPTER 3

THE POUNDING WOKE HIM. HE LAY WITH HIS EYES SHUT FOR a few more seconds as the banging on his at-sea stateroom door continued. He knew who was on the other side of that door, and he promised himself he really was going to talk to her. He blinked his eyes, fully awake, but hating the idea of rising. Another round of loud raps on the door vibrated through the compartment. He bet her parents and brothers danced and shouted for joy the morning she left for the Naval Academy. Xavier Bennett pushed himself up onto his elbows. The faint breeze from the circulated air brought a band of coolness across the back of his head where sweat had stuck the hairs to the pillows.

"Come in," he said, waiting for the door to open to confirm what he already knew. There was only one person who moved through the ship with the grace of a sledgehammer and the presence of a storm. He leaned over and grabbed the plastic bottle of spring water from the small bedside table, knocking the report from earlier onto the deck. Only captains of large ships had bedside tables. *Be a Navy captain and have a bedside table.* The caption might be competitively appealing against the decades long "Army of

One" mantra. He reached down, picked up the report, and set it back on the side table.

"Come in," he said louder.

He tilted the full bottle slightly to the side as he drank so he could watch his XO, Commander Elinor Fulbright, open the door. *Open* was the wrong word. Ellen never "opened" anything. One moment the air in his stateroom moved languidly to the soft whirl of the circulating fan, and next moment she burst into his at-sea stateroom, her broad shoulders blocking his view of the passageway behind her, causing him to feel the change in the air as it brushed against his face.

"Sorry to wake you, Skipper," she boomed, her raspy voice bouncing off the bulkheads. "Didn't want to . . ." She stopped for a moment and put her broad hand against her chest. "Whew! Those ladders could kill a girl!" She took several deep breaths, expelling them through her nose.

The sound reminded Xavier of a horse snorting. He shook his head. Horses were beautiful animals, but women tended to get upset if you compared them to one. Wasn't meant to be an ill thought. Maybe somewhere within that broad chest hid a bullhorn.

"There!" she said, dropping her hand from her chest. "Skipper, Admiral Holman is holding on the secure telephone for you." Her thick eyebrows furrowed into a shallow V as she emphasized the importance of the telephone call.

Xavier slung the covers back, revealing the gray gym shorts and shirt in which he routinely slept, "USNA" embossed in blue on both. Gym attire was the most suitable alternative for sleepwear in a coed navy. He was up and out of the full-size rack in seconds.

"I'll be right there, Ellen," he said. He yawned, reached up nonchalantly, and ran his hand once through his thinning and graying brown hair. He caught the slight shake of her head from the corner of his eye and wondered for a brief second what that was about.

Which would win, he wondered briefly? Would he have

a head full of gray hair or a head with no hair at all? He smiled at Ellen. She nodded sternly back as if recognizing that he understood the importance of a telephone call from their boss, the Commander Amphibious Group Two. He sighed. His executive officer had little tolerance for those who failed to see how important everything was. He knew she was waiting for him to follow her regardless of his dress, but admirals didn't hold on telephones, someone else did it for them, so he took his time. It looked as if he was going to have to order her out of his stateroom so he could get dressed.

As if reading his last thought, Fulbright blushed slightly, saluted, and with marching decibels shouted, "Aye aye, Skipper!" She did a smart about-face and slammed the door behind her. "I'll head back to Combat and tell him you're on your way!" she shouted from the other side of the door, her voice fading ever so slightly as she marched off down the passageway.

"You do that, XO," Xavier replied softly. No one to hear his comment in the empty compartment. He shook his head and grinned. It wasn't hard for anyone to realize Elinor "call me Ellen" Fulbright loved her job, loved the Navy, loved the adventure, and loved being XO. If she had a sense of humor to oppose her seriousness, she'd have a lot more fun in the Navy. He chuckled as he recalled, at his urging, her attempt to tell a joke at the last "dining-in" in Norfolk. Admiral Holman had been their guest speaker. Everyone had edged forward on their seats, listening to Commander Elinor Fulbright tell a joke. The wine glass in her hand sloshed the stuff onto the table and on the heads of those with the misfortune to be seated beside her while she stammered through the tale. Some have this intrinsic skill to be able to tell the most casual of tales and have everyone rolling on the ground in laughter. Others take jokes and humor and, with little attempt, kill them at the first word. Ellen was one of the latter. She had finished the only joke she knew and shoved the wine glass forward in a mock toast. This sent the contents halfway across the open area within the tables, nearly splashing Admiral Holman. Laughter brought the place down. Not because of the joke, but because it was the first time any of them had ever heard her try to tell one. The Navy was just going to have to have Ellen as she was. She was ecstatic. Now the challenge had been to convince her that everyone had already heard the lone joke of Ellen Fulbright so she'd never tell it again.

He pulled a pair of socks from his chest of drawers and tossed them on the bed. Bottom line was she was good. He was happy with her. She met Xavier's concept of a good XO. Unafraid to tell him what she thought, even when it conflicted with his ideas. Sometimes he agreed, and they went her way. Sometimes not. When they went his way against her advice, an outsider could never tell the two had differing opinions. She was pure Naval Academy, acting as if she fully and wholeheartedly supported whatever the old man wanted, even when he knew in her heart she still thought he was wrong. Xavier long ago discovered the old adage about there being "more than one way to skin a cat" was a good leadership philosophy. Tell them what you want and see how they go about doing it. Sure, they'd do it differently than you would, but in the process they learned, and sometimes you did. It also built loyalty because it showed trust. Allowing subordinates to argue their recommendations was an important element of leadership and developing future captains for the sea. It didn't matter whether he thought the advice or recommendation was doable or valuable—sometimes he thought it ludicrous— but what mattered was that they knew he would listen. Being a great listener was a more valuable leadership trait than being a great speaker.

He lifted the report from the bedstand, thumbed quickly through the ten-page, single-spaced package. Several things in it concerned him. The low morale within the wardroom that the lieutenant implied was in itself enough to merit an inspector general visit. But if what his lieutenant, who had been the exercise observer on the *Churchill* the day of the F-16 formation disappearance, wrote was accurate, then he had more than a legal problem. Why would that upstart Harrison deliberately lock a fire control radar onto a non-hostile aircraft? It made little sense for a man on the fast-track to Admiral to do something this childish, this illegal, and this stupid. International convention marked such deliberate events as acts of war.

He would do what he always did when confronted with something so important that it could have far-reaching consequences, but didn't require an immediate decision. He would think about it. Give this one a well-thought-out decision. One to two more days weren't going to kill anyone—at least he hoped not.

He knew he was going to have to assign an officer to conduct a Judge Advocate General Manual, a JAGMAN, investigation to gather statements and develop a better picture of what had happened. A regular line officer did these, with the legal animals of JAG reviewing the work when completed. A JAGMAN would provide better information than half-heard and half-seen perceptions from his lieutenant. As he pulled on his underwear, his thoughts were on sending Admiral Holman a "personal for" message later with the details, and sometime today issuing a SECRET operations report on the incident. He knew that when he did, it would be like a dam blowing, releasing millions of gallons of water. The flood of requests, questions, and directions would fill his radio shack and a number of careers could be washed away. Meanwhile, he still had a couple of days to refine his course—or courses—of action.

Captain Xavier Bennett slipped on his bedroom slippers and stepped into the private bathroom on the starboard side of his at-sea stateroom. With the exception of when an admiral occupied the lone flag suite on board the *Mesa Verde*, Xavier was the only person on board with his own private head. Another perk of command at sea. He pushed the thoughts of the report aside. Take the telephone call first, then tomorrow morning ask his legal officer to look at the lieutenant's report.

The sound of water flushing down the commode filled the background as he quickly finished dressing. Walking toward the door, he pushed the end of his belt through the buckle, pulling it back slightly to lock the clasp. He stepped through the door, gently shutting it behind him.

The radio shack was nearer, but the people most interested, who would have to act on orders resulting from the upcoming conversation with his boss, the Commander Amphibious Group Two, would be in Combat, so he'd go down the extra deck and cross the extra frames so they wouldn't feel left out. He smiled, knowing his XO was tapping her fingers on something, worried that his slow pace to answer the call would reflect badly on him and the *Mesa Verde*. He didn't worry about the admiral tapping his fingers on the other end, waiting impatiently for him to pick up. The admiral had his time at sea and knew the routine. One of the admiral's officers, most likely his executive aide, would be the one on the other end waiting patiently for Xavier to acknowledge his presence. Then the admiral would come on the line.

Xavier ducked as he stepped through a watertight hatch between frames along the passageway. He smiled, recalling a two-star admiral he served with years ago who enjoyed making his own telephone calls. His favorite game was when someone on the other end made the faux pas of putting him on hold. The admiral would hang up and go about his business, knowing that on the other end, bedlam was breaking out as the officer he called was either dialing him back ASAP, or, worse, the young sailor or junior officer who answered the telephone failed to catch the admiral's name. When that happened, the bedlam was vivacious, with much wailing and arm waving. Xavier also knew from experience that it was mouth drying, because the admiral had a reputation as a screamer. It had been a mean habit, with only the flag officer enjoying it.

Ten minutes after Elinor Fulbright had shocked him from sleep, Bennett stepped over the transom of the watertight hatch into Combat. He stopped for a brief moment to allow his eyes to adjust to the soft blue light of the compartment. Then he moved between the consoles, working his way to the Combat Information Center Watch Officer and took the proffered handset from him without a word. The First Class Operations Specialist, the leading petty officer for the mid-watch hours, handed him a cup of coffee. He nodded at the man and took a quick sip as the petty officer faded into the shadows of the darker spaces. Good. No milk. No sugar. And, most importantly, fresh.

The faint ozone smell of electronics wafted along with the odor of fresh coffee, riding the light breeze of cool air circulating through CIC. Below the soft murmur of CIC conversation and sound-powered telephone reports, a constant hum from the electronics provided a steady background noise. These electronics analyzed and displayed a continuum of data that poured into giant computer servers buzzing away in a compartment several frames from CIC. Giant computer servers, acting like gigantic data mixing bowls, churned the new data, updated the old, and created a common operating picture for the users. Data from organic sensors on the *Mesa Verde*, data from satellites passing overhead, data riding a line-of-sight communications link from the USS *Winston S. Churchill*, steaming twenty miles north of their position, and data pushed by intelligence agencies and other commands thousands of miles away in the United States arrived via satellite links into the information cauldron of the servers. The servers then mined the millions of bits of data sent to the *Mesa Verde* and graphically displayed the results on the consoles. Hidden away from day-to-day operators who used those consoles, a small group of system administrators worked constantly to keep the information flowing by manipulating the cyber world and keeping communication ports and protocols working.

Xavier pushed the small diamond-shaped transmit button on the red handset. The musical notes of the cryptographic keys synchronizing filled the speaker. "Captain Bennett here for Admiral Holman." He put his hand over the mouthpiece. "Lieutenant," he said softly to the Combat

Information Center Watch Officer. "Take this off the speaker while the Admiral and I talk."

A few seconds later, the Commander Amphibious Group Two picked up on the other end.

"Harry, Dick Holman here. How's everything going?"

Only a few, such as his mother, called him Xavier. Even his wife called him Harry.

Admiral Holman started to say something and the circuit lost contact, cutting the admiral off abruptly. Xavier waited patiently with the handset to his ear. It was not an unusual occurrence at sea, where most communications were via satellite.

Hearing the admiral address him as Harry caused Xavier to recall how his oldest, his daughter Mary, had come home upset when she was in the third grade when she discovered her father's real name was Xavier, not Harry. He grinned at the recollection.

Static stopped abruptly on the line. Xavier nodded. It meant that the information technicians were resetting something or switching to another communications portal.

Yes, his daughter had been almost as upset as when she discovered at age sixteen that she had no college fund. *Why?* she demanded. *Everyone at school has one; some have as much as two thousand dollars in theirs.* Probably if he hadn't laughed, she wouldn't have been as upset as she had been. College funds were unnecessary for a Bennett. Bennetts went to the Naval Academy. He did, his father did, and his grandfather did, and eventually Mary did. He hoped she was enjoying her new assignment as the assistant operations officer aboard the guided-missile destroyer USS *Stribling*. Her ship was engaged in gunfire support to the Marines ashore in Indonesia. Even though she was a mile or so offshore, he still worried for her safety.

The static came back for a moment and then cleared.

"Harry, you still there?"

"I've got you fivers, Admiral. We're fine out here. We're still searching for survivors, but after this long a period, it is very doubtful there will be any. The sea's been calm,

increasing our visibility. We've found lots of debris, but
nothing of the pilots. I believe we've found everything floating. Some of the search areas we've covered three times,
hoping something might pop up to the surface."

"I've been reading your reports. They're all starting to
look the same."

"Like I said, Admiral Holman, we haven't found anything new in the past thirty-six hours. Most everything we
recovered was during the first day of the search."

"I understand, Harry," Holman said. Xavier detected the
resignation in his tone. No one wants to give up hope for
the fear that a survivor is out there waiting for rescue. Also,
there is the knowledge that someday you could be the one
floating out there waiting for someone to pull you out of
the sea.

"Admiral, I received the Second Fleet deployment order
this morning detailing USS *Grapple,* ARS 53, from Little
Creek to the area to probe beneath the waves. I think it's
the right move. We've reached the point where a rescue
and salvage ship is the only feasible way we're going to recover the bodies and possibly additional wreckage."

"Yeah, Harry, I talked with Second Fleet before the
message went. The *Grapple* is deploying with one of our
two east coast deep submersibles on her."

"That's good. Do we have an arrival date, and do you
want me to continue the SAR until she arrives?"

"What's your recommendation, Xavier?"

Xavier smiled. The admiral switched between Harry
and Xavier as if unsure which one Xavier preferred. To
Xavier, he answered to both as easily as to one. "Admiral,
we just ended our third day of searching. The *Churchill* is
twenty miles north of my position—you have those positions, sir?"

"I got them right in front of me, Xavier. I'm playing
combat information command on my desk like a grammar
school kid—with a chart, a pair of calipers, and a couple of
number-two pencils."

"Yes, sir. As you know, we're conducting a coordinated

grid search. My ship is two nautical miles west of the center grid at—"

"I have the coordinates, Harry." Xavier heard a huge sigh come through the speaker. "Xavier, I don't want to tell you to quit, but I agree with you. I think you've found all you're going to. We need to free you up to let you continue on to Harper, Liberia, and discharge the 133rd "kangaroos can do" Seabees. General Thomaston says if they don't start their work on the port and airport soon, they'll run the risk of being caught when the monsoons hit next year," Holman said.

Xavier hadn't had the pleasure of meeting retired Lieutenant General Thomaston, late of the 82nd Airborne. General Thomaston was fast becoming a legend not only in America, but throughout Africa. The retired three-star Ranger immigrated to Liberia with nearly a hundred families several years ago. Two years ago, after defeating a rebel army lead by the notorious terrorist Abu Alhaul, General Thomaston had become the president of the interim Liberian government.

"Roger, sir. I understand. My recommendation, Admiral, is for us to run into Harper and discharge the Seabees. Then, if the situation merits it, we can return to the search area to help the *Grapple* while its deep submergence vehicle searches for additional debris on the bottom. It's only a couple of hundred miles from here to Harper. We can leave the USS *Churchill* as Officer in Tactical Charge of the search effort. My helicopters have the legs to stage from the *Mesa Verde* flight deck while we're tied up pierside in Harper."

"Sounds good, Harry. You go ahead and make it happen. That way we can continue a search for survivors while making both the acting president of Liberia and your Seabees happy. I've already received two telephone calls from the head Seabee himself stressing the importance of getting them off-loaded and working."

"Aye, Admiral. Will make it happen. Anything else?"

"A couple, Xavier. One, once you reach port, remain

port-side until told otherwise. I don't want you rushing back out to sea unnecessarily."

"Roger, sir."

There was a noticeable pause before the handset crackled in response to the person on the far end pressing the talk button. "Just you and I on this circuit, Harry?"

"Yes, sir."

"This is sensitive, and I'm having my intelligence officer Mary Davidson send you more information."

"I'll be looking for it, Admiral," Xavier replied, wondering what information could be so sensitive that instead of passing it via secure voice, the admiral insisted on sending it via message. "Anything you can tell me until Mary's message arrives?"

"I'll tell you this, Xavier. There's a possibility that the loss of those F-16s wasn't accidental. There's a chance they were shot down."

A chill went up Xavier's back. Mentally, he quickly reviewed the series of events before responding. "Sir, that would be impossible. There was nothing in the area with the missiles to shoot them down but us, and we didn't even fire our guns. There were no foreign warships in the area, and the only other visitor was a French Atlantique reconnaissance aircraft, which fled the area when the F-16s collided."

"We're not sure they collided."

"Admiral, that's the only explanation that we can come up with."

"Apparently, there's another one, but you'll need to read the message when it arrives. You've got to ask yourself, Xavier, how do you know they collided?"

Xavier shrugged his shoulders. "It's the only explanation, isn't it, Admiral? The four were reforming, about to turn, or in a turn. Plus, they'd been formation flying for over eight hours. I mean, the fatigue . . . It's no wonder one or more of the aircraft collided causing a cascading effect that downed all four. I'm not an aviator, but even surface ships maneuver independently when we're traveling in formation. It breaks the tension and keeps the mind sharp."

Xavier heard a deep breath from the other end. "Keep this to yourself, Xavier, until you read the message. The information from Captain Davidson will tell you more than I can say. You recall the arrest—I think it was about a month ago—of a government employee at the Missile Research Defense Agency?"

Xavier's eyes squinted for a moment as he sought to recall the finer points of that arrest. "I recall the arrest," he drew out. Then, speaking normally, he continued, "But I have to admit I didn't follow it closely. I was in Pascagoula loading Naval Mobile Construction Battalion 133, which is a story for several beers one day, Admiral."

Laughter came from the other end. "I know. I've had the pleasure of keeping company with the Seabees. I think of them as the other half in a marriage—can't live with them, can't live without them."

He chuckled. "You're right. Thought I was going to have to take them everywhere twice; second time to apologize."

"We're getting off the subject, Xavier."

"Yes, sir. You were telling me about the arrest."

"Seems our little government spy had his fat little heart set on selling to our French allies information on a special laser weapons program called "Phoenix." He had classified CDs on him when they arrested him. Seems to me they took their sweet time in grabbing him off the street. They'd been watching him for months. Only arrested him when they realized he had cleared out his bank account—figured he was about to run. From what they've managed to get out of the man, apparently those classified CDs found on him were the final delivery to the French." He chuckled. "Ironically, the laser weapons program has lots of problems and has yet to perform to expectations. We think the French were sold a load of crap, which makes me happy from that perspective. The Defense Information Systems Agency did an analysis of the CDs and found test results with recommended technical corrections to the Phoenix program. The problem is, the technical corrections have already been tried. They don't work. Phoenix still has a long way to go before we can cry *Eureka!* Guess if we go down enough roads, we'll discover one that runs all the way."

The secure voice synched suddenly, disrupting the conversation as the communications equipment, with the help of information technicians, automatically sought to reestablish secure communications between Admiral Holman and Captain Bennett. One on a ship sailing two hundred miles off the west coast of Africa, and the other ashore in the headquarters building of Commander, Amphibious Group Two, on Little Creek Amphibious Base, Norfolk, Virginia. The link passed between ground and ship through a stationary satellite orbiting over the middle of the Atlantic Ocean.

Xavier lay the handset down after a minute. He'd hear the static announcing circuit restoration when it occurred. He picked up his cup and took a big swig of coffee, shutting his eyes briefly as he enjoyed the taste. Last night had been the first time in three days where he had allowed himself to sleep in his rack instead of power napping in the captain's chair on the bridge. He looked at the clock on the bulkhead and wondered if he could sneak in another couple of hours before reveille. He heard the burst of static from the earpiece, reached down, and put the handset against his ear.

Another couple of seconds passed before the communications link reestablished and the digital readout showed the two men cleared to talk at the top-secret level.

"Sorry about that, Admiral. Must be the summer night."

"I had my joys with communications two years ago when I was off the coast of Liberia. You don't know how important information is until you can't get it or those whom you expect to provide insight to a situation suddenly seem unavailable." A grunt came across the handset.

Xavier had heard rumors of how Holman had been left on his own to handle a French-American confrontation. Apparently, Washington could have disappeared from the face of the earth for the lack of advice and insight they had provided the Commander, Amphibious Group Two. A long, successful career in the Navy, reinforced by two tours at the Pentagon, had taught Xavier that rumors were rumors and most rumors were born from someone somewhere with his or her own agenda and interests. No one ever lied; everyone just had different perceptions of the truth.

"When you get back, Harry, we'll have a couple of beers. Throw some dogs and hamburgers on the grill and you can tell me your stories of loading the Seabees and I'll tell you mine about communications in your area of the world."

"Nothing stirs my soul more, Admiral, than talking techno-geek stuff such as communications. You'd better bring more than a couple of beers if we're going to talk comms long," Xavier said, smiling. Then he added, "I'll bring Linda, also. She'll enjoy learning from your wife." The communications link dropped again. His mind wandered as he waited for it to be restored again.

"Good," Holman said, jerking Xavier back to the conversation. He hadn't heard the line resynchronize. "Xavier, Commander Tucker Raleigh is arriving in Monrovia tomorrow afternoon on the daily Air Force C-141. Chances are he'll arrive before you dock in Harper. He's coming down to help Thomaston train the new Liberian army, so technically he's not a SEAL for a while."

"Roger, sir. We'll help him when he shows up. Not a SEAL for a while? That must be like being thrown out of the family for one of them."

"Could be. Another thing, Xavier. I know you and I discussed this, but I was in Washington last week and had a chance to spend a few minutes with the Vice Chief of Naval Operations. The subject of my replacement came up, since I leave next year. He asked me my thoughts and I told him. I think you're the right person for the job. He has approved my request to frock you to Admiral when the next fiscal year begins on October first."

Frocking was the administrative action of allowing someone selected for the next rank to wear the rank and have the privileges of that rank, but without the pay and monetary benefits. More work for the same pay and privileges.

"It will give you some time to get used to the stars while you continue as commanding officer of *Mesa Verde*. Next summer you'll roll to Fort McNair in Washington, D.C., and go through the flag officer CAPSTONE course to learn the secret handshake, how to hide the effects of that third glass of wine, and what not to do when groupies flock after you—along with other maritime secrets of those wearing the rank of admiral."

"You've had groupies, sir?"

"Well, *I've* never had any, but I've seen some who have."

"You have?"

"Yep, they retire early, and if they're lucky, at the same pay grade. Good try, Harry. Bottom line is you're coming to the vacation spot of the Navy—Little Creek Amphibious Base in Norfolk or Virginia Beach, depending on which mayor is speaking. You're going to be the next Commander, Amphibious Group Two. And you're going up to Washington for CAPSTONE where you'll hobnob for a couple of weeks with future flag and general officers of all four military services."

Linda would enjoy the short visit to Washington. She would enjoy remaining in the Tidewater area. When Holman had offered it to him back in February after the flag selection list came out with his name on it, Xavier had been reluctant to accept. He and Linda had been looking forward to returning to their country house in Maryland. They had even discussed planting a half-acre garden. Their friends teased that a half-acre was more farming than gardening. Linda was a Norfolkian. A former cheerleader of Norfolk Catholic High School. Plus, she was quick to point out a long line of ancestors who called Norfolk home. With her younger sister in rehab and her sister's children staying with Linda's parents, his wife was sorting through her own feelings of guilt over the chance she might have to leave the family before this crisis was over. The other side was that she really wanted to return to Maryland.

"Thanks, Admiral. Linda and I have discussed the idea of me relieving you. If the Navy feels I can best serve it as your relief, I would be honored."

"That's good news, Harry. All things being equal, I hope this is something you're looking forward to and not something you're accepting out of obligation and Navy loyalty."

He grinned. "Admiral, it's all of the above."

BEHIND XAVIER, OUT OF SIGHT, COMMANDER FULBRIGHT elbowed Lieutenant Embrey. "See, I told ya," she whispered.

Embrey rubbed her rib cage. "Yeah, but you're leaving soon after he does. I have two more years here and it would be just my luck to get one of those testosterone-laden Naval Academy types whose "A-type" personality is tipped with titanium. A tip that will bore through all of us when he realizes his predecessor made Admiral out of his tour on the *Mesa Verde*."

"Shit, Teresa. Don't be paranoid. Captain Bennett is Naval Academy."

"I'm not paranoid, and he doesn't count," Lieutenant Teresa Embrey pouted.

Lieutenant Patrick Macmillan, the CICWO, leaned toward the two women. "What are you two whispering about?" he asked quietly, his elbow lightly touching Embrey's shoulder and enjoying the slight pressure the petite woman officer pressed back in return.

"The skipper just accepted orders to relieve Admiral Holman."

"He's going to be COMPHIBGRU Two?" Macmillan asked incredulously. Then he turned around, bent his head down to the chief standing beside him. Like wildfire, the news about Admiral-select Bennett becoming COMPHIB-GRU Two circulated through Combat. A few moments later the sound-powered telephone operators blazed the news through the ship. Nothing made a crew prouder than when one of their own succeeded. Nothing made them sadder than when someone undeserving succeeded.

"OKAY, XAVIER. I'M SIGNING OFF. I APOLOGIZE FOR GETTING you out of the rack. You should expect to read the flag message from Chief of Naval Operations sometime this spring directing you to report to Amphibious Group Two as my relief. My staff is already looking forward to you coming. I have told them how you will be a lot more involved than I am in their day-to-day operations, providing minute guidance to make their job easier. Told them the thing I admired the most was your leadership style of gathering the wardroom together every morning around 0800 for a fifteen-minute prayer session to set the tone of the day."

"You didn't!" Xavier gasped.

Holman's loud laughter erupted from the other side. "Harry, you should see the number of transfer chits I have on my desk."

"Admiral, surely someone on your staff knows me well enough—"

"Just kidding, Harry. You're too well-known. I did tell a bunch of junior officers that tall tale, but my chief of staff, Leo Upmann, couldn't keep a straight face. I may leave him here for you as punishment for ruining my fun."

"Thanks, Admiral. I can tell that I can only go up once I relieve you."

"Sometimes, Xavier, I think I'm walking a fine line between Washington wanting me relieved and the thoughts of doing it taking over the minds of both Commander, Fleet Forces Command and Commander Second Fleet. There are always toes to step on when tact is a four-letter word."

"Would that mean I'd transfer earlier?" Xavier replied, a hint of amusement in his voice.

"Don't be too pushy. You surface warfare types are all

alike. You see a person with more work than you have and you're immediately jealous for his job."

They both laughed.

A few more exchanges occurred about the planned cookout before Admiral Holman ended the conversation. Xavier pushed the handset back into its cradle. Looking up, everyone was staring at him. "What?"

"Congratulations, Boss!" came Ellen's boom. She started clapping, and soon everyone in the *Mesa Verde* Combat Information Center joined the applause.

His face grew warm. A path of red light broke the blue of Combat for a moment as someone entered through the watertight hatch leading from the 03-level passageway. He glanced over and recognized the thin waist and bulldog chest. It was Commander Teddy Klein, commanding officer of the Naval Construction Battalion 133. The sandy-haired Seabee had upper arms like giant pistons that moved when he walked, stretching the short cotton sleeves of the khaki shirt to where Xavier expected the shirt to split at any moment. The Seabee's legs bowed slightly as if the muscle weight of the huge chest pushed them outward to their limits.

"Thank you! Thank you!" Klein shouted from the door, smiling, his voice as strong as his arms.

For a moment, Xavier thought of how much noise and bedlam a bevy of offsprings from the likes of Klein and Fulbright could bring to a neighborhood. He shook his head, ridding himself of the horrible thought.

The applause died as those in Combat turned toward Klein.

"Thank you, all! Captain, your ship really knows how to make a sailor feel at home!" Klein shouted, continuing to wave his hands about his head as he walked toward Captain Bennett. A trace of humor rode beneath the comment.

Laughter filled the compartment. People such as Klein were always good for morale. If he'd only get a haircut. No one could ever accuse Klein of being too military. Klein's ballcap had the hopping kangaroo emblem of the

NMCB-133 sewed above the scrambled eggs on the brim. The emblem evoked the NMCB-133 mantra of "kangroos can do," which was why Xavier always heard the Seabees respond to orders with a loud "kangroos can do." Of course, the mantra caused the war-fighting arm of the Navy to roll their eyes when they heard it, but not so those muscle-bound, hell-raising Seabees could see them. You never knew when a Seabee was going to build something or rip it down with their bare hands—bare hands the rest of the Navy would prefer they keep away from them. Seabees sure as hell made life a lot easier for the war-fighting forces when the fight moved ashore. They were renown for their skills in turning swamp-ridden everglades into airfields and barracks with running water. And they could do it nearly overnight. Seabees were legendary, and for the most part forgotten until needed.

"Captain," Klein said as he reached the master bank of consoles. "Sir, I wasn't expecting you to be up at this time of night."

Xavier looked at Ellen. "And, I wouldn't be, Commander, if my XO hadn't asked me to come to Combat. I would also say the same for you."

"I've just finished a meeting with my officers, sir. You know we're nearly six weeks behind. We were a month behind before we left Pascagoula and now we've been delayed another week out here—"

"Three days."

"Sir?"

"Three days. Not a week."

Klein nodded, a slight grin complementing the twinkle in his light-blue eyes. It was hard to be upset with this gregarious officer, and the fact that he could easily rip Xavier's head off and use it as a step stool had nothing to do with it.

"Yes, sir. Three days. Figured after the past couple of days, you'd be catching up on some valuable shuteye."

Xavier glanced at his XO. "I did have a short rest, Commander. Nice of you to ask."

"Yes, sir. Captain, do we have a date as to when we're going to get into Harper, sir? For the past week, even before the F-16s disappeared, we've been going over our construction plans, looking for ways to cut days of work. The bad news, Captain, is that regardless of how well we plan, Mother Nature always throws curves at us Seabees, and if we have to face the monsoon season next year—"

Xavier held up his hand. "Commander Klein, I have ordered the ship to start toward Harper. With luck, we should start off-loading you and your Seabees sometime within the next seventy-two hours."

Klein let out a deep breath. "That's great news, Captain. I'll tell my men and women tomorrow morning." Klein nodded once and walked around the captain to where Lieutenant Emery stood.

Xavier rubbed his right thumb along the side of his hand, a nervous gesture he'd inherited from his father.

"Ellen, I'm heading back to my stateroom to try to steal a couple more hours of sleep before reveille."

"Yes, sir."

He walked by her, stopped, and turned. "By the way, XO, leave word for our young legal-beagle to have breakfast with me. I want to go over the report Lieutenant Sanchez wrote with him." He looked down, biting his lower lip for a moment before he continued. "Did you get a chance to read it?"

She nodded. "Yes, sir, I did. And I gave a copy to Lieutenant Commander Kilpatrick after dropping off the original with you."

"Good. Then, I shouldn't have to prep him about the contents?"

Fulbright shook her head. "I don't think so, sir. He's usually pretty thorough on things."

"That may be, but he has a lot on his plate right now with the letters from Pascagoula about our Seabees' last night in port—"

"—And the two captain's masts scheduled for late tomorrow morning."

"Yeah, those two we may delay until we arrive in Port Harper."

"Sir, one of those going to mast is a Seabee. If you wait until we tie up, then he has the option of a court martial. Not to mention, if he disembarks, it will be Commander Teddy Klein who will do the mast."

He sighed. "Have Legal draft the paperwork for me to authorize Commander Klein to do the administrative punishment on his people."

She nodded.

"What did you think of the report?"

The XO's eyes locked with his. "If half of what Lieutenant Sanchez says is right, then the *Churchill* has a lot of problems."

He bit his lower lip, nodding. "You could be right, but perceptions and half-truths have ruined many a Navy career."

Xavier didn't wait for a reply as he turned and departed Combat to the traditional "Captain out of Combat" cry coming from behind him. On the bridge, they'd duplicate the operations log in Combat with a notated time of his entry and exit from the compartment. His mind felt foggy from the fatigue of being awake for nearly three days with only short naps on the bridge or a few power naps in his at-sea stateroom. This wasn't his first search for survivors at sea. People lost at sea had only minutes in the worst case, hours in the best, to survive. Many times, it's serendipitous luck when a ship recovers a survivor. Helicopters cover more surface and have more flexibility to rescue someone than a surface ship that must maneuver against tide, waves, and wind.

He closed the door to his stateroom and flipped on the bedside lamp. Xavier unclasped his trousers and let them fall on the deck. He lay down, reached over the side of the bed, and lifted the trousers off the deck and tossed them onto a nearby chair. He made the slam-dunk sign with his two fingers. "Dos Puntos!"

Three days they had searched. If you haven't recovered

a survivor in three days, the prognosis was slim that you ever would.

IN COMBAT, COMMANDER FULBRIGHT PICKED UP A SHIP'S telephone and dialed the ship's judge advocate, Lieutenant Commander Thomas Kilpatrick. It never occurred to her to wait until reveille. An order was an order was an order, and you executed orders immediately. Plus, the last thing Fulbright wanted was an officer of hers blindsided. Though she had told the captain that Kilpatrick was aware of the report, it never hurt to double check your statements and confirm information.

CHAPTER 4

ADMIRAL DICK HOLMAN, COMMANDER, AMPHIBIOUS Group Two, jiggled the handset into the metal holders of the cradle. "Well, Leo, looks as if Rear Admiral Lower Half—*selectee*—Bennett is going to be your new boss sometime next year. Maybe he can straighten out your lax nature."

"Xavier's a good man, Admiral, even if he is Naval Academy. I look forward to serving with and under him until he can bring someone in to relieve me."

"Relieve you? What a fantastic idea, Leo. I should have thought of that years ago." Holman pushed his chair away from his desk and stood, holding his hand over his eyes. "Shut the blinds, if you would, Leo. These Virginia suns are too bright in the afternoon. Where's the clouds when you need them?" Holman scrunched his face. "We've been ashore for nearly a month."

"And we notice it, too, sir."

"Don't give me that crap about me being irritable when I'm ashore too long. I'm an aviator. Being at sea doesn't count; buzzing clouds in the sky does. Besides, what's the purpose of being in the Navy, if you can't be at sea, above the sea, or at least pulling into some exotic port?"

"Don't forget under the sea."

Holman faked a shudder. "Right, you can't bail out of a submarine if something goes wrong."

"As a submarine captain told me once, Boss, there are more aircraft in the ocean than there are submarines in the air."

"Leo, don't you have something to do?" He leaned back in his chair and crossed his legs. "We ought to be doing something. The *Boxer* finish with its dock-side repair work?"

Captain Leo Upmann pushed himself upright off the couch to the side of Holman's desk. "No, sir. They need another couple of weeks, Admiral. They're working on the turbines and apparently believe one of the shafts is bent. They're seeing if it's fixable or if they're going to have to replace it." He started twisting the round plexiglass rod that controlled the blinds.

"How long will that take?" Holman asked sharply, referring to the engineering problems on his flagship. "I thought the major work they had to do was upgrading some combat systems on board. The engineering casualty was supposed to be easy to fix."

Holman's flagship, the USS *Boxer,* was tied up at Norfolk Naval Station where deep-draft warships moored. Here he sat at Amphibious Group Two headquarters on Little Creek Amphibious Base shuffling papers and waffling platitudes about shipboard readiness and personnel retention. Granted, you couldn't fight and win wars if ships weren't ready, and people beat feet for the civilian world. They were very important items for a great Navy, but couldn't he do that at sea—off the coast, out of sight of land and bureaucrats—as well, if not better, than day-in and day-out, pulling-in and pulling-out an office chair as he rushed to beat the administrative traffic pouring into his inbox?

Being at sea meant no inbox; hence, the administrative burden of command remained ashore with a senior Navy captain who had the fun of sitting in his chair doing what he was doing now—only without his cigars. He always took those with him. Others would say he might be shirking his duty, but he preferred to think of it as training his subordinates. Then, there was that one asshole he overheard at the Officers Club who commented that the best captain's job in the Navy was Commander, Amphibious Group Two. That was Holman's job, and it was a two-star admiral's job, which he knew also brokered discussion as to why after two years as COMPHIBGRU Two, Holman was still a one-star.

Bright sunlight flooded the room as it reflected off the edges of the half-closed blinds from Captain Leo Upmann's efforts to execute the admiral's orders.

"There you are, Admiral. Should give you that cramped feeling you enjoy when inside the skin of the ship." Upmann twisted the rod a couple more times and the sunlight reflected onto the floor between Holman's desk and the windows.

"If I saw sunlight filtering through the sides of the ship, it would give me cause for concern." Holman flipped open the humidor. He rolled the cigars inside it back and forth, searching for just the right one. "Let me see . . ." he mumbled to himself. Glancing up, he saw his reflection in the glass of the large framed photograph behind his desk. For a short, chubby Navy officer, he'd at least managed to keep some of his hair. He grabbed a cigar. "Well, my fine Chief of Staff, shouldn't we go to the roof of this landlubber building and see what the fleet is doing?"

Upmann laughed. "Let me see, Admiral, if I have this right. Shut the blinds because it's too bright, and now rush up to the roof so we can stand directly in the sunlight?"

Holman looked over the top of his glasses at the tall African-American. Upmann had accompanied him into harm's way in rescuing the Americans in Liberia and most recently in stopping the terrorist attempt to land a weapon of mass destruction in America. Holman removed his aviator glasses and tossed them gently onto the center of the huge calendar that covered most of his metal desk. "Captain Upmann," he said, punctuating his words with his cigar. "When you make Admiral, you will understand that there is nothing those of us who wear the stars do that doesn't have a hidden meaning specifically designed to build leadership qualities in young Navy captains such as yourself."

Upmann opened the door. "After you, sir. Seems if I recall correctly, I'm a couple of years older."

"And uglier."

"And taller."

"There you go again with those short men jokes," Holman said as he walked through the door.

A couple of minutes later they stood on the flat roof of Amphibious Group Two headquarters. The roof had been remodeled at Holman's direction last year when leaks forced them to contract for a new one. If you had to put a new roof on an old building, why not take advantage of the view and build something everyone could enjoy? With a deck, a couple of picnic tables, and benches running around three sides of a raised wall that encompassed the roof area, the top of Amphibious Group Two headquarters had become a favored place for the sailors to take lunch, rest, and—heaven forbid—enjoy a fine cigar.

Three sailors laughed at something one of them said as they sat at one of the three picnic tables on the far side of the roof. In front of Holman and Upmann, a set of binoculars, similar to the ones installed at scenic outlooks, was mounted atop a large metal pole. A small metal stool for standing allowed everyone regardless of age or height a chance to use them. The binoculars looked out across Hampton Roads Channel so the user could watch the continuum of maritime and naval traffic as it entered and departed the deepwater port of Norfolk. Upmann had his own binoculars hanging around his neck.

"Right, red, returning," Upmann said, referring to the maritime navigation "rules of the road" for ships entering a port. Entering ships stayed to the right inside the red buoys that lined a harbor channel. Green buoys lined the other side of the channel.

"Weapons free, tally-ho," Holman responded.

"What was that about?"

"Look, if we're going to come out here for fresh air and light conversation, then the least you can do is quit this surface warfare stuff about boring holes in the ocean."

"Moi?" Upmann responded, his open right hand patting his chest.

"Oui, you."

Holman lit his cigar, worked it for a half-minute to get the ember fully spread, and then leaned forward bracing his arm along the top of the wall, staring at the nearby channel that led from the largest Navy base in the world out into the Atlantic Ocean.

"Think it's about time to head back out to sea, Leo?"

"Sir, we just got off the *Boxer* a month ago. Some of those officers and sailors on board have families. And before we departed the great accommodations of the *Boxer,* we took the flattop over to the east Atlantic to help our stout British ally and our part-time French comrade search for that terrorist merchant vessel that eventually was captured right out there." He pointed out to the ocean. "If bad weather and good luck hadn't intervened, it could have been quite a catastrophe here."

"As it was, we still had twenty-six deaths in Florida and four in Georgia before the health community came to grips with it."

Upmann chuckled. "No one can accuse you of not having a way with words, Admiral. Tact is your best quality."

"How about that?" Holman muttered, pointing at the bow of an aircraft carrier emerging into view. "That's what keeps the terrorists at bay, my fine surface warfare warrior. Without those acres of America sailing on the oceans and seas of the world, we'd find our job in the amphibious Navy a hell of lot harder to do." He took a deep puff on his cigar. "Hell of a sight." With his fist, he struck his chest a couple of times. "Gets you right here."

As the starboard side of the huge warship slid slowly into view, the forecastle became visible. "72" in large white paint broke the gray symmetry of the aircraft carrier.

"*Abraham Lincoln*," Upmann said.

"Wonder what she's up to today."

"The morning activity report from Naval Air Force Atlantic says she's heading out to sea so those flyboys—and girls—from Oceana can keep their carrier qualifications up to date."

"Going to be boring holes in the VACAPES operations area," Holman added, using the acronym VACAPES instead of Virginia Capes. He sighed. "Wish I could do a few cats and traps on her."

"You ever missed a landing on one of those floating airfields?" Upmann asked, watching the ship move across the water. "What do you call it when that happens? A bolter?" A bolter was when the aircraft tailhook missed one of the four trap wires crossing the deck at the rear of an aircraft carrier.

"Every Navy pilot who ever flew a carrier-based aircraft has missed those wires at one time in their flying career. If they say they haven't, then they're lying."

Holman flicked the ash from his cigar into a nearby red bucket filled with sand. "Landing on an aircraft carrier is more of a controlled crash than a landing." He slapped his right fist into his left palm. "You slam down on the deck, wait a second, and, if you don't feel the immediate grip of the wire jerking you to a stop . . ." He lifted his right hand and, holding an imaginary throttle, shoved his hand forward. "You push the throttle full bore and fly around again."

"How many times—"

"About three, then you either get a drink from the A-6 tanker orbiting overhead, or the flight boss will bingo you ashore, if you're close enough." Holding the cigar between his fingers, he jabbed his hand at Upmann a couple of times, and in a smooth motion he put the cigar back between his lips. "I can tell you, if you've missed the wire three times, it's a butt-tightening experience. Leo, those bolters are what separates the men from their underwear."

The two watched silently as the USS *Abraham Lincoln* sailed past. The deck of the huge ship was higher than the roof upon which they stood. There were no aircraft on the *Lincoln* deck. Yellow deck cats that normally would be shuttling between parked aircraft, towing others, and waiting for instructions stood parked in a line near the forecastle. When aircraft carriers returned from deployment, the air squadrons flew off to their own base before the carriers entered port. They landed on board an aircraft carrier after it was underway and far enough out to sea so it could maneuver for best winds.

Signal flags flew from the lines running from the signal bridge to one of the transoms on the main mast.

"Don't see Commander Carrier Group Four's flag, do you?"

"No, sir. He must be ashore, but I'm sure some of his staff is on board. After all, COMCARGRU Four is responsible for carrier training and readiness."

Holman wished he could be on board the carrier. He would have given his left nut to be given a carrier group command because so much of his Navy career had been spent on board those floating airfields. Not that being the admiral in charge of the largest amphibious command in the world wasn't great. It was. Those large flattops he commanded, such as the USS *Boxer,* were larger and more capable than any World War II aircraft carrier. This new concept of Expeditionary Amphibious Warfare that combined surface warships, a submarine, and maritime patrol aircraft made his forces capable not only of projecting power ashore, but it also allowed him the one advantage he had over carrier battle groups: once he had embarked Marines, he could land.

He may be a pilot, but he knew wars were won by taking land, and no matter how many times the Air Force and Naval Air had tried, you can't take land from the seat of a fighter aircraft bombing unseen targets twenty thousand feet below. You took land by putting boots on the ground. He puffed out a large cloud of smoke. Still, he was a fighter pilot, an F-18 Hornet fighter pilot, and that was what he knew.

Behind the huge ship, an older Spruance-class destroyer followed. The destroyer would be the plane guard for the flight operations, following in the wake of the floating airfield, prepared to pick up pilots or carrier crewmembers who may find themselves in the drink. The other, less talked about, mission of the destroyer was to serve as a fire ship in the event the aircraft carrier suffered a catastrophe at sea. Aircraft carriers were so large that a fire burning around the hull of the warship was hard to fight with ship's company. The destroyer could close alongside, covering the exposed hull of the aircraft carrier with firefighting foam and water. Holman took a puff on the Cuban cigar and let the smoke out slowly. He recalled the 1960s, when three major aircraft carrier fires cost the lives of many sailors. To him, the *Forrestal* fire in 1967—he thought, *July*—off Vietnam was the worst. The fire burned for hours at an awful loss of over 130 sailors. A former U.S. senator had been one of the fighter pilots who had had to run from his burning fighter on the *Forrestal*. There was the *Oriskany,* earlier than the *Forrestal* fire, that killed nearly fifty sailors, and the *Enterprise* fire, which burned for four hours. Hard to compare the *Enterprise* fire with the other two. Then there was the USS *Kennedy* fire in the Mediterranean in the early 1970s after it collided with the cruiser *Belknap*. There was a slew of carrier fires during World War II, and every carrier fire had a common firefighting response involving destroyers coming alongside, throwing everything in their firefighting arsenal to save the burning flattops.

Even with their bombs exploding and aircraft burning, every one of those carriers survived. They were magnificent killing machines that could take nearly anything an adversary could throw at them, but, like all ships at sea, fire was ironically the scourge of the ocean; the fear of the sailors. You could always refloat a ship if it flooded, but when it caught fire there was nothing between the sailor and the deep blue sea but those gray hulls. When your ship is burning there are only two courses of action: save the ship or swim for shore.

Upmann lifted his fist to his lips and coughed, bringing Holman out of his aircraft carrier reverie. "Admiral, Captain Davidson handed me a report today showing that Abu Alhaul and his minions may be returning to the border areas around the Ivory Coast and Liberia. Possibly setting up camps in the jungles of the Ivory Coast. Not much chance of us going in after him there."

"Does that mean we may have shoved the terrorist and his "I wanna die" followers out of the picture for a while?"

"No, sir. I think it has more to do with this African nationalist who is organizing north of Liberia—in the jungles of Guinea around the northwest Ivory Coast border. Captain Davidson was very graphic in some of the *things* this African Nationalist Army is doing, and, with the exception of their methods, it appears the ANA likes the terrorists as much as we do. This new player on the African continent is killing Islamic militants, overrunning the Wahabi-led schools that had sprouted up in West Africa in the last decade, and killing anyone suspected of being a Moslem."

Holman waved his cigar at Upmann. "I've been following it on Fox News Channel. I've heard that European Command has deployed or is deploying one of Fleet Air Reconnaissance Squadron Two's EP-3E reconnaissance aircraft to Monrovia to fly some recce missions against them."

"Against the Africans?"

Holman lifted one shoulder for a second and dropped it. "Don't know. Most likely, knowing the aircraft capability, whatever they find, they'll collect. Eventually the raw data will be analyzed by some souped-up intelligence type who will tell us what he saw."

"It's a dirty fight."

"I imagine it is. Africa is full of dirty little fights that kill more people in a smaller amount of time than most of our upper-world-hemisphere conflicts."

Upmann put a hand against the binocular pole as he

looked at the admiral. "The fight is outside Liberia right now. Hopefully it will stay outside Liberia."

Holman nodded. "Let's hope you're right. Thomaston is holding the democratic elections he promised when he seized—wrong word. He was more a benevolent caretaker of Liberia while they wrote their constitution, and now they're going to elect a congress. When Liberia finishes its path to democracy, it will be a miniature twin of our own government, even down to a Supreme Court." Holman shook his head back and forth. "You know what'll happen next, don't you?"

"Statehood?"

Holman shook his head. "Not without another country or territory that could be annexed to offset the obvious democratic lean such a state would bring into the union."

Upmann's head jerked back. "You don't think they'd keep a state from becoming part of the United States because of politics, do you?"

Holman laughed. "That's why they call it politics, Leo. Truth is, I really don't know if Thomaston will pursue that aim or not. When they evacuated him and his followers from Kingsville to the *Boxer* two years ago, he remarked how he equated their fight against Abu Alhaul—who had them trapped inside their armory and who outnumbered them ten to one—as their Alamo. So, he never said Liberia would eventually pursue statehood, but I came away with the impression that that was what he meant."

Upmann shuddered slightly. "I can't imagine us accepting another state. We haven't done it since Hawaii and Alaska, even when Puerto Rico voted for statehood."

"Puerto Rico would have been another state that would have given one political party an edge over the other."

"Then, having Liberia and Puerto Rico as states—"

"Double the reason why it isn't going to happen."

"Guess we'll have to wait and see."

"Wait and see," Holman repeated. "It's what we do best. Leo, who is the leader of this African Nationalist Army?"

Upmann's lower lip pushed up, his eyebrows scrunched together. "I'm not sure," he said finally. He lifted his binoculars as if he were going to scan the horizon.

"It's Fela Azikiwe Ojo," Holman said, rolling the African name out as if it were one word.

Upmann dropped his binoculars. They swung from the cord around his neck like a clock pendulum. "How the hell did you know that? I can't even pronounce one of his names, much less all of them."

Holman smiled. Davidson had briefed him early this morning before Upmann arrived, and they had spent some time going over the intelligence analysis of the African leader's name. He started to tell Leo about the earlier briefing, but decided not to. It was amusing to amaze his chief of staff. "Seems the three names this African leader chose—by the way, he refers to himself as a general— originate from three different areas along Western Africa, which is why the intelligence agencies reached the conclusion it was an assumed name. A name given at birth would originate from names common to a specific area. Fela Azikiwe Ojo translates as 'full vigor warrior of a difficult birth.' Fela means warrior, Azikiwe is a male name for 'full of vigor,' and Ojo is from a West African name for someone who was a difficult birth."

"Admiral, you've definitely got to bone up on your conversation topics."

"I know, but I think you'll find this interesting, Leo. He chose the name from a broad spectrum of West African male names. No single name he is using came from one location. *Fela Azikiwe Ojo.* Try to say it, Leo. It has a sing-song quality to it. A pleasing quality that rolls off the tongue. Creating a name with a wide geographical disparity is a great example of psych-ops; it's another way to encourage Africans to rally to his cause."

Upmann tried it a couple of times with ill success. "Quit laughing, Admiral. Foreign languages have never been my forte. It's easy for you, but it's a tongue twister for me."

Upmann cocked his head to the side, running his hand over the top of his bald head, his broad hand lightly touching the gray hair along the sides. "How did you get this information? CNN? I know Mary must have provided some of it, but I read her reports when she debriefed me earlier, and none of this was in it."

Holman and Mary Davidson had sat in his office practicing the name back and forth to see who could say it the quickest and clearest. Holman nodded to himself. "Leo, when you make Admiral, you'll discover how we flag officers are able to reach into thin air and discover little-known facts others are unable to see—or even comprehend."

"Oh, I don't have to wait until, or *if,* I make Admiral, Admiral. I've seen flag officers pull facts out of thin air numerous times."

"Admiral!" came a shout from behind them.

Holman turned.

The Officer of the Deck rushed toward them, the man's face red from running up three decks of stairs. The officer stopped in front of them and stood there, his chest heaving as he caught his breath.

"Admiral," he gasped.

"Take your time, son. Nothing's so important you have to die from lack of breath." A puff of cigar smoke enveloped the poor man's face for a moment before the slight off-sea wind blew it skyward.

"Probably, Lieutenant," Upmann said, "if you ran more and worked out more, you wouldn't be out of breath."

Holman cut his eyes at his chief of staff, knowing Upmann's comment was also meant for him. He didn't need others reminding him of his own battle of the bulge.

"Yes, sir, Chief of Staff. Admiral, we just received a telephone report from Admiral Duncan James's office at the Pentagon. Commander Raleigh's home in Urbana, Maryland, was bombed about an hour ago."

"Captain Upmann, Commander Raleigh on that airplane?"

"Should be on the Air Force Transport out of Norfolk, Admiral."

"Double check," he ordered. Holman turned back to the OOD. "Lieutenant, any casualties? What else do you have?"

"Not much, sir. Just Admiral James's office called and said I was to pass it along to you ASAP. Said you would know the why of the bombing."

"Abu Alhaul," Upmann offered.

"Of course. Doesn't seem the asshole is getting the message, is he?"

"Sir, should I relay anything back to Admiral James?"

"Not until we ensure that Commander Raleigh is airborne and on his way to Liberia."

"Sir, do you mind if I ask as to why Abu Alhaul would bomb Commander Raleigh's home?"

"No, Lieutenant, I don't mind you asking, as long as you don't mind me not answering. Dismissed."

The lieutenant saluted and quickly disappeared down the stairs leading back to the quarterdeck on the ground floor.

"Abu Alhaul is sending a message to both Commander Raleigh and to us that his reach continues to penetrate America and that he hasn't foregone his vendetta against the American he blames for the death of his family."

"Stupid, isn't it."

"What is?"

"You're a known terrorist with equally dangerous people searching for you, and you're so arrogant that you think you can have a normal life with family and friends surrounding you? And never expect some of them to get killed?"

Holman scrunched the cigar out in the bucket of sand serving as an ashtray. "On the other hand, our knowing that he wanted to get to Tucker Raleigh was what proved Alhaul's downfall when he tried to sail a weapon of mass destruction into Norfolk Harbor earlier."

"I guess the question is, if Abu Alhaul is targeting this one man for past transgressions, and Abu Alhaul is currently in Western Africa, then why are we sending Raleigh to where he will be more vulnerable?"

Holman shrugged. "Don't know, but I would suspect—knowing Admiral James and having spent some quality time with Commander Raleigh—that neither of them intend to allow Abu Alhaul to dictate Raleigh's way of life."

"They could have sent another SEAL to train the new Liberian Army."

"Sure, they could have, but Tucker Raleigh is attached to the staff of Admiral James. I'm unsure what his specific job title is, but I know it's in the SEAL training field."

"Still seems like a bad idea to me."

"Have to admit, I don't know why they're sending him either; unless it's meant to send a message to Abu Alhaul that we're not scared of him or his threats."

Upmann nodded. "If someone bombed my house, he'd have earned my fear."

"Then again, Leo, you and I aren't Navy SEALs."

"True, sir," Upmann said. "Admiral, with your permission, I'll get below and make sure Commander Raleigh is airborne."

The two started toward the stairs.

"I'll brief you as soon as I know anything else."

Holman led the way down. "As for myself, I'll be in my office, calling retired Lieutenant General Thomaston in Monrovia. I don't want Commander Raleigh to land in Monrovia without some additional security. It'll also give me a chance to see if Thomaston has any additional data on this Fela Azikiwe Ojo."

Admiral Holman reached the bottom of the stairs.

"Sir, you know it's pretty early in the morning in Liberia."

"What are you trying to say, Leo? Not to call the interim President of Liberia when we have concerns over a Navy officer's safety? Besides, Leo, it's only about one in the morning there. Army Rangers don't sleep, so Thomaston is probably lonely for company. Even with all of this, Leo, we can't forget what may have happened to those Air Force fighters. Any death is bad, but in this instance, let's hope they collided with each other." Holman reached to open the side door of the building. "The other prospect is something I've never envisioned."

"Me neither, sir."

"But, it's something we can't talk about out here in the open."

CHAPTER 5

ANY DAY THAT BEGINS WITH A TELEPHONE CALL FROM THE
Pentagon is a bad day. Means someone somewhere is excited about something and when someone in the Pentagon
is excited, it means a lot of work for those further down the
food chain. And it must be important for them to catch him
before he even sat his first cup of coffee on his desk.

The day grew worse when he stepped off the helicopter
onto the Pentagon helo pad and saw the brown smear, from
God knew where, running along the bottom two-button
line of his white summer uniform shirt and touching the
edge of his belt line. He thought, *Holman, you stupid shit.
You really know how to make a damn good first impression.*
Little things such as this were ankle biters. Ankle biters
were never huge problems, but small ones that detracted
from whatever major issue you were pursuing. The stain
just added to the disruption Washington causes when it
comes calling.

The lanky lieutenant stepped behind Holman, changing
from the admiral's right side to his left, where juniors
walked in deference to their superiors. Holman's head followed the position shift as they walked toward the Pentagon

entrance. *Man's got no waist!* he thought. If Holman had been with someone he knew, he'd have said something about the stain. He glanced down, touched it briefly, and for a second nearly touched his finger to his lips. He dropped his hand. *What if it's not coffee? What if it's some sort of oil product from the helicopter? Helicopters always had some kind of leak.*

The lieutenant dashed ahead and opened the door for Holman. "Admiral," he said, gesturing toward the hallway inside the Pentagon.

What in the hell did he think I was going to do? Stop at it and ask what was inside?

He's probably a fine young officer, Holman argued with himself, but no way was he going to ask this lanky, physical-readiness Mafiosi—*if they have thin waists, then they exercise too much*—whom his Chief of Staff Captain Leo Upmann set up on the spur of the moment to be his executive aide for the trip. He didn't like EAs. Not because they couldn't be useful, but because they were too useful. You couldn't open a door, pull out your chair, or grab a cup of coffee. About the only thing remaining they didn't do for you was unzip you and zip you back up when you were finished. Admiral Dick Holman, Commander Amphibious Group Two, walked along the eighth corridor of the Pentagon. Portraits of past Chairmen of the Joint Chiefs of Staff stared down on him from both walls as he headed toward the "E" ring. He glanced at each row of medals aligned beneath each portrait. It was a matter of interest to see what the highest military medal each one wore and which had the Purple Heart. The Purple Heart medal identified the bearer as wounded in the service of his country. Holman's eyes may have been following the displays of military award, but his mind drifted elsewhere.

His eyes avoided contact with the young lieutenant as they shifted from one wall to the other, tracking the portraits as they trailed past. This young lieutenant had immediately jumped into the fun of being an executive aide, bossing him around, as if he owned him. Even to the point of tactfully insisting, "The Admiral might want to wear his khakis or flight suit and change into his whites once in Washington." But, no, he had to show he was an admiral.

One of these days, he would listen to those whose duties it was to provide him advice. Now, when he returned to Norfolk, he was going to have to listen to a tall, African-American surface warfare officer give a protracted diatribe about why airdales never listen. Almost like a Jerry Springer show: "Airdales never listen, and their mothers who made them that way."

If Leo wasn't such a damn good chief of staff, he'd have shitcanned him to some cruiser command months ago. Unfortunately, though they'd never publicly admit it, airdales lacked in-depth knowledge of how to drive ships, so they depended on deputies such as Upmann to keep them from running a task force aground. He knew Upmann knew this, but damn if he was going to give a surface warfare officer the pleasure of admitting it. Moreover, he wasn't going to send him to command a cruiser, damn it. The man had already done a tour as a commanding officer of a Ticonderoga-class cruiser, enjoyed it too much, and was ranked number one of twenty-five commanding officers. No, he had worse plans in store for his chief of staff. He was going to see the man put on an admiral's star and watch him pace the time away, pining for the smell of salt water across a rolling deck instead of manning a desk. Holman smiled as he imagined the words Upmann would use when the epiphany of how hamstrung admirals actually were in determining their future came over him like a bad dream.

Dick reached for his handkerchief as he neared the second stairwell to his left. He nearly had his hand in his back pocket when he stopped and pulled it back. He had touched that brown smear only moments ago. What if he had dirt, oil, or something on his hand from touching it? He didn't need more accidents to further mar the summer uniform, and he wasn't going to draw more attention than necessary to himself by reaching completely across his rear end with his left hand to get that handkerchief.

Dick spotted the head to his left and quickly swung direction toward the men's room. Quick pit stop to see if he could do something about the brown spot. The young, spry lieutenant, wearing the gold epaulet of a one-star admiral's aide, slowed so Dick didn't run into him as he crossed the young man's bow.

"I'm going to hit the head," Holman mumbled.

"Yes, sir. I'll wait here."

"Good. This is something I can handle alone." He caught the creep of red up the young man's neck as he pushed the door open. He should let up, but damn it. It just wasn't the Navy way.

Pat Willis . . . that was the young man's name. Willis hadn't been aboard Amphibious Group Two three months, and other than the "welcome aboard" meeting with Holman the first week, Holman hadn't seen the man again.

"Pat, what time's our meeting with the chairman and that lady from the National Security Council?" Holman asked as he pushed the door to the bathroom open.

"You have twenty-eight minutes, sir," the EA replied. "Admiral, would you like me to see about replacing that shirt?"

"Lieutenant, where are you going to get a replacement shirt at this short notice? The Navy Annex, up beside Arlington National Cemetery, is the nearest, and you'd never make it there and back in time." He paused and looked back at the aide. "Pat, next time look at your watch as if you're checking the time. At least pretend. If you're going to be my EA, make your job look hard, so the other admirals will be impressed," Holman said, trying to sound friendly. He disappeared into the head before the man could reply.

Minutes later he emerged. The brown recycled paper provided by the Department of Defense for drying hands had smeared the stain into a broad streak. Now, it ran from the second bottom buttonhole above the waistline and across the top of the belt line. Made it looked as if he had a mishap on the toilet. He caught the quick glance of his EA's wide eyes staring at the spreading stain.

"Dick!"

Holman looked back toward the center of the Pentagon. Walking toward him from the "A" wing was Rear Admiral "two-stars" Duncan James, head of Navy SEALS, a tall, muscular, mid-fifties warrior with close-cropped graying hair and a pair of knees that had long ago lost their warranty for combat.

"Duncan, I hear you and I have been invited to some sort of top secret meeting with some demon from the National Security Council," Holman said as they shook hands.

"It seems this is the only time we ever meet, Dick. When you're in trouble, getting out of trouble, or about to leap or be thrown into trouble."

They turned and walked side by side down the corridor toward the outer "E" ring. Lieutenant Willis took position several steps behind the two admirals. Close enough to respond if Holman called and far enough way so they could talk in a semblance of privacy.

"You're looking good, Duncan," Holman said. "And, you're walking as if your knees are better."

"I should be so lucky. I think Bethesda Orthopedics has given up on me, so I've been taking . . ."

The two of them had met several years ago when both were captains. At the time, Holman was a pudgy commanding officer of an aircraft carrier and Duncan was on the verge of being forced to retire by a vindictive flag officer. Friendship forged in combat is like steel: it survives a lot of punishment before it bends. It had been the summer of 2011 when a Libyan Islamic madman had nearly united the whole of North Africa from Morocco to Sudan under the banner of radical Islam. The potential power of such a nation threatened the stability of the world and the security of the United States.

Duncan had gone into Algeria with two teams of SEALs

to rescue its last democratically elected president, only to return a couple of weeks later into Algiers to rescue a bunch of American hostages being held by Islamic terrorists.

During the conflict, Holman had been "fleeted up," as the term goes when you ascend to authority from within the chain of command. One moment, he was commanding officer of the USS *Stennis,* a mighty aircraft carrier that he had sailed through a mined Strait of Gibraltar, and the next, he was a four-striper captain in charge of all air power in the Sixth Fleet. It had been Holman's aircraft that had saved Duncan when he and his SEAL teams attempted to escape Algeria the first time only to run into the remnants of the Algerian Navy. When the crisis passed, the United States Navy selected both of them for Admiral, and along with the selection came awards of Silver Stars for both of them.

Something involving the head of Navy Seals had happened to Duncan James before he arrived in the war theater. Lots of unknowns, even to Holman, who was a close friend of James. What little Holman knew had to do with a female officer who wanted to be a SEAL and a now long-gone admiral who had ordered James to retire. Duncan James had never deemed it necessary to share any of that information with Holman, as much as Holman would have enjoyed hearing it. Whatever happened, the previous chief of Naval Operations had had a closed-door discussion with the old head of Navy SEALs, and when the door opened, the troubled, pale-faced Navy SEAL admiral had requested immediate retirement. James had been promoted directly to two-star and ordered to the Pentagon as his replacement.

As they exchanged small talk, Holman noticed James still had the hard figure of a Navy SEAL. Tight skin around the neck and a waist significantly smaller than his chest. Holman hadn't changed either since the North African crisis. He was still photogenic but pudgy, though he never failed a Navy physical fitness measurement. He nodded curtly to himself. While he was a pudgy one-star, Duncan was still a muscle-bound, desk-bound Navy SEAL who, like him, missed the field, missed doing what they were trained to do. But the good thing about being commander of the world's mightiest amphibious fleet was that he could go out to sea anytime he wanted, even if the Navy had decided his flying days were over.

". . . so, they seem to be getting better."

"Sir, if I may," Willis interjected as they neared the end of the eighth corridor. "If Admiral James will escort you to the Tank, I will see if I can find a replacement shirt for you."

Holman saw Duncan's right eyebrow rise as he looked down at the stain.

"You've had something like this happen, I'm sure," Holman offered.

"Yeah, but at the time I had about a hundred screaming Jihadists begging for martyrdom charging at me. Of course, my stains weren't around the waist. And I ended up giving them their martyrdom."

"Lieutenant," Holman said. "Go. Your ears aren't meant to hear what two of the finer admirals in the Navy are discussing."

With a quick nod and acknowledgment, Lieutenant Pat Willis headed down the hallway, his steps rapid as he hurried toward the center court of the Pentagon.

"Who's your EA? He your physical trainer?"

"He's a young lieutenant who is making it a habit of being up my ass at every moment. And he takes too much pleasure in physical fitness," Holman complained, adding, "Leo assigned him this morning for the trip."

"Dick, you ought to keep him. EAs are a Godsend when you're hurrying from one place to the next."

The two men turned and continued down the "E" hallway, exchanging small talk, and discussing the new chief of Naval Operations who had started a series of Naval Administrative messages, called NAVADMINs, detailing several new initiatives designed to encourage sailors to make the Navy their career. Most the information wasn't new, just repackaged encouragement both had seen in past

NAVADMINs, but it didn't mean the information wasn't
pertinent. They knew that, periodically, leadership mandated you reemphasized policies so they were forever anew.
The Navy, like a commercial firm, changed as its manpower
aged and new leaders ascended to the forefront.

"Ever been in the Tank?" Duncan James asked as they
passed through a set of double-glass doors.

"Only a couple of times. I try to steer clear when and
where elephants dance. Don't want to find myself a smear
between their toes." Holman glanced down at the brown
smear on his shirt and shook his head slightly. *What a fool
I am sometimes.*

Many believed the Tank to be a fabrication of a bunch
of wild-eyed fringe conspiracy elements that believed a
shadow government met within its sound- and electronic-
proof walls. However, the Tank was real. It existed, and
the shakers and movers of government, and those within
the Defense Department, used it. It wasn't a big compartment, but it was secure from penetration by any known
technology that might try to discover what was going on
within its four sides. Members of both the United States
military and the notorious Defense Security Service
guarded it. Each carried an automatic weapon and a
sidearm. Discussions in the Tank had the potential to
cause grave consequences for the nation, hence the checks
and balances of two differing teams of guards who eyed
each other with distrust and whose members were rotated
in such a fashion that discouraged any bond of friendship
between members of the two teams.

At any time of the day or night, the Tank may host senior
officers of the military and senior civilians of government
to discuss critical items of national security, items best resolved out of the public eye. The Tank was where the military met to develop overall missions and strategy for the
armed forces, to determine how the four services would di-
vide the funds Congress gave, and to develop a vision of
where the military needed to be ten, twenty, and thirty years
hence down the road. Without those decisions, America's

power would slowly degrade over the years, and the lone superpower status enjoyed for so many decades would one
day evaporate.

Holman and James usually discussed the still-secret,
while the public debated decisions made many years ago in
the Tank. Today, though, they were discussing one of those
now-public topics which came out of the Tank years ago.
The Joint Chiefs of Staff at the time—who all serve for two
years at the request of the president—voiced during a press
interview that probably within the next ten to twenty years
America would have to fight China unless certain geopoliti-
cal changes occurred much sooner. It was not greeted with
enthusiasm by the administration in office at the time. Quite
the opposite; headlines blaring to the world that America
was *planning* to fight China within the next ten years made
the chairman an overnight pariah within an administration
which was quickly distancing itself from such an idea. After all, China was America's number one trading partner,
where the bulk of factory-made goods that serviced the
American economy now originated. The chairman had retired shortly thereafter.

Holman subscribed to the conservative belief that the
People's Republic of China had been for years engaged in
a secret economic war against the United States. And he
liked to talk about it. The Chinese government had taken a
lesson from the U.S. economic defeat of the Soviet Union
and was waging it against us. Economic warfare didn't
mean economic conflict. With a world economy, you could
just as easily degrade a nation's capability to fight by luring
its elements of national security, such as factories and
mills, away to another country. What remains are service-
related businesses that don't manufacture anything. It's
hard to build weapons in a service economy. At least, this
was the point Holman was trying to make now.

Holman had been in the Tank a couple of times for
briefing workups being prepared for the Joint Chiefs of
Staff. You never went into the Tank cold, flipped open your
notebook, and started briefing the Joint Chiefs of Staff.

There was a long road to reach that point, and Holman had been involved in some of the preliminary tasking of developing such briefs. The Director of the Joint Staff, lovingly referred to as the "DJS," was the real power behind the throne. The one in charge now was a Lieutenant General Winifred Hulley, United States Army, known as "Win" by his friends. From his well-earned reputation, those friends were few and far away. Hulley ripped briefs to shreds. No brief survived unscathed the first time across his desk, and only a few survived the second and third times.

By the time a briefer reached the chairman and his four Joint Chiefs from the services, the brief never resembled anything the originator intended.

The two men passed the "River Exit." A man in a dark blue suit leaned against the outside wall of the hallway, his eyes sweeping back and forth. His suit buldged slightly under his left arm where a concealed weapon disrupted the symmetry. The man's eyes swept across Holman and James, lingering for a moment before continuing their sweep. A coiled wire ran from an earpiece, disappearing beneath the back collar of the man's suit coat. *Secret Service or Defense Security Service,* Holman thought as he listened to Duncan finally turn away from the coming war with China to discuss the challenges of the upcoming fiscal year budget.

Holman was glad he didn't have to fight budget-weenie battles at the Pentagon level. It was bad enough at the Group level fighting with Commander Second Fleet and Fleet Forces Command for his paltry amount. If he had to do what Duncan James did on a daily basis, he'd drive into North Parking in the morning, open up the trunk, and toss his integrity into it. At least it'd still be there when he left at night.

"What do you think they want to discuss that is so critical and so super secret that we have to come to the Tank to hear it?"

James shrugged. "Don't know. I know about as much as you do, Dick. I didn't even know they called you until I saw the attendee list. When I saw your name, my first thought—or question—was who did they call first, you or me?"

"Why would that matter?"

"If they call me first, then it's something to do with sending Navy SEALs to your command to do something neither of us probably wants to do."

"Duncan," Holman said with a slight smile. "You've been in Washington too long if who gets called first carries such unintended consequences."

"When you've been in the Pentagon more than six months, you discover quickly that no meeting is held without each participant having their own hidden agenda." He laughed. "Not everyone is as up front as I am."

"Either way, my friend, I would have to give it a lot more thought than you did to determine why they would call one of us ahead of the other."

An Air Force sergeant wearing five stripes stood outside the Tank, near a square sign with the words QUIET MEETING IN PROGRESS. On either side of the door stood two guards, a U.S. Army officer wearing a Ranger badge on his left shoulder, and a member of the Defense Security Service. Both men watched the two admirals approach. Holman had never figured out whether they were there to keep people out or keep those inside in. The couple of times he went, all he wanted to do was leave; but once you were inside and those massive doors locked, you were in for the duration. Water and coffee were available, but there were no head facilities within, which can be a killer if you have a fifty-something-year-old bladder. *Maybe that's why there's an informal law that says no brief to a flag or general officer can be over thirty minutes long,* he thought.

You didn't walk out during a Tank meeting.

"Sir, are you here for the meeting with Ms. Chatelain-Malpass?"

Holman looked at Duncan. "Is that who we're here to meet?"

"Got me, Dick. What time is this meeting with Ms. Chatterly . . . ?" his voice trailed off.

"Ms. Chatelain-Malpass, sir, and the meeting is scheduled to start in seventeen minutes."

"How do they do that, Duncan?" Holman said in an exaggerated whisper. "Is there some sort of internal timing mechanism where they don't need watches?"

James turned his head and nodded over his shoulder. On the wall behind them was the standard government-issue white-faced analog clock. The hands showed seventeen minutes to ten. Here they were, near the quarter–twenty-first century mark, and the Department of Defense still had those battery-driven clocks mounted on walls and bulkheads throughout the military.

"I guess we are, Sergeant," Admiral James said, "if this is the one the Chairman and Admiral Yalvarez are also attending."

"Yes, sir, it is. Ms. Chatelain-Malpass will be a few minutes late, sir. She has to come from the White House."

Two minutes later, after having their security clearances verified and signing the attendance log, the two men were ushered into the Tank. Inside, behind those wooden walls, were half-inch-thick magnetized metal plates designed to thwart outside attempts to monitor what was going on. Both men discovered nameplates at the rectangle mahogany table that filled the center of the room. A chair for the chairman was placed at one end of the table so he could look directly at the two gigantic split-screens on the far wall.

"Never sat at the table before," Holman confessed.

"Makes two of us," Duncan said. "Most times, I'm relegated to one of those six chairs—" He pointed to the chairs lining the wall nearest the "E" corridor. "—and then, only after being admonished to keep my ears and eyes opened and my mouth shut. One and two-stars are seldom in here."

Holman pulled his chair away from the desk. James walked around the table, stopping for a moment in front of each nameplate.

"Here is Ms. Alice Chatelain-Malpass, Dick." James lifted her nameplate for a moment and then set it back down. "Says she's from National Security Council." He moved to the next one. "Looks as if the DJS is going to join us for the meeting." He reached forward and lifted this nameplate, turning it so Dick could see it. "Lieutenant General Win Hulley," James said with a trace of humor. "Wouldn't want to use his real name."

At the head of the table was the chairman's plate. "Can't say he takes himself too seriously, Dick." He held up the nameplate. It read HALFPENNY. "Of course, if you're the chairman, you don't need a nametag to tell people who you are." James walked around the head of the table, crossing to the side where Holman sat. "Admiral Jesus 'Jay' Yalvarez," he announced, nodding at the place directly left of the chairman's seat. "And, here I am. Right beside the Chief of Naval Operations. How about that for career opportunity, Dick?" James pulled the chair out. "Looks as if you and I have two grand opportunities here, Dick. We have an opportunity to make a lot of brownie points and to catapult our careers onward and upward." He sat down. "Or, when we leave here we could see our career in handcuffs, heading for the Devil's Island of the Navy—forced retirement."

They laughed.

Large plastic bottles of spring water were set in front of the five spaces. The two men opened theirs and sipped. The wall clock showed ten minutes until the meeting started. Time was a precious commodity in the Pentagon, and seldom did anyone arrive for a meeting until seconds before it began. Less wasted time made meetings less boring. But when you were the junior trooper on the roster, it helped to be a little ahead of time, and Holman and Duncan were the two junior people at this important, urgently called meeting.

Holman's executive aide walked into the compartment. A sprinkling of perspiration dotted the lieutenant's forehead. "Admiral," Willis said, holding up a milky-white plastic bag with the blue-red logo of ARMY-AIR FORCE EXCHANGE SERVICE on the side. "I have your shirt, sir."

"How'd you do that?" he asked, his eyebrows rising.

Pointing at the sweat on the man's forehead, Holman asked, "And, don't tell me you jogged up and back to the Arlington Annex? That's a good two miles away."

"There's a small Army-Air Force uniform shop on the fourth deck," Duncan James volunteered. "Does't have much of a Navy selection, but they do carry a few shirts." He touched Holman on the shoulder. "Primarily size Small."

"Admiral, there's a small room next door where I've arranged for you to change."

Five minutes later, Holman was back. Sitting and talking with Duncan James now was the new Chief of Naval Operations, Admiral Jesus Antonio Yalvarez, called "Jay" by his counterparts. Counterparts who consisted of the other thirty-four four-stars in the military. Holman shook the newest Chief of Naval Operations's hand before he sat down beside Duncan. Jay was the first Hispanic Chief of Naval Operations in history, and one of only five Hispanic four-stars on active duty. While he had the Hispanic countenance of graying black hair and brown eyes, the accent was flawless American English, which, *if referenced,* received a curt admonishment by Admiral Yalvarez to the fact that he was an American; why would he have an accent? The ribbon of a Silver Star led the CNO's seven rows of medals. Yalvarez had a colorful reputation loved by the news tabloids. Even the supermarket tabloid the *Sun* periodically carried tales of the Navy's leader.

Yalvarez was a folk hero to the Hispanic communities, not only in the United States, but throughout Latin and South America as well as with Spaniards. Colombia even had a statue of this American in the main square of its capital. They loved him. A decade ago, when Yalvarez commanded a small U.S. frigate patrolling the Colombian coast during the Colombia police action, he had successfully defeated a multiple-small-boat attack launched by rebels associated with the drug cartels. He had sunk two of the boats, rammed a third, and when his gunfire disabled the fourth and largest boat, he personally led the boarding party. It was the first hand-to-hand combat at sea by American sailors boarding another vessel since the age of sail. The newspapers and news magazines ate it up. They wrote about the exploit for months, and the photograph of Yalvarez, taken by a signalman from the top deck of the U.S. frigate, became an instant icon for America's commitment to freedom. It showed Yalvarez holding a Navy sword above his head as he leapt onto the disabled drug cartel warship. To the side of him and behind him, tens of sailors with carbines blazing followed. The photograph earned the signalman ten thousand dollars and made the cover of *Time* magazine.

People just didn't fight with swords anymore, in this era of guns. Holman always wondered why Yalvarez went with a sword when a fully loaded M-16 would have been more effective, but the impact of that photograph sent Yalvarez's popularity soaring past rock stars and movie stars. Women wanted his baby. Several men did, too. Movie companies wanted his life story. Nike offered him a contract, but the shoes weren't Navy regulation and that was where Yalvarez confessed his loyalties lay. In another first, he was the *youngest* Chief of Naval Operations, surpassing the great Admiral Zumwalt, who in the seventies was leapfrogged over many senior flags to lead the Navy. The same thing happened with Yalvarez. Sure, the CNO had his detractors—those who believed him to be too political, or too self-serving. Holman didn't know the admiral other than through word-of-mouth reputation and newspaper articles, of which there were many. Christ! Being too political didn't sound like a negative point to Holman. You wouldn't survive a junior officer tour in the Pentagon if you didn't have some political savvy.

Admiral Yalvarez leaned forward, resting his elbow on the table, so he could look around Duncan James. His eyes stared directly into Holman's. "Dick," he said, "what's the latest on the loss of those Air Force F-16s? I read the latest in your Operations Report series this morning, but OPREPs seldom tell you everything."

No greeting. Just down to business. Another reputation

Admiral Jay had was for directness and a paucity of small talk.

"Sorry, Admiral. I don't have any additional information other than what is in the OPREP. I know Captain Bennett has already started a JAGMAN. The MISHAP report was issued yesterday—"

"I know all that, Dick. I want to know what you and he are discussing informally. Surely he has an idea as to what happened and if the French used some sort of laser weapon to destroy them?"

Holman shook his head.

"Laser weapons?" James asked.

Admiral Yalvarez waved his question away. "Later, Duncan."

"Sir, we're still leaning toward the idea that the pilots were fatigued after such a long flight, and one or more of them collided in mid-air, causing a cascade effect that sent the four aircraft crashing into the sea."

"I talked with the Air Force Chief of Staff and he disagrees with the theory." Yalvarez fingers tapped the table a couple of times. "Of course, he has a reason to believe it was something other than fatigue. If those pilots crashed because the flight time is too tiring, then it has a direct impact on Air Force strategy of being able to reach anywhere in the world within seventy-two hours. And that is from bases within the United States."

"I'll ask Captain Bennett to add more detail to his reports."

Yalvarez raised his hand off the table, palm toward Holman for a couple of seconds. "The reports are fine, Dick," he said with a smile. "They're right on target. They meet expectations. I just wanted to know what you and Captain Bennett are discussing informally. Wanted to know the rumors you're hearing. What's behind the facts that we haven't been able to substantiate yet. All of those are questions I would prefer answered before reading about them, if you get my drift."

Holman glanced at Duncan, who had leaned back in

his chair so the Chief of Naval Operations could talk to the Commander Amphibious Group Two. James's lips were pursed together and he stared at the ceiling.

Gee, thanks, Bud, Holman thought as he turned his gaze back to the CNO.

"Admiral," Yalvarez said, a hint of steely firmness in his voice. "Duncan can't help you. He wasn't there. You weren't there either, but you have a more rounded picture of what happened than what the OPREPs will be showing." When Yalvarez said "rounded" he cupped his hands for a moment as if he were holding a ball.

Holman cleared his throat. The problem with relaying third-hand information about something as serious as this is you risk having it confused with known facts. He knew how rumors, innuendoes, and partial facts of events such as this one could cloud the truth. He kept to himself these rumors and half-truths, waiting for Mary to lay out the events in chronological order. Time is always the deciding factor when determining fact from fiction. Events always unfolded to second- and third-hand listeners in chronological order, and when displayed in that way, why certain things were done or why things happened became clearer.

"Don't worry," Yalvarez said, making a downward motion with his hand. "I know how to keep fact and hearsay separated."

Holman had heard that mantra before, only to discover that those who believed themselves capable of doing it didn't do it well at all. Maybe he was in that group; he hoped not. Yalvarez, three years younger than Holman, wearing the solid gold epaulets with four embroidered stars, and who was his boss, was asking for insider information. This wasn't like the stock market where they made you do the perp walk and sent you off to jail for insider information, but you sure could find yourself in cold waters if you didn't share what you knew when asked.

Holman took a deep breath and let it out. *I hope this doesn't backfire.* "Sir, there is one thing that I have asked

Captain Bennett to chase down, and that is the precise events surrounding the anti-cruise missile exercise the *Winston Churchill* was conducting at the time the F-16s disappeared."

The CNO leaned back in his chair. "Tell me about it," Yalvarez ordered in a voice that seemed to Holman to say "I already know, but I want to see if you'll tell me."

"Admiral, from what I've been able to find out, *Mesa Verde* had an officer on board *Churchill* as an exercise observer. When the officer returned to his ship, he turned in an unsolicited report accusing the *Winston Churchill* of locking its fire control radar on a French Atlantique reconnaissance aircraft flying in its vicinity. This, coupled with the intelligence reports suggesting that a laser weapon—a laser weapon based on stolen U.S. technology—may have destroyed the Air Force fighters, led me to ask for more information."

"Thanks, Dick," Yalvarez said, his head nodding in agreement. The CNO leaned back in his chair, his finger drumming on the table. "You've confirmed what the director of Navy Intelligence told me this morning."

Holman swallowed. *So, I was right. He knew all along and was testing me.* Holman leaned forward so he could see the CNO's face. Maybe the CNO knew something concerning his Expeditionary Strike Group. If so, then he wanted to know, too. Before he could ask, the door to the Tank opened and the burly Air Force sergeant from outside announced in a loud voice, "Gentlemen, the Chairman."

They stood, their chairs creating a muffled sound as the legs slid back across the thick carpet. Holman's chair snagged, nearly causing him to fall back into it.

General "Halfpenny" Baines entered, wearing the Air Force blue tie.

Holman loved the Air Force tie for the great uniform concept it carried. The Air Force blue tie was the centerpiece of their uniforms. Without the tie, the uniform was just the working uniform of the day. But, when emergent occasions dictated, an Air Force member could jerk that tie out of a top desk drawer, whip it around his neck, and, while on the run toward the wine and nibblies, tie it. Tie it so fast and neat that by the time he reached the end of the passageway, *voila,* he was dressed for any confrontation on the dance or dinner floor. Holman kept such observations to himself. Somewhere, out of sight, during boot camp, they probably practiced the art of the quick tie.

"Morning, Admirals," Halfpenny said, strolling quickly along the opposite side of the table. Behind the Chairman trailed his Director of the Joint Staff, Army Lieutenant General Winifred Hulley, displaying the slack-jowl scowl political cartoonists had satirized during the Colombia police actions. He nodded at Holman.

Holman returned the nod, wondering if he heard a growl with that nod or if it was his imagination.

"Admiral Yalvarez, good to see you, sir," Hulley said, his voice deep and vibrating.

Holman thought, *Must know each other from the Colombia police action.*

"We're waiting for Miss Chatelain-Malpass, gentlemen," the chairman said. He reached forward and twisted the plastic top off the water bottle near his nameplate. Instead of pouring it into the glass, he took a deep swig. "Ah, that was good." He pulled a handkerchief from his back pocket and wiped his forehead. "You gentlemen will have to excuse me, I just came from the POAC. Managed to get in a few miles this morning."

POAC was the acronym for the Pentagon Officers Athletic Club. The POAC was a holdover from the era when Holman was a young lieutenant and it had been shoved into a separate building near Pentagon North Parking. The new one was named the Pentagon Athletic Club, but old-timers like the chairman still referred to it as "POAC."

They watched, but no one spoke as the chairman pulled out his chair. When he sat down, they followed suit. The chairman crossed his legs, left ankle over right knee. "Admiral James, we've met, but Admiral Holman—Dick, isn't it?"

"Yes, sir."

"Good to meet you, Admiral." Holman nodded. "Now, I know you two," he said, pointing at Duncan James and Holman, "are both wondering why you've been unceremoniously invited to the Tank, and the fact that I'm sitting here with you probably makes you even more nervous about why you've been called. Well, I'm not even in your shoes and I'm nervous. Admiral Holman, first let me apologize. I know it must have been quite an obstacle to break away from the battle groups you command to fly here today, but I think once you hear what Miss Chatelain-Malpass has to say, you'll understand why Admiral Yalvarez insisted on your presence."

Holman glanced at the CNO. Yalvarez's eyes were on his hands in his lap, one hand working slowly on the nails of the other.

"Before our distinguished visitor arrives, let me give you a heads up on what I think she is going to tell you and then ask you to do something which has the blessing of the Secretary of Defense. SecDef won't be joining us, but as you listen to what Miss Chatelain-Malpass has to say—"

The door to the Tank opened. General Halfpenny Baines abruptly stopped talking. The Air Force sergeant stepped into the room and held the door. A woman stepped inside the Tank, stopped briefly, and nodded to those around the table.

This must be Miss "however you say her name," thought Holman. She was tall, what his mother would have called a 'drink of water,' and she moved gracefully toward the seat beside Lieutenant General Hulley, standing beside the chair with her nametag in front of it. Her body was a plane of symmetry as if the slightly above-knee bluish-green dress had been purposely designed to hide any curves, though it failed to hide a pair of thin, shapely legs.

Holman was momentarily caught off guard by the men

standing and barely made it to his feet by the time the lady sat down in the chair that the director pulled out for her. You never knew what reaction you would get from some women in power when they were honored with a traditional gentlemanly act. Holman watched Chatelain-Malpass's face to see what the reaction might be, but she nodded with a smile, thanked General Hulley, and sat down as if this was normal wherever she went. The five of them followed suit.

She pulled her chair closer to the table as the men adjusted theirs.

Holman shifted slightly. Chatelain-Malpass's brown hair was pulled tight into a bun, almost as if intentionally tight so the skin on her face would have no flexibility to reveal any emotion. This was not a woman he would want to wake up with in the morning. *Where in the hell did that thought come from?* All she needed was a pair of half-moon bifocals and she'd epitomize his perception of a stereotyped librarian.

"Gentlemen," General Baines said, "allow me to introduce Ms. Alice Chatelain-Malpass from the president's National Security Council."

"Please call me Alice," she said. "I cringe when I hear people try to pronounce that hyphenated name of my parents."

Single, thought Holman, *and wants people to know the hyphenated name isn't a married one.* She smiled at Duncan James and nodded at Holman. A nice voice, smooth.

Holman twisted his wedding band several times.

"Alice, this meeting is yours, ma'am. As you know, the president's National Security Advisor asked for this meeting late last night," the chairman announced. "The secretary sends his regrets." Halfpenny pointed toward Holman. "This is Admiral Holman. He commands the Amphibious Group Two out of Little Creek Amphibious Base in Norfolk; and sitting between him and Admiral Yalvarez— Chief of Naval Operations—is Admiral Duncan James, head of Navy SEALs."

She nodded, a thin smile across her lips. *Was there anything about this woman that wasn't tight?* He felt a slight blush along his neck.

Holman took a deep breath, glancing down at the table a moment. When he looked up, she was staring at him, as if she had read his thoughts. He felt the red creep up his face. *Don't tell me I've got to watch my thoughts, too.*

General Baines paused.

"Thank you, General," she said, the forced smile still on her lips. She turned her attention to Admiral Holman and Admiral James. "I apologize for taking you away from your important jobs on such short notice, and on behalf of the president, I would like to extend his compliments and his knowledge that you will perform the mission which you are about to be assigned with courage, stealth, and success."

Holman rested his right hand on the table. There it was—that sinking feeling in his stomach. He reached forward, grabbed the water bottle, and took a deep swallow, knowing as he did it that it wasn't going to take away the dry feeling in his mouth. Missions weren't assigned this way to naval forces—in the Tank, by the White House, and with the chairman acting as a benign observer. Missions were planned and re-planned; beaten to death in a compartment full of devil's advocates in an attempt to identify everything that could happen. Even then, once a well-planned mission started, the fog of war sometimes made it go to shit in a handbasket. Bottom line was a mission may end that way, but you didn't start it already in the handbasket.

James and Holman exchanged a quick glance. Holman knew without asking that Duncan would be thinking the same thing.

Chatelain-Malpass lifted her briefcase to the table, opened it, and removed several binders before setting it on the floor beside her. "I have some data for you to read while we are here, but I have to take everything back with me when I leave." She shoved three of the binders across the table to the three admirals. Lieutenant General Hulley took another one and eased a fifth to the chairman, who immediately lifted it and flipped through the pages.

Holman caught a flash of irritation on Chatelain-Malpass's face when she saw the chairman flipping through her brief. *So much for a tight bun hiding emotions.* All the artificial tightening in the world couldn't hide the momentary burst of fire in those baby blues. Holman pressed his lips together to stop the slight urge to smile.

Chatelain-Malpass reached down and pulled a small black notebook from her briefcase. She opened it and, with a quick glance at Holman, started talking, never looking down at it again.

"Before I start, gentlemen, the classification of this discussion and anything else said while I am here is top-secret compartmented eyes-only. We would also prefer that my name and presence not be mentioned in follow-on discussions after I leave. That means only you five, outside of the National Security Council, are aware of everything I'm going to tell you today. It's not to be discussed outside this room. It's not to be discussed with others as to how you came about the mission to be assigned today, and only the information necessary to do the mission will be used, and that information will be attributed to some unnamed intelligence source. Admiral Holman, this secrecy applies to conversations with your wife, also. We're on the verge of a great success, if you do your job right."

He stopped turning his wedding band. "I beg your pardon."

She gave him a slight nod with that tight smile, but continued with her remarks. "Is that understood? I was never here today and what I am asking you to do did not come from the White House."

Don't underestimate her, Holman thought. Alice Chatelain-Malpass was a timber wolf. They ate men for fun. *"On the verge of a great success"—is that kind of like nearly being a virgin?*

The vision of a clothesline with the caption "left out to

dry" crossed Holman's mind. Whatever he and Duncan were about to be *asked* to do was going to be something that, if it became "fucked up beyond all recognition," *fubar* as the acronym goes, the blame wasn't going to go higher than him and Duncan. *Wonder why that sounds familiar?*

"Does everyone understand?"

"I think you've made it clear, Alice. Bottom line is that whatever happens, it won't roll uphill," Lieutenant General Hulley said with a trace of anger.

Holman could grow to like this gruff old warrior.

Chatelain-Malpass turned her head and met the director of the Joint Staff's eyes for a second before she returned her attention back to Holman and James. Holman patted his pocket. Obviously, she considered Hulley beneath her concern. He hoped his EA had his cigars, because he was going to need one after this.

"First, we have a problem, gentlemen. The problem is that the French have gained possession of classified data on the development of a new laser weapon we were working on. As you are aware from your own closely held intelligence reports, there is an analysis circulating around the intelligence community at the higher levels of command that offers an opinion that the disappearance of the Air Force F-16s was caused by a laser weapon." She paused for a moment, her eyes shifting from Holman to James. "The code name for the laser program is Phoenix Depth, not to be confused with some of the other more super-secret Defense Department Phoenix programs."

So far, nothing new. Holman took another sip of water. A cup of coffee would be nice.

"If you will look at the package I brought from the White House," she said, nodding directly at Holman.

She enjoys using the term "White House," thought Holman. It wouldn't have surprised him if she had lifted her hands each time she drew out the words and put "air quotes" around them. *Doubt her feet ever touch pavement when she's walking.* He nearly smiled at an image of her stopping complete strangers on the street to tell them she worked at the *quote,* White House, *unquote.* Holman sighed, immediately aware it had been loud enough to draw everyone's attention.

Regardless of what Holman thought, this lady represented the White House—whatever she wanted, he knew he was going to do it, as long as it didn't violate the Constitution or laws of war.

Holman opened the red-striped folder in front of him.

"The French have perfected the weapon, we believe," Chatelain-Malpass continued. "Having possession of our data showed them what didn't work, so they were able to avoid duplication of failure. Reducing the number of false starts apparently allowed them to perfect the weapon. The data Mr. Vernigan was caught with when the FBI arrested him would neither have helped nor hurt the French program. We can only speculate that they wanted the information to make sure our own laser weapon program was still having problems. While we work toward resolving the technical issues of the weapon, they have one that works fast, accurately, and reliably. Having our technical data gave the lead to the French."

Chatelain-Malpass reached forward and took a sip of water. "In short, our laser weapon program is sliding to the right, and if it isn't brought back on track by the time Congress returns from its summer recess we can expect Phoenix Depth to be cut. Do you know what that means?"

"Means the French have a laser weapon and we don't," Halfpenny volunteered. "But, if that's true, Alice, why don't we tell Congress. That should—"

"We can't, General. Intelligence funds were used to develop this project. Funds that were supposed to be used for other functions. And there would be an uproar over the misappropriation. No one in the administration approved this diversion of funds." She covered her mouth for a quick cough. "I know this sounds political, but it was the previous administration who diverted the funds . . ."

Sounds familiar, thought Holman. Teflon politicians were a great commodity in Washington.

"The problem is far worse as the SecDef can tell you. Right now America is a hyper-power. No one, anywhere, can stand up to us. With another nation having an effective laser weapon and America lacking parity in that technology, it could have a profound effect on us. See what I mean?"

The chairman looked at her. "I think it's worse than what you present, Ms. Chatelain-Malpass. If the laser weapon is everything you say, then it might be possible for it to take out whole fleets of ships and flights of aircraft in a single burst. It could reduce America to a second-rate power."

Holman looked up from the cover page, closed the folder, and crossed his hands on top. A few chill bumps creeped up his back. The chairman was right. The nation that possessed a weapon that had the capability of wiping out everything within a broad swath, without regard to whether it was aiming for it or not, would change the face of the world. Strength through numbers would be rendered obsolete. America's military strength would be threatened by any nation that wielded such technology. *We would cease to be the lone superpower,* Holman said to himself.

The ramifications flew through Holman's mind—the tactical implications of fighting a war at sea. Missiles would die in the air as the platforms that fired them erupted into flames. *The chairman is right. We're dead if we don't have weapon parity.* The White House was concerned about another nation having technology we don't, but Halfpenny Baines had thought the problem through and gone a step further in the implications, pointing out that we could quickly become an equal or less player in the world of global politics. America's national security was at stake.

"Then I guess I bring good news, General," Chatelain-Malpass said. "The French only have a prototype of this weapon."

"If it's a prototype, that means they have to test it or are testing it. Do we know where this is taking place?" the chairman asked.

Chatelain-Malpass cleared her throat. "General, they are already testing the laser weapon. Have been for a couple of months. Our reports through certain channels indicate the tests have been very successful and the French are very pleased with it."

"Then, ma'am, you ought to have those channels get us a copy of their test results and something on the laser weapon so our people can duplicate it."

"Mr. Chairman, I am afraid that is impossible. The weapon is beyond our operative's reach, and if he tried to obtain any data on it other than the briefings to which he has been invited, the French espionage service would quickly catch on and we would lose one of our most valuable resources. Even if we were willing to take that chance, the prototype is out of his reach regardless."

"Where is it?" Admiral Yalvarez asked. "I think I know from the presence of Admirals James and Holman where it is, but—"

She nodded at the chief of Naval Operations. "To test their version of the weapon, the French military installed the prototype on one of their Atlantique reconnaissance aircraft."

"The one in West Africa?" Holman interrupted, leaning forward. If so, he knew what she was going to tell them to do. He wanted her to say it, though, and he wanted every bit of knowledge she had before she disappeared from the Tank and he'd never see her again. After that, she'd be stacking sandbags of denial around her.

Chatelain-Malpass nodded curtly. "Correct. That very aircraft. And, Admiral Holman, that"— She glanced down at her notes —"Atlantique aircraft was the same one flying south of where the Air Force F-16 aircraft disappeared near your ships. We can't prove it yet—even if we could, we aren't sure how we would handle it—but we believe they deliberately chose this venue to test the laser weapon on our military aircraft."

"Alice," General Halfpenny Baines interjected, "I, too, have read the CIA report. And the British MI-5 report that supports it. What both reports say is more conjecture than fact. Even our own Department of Defense Intelligence Agencies find it hard to believe that the French would deliberately attack our aircraft. They haven't ruled it out, but their analysts fail to understand why they would do something such as this when we've come so far in mending fences between our two countries. Plus, there are better ways to test a weapon than shooting down another nation's aircraft. They could use unmanned drones or missiles without taking the chance of compromising their possession of such a weapon." He shook his head. "A weapon that would transform the act of war." He shook his head again, more briskly. "Just doesn't make good operational security sense to me."

"Unless, they believed themselves under attack or under threat of being shot down," Admiral Yalvarez added.

"I can't believe that," Halfpenny Baines replied.

Chatelain-Malpass's pencil-thin eyebrows scrunched into a shallow V. "Why would you say that, Admiral?"

Yalvarez nodded toward Holman. "Dick, tell her."

How did the saying go? There's three ways to skirt the truth; lies, half-truths, and statistics. Right now, none were applicable, and even he didn't know the truth. That metaphorical itch between his shoulder blades was the knife the CNO had just shoved into him. He had a vision of himself walking the plank with sharks circling beneath him.

Holman cleared his throat and repeated what he had told the chief of Naval Operations earlier about the possibility that the USS *Winston S. Churchill* had inadvertently locked its fire control radar on the French reconnaissance aircraft. He threw in as many "possibles" and "probables" as he could, knowing it made him sound like some gawldamn intelligence officer. And Bennett was still investigating the events surrounding the exercise. May be nothing there but the untrained eye of some junior officer. Lord knows, he'd seen plenty of "shoot first, put the bullets in later" officers in his career, who could say just what they were thinking when they did what they did with little regard to truth or consequence. The *Churchill* incident was like a first report from a combat zone. They're seldom accurate, emotionally written, and always subject to change.

Chatelain-Malpass listened, her face never betraying her thoughts. Holman thought he saw the fingers on her hands spread when he reached the point about the fire control radar. "If the *Churchill*'s fire control inadvertently locked on to the French aircraft, it could be construed as a violation of international law—an act of war. The time of possible fire control lock-on also matched the flight pattern of the four Air Force F-16s, heading outbound from the exercise on a direct course that could have been misinterpreted as intercept bound. Intercept-bound against a French reconnaissance aircraft operating over international waters."

He finished and leaned back in his seat. The water bottle was nearly empty; he gulped the last of it down.

A couple of seconds passed with everyone looking at the woman from the White House.

Chatelain-Malpass nodded curtly. "Thank you, Admiral, but that doesn't change one damn thing about the mission. It only explains why the French would reveal their weapon, if they thought they were under attack. Weighing the chairman's earlier assessment, it only serves to show that the French have already reached a conclusion as to how this weapon will transform global power overnight. Otherwise, they wouldn't have had the confidence to use it."

"We haven't had a confrontation with them since Admiral Holman braced Admiral Colbert and his French carrier battle groups."

"In the same area, wasn't it, General Baines?"

The chairman nodded. "Yes, Alice, it was."

"Just further complements these pieces of the puzzle falling into place."

"If I may ask, ma'am," Holman said. "What is the mission you want us to do?"

He seemed to have gained the attention of the table, but

the earlier coffee was working its way through him. No one ever mentioned it in the Pentagon, but the duration of many meetings depended on the strength of the chair's bladder. He hated the thought of having to stand up and excuse himself, because the reason they were there was for him.

"The mission, Admiral, is to go and get that laser weapon off the French aircraft. If we're unable to do that, then destroy it. We can't have the French or anyone other than ourselves possessing a weapon with such potential."

"Destroying it wouldn't stop them from building another prototype, or—let's hypothesize for a moment," Halfpenny Baines offered, interlocking his fingers and resting them beneath his chin. "Let's say the French did use the laser weapon to shoot down the F-16s. Add that to two weeks of field testing and you've successfully proven the utility and value of the weapon. You don't need to build another prototype. You could, *conceivably*, go right into production."

"If we destroy it," Lieutenant General Hulley added, his voice betraying a slight tremor from the massive jowls alongside each cheek, "then, we only destroy the prototype. If we bring it back, or bring the computer system that controls it back, then we have two things to keep in mind"—he held up two fingers—"one, we will be able to recover the data; and two, we have to do it without them knowing we were the ones."

"General Hulley is correct, Ms. Chatelain-Malpass," Halfpenny Baines argued. "If we're going to do this, we're going to have to be careful."

"It will take time to arrange the mission," Admiral Yalvarez said.

"It would only take four or five days to prepare a SEAL team—"

"Or Delta Force," General Hulley added with a quick smile at Yalvarez.

Chatelain-Malpass shook her head. "Gentlemen, the

French will fly the aircraft out of Ivory Coast to France within the next seventy-two hours. We had considered sending in SEALs, or Army Special Forces, to steal the weapon systems, or, failing that, to destroy the aircraft . . ."

"We can destroy the aircraft, Ms. Chatelain-Malpass," Halfpenny Baines responded.

"Yes, General, I'm sure you can, but can you destroy it without the French knowing we did it? While we're prepared to take the chance of the French discovering we were the ones responsible for blowing it up, we would prefer that they never have concrete evidence just the same."

"I understand."

James shook his head. "This is going to be hard to do. I don't have any SEALs in Liberia, ma'am." James took a deep breath and let it out. Holman knew even as James spoke that the head of Navy SEALs was trying to figure a way to get teams to Liberia in time. "What I have is a lone SEAL commander attached to Admiral Holman's command who is in Liberia to discuss with the government special operations training. We are going—"

"I don't care," she said. "Admiral, it's not my job to figure out how you're going to do it. What I—we—want is for the Navy to execute the mission. Retrieve the laser weapon technology. While we thought about using SEALs or Special Forces for this mission, we can use neither. No SEALs or Special Forces can be involved."

"What!" Lieutenant General Hulley cried. "What do you want us to use? Military Police in a Humvee?"

The chairman reached over and touched his director of the Joint Staff on the arm.

"Alice," Halfpenny said softly. "Our SEALs and Special Forces are the only ones qualified to do this mission."

"I know, General, but laws passed years ago require the president to authorize such a mission. We must have separation from the president on this mission. If it fails, it must not be linked to him. And if it succeeds, and the French discover it was the United States who made off with their laser technology, then it still must not be linked to him."

The military officers exchanged glances around the table, no one eager to say anything.

"Well?" Chatelain-Malpass finally asked.

"Ma'am, we can destroy the aircraft easily," Holman volunteered. "The Air Force has six F-16s forward deployed to Monrovia. They can be across the border and back, mission accomplished, within—"

Chatelain-Malpass leaned forward, her face still expressionless, and in the level tone she used for her briefing thirty minutes ago, she said, "There must be something wrong with the tone of my voice, gentlemen. It's not the Air Force we want to go in there with guns blazing, singing yippee-kie-oh. There are political considerations. We will not have our political détente with the French destroyed by an overt military action."

General Baines leaned forward as if to say something.

Chatelain-Malpass, palm out, held her hand up at him as she continued. "If it was just to go in and destroy the plane, any military action could do it, but the political reverberations would be unacceptable. The French aircraft is in the Ivory Coast. It's on the west coast of Africa where 'things happen.' Things that never make the papers or, when things do, can be better explained. If we are going to detour the French laser weapon program we have to do it in Africa. Once that aircraft is back in France, the mission is over. We aren't going to try anything on French soil. You have to ask yourself, why would we ask for you to keep this meeting top secret if we wanted to just destroy the weapon and not worry about them knowing who did it?" She stopped abruptly.

"I think you misunderstand—" Holman started.

"Can we expect a warning order from the president to do this mission?" Halfpenny Baines interrupted.

"No," she said. Poking herself in the chest with her finger, she continued, "I'm your warning order and your tasking directive. Your job is to execute it. The President must be kept separate from this mission for all the reasons I have noted."

"Without SEALs, we would have to send untrained personnel to do this mission," Admiral Duncan James said sharply.

"That's not my problem, Admiral. That's your problem. You can use the average sailor if you so desire, as long as the mission is a success. Tell them the French have free beer and they'll take the whole continent."

Admiral Yalvarez's head shot up. "I think you're overstepping your bounds, young lady."

Whew! thought Holman. That's the *Time* magazine admiral he'd heard about. And apparently Chatelain-Malpass was aware of the danger of taking on such a popular American hero because, to the surprise of those around the table, she apologized for her "sailor" comment.

TEN MINUTES LATER, HOLMAN WALKED OUT OF THE MEN'S head on the eighth corridor. "I thought two years at the Pentagon had stripped me of the minimal amount of integrity I had when I arrived here, but after meeting with this National Security Council representative, I realize we aren't so bad off in the field of integrity. Well, what do you think, Duncan?" he asked Admiral James, waiting in the hallway for him.

"I would say she has that special appearance and voice—that intrinsic talent that comes together in a special way—that just pisses you off when she says, 'hello.'"

Holman chuckled. "Could be true, but what I meant was, what do we do?"

"You have the only SEAL I have available, but he comes with baggage, Dick. His house was blown up two days ago, and he's on the continent where the terrorist leader Abu Al-haul has sworn to kill him. Means if you use him, and I think you have little choice, he's not only going to have the French Foreign Legion to worry about, but this Islamic Jihadist who blames him for the death of his family in Yemen."

They walked toward the inner circle of the Pentagon. The windows ahead reflected the sunny day, lighting up the central courtyard of the Pentagon.

"There's also this African army that is somewhere around the border areas of Liberia and Ivory Coast. Our Islamic enemy may have his hands full trying to avoid those Africans, then again, he may not. I understand they're wiping the land free of Jihadists, though, using methods that would make the average American throw up."

"And they're ridding themselves of our missionaries, also."

Lieutenant Willis, who had been trailing Holman since the head, slowed slightly to give the two admirals comfortable distance to talk freely. Holman noticed and thought, *Maybe I'll keep him as my EA.*

"I do have some Seabees disembarking at Harper, Liberia, off the *Mesa Verde,*" Holman offered, trying to see what James would propose. Seabees may have some combat training, but they weren't Marines or SEALs. They built things.

Instead of turning down Holman's half-suggestion, Holman was surprised to hear James discussing the combat training Navy Seabees go through. James further offered that, with the exception of Navy SEALs and EOD, the Seabees were the only other group who received combat training *en masse.* Granted, Seabees were not trained in covert operations, but at a minimum they knew which end of the gun the bullet came out, which was more than most sailors.

"Good idea, Dick. Damn," James said as they reached the "A" ring, "wish I'd thought of it."

"My idea!? I didn't say I would use Seabees. You told me they *could* be used. And even if I accept your logic, Duncan, they'd still need a Navy SEAL to lead them."

The two exited into the open garden center of the Pentagon, commonly referred to as "ground zero," a term left over from the Cold War days when rumor had it that the Soviets had a missile aimed directly for the center of the open space. Standing to the right of the two men were several Navy captains and a couple of Army colonels, all smoking cigars. Holman patted his pocket and for a brief second nearly excused himself to join the officers. Even from here, it was apparent from the laughter and body language that the men were close friends. *Probably the Ground Zero cigar club he'd encountered last time here. Looks as if they have some new members. Wonder if they have temporary memberships?*

"I said, what are you going to do?" James asked.

"Sorry, Duncan, I was just thinking—"

"—how good a cigar would be right about now?"

The two laughed as they continued walking across the open space.

They walked through the arch leading to corridor four. Holman glanced at the number above his head. This was the corridor where American Airlines flight 77 entered the Pentagon "E" ring on its deathly journey on September 11, 2001. Things had changed a lot since then.

"Look, Dick. I'm going to leave you here. I'll detach two teams to you from somewhere. The USS *Detroit* is doing an around-the-world show of the flag during its return to its homeport of San Diego. We have SEALs on board. I'll contact Commander, Special Warfare Group One in San Diego and have them shift two teams to you when their Expeditionary Strike Group rounds South Africa. They won't be there before you execute the mission, but if things go to shit, you might be able to use them. At least they'll give you additional options."

"Thanks, Duncan," Holman said, shaking hands with his friend. "Get them to me as soon as you can."

As they shook hands, Duncan leaned close. "There is one other thing I'm going to do. I am going to relieve Commander Tucker Raleigh as a Navy SEAL. It'll be a good way to circumvent protocol. I'll draft a letter telling him something about his wounds making him unfit. I'll also call him and explain the rationale. Tucker is a player. He'll understand. May not be happy, but he'll understand.

If this goes off well, then we'll return him to full duty. This way, we avoid asking for presidential authority."

"That would help immensely, having Raleigh in charge. Can you have him report to Captain Xavier Bennett, commanding officer of the *Mesa Verde*? Since this is such a super-secret quagmire they're sending our way, I guess he'll be the commander of this 'Joint Task Force France,' for lack of a better operational title."

"We both know that if we do well and succeed we'll never hear a word about it; but if we fail, they'll hang our asses out to cover theirs."

Holman laughed as he dropped James's hand. "Damn, Duncan, I never would have figured that out if you hadn't told me."

Duncan James slapped him on the shoulder. "You take care, my friend. By the way, I wouldn't use 'Joint Task Force France' as my operational title. Doesn't sound too meaty, if you know what I mean."

Holman grinned. "Wasn't supposed to."

He looked toward the end of the corridor where the faint sound of rotors could be heard. "Guess I'll use my trip back to Little Creek to think about this problem."

"Think hard, my friend," Duncan James replied. He winked before turning on his heels and heading up a nearby staircase to an upper level. Someone entered the Pentagon from the door leading to the helo pad. Holman's nose wrinkled from the smell of exhaust that followed the Army colonel who saluted as she passed.

Thirty minutes later, Holman was strapped into the web seating of the CH-53 Sea Stallion helicopter. He leaned against the vibrating fuselage as the helicopter lifted off from the Pentagon helo pad and turned south to take him to Little Creek Amphibious Base. He shut his eyes. Commander Tucker Raleigh had saved America from an attack only months ago, and now Holman was going to ask him to risk his life again. If there were any other way, he'd do it. The man had suffered enough in this ongoing war on terrorism, but when duty calls, you can't use "get out of jail free" cards from your past exploits. Duty expects you rise to the occasion, surge forward, and do your best. If your best fails, then a grateful nation will send another.

Of course, that's easy to say—easy to envision. Holman was the one who was going to have to explain to Rear Admiral select Xavier Bennett why Seabees would do a SEAL mission. He had no doubt the Seabees would do it; it was just they weren't trained to muck silently about in the jungles. They were trained to build and fight; if necessary to do both at the same time. *"Joint Task Force France"—sounds like a bunch of sailors dating a barmaid.*

CHAPTER 6

"THEY WANT ME TO DO WHAT?" COMMANDER TUCKER Raleigh said, his voice rising. "That's bullshit, Skipper. You're telling me to jump in a helo four hours from now with three Seabees—*who have no idea how in the hell to survive in a Special Forces–type operation*—traipse up to an aircraft, dash into it, rip out some sort of technology—stolen weapon or whatever gadget it is—and return here safely?" He lifted his hands above his head. "I can't imagine anyone believing there may be something wrong with this scenario!"

Tucker took a couple of steps to the right, reversed his pace, and walked back to where he originally stood. He dropped his hands by his side. Shaking his head slowly, he thought, *Who in the hell came up with this brilliant idea? It had to be some desk jockey in Washington; someone who's never been in harm's way to come up with this Keystone Cop of an idea!*

If Bennett's in-port stateroom had been bigger, Tucker would have continued pacing back and forth. "This is ludicrous," he mumbled. "Not to mention it's most likely a one-way trip." He turned to Bennett. "Captain, just because they blew up my home and I don't have anything to go back to doesn't mean I'm expendable."

Captain Xavier "Harry" Bennett motioned downward with his right hand. "I know how you feel, Commander Raleigh. I'm not happy with the orders either, but let's not exaggerate. Admiral Holman is as concerned as you and I are. As to where this mission originated, I can only speculate, but it definitely was outside the Pentagon."

"I wish I was exaggerating," he said. Captain Bennett seemed like a nice guy, but what would a Surface Warfare officer know about SEAL operations? Dangerous enough when a team was forced periodically to take a non-SEAL with them because of a person's special talents, but for one SEAL to take three untrained, untried, and unknown sailors into hostile territory! Abu Alhaul hadn't succeeded in killing him, but his own bosses may be more successful.

He turned and walked toward the bulkhead, stopping at the porthole to look across the small port of Harper, Liberia. His mind raced over the unexpected mission and concerns with how in the hell he was going to do it without getting himself and whoever went with him killed. He didn't mind going into the field, doing the covert shit SEALs could handle, but someone somewhere apparently had not one iota of an idea how to work up for those missions.

Cool air from the ship's air conditioning system blew from the vent above his head. Directly outside the porthole, three sailors, hand over hand, tugged at the pulley lines, slowly bringing the portable stand up from the side of the ship. Once even with the deck, they began to crawl over the safety lines, toting paint buckets along with them. Tucker thought, *You don't drive up to the front gate, step out of a cab, and sneak into a facility!*

He watched the scene outside the porthole without really seeing it; his mind was elsewhere. The petty officer in charge cradled plastic bottles of water in his right elbow and handed the first sailor a bottle. The first sailor flopped down on the deck, using a dirty towel to wipe the sweat from his face. As the others crawled back onto the main deck, the petty officer handed each a bottle before they eased themselves onto the deck. Tucker watched the short tableau of ship's work, sweat rolling down faces onto already soaked T-shirts yellowed by the labor over the side of the ship. The late-afternoon humid heat of Africa sucked moisture like some invisible vampire from those who lingered topside too long. The petty officer was speaking while those on the deck nodded, with the exception of one sailor who appeared to be arguing with him. The others laughed, raising hands to slap high-fives among them. Tucker didn't need to hear the words of the sailors to have a good idea what they were saying. The petty officer also laughed and opened his own bottle of water.

Forty-eight hours ago Tucker was on an Air Force C-141 flying into Monrovia supposedly to discuss the training of select soldiers within retired Lieutenant General Daniel Thomaston's new Liberian army so they could do a Special Forces–type mission. Complicating his own mission was trying to find out how much of his household goods were destroyed in the bombing of his home. The house was gone; that he knew. Other people have fires and floods, but not him—no, he had to have his own devil chasing him with gunfire and bombs. He briefly touched his left shoulder. If the bullet from the first time had been two inches lower and slightly left, he wouldn't be here today, and his organs would be living inside other people. *I wonder if Abu Alhaul would have chased them down to make sure every bit of Tucker Raleigh was dead?* He hoped that someone had called Allegheny Power and Washington Gas and told them to turn off the utilities. Be just his luck to return and discover hundreds of dollars in bills accumulating to run a destroyed house.

He had expected Admiral James to allow him to return to take care of this catastrophe, but instead of heading back to the States, he stood in the stateroom of the skipper of the USS *Mesa Verde* listening to some God-forsaken plan. *Well, that's one way for the Navy to get out of paying him for the household goods destroyed in the bombing. Get him killed.* And his homeowner's insurance hadn't been much help. The agent had almost sounded happy as he told Tucker, "I'm really sorry, Commander, but if you read your homeowner's insurance, you'll see we are unable to cover acts of terrorism." Nor sinkholes, nor earthquakes, nor floods, but if someone breaks in and steals your groceries, they'd be jolly on the spot with a claims adjuster to prorate the estimate.

The sailor who had been jawing with the supervisor of the working party stood and grabbed another liter of bottled water from beneath the porthole. Tucker couldn't see the container, but the sailor ran his hand over the outside of the bottle, gathering flakes of ice in his hand, before rubbing it across his face. Then he ran his tongue across dry lips.

The sun broke from behind the stanchion to the east, the heat almost palatable as rays burst through the porthole, a more intense glare off the waters of the harbor adding to the heat. Tucker turned away from the sailors on the deck and back to Captain Xavier Bennett, lifting the bottle of water Bennett's aide had given him earlier.

The reed-thin skipper of the amphibious ship *Mesa Verde* leaned against the metal desk in his in-port cabin. The taller Surface Warfare officer had his arms folded across his chest and his legs crossed at the ankle, watching passively. Bennett had said he and Admiral Holman agreed with his bleak assessment, but Tucker really had no way of knowing if the disbelief expressed by Captain Bennett was truly accurate. Even if it was, they couldn't be as concerned as he was—they didn't have to go into the field. They could sit back here and commiserate all they wanted; they didn't have to dodge the bullets. All they had to do was make the decision.

Neither could Tucker know the acrimony with which Bennett reacted when he received the orders. Though Bennett and Holman were professional friends, it finally had reached the point where Admiral Holman had to order the Naval Academy officer to accept and execute his orders. At that point, Bennett stood straight, acknowledged the order with a vocal "aye aye, sir," and hung the telephone up after assuring Holman he would keep him informed.

"Is this some plan to lure Abu Alhaul out into the open, sir?" Tucker asked softly. "It's not like it's unknown intelligence that the man has a hard-on for me just because I blew up his wife and children—unintentionally—because at the time I was trying to kill him."

A knock on the stateroom door drew both their attention.

"I don't think so, Commander Raleigh. Enter!" Bennett shouted at the door.

"The Navy used me as bait once, sir. I'm not opposed to it. If using me brings Abu Alhaul out of hiding and gives us a chance to kill his ass then I'm willing to be bait. I'd just like to know about it first."

Tucker looked over his shoulder. The Marine sentry had stepped inside the compartment and was holding the door open. The commanding officer of the Navy Mobile Construction Battalion-133 stepped inside while the Marine stepped out and shut the door. Tucker nodded at the sandy-haired commander wearing battle-dress utilities.

"Captain, you sent for me, sir?" Klein asked.

"Teddy, this is Tucker Raleigh." As the two shook hands, Bennett continued. "I won't go into details as to his initial mission in Liberia, but a couple of hours ago we received a change in operational orders. He is going to need two—"

"Three, sir," Tucker interrupted.

"Three of your people to give him a hand."

Klein smiled. "Should be no problem, sir." He nodded at Tucker. "What is it you need built, Commander?" Klein reached up and lightly tapped the SEAL emblem over Tucker's left pocket. "We specialize in helping anyone, especially you SEALs. My people can throw a barracks up in hours or build you a landing strip in a day." He held up one finger. He was suddenly a salesman working his pitch. "And, outdoor heads or latrines are part of the package—two seaters so you've got someone to chat with if you forgot reading material. Newspapers and toilet tissue will be your responsibility, of course."

"Not exactly what I need." Tucker paused for a second. "Your people good at building hospitals?"

"I suppose it's something like that covert camp we built for you people last year in Ethiopia?"

Tucker chuckled, shaking his head. "You have no idea, my friend, what's going to be asked of you."

Klein turned to Captain Bennett.

Tucker looked at Bennett and smiled. "Captain, I believe the pleasure is all yours, sir."

Klein turned his head toward Tucker. "Whatever you want constructed, my battalion can do it."

"I think *deconstructed* might be a better word," he replied, wondering about the small feeling of comradeship he felt. Maybe it was the wariness registering in Klein's face. *Yeah, this could be the only highlight of the day— finding someone else who feels the same way I do.*

He glanced at his wristwatch. In hours, he was going to be helo' ing with a group of sailors—sailors whose combat skills and bush qualities were uncertain. If they came back alive, it would be because of luck on their side and shitty professionalism on the French side. Anything could happen. Not to mention this "jack-in-the-box" terrorist who blew up his new home and kept trying to kill him. Oh! And don't forget the African National Army that intelligence was still trying to decide whether it truly existed or was just a rabble of rioters looting the countryside. He glanced out the porthole again, listening as Bennett explained to Commander Klein what was going to happen. Tucker smiled every time he heard Klein's exclamations of disbelief.

At least it was a nice day. When they arrived later near this covert French military airport some thirty plus miles from the Liberia border, it would be near midnight. *Oh, yes, Skipper, don't forget to tell him how far we're going to be from backup if this goes downhill.* Tucker shifted left slightly so the sun hit him squarely in the face. He shut his eyes. Somewhere on this floating hulk of gray, the ship's young intelligence officer was rounding up some satellite photographs of the airfield and printing them some charts. The charts he'd need if they were forced to work their way back cross-country. He shook his head. Alone, he probably stood a chance. A chance if he was only reconnoitering. Escorting a bunch of untrained Seabees heightened the odds in favor of the French.

Bennett straightened up, uncrossing his arms and legs, to face the two men. Tucker heard the movement, opened his eyes, and turned around, stepping forward out of the patch of sunlight.

The happy face Commander Klein had when he entered the compartment had melted like a candle in the African sunlight. *I know what's going through your mind, my fine Seabee friend.* Tucker's ire over the mission was diminishing as his thoughts turned to how to accomplish it once inserted. The other thoughts were on how they were going to survive long enough to be picked up.

". . . and that's about it, Commander," Bennett finished. The captain held his hands out to the side. "Any questions?"

Klein raised his head. A slight smile crossed his lips. He stretched his neck and looked quickly around the compartment as if searching for something.

"Sir, is there a camera here?" A forced laugh came from Klein as he waved his finger at the two unsmiling men. "I was warned by my boss to beware of Surface Warfare humor. Having a SEAL here could make this almost believable. If it wasn't that what you propose is, I believe, a violation of the Geneva Convention, I'd have bitten." He bent down and looked under the desk for a hidden camera, craning his neck so he could see around Bennett's legs. "My boss said SWO humor was somewhat disgusting and sordid. I didn't believe him. I definitely owe him an apology when I get back to Gulfport."

Bennett shook his head. Tucker saw the tight smile fade from Klein's face. "Okay, I'm done clowning, captain. There is no way my people can do this. We aren't properly trained for such a mission, and, while I may have some in physical shape to do it, they didn't get in that physical shape by preparing to dash through jungles, eating snakes, and shooting people."

"I wish I was kidding, Teddy," Bennett sighed. The captain uncrossed his legs, turned, and lifted a sheet of paper from the desk. Bennett tilted his head so his bifocals shifted into place. "There are other things you need to know. Commander Raleigh has already been briefed—"

"Sir, this is a load of bullshit! What you're asking me to do is send my men, or women, who are not trained for this, into a mission where they stand a good chance of being killed, wounded, or captured." Klein had extended his right hand, palm up, at Bennett. "This can't be right."

"They're trained to fight, aren't they?" Bennett snapped. "Don't tell me what's bullshit and what isn't on my ship."

Tucker slipped his hand into his right rear pocket. After his own tirade about this asininity, he could understand why the captain's patience was wearing thin. His would be, too, if he had to overcome the skepticism this order generated. It wasn't as if anyone gave great thought to it. Maybe it did come from the White House. Although great thoughts seldom come from an administration. *"Boys, America needs you to just go in, stomp ass, and take names. The American people will love you."*

"Yes, sir. It's your ship, but these are my men and women, and if you're ordering them into harm's way then they deserve to know who ordered this and for what goddamn reason it is so imperative that I'm being asked—no, ordered—to send sailors to risk their lives unnecessarily."

Just what I need, Tucker thought, *having to jump in and separate these two.* SEALs were trained to think fast and act faster. Without realizing it, Tucker compared his six-foot-one frame against the older captain and the shorter but stockier Seabee. Tucker ran his hand through his short sandy-brown hair. The Seabee may be a problem. Klein's upper arms stretched the fabric of the uniform to near ripping tension. If he had to step between these two, he hoped the Seabee commander was reasonable. He could fight . . .

Bennett lifted the sheet. "The order came from the White House, was passed via the chairman of the Joint Chiefs of Staff to Admiral Yalvarez, who gave it to Admiral Holman, who, graciously, a couple of hours ago, gave it to me."

"Can I see the operational order, sir?" Klein asked, holding his hand out.

Bennett waved the paper in the air before bringing it down. "This isn't the OPORDER, Teddy. These are notes I made from the telephone call."

Tucker studied the Seabee commander in front of him. The man had the build and physical bearing of a warfighter, but behind those muscles beat the nerves of an engineer. Anyone could look the part. Most Navy SEALs didn't look anything like the movie-generated versions. Most were wry and nondescript. It was the mental attitude and ability to remain calm when hell was breaking loose around you that separated the Navy SEALs from everyone else. Of course, on the other hand, if you're calm while everyone around you is running and screaming, maybe you don't fully understand the situation. Could the Seabees keep their calm when the bullets started flying? Being calm didn't mean being unafraid; it meant overcoming and suppressing your fear so you could function in combat.

"Then when can we expect the OPORDER?"

"There won't be one," Tucker said, shaking his head. "There won't be an OPORDER because this mission doesn't exist. It doesn't exist on paper and it doesn't exist at the White House either."

"I don't like this."

"Well, Commander, that makes three of us," Captain

Bennett added. "But, regardless of whether we like it or not, the orders are valid and they are legal."

"And what happens if I send some of my men along with Commander Raleigh—it is Raleigh, right?"

Tucker nodded. "Tucker Raleigh."

"What happens if they become stranded?" Klein asked, turning back to Captain Bennett. "Are we going to rescue them, or is this going to be a Laos–type mission we studied at Georgia Tech?"

"You studied the Vietnam war at Georgia Tech?" Tucker asked.

"Of course," Klein replied. "You don't think us Yellow Jackets do nothing but study engineering, sing songs, and drink beer do you?"

"You sing songs and drink beer, too? I am now fully amazed," Tucker said. Klein didn't smile in return. *Well, that went down well,* Tucker thought.

"If they get trapped and we can mount a rescue, we will. Tucker and I have worked out a quick operational plan that calls for him and three of your men—and I know you'll select your best qualified—to be helo'ed within a few miles of the airport where the French Atlantique reconnaissance aircraft is based. Commander Raleigh will brief his team once you two have put it together. Three hours after they're inserted, I expect the helicopter to pick them up where it dropped them off. Barring any problems, this mission will be over by sunrise tomorrow morning." Bennett nodded toward Tucker. "It's a legal order, Commanders, and you will obey it, understand?"

Klein stood straight. "Sir, I never intended to disobey the order," he said, his voice betraying his irritation. "My only intention is to find out where this stupid idea originated so I can tell my grandchildren some day when they read about it."

Bennett reached out and briefly touched the stout young commander on the shoulder. "I know, Teddy. And I know this is foreign to you and something the Seabees haven't been asked to do since World War II, but your people are the only combat-trained personnel I have. My sailors on the *Mesa Verde* and those on the *Churchill* don't have the fire training your people do."

Klein nodded, his upper teeth biting his lower lip for a couple of seconds. He looked up, making eye contact with both Tucker and Captain Bennett. "You're right there. Most of Charlie Company wears the Seabee Combat Warfare Breast Insignia. That's not to say the other two companies aren't as proficient, but Charlie Company's commander, Lieutenant Peal, has been proactive in getting his people qualified. Plus, Brute's in Charlie Company."

"Brute?" Tucker asked, rolling the name a couple of times off his tongue. "Got a nice ring to it."

"Brute has been a source of . . . let's say conversation aboard the *Mesa Verde* since we departed Pascagoula, Mississippi," Bennett added. He crossed his arms across his chest and leaned back against the desk. "Yes, Brute would be a great asset to Commander Raleigh. A greater asset if they run into the French."

"Brute?" Tucker asked again. "I take it that's a name of a person and not an animal."

"The jury's still out on that," Klein replied.

"Brute isn't this Seabee's real name, as you probably guessed, Tucker. Brute is a second-class Builder," Bennett offered.

"Third class now, sir," Klein said. "I busted him for that brawl in Pascagoula. He'll be second class again in a few months." Klein turned to Tucker. "He's made second class petty officer more times than most people get promoted in a career in the Navy, and he's only been in the Navy five years."

"Brute is about six-foot-six and somewhere in his life his neck disappeared into his chest," Bennett continued. "His chest starts somewhere just below where his neck used to be and tapers down to his waistline."

"If it were possible, he'd be negative body fat on the

Navy's physical fitness body measurements. He's not only a builder, but he specializes in underwater construction," Klein offered.

"That'll come in handy in the middle of Africa," Tucker said sarcastically.

"All right. We're done here, gentlemen. I expect you back within ninety minutes with the names of those going."

"Sir, I will be one of those going," Klein said.

Tucker could tell from the way Bennett's eyes narrowed that he was on the verge of telling Klein no, and he was surprised when the man said, "That's between you and Commander Raleigh. You two work it out."

THE TWO COMMANDERS, ONE IN WORKING KHAKI WITH silver oak leaves on the collar and the other wearing battle dress utilities with embroidered black oak leaves on the collar, walked side by side down the passageway.

"Where can we go to work this out?" Tucker asked. He had only been aboard since this morning, and, with only a stateroom assigned to him, he had no working space.

"We can go to my office."

"So, what was this brawl this Seabee Brute got himself into in Pascagoula?" Tucker asked as he followed Teddy Klein down a nearby ladder.

At the bottom of the ladder, Klein looked both ways, and, seeing no one in the passageway, he turned to Tucker, shrugged, and said, "Just your typical brawl. My people had finished participating in a military funeral at the local American Legion. They were wearing whites. Afterward a few of them, along with Brute, stopped at a local bar for a few post-service observances before returning to the ship. Seems several of the locals had arrived much earlier than Brute and his buddies."

A sailor emerged from a nearby office. Klein stopped speaking. The sailor excused himself as he walked between the two officers and scurried up the ladder the two men had just come down. When the footsteps faded, Klein continued.

"One of the locals saw the summer whites and asked what type of ice cream they served. Probably would have been laughed off, but they apparently were amused over their own humor and kept it up until one of them—feeling suicidal, of course—pointed at Brute and asked him what type of ice cream he was. From what the other sailors said, Brute told him, 'Rocky Road, because it reminds us of your face.' And when the man stepped forward, Brute knocked him into his friends. It went downhill from there."

Klein turned and continued aft toward his office.

"You're lucky the sheriff didn't lock them up."

"What's lucky is the sheriff was a Navy veteran and the locals Brute beat up 'needed it' according to the sheriff. In Mississippi, it's a legal defense: 'Yore honor, I beat the shit out of him because he needed it,' " Klein said, deliberately deepening his Georgian accent. "So, the sheriff gave me custody with the understanding Brute wouldn't be allowed off the ship again and I would take him to mast. In return, when the two locals got out of the hospital, the sheriff would conveniently lose the incident report."

A master chief dressed in cammies and holding his hat in his hand stepped over the knee knocker of the opening ahead of them. Thick steel frames protruded along the deck, around the bulkheads, and overhead to provide better watertight integrity to the ship in the event of catastrophic damage. This metal frame gave the watertight door purchase when the lever was shoved down, locked, and secured. Sailors referred to this watertight frame as a knee knocker because sailors tripped and fell over them continually, even bumping their heads on the protruding frame curving overhead.

"That's Master Chief Collins," Klein said, his head motioning ahead of them. "He's my Command Master Chief."

"Sir," the master chief said when the two men reached his vicinity. "We've managed to off-load your Humvee, sir. It's on the deck."

"Thanks, Master Chief," he said. Klein introduced Tucker Raleigh to the older man. The three turned and continued back the way the master chief had just came. Along the way, Master Chief Collins gave Commander Klein the status of the off-load and let him know that the forward party had already arrived at the airfield. From what they said on the walkie-talkies, it sounded as if they were going to have to clear the old airfield before they could start to broaden and widen it for U.S. military use.

"Old airfield?" Klein asked. "We're just supposed to extend the current airfield and do any repairs necessary so our aircraft can use it."

"Yes, sir, but the current airfield is an unused airfield. The data we were given to work up our work plan was erroneous. Lieutenant Wilson-Fran is working up a new one out at the airfield now."

Tucker listened as the two men shifted into engineer and *Seabee-speak*. He could tell from the short answers Klein gave the master chief that the leader of these Seabees had other concerns on his mind, and he'd bet his life they were the same concerns he had.

As the conversation faded, the master chief never noticed Klein's answers were shorter, he just kept bringing his skipper up to date on everything from tents to water to status of the off-load. Like most master chiefs, Collins was older than his boss by a few years.

Tucker listened until Klein's interest peaked again and he started exchanging mathematical equations with Collins. He gathered from their discussion that the NMCB-133 was expected to expand the airlift capability on an operational, but small, local airport. From the time they received their mission orders in Gulfport, they had planned their work-load, work schedule, and task plans according to that premise. Even the construction equipment the NMCB-133 brought with them had been itemized against these plans. Instead, what they found was an airfield that had been abandoned years ago and most of what was loot-able had been looted. There was an empty shell of an airport control tower where even the huge windows overlooking the airfield were missing.

The master chief had his people identifying the work they would have to do to make up the difference between starting construction on an operational airfield and the one they discovered. No water. No toilets. No air conditioning. Collins had doubled the number of port-a-potties and portable showers to be installed at the airport. Collins told Klein that he had ordered one of the water sterilization plants unpacked.

They turned and started walking from the starboard toward the port side of the ship. Tucker really needed a few minutes with Klein to discuss what type of combat training his men and women had gone through; although, unlike his boss, Admiral James, he had no intention of taking women along in this mission.

Klein stopped and opened a door. A small plaque in a metal holder identified the compartment as belonging to the commanding officer, NMCB-133, and above it was the bold black name of Commander Teddy Klein. The master chief mentioned Brute. Hearing the name, Tucker refocused on the conversation long enough to hear that the new third class was at the airfield.

"Commander Raleigh, I think we're going to have the pleasure of sharing this new mission with my favorite command master chief," Klein said as he opened the door.

"I should be. I'm the only master chief you've got, Skipper."

Klein put his back against the gray door that opened inward and, in an exaggerated bow, motioned Master Chief Collins in ahead of Tucker. "Master Chief, have we got some wonderful news for you. When the two of us finish bringing you up to date, you're going to be so grateful that you volunteered to stay with the fighting 'roos of NMCB-133 for six more months you'll bow down and kiss my feet."

The master chief shook his head. "Yes, sir. That's gonna happen." Collins entered the compartment shaking his head. "I have this sinking feeling, Skipper, that I should have accepted those orders to Rota, Spain."

Ten minutes later, two Seabee sailors heading aft toward the smoking deck ambled by the closed compartment door of Commander Teddy Klein's office just as the two commanders finished briefing Master Chief Collins.

"Who the fuck thought up this asinine idea?" came a shout of disbelief from inside the compartment.

The sailors jumped and then laughed as they picked up their pace.

"Recognize that voice anywhere."

"Yep, Master Chief Collins."

"I guess when you're a Master Chief you can talk like that," one of them said as they neared the corner of the passageway.

"Not every master chief. Just Master Chief Collins. He's not a bad sort. His arms remind me of Popeye."

"I can see that. You see the anchors tattooed on both of them?"

The other sailor nodded. "Brute says he's got the heart of a little boy."

"Yeah, and he keeps it in a jar on his desk." They both laughed.

They turned the corner, pausing for a moment to glance back to see if the door had opened.

"I'll be glad when I make Master Chief," the one who offered the advice on Master Chief Collins said.

"You ought to try staying a third class first."

"I can't help it if the skipper has no sense of humor."

THE HUMVEE BOUNCED AND JOSTLED OVER THE ROUGH dirt road that led from the southernmost Liberian town of Harper to the abandoned airport northeast of it. Tucker had already taken his cap off and had tucked it under his thigh. Tire marks from vehicles passing earlier marked the center of the little-used road, probably from earlier Seabee vehicles. The right tire of the Humvee hit a hole as they sped around a curve, throwing the vehicle into the air to land with a jolt that caused the rear seat belt to jerk him back. It was a good thing this Humvee had no top or his head would have creamed the roof. Tucker reached down and touched his hat, making sure it was still there.

The engine revved up as the master chief pressed his foot down on the gas pedal, ignoring the condition of the road as if daring it to stop his Humvee. Tucker knew the master chief was still upset over the idea of having to send three of his men off on some "God-forsaken" mission that didn't have anything to do with building an airport.

Behind the Humvee, a roiling dust cloud rose into the air, twisting and weaving in the wind created by the speeding vehicle, rising forty to fifty feet into the air before losing momentum and sifting out to the sides to rain fine dust over the African bush, the livestock, and the Liberian herders whose eyes followed the Americans as they sped down the road.

"Stupid, stupid, stupid," said Master Chief Collins, his voice loud enough to carry over the noise of the vehicle.

Tucker sat in the back of the topless Marine Corps green Humvee, his eyes squinting to keep the dust that rolled under the sunglasses from caking them too much.

"Great plan, great plan, great plan!" Klein shouted back. "Just keep thinking and saying that over and over, Master Chief. We haven't done something like this since—"

"John Wayne in *The Fighting Seabees*. I hope the skipper remembers that was a movie, sir!"

The master chief jerked the steering wheel to the left to avoid a deep hole in the middle of the road. Tucker and Klein fell to the right, bouncing off the side of the vehicle. Klein grabbed his hat, holding it on his head.

"You did that on purpose!"

Collins turned the wheel to the right, jerking the Humvee back into the center of the road.

"Yes, sir, I did. I thought if we die right here, we won't look as foolish as we're gonna."

Tucker's admiration for the Seabee officer had grown since their first meeting. He had respect for an officer such as Klein who was adamantly opposed to the orders, but in front of everyone—including Tucker—accepted and embraced them. It was also obvious that between the commanding officer of the Seabees and his command master chief there was a bond of fidelity and respect where each was at ease to air his concerns and differences while sharing opposite opinions. Klein was lucky to have a command master chief like Collins. A commanding officer never commanded alone. He or she might have the ultimate responsibility, but without an executive officer to loyally execute day-to-day operations along with a command master chief who wasn't afraid to tell you what you didn't want to hear, a commanding officer seldom enjoyed a successful tour.

Ahead and to the right of the road, the top of a dilapidated airfield control tower appeared above the tree line of the jungle. Ten minutes later, they rolled to a dusty stop beside it. Two huge tents were set up on dirt plain next to a cracked and weed-ridden parking apron adjacent to the tower. A third tent was directly ahead of them, and, from the activity beneath it, this tent had to be the Seabees command post. The rolled sides of the three tents allowed the minute breeze to circulate through the late-afternoon African sun. Several Seabees sat on folding chairs inside one of the tents while other Seabees, their cammie sleeves rolled down, offloaded supplies and gear from a truck.

Master Chief Collins turned the engine off and was first out of the vehicle. "That's water and food mostly, Skipper," he said, pointing at the working party off-loading the truck. "With this heat, we need to make sure the troops drink plenty of liquids, and I don't mean beer."

"What's wrong with the ones lounging around under the tents? Why aren't they helping?" Tucker asked as they walked toward the group.

"There's nothing wrong with them, Commander. What they're doing *is* helping. With the heat and humidity so high, we have two working parties switching off at thirty-minute intervals." He pointed to the sailors beneath the nearest tent. "That bunch will relieve those in the sun shortly, and those in the sun will take a short break to chug water and grab a bite to eat, if they're hungry. They can even sneak in a power nap, if they want—if they can." Collins pointed at the ground. "Watch the hole," he said.

They stepped over the hole in the concrete. Tucker glanced down into it, but couldn't see anything.

"I think it'll take a week for our people to adjust to the climate, then we can work their balls off." Master Chief Collins paused. "Well, those that have them," he added softly.

The three reached the end of the tower wall. Smaller tents appeared to the right. A Seabee working party was setting up more tents.

"You're going to sleep out here?" Tucker asked, slightly bewildered. The *Mesa Verde* was only thirty minutes from here. The Seabees could commute.

"Probably not all of us, but eventually the *Mesa Verde* is going to get underway and then we'll have little choice. Besides, we'll build some barracks in the next couple of weeks."

Tucker ducked slightly as they stepped under the edge of and into the command tent. The temperature dipped as they stepped out of the sun. Tucker removed his hat and wiped sweat from his brow with the back of his hand. *It's amazing how much a shade will drop the heat, and with the right amount of breeze, it's almost like walking into an air conditioned room as your sweat cooled on your skin.* He thought, *Well, maybe not air conditioned, but there was a difference.*

A young baby-faced lieutenant straightened up from where she was leaning over a table at the far end of the tent.

"Captain," she called, referring to Klein.

Klein turned to Tucker as he waved in acknowledgment. "That's Lieutenant Wilson-Flan; Carol Wilson-Flan. She's my XO," he said softly. "She'll be our main problem."

"How's that?"

"She truly believes a Seabee is worth more than any other sailor in the Navy."

"Well, she's right about that at least," Master Chief Collins interjected, as he beat his cammies with his hat, dismayed over the dust clouds rising from his uniform.

"Sir," she said when they reached where Wilson-Flan, two chief petty officers, and a construction mechanic first class from Alpha Company stood. "We're working up the game plan for getting this construction back on track." Before Klein could reply, she started rattling off the challenges facing them from water to sewage to weather to building material. After a few minutes, she paused.

"That's good, XO," Klein said. He looked at the others standing around the table. "You men continue with this. I need to talk with the XO for a moment."

Ten minutes later, she had been brought up to speed on what they had to do. Unlike Klein and the master chief, Tucker saw the sparkle of excitement in her eyes. Klein was right. This one was going to go, if she had any say in it. Luckily she didn't.

Tucker caught movement out of the corner of his left eye. He turned. A few hundred yards away, toward the cracked concrete and bush-covered runway, four Seabees walked toward them. The one in front was gigantic. Even from this distance he towered over the two walking alongside. One of the sailors broke away from the group and ran toward the command tent. Tucker couldn't make out what the big man was carrying. Must be a sack or something from the way it was thrown over his right shoulder.

The Seabee running toward the tent was shouting and waving his hand. Tucker couldn't make out what he was saying, but the urgency in the tenor of the voice was unmistakable. Four sailors hurriedly rose and dashed to a nearby Humvee. With a couple of quick flicks, they freed a stretcher. Two grabbed the ends, and, with the other two on each side of the stretcher, the four ran toward the group, skirting the edge of the tent and barely avoiding the lines running the surrounding stakes.

"What's going on?" Klein asked.

The sailor was fifty feet away, breathing hard, when he stopped and put both hands on his knees. "It's Palma, sir! He's been snake bit!"

Klein turned to the construction mechanic. "Get over to the medical tent and tell Doc what's happened." Klein dashed from under the tent at the same time the chief petty officer dashed out the other side. Klein caught up with the stretcher-bearers and passed them as he ran toward the injured sailor.

Tucker realized that the huge man was carrying this Palma. As they approached, he could tell the sailor lying over the man's shoulder wasn't small. The man must weigh in excess of a hundred-eighty, Tucker told himself. He was mesmerized by how the big sailor walked as if the weight thrown across his shoulder was nothing more than a minor inconvenience: each step steady and smooth—the left arm swinging freely. The sun glistened off the sweat coursing down the man's face, but other than this small indication, there was no expression to indicate strain from the exertion. Tucker shielded his eyes and glanced at the African sun, low in the sky, burning down on the naked head of the giant. Somewhere, the man had lost his hat.

The man placed one foot in front of the other as if out on a leisurely stroll. Why should Tucker expect him to be running with this load? It wasn't easy, it wasn't fun, and it sapped the strength of those who had to do it; but you did it because someone someday may have to do it for you.

Tucker thought about going out there, but knew he'd only be in the way. He looked around for the XO, but she was gone. He searched the tent for a moment and finally saw her near one of the parked Humvees with a couple of sailors. She was motioning the driver, who was turning the Humvee around, so they could load the sailor on it for the race back to the ship. They work well together, these Seabees, Tucker realized; and at that moment, he knew he was seeing something that few did in the Navy. Everyone knew about fighter pilots, surface warriors, and

SEALs, but few saw what he was seeing or realized what he was realizing. Seabees were warriors. Behind the scenes of the glory elements of the Navy, the Seabees forged their own ethos—their own way of surviving against the elements and in any kind of environment. Environments few encountered and even fewer lived through. As if having an epiphany, at that moment—that very moment—Tucker knew that they were going to succeed in this mission from hell, and they were going to succeed with sailors from a much-unheralded group: the United States Mobile Construction Battalion—the Seabees.

At the far end of the tent, Master Chief Collins was talking with the man they called Brute, the one who had carried the injured Seabee back from the end of the runway, and a slender, tall African-American sailor who kept poking himself in his chest as they talked.

Master Chief Collins rubbed his face and then lowered his hand to point at the giant sailor. The African-American sailor leaped forward and pushed Collins's hand down. The master chief nodded at him and continued asking questions. Tucker thought, *Wonder what that was about?*

Tucker was finishing his water bottle when the Humvee departed in a shower of gravel and dust, racing to the ship. Klein and Wilson-Flan, outside the tent, watched until the Humvee disappeared down the road and the dust from its departure enveloped them. Then they turned to join him under the protection of the large open tent.

"He'll be all right," Klein said to Tucker. He reached into the ice chest and pulled a couple of waters out, handing one to Wilson-Flan. "The doc," he continued, referring to the first class corpsman assigned to his battalion, "gave Palma an anti-venom injection that should keep him until they get him to the ship."

"What happened?"

"Well, they have a hundred species of snakes here in Liberia and ninety-nine of them are poisonous. The other one swallows you whole."

"I've heard of that one."

Klein shrugged his shoulders. "Just stepped on the wrong thing in the wrong place at the wrong time. Good thing Brute was with them. I don't think the other three could have hauled his ass back here in time. Palma must weigh two hundred pounds."

Master Chief Collins joined them.

"Commander," Collins said, addressing Tucker. "I've got your three volunteers for this mission."

"Master Chief, we haven't discussed this," Klein objected.

Collins held up his walkie-talkie. "They just called from the ship and Captain Bennett wants the team back ASAP. Couldn't tell me what was going on, but I've been around the Navy long enough to know it means something's changed."

"And who are these three, Master Chief?" Klein asked, his head tilting to the side. "I think I should have final say on who goes and who doesn't."

"Yes, sir, you should; but I have this itch that tells me you think you're going to be one of those going. That means that we'd have to argue for an hour while I convince you that the commanding officer can't do this and why I, who wears the Seabee Combat Warfare Breast Insignia, should."

"Oh, I see," Klein said, his voice tight. "You can go, but I can't."

"Sir, of course you can go, but then the XO would be in charge and she'd want to go. This way, if I go, you two with Chief Brown and Chief Dickens can get the job started here. Besides, it's not as if we're going to be gone long. An overnight hop in, do what our great nation wants us to do, and then a quick hop out. It can't be easier, right, Commander Raleigh?"

Tucker chuckled. "Of course, Master Chief. Every well-planned mission goes according to the plan."

"This is not what I would call a well-planned mission," Klein said. "It hasn't even been diagrammed on a chart."

"Diagrammed on a chart?" Master Chief Collins asked.

"Of course. Every well-planned mission has a chart."

Tucker grinned at the master chief, who tilted his head to the side. "He's got you there, Master Chief. It's a well-known fact that good missions have a chart."

"Sir, I'm a Master Chief. I don't need any damn chart to be able to ride a helicopter to point A, walk to point B, snatch whatever is there they want snatched, and hightail it out of the country. I'd say this makes your argument another good reason why I have to go instead of you." He nodded curtly as he crossed his arms across his chest. Collins's eyes moved from Klein to Wilson-Flan to Tucker. When no one said anything, he uncrossed his arms. "There, sir. I'm glad we agree on this. Since officers need a chart, I have a road map of Liberia we can take with us."

"But, we're going into Ivory Coast," Tucker offered.

"Yes, sir, but I have this feeling that if we don't make that helicopter, we aren't going to need a map of Ivory Coast."

"And Liberia? We need a road map of Liberia?"

"Sir, I don't need a chart or a road map; but if it makes you feel better, then at least we'll have something."

"Okay, you win, Master Chief," Klein said. "I presume Brute is one of those you're recommending. Who's the other?"

Collins jerked his thumb over his shoulder a couple of times. Brute was standing on the far side of the tent beside the tall African-American Tucker saw earlier with the master chief. The tall sailor smiled, uncurled his folded arms, and waved at them.

"You're going to take Ricard?"

"Yes, sir, Skipper. Petty Officer Ricard is a washout from Explosive Ordnance training, but he's earned his Seabee Combat Warfare Breast Insignia."

"A washout?" Tucker said.

Master Chief Collins turned to Tucker. "Sir, a washout is better than never attending. At least he's had some combat training. That's on top of the defense combat techniques and tactics we have to learn, even if his was nearly two years ago. He jogs well, also. Plus, he's qualified on the heavy machine gun—the .50 caliber—and I figured you might want a heavy gunner along with us. But, most important, Commander, is that Ricard is our explosives expert. If we can't grab that technology they want off the aircraft, then at least we can blow it up."

The walkie-talkie on the side of the master chief's belt squawked. "Hey Forward One, this is Mother. You guys left yet? The old man is chomping at the bit. So, Master Chief, you gotta get those zeros moving before this skipper picks me up and throws me overboard." "Zeros" was a slang term for officers that was derived from the pay scales promulgated by the military. Officers were identified by O-1, O-2, etc., while enlisted men, sometimes referred to as Es, were identified by E-1, E-2, etc.

Collins unhooked the walkie-talkie from his belt and pushed the speak-to-talk button as he brought it up to his mouth. "Wallens, he ain't going to throw you overboard; and if he does, you don't have to worry. They don't have sharks inside the harbor."

A second passed before the radio squawked again. "Thanks, Master Chief. You may know that, but you're miles inshore where they can't get to you."

Collins shook his head. "Wallens, tell the old man we're on our way." He paused, then pressed the button again. "Wallens, I don't need to be there to know there's no sharks. Sharks don't swim in shit, and that harbor's full of it."

Two clicks came across the airways as Wallens roger'ed up the master chief's transmission.

"Looks as if we'd better get on our way, Skipper," Collins said to Klein.

Tucker knew that the senior enlisted man for the entire NMCB-133 battalion was giving his commanding officer a last chance to nix his plan. This was the give and take of command, but the final decision always lies with the commanding officer, and if Teddy Klein wanted, he could change the master chief's recommendations. Additionally, Tucker knew that if that happened, the master chief wouldn't be happy, but he'd march away and fully execute his orders as if he himself had made the decision. Tucker relaxed when Klein nodded in agreement. He had already developed a degree of confidence in the master chief; a confidence that later would be fully justified.

CHAPTER 7

TUCKER SHIVERED SLIGHTLY AS HE STEPPED FROM THE passageway into the captain's in-port cabin. The sudden drop in temperature brought by the air conditioning of the ship rippled across wet clothes and a body covered in sweat from the high temperature and higher humidity of the African summer. He paused long enough to use his handkerchief to wipe the stinging sweat away from his eyes while the other hand shut the door.

On the other side of the short conference table that doubled as Captain Bennett's private dining table, the intelligence officer was busy laying out photographs and papers. Master Chief Collins stood quietly near the porthole behind the Intel officer with his hands clasped behind his back. Tucker was glad Klein had elected to stay with his battalion instead of coming with him, the master chief, Brute—he still wasn't convinced that big was better—and Ricard—*why did he washout of EOD?*—who was going along as the explosive expert. Washing out of a Navy school was considered a mark against you. That wasn't something he and other Navy officers discussed, but in the back of Tucker's mind was the unwritten Navy belief that it was better to never have tried than to have tried and failed.

Explosive Ordnance Disposal personnel were trained to disarm mines and bombs both ashore and beneath the waves. Their training dovetailed slightly with the SEALs when it came to weapons training and learning how to jump out of perfectly good aircraft expecting twenty pounds of silk to safely carry you to the ground with a hundred pounds of gear strapped to your back. His eyes lingered longer than he intended on Ricard, who stood next to Master Chief Collins. Tucker might feel better about the sailor who was going to be carrying twenty-five pounds of C4 explosives if he knew why he had washed out of EOD.

Ricard raised his head slightly and met Tucker's stare. Tucker nodded and moved his gaze around the compartment. It wasn't lost on him that Ricard neither acknowledged his scrutiny nor his nod.

The skipper of the USS *Mesa Verde*, Captain Xavier Bennett, was talking softly to a lieutenant commander. The exchange between Bennett and the unidentified officer showed an easy confidence between the two Surface Warfare officers. Easy confidence between Surface Warfare officers was an anomaly as far as Tucker was concerned. A happy Surface Warfare officer was one who had no time for friends, too much work to ever complete, and an opportunity to take work from others. How did the Navy story go about Surface Warfare officers—those officers who commanded ships at sea and got woodies at the idea of getting underway? Oh, yes: *"Put a surface warfare officer in a room by himself with only a pencil and a piece of paper and within thirty minutes he'll have developed a watchbill for himself."*

Master Chief Collins moved away from the porthole, through the patch of sunlight, to the coffee pot against the aft bulkhead. "Light's on," the master chief said to no one in particular, referring to the red light above the spigot of the thirty-cup pot that indicated when the coffee had finished percolating. His rolled-up cammie sleeves revealed the twisted anchor tattoo of a chief petty officer on his left lower arm with a date beneath it. Tucker thought, *Probably the date he made chief.* Tucker saw the telltale blue of another tattoo on the right arm, but his quick glance couldn't tell what it was.

Collins stuck one of the ceramic visitor cups, embossed with the ship's shield, under the spigot and filled the cup. The action revealed sinewy arms while the fluorescent lights highlighted a slight five o' clock shadow on the sunned face of the Seabee. *All that time outdoors had baked the man's face into leather, but, then again, he's in good shape for someone in his forties.* Tucker smiled. *I'm in my forties.* The master chief turned, saw Tucker looking at him, and raised his cup toward him in an informal toast while silently mouthing the words, "Fresh, sir," to him.

Tucker smiled and nodded. Collins pulled a handkerchief from his pocket and ran it across the short stubble of hair covering his head. Then he poured another cup, walked the few steps to Tucker, and handed it to him. "Wouldn't drink too much, Commander. I doubt they have head facilities on the helo."

"Doubt it, too. But, then again, Master Chief, this may be our last hot drink for a while."

"Or, forever," Brute added.

"Thanks, Brute. I needed that," Collins replied.

Collins winked at Tucker. "Sir, I intend to hold the commander to his word that this is a "quick in, quick out" mission where for once in our careers we Seabees are going to get to destroy something that is in perfect working order and doesn't require us to rebuild it."

"I should have this ready in just a moment," the ship's intelligence officer, Lieutenant Commander Portnoy, announced.

Captain Bennett moved away from the lieutenant commander he had been talking with and over to the table. "Commander Raleigh, this is for you and your team," he said, motioning Tucker nearer the table.

A drop of sweat ran around the corner of Tucker's eye

and into it before he could wipe it away. The salt sting added fresh tears to the sweet that ran down his cheek before he could catch them in an already soaked handkerchief. Bennett set a few vials and canisters on the table.

"Yes, sir," Tucker acknowledged, wiping his forehead. On the other side, Ricard walked around behind the ship's captain to where Tucker, the master chief, and Brute—the enigmatic giant, the hero of the Seabee battalion—stood.

Everyone was going to have to shower and change into dry clothes before they left. Tucker thought, *Going into battle was bad enough in fresh attire, but going into an operation intentionally wet only added the danger of disease and sickness; plus it caused the skin to rub raw, or you had the pleasure of a combination of all three.* He'd seen others emergency evacuated from missions because their skin failed. No other way to describe it—skin failure. Wasn't much you could do about an enemy throwing bullets at you, but you could do something about keeping your skin dry, taking extra socks and underwear. The few things veterans understood and newbies soon learned.

"Bactine and talcum powder."

"Yes, sir," Collins said softly. "Bactine and talcum powder."

Tucker turned slightly to his left. The giant Brute stood quietly behind Collins and Ricard, his eyes focused intently on the intelligence officer who had pulled another batch of photographs from the leather courier briefcase. Tucker caught a glimpse and thought, *satellite.* Satellite photographs were only as good as the analyst who interpreted them.

His gaze wandered back to the giant Seabee. Other than the comment at the coffee pot, Tucker couldn't recall hearing the newest third class petty officer of NMCB-133 say a complete sentence since they'd left the Seabee encampment. *What was his story?* Tucker wondered. Everyone has a story, some were just better than others. What little he knew wasn't sufficient to form an opinion on how this man would perform in combat. Being good in a bar brawl was a lot different from dodging bullets in unfamiliar jungles. For that matter, this whole thing was ludicrous. Tucker had no idea how well these three would support the four of them in a firefight, and the three of them had no way of knowing how competent he was. Combat was a poor training field for coordinating teamwork. Teamwork and an appreciation for your shipmates' combat skills needed to exist before you charged over the proverbial hill to confront the enemy on the other side.

Brute shifted his weight from one leg to the other and crossed his arms. Tucker thought, *Probably weighs two-fifty or more. Look at those biceps!* The Seabee's upper arms stretched the fabric of the sweat-soaked cammie sleeves. Tucker glanced at his own rolled-up sleeves, stained with water from the elbows to the shoulders. He lifted his arm slightly. Dark wet areas bathed the armpits. This one had better hold his own in combat, especially if things go to hell in a handbasket like Tucker's inner voice told him they would. No way he and the others would carry this mission out without some sort of hiccup. Even trained SEALs encountered hiccups in a mission regardless of how well trained, well briefed, or how well the mission was executed. The adage of "shit happens" was never more evident than in the fog of war. Brute glanced up, unsmiling, and met Tucker's gaze. They nodded at each other. *There's more than air between those ears,* Tucker thought.

Lieutenant Commander Portnoy stepped back and looked at Captain Bennett. "Skipper, I'm ready, sir."

"Good, Allen. Commander Raleigh, you and your team gather closer around the table, our intelligence officer Lieutenant Commander Portnoy will give you our intelligence brief. Before he starts, let me remind everyone here in the compartment that this brief is classified top secret. It's not for general discussion outside this compartment. When you return early tomorrow morning, I am under instructions to conduct a debrief at which time each of you will sign a non-disclosure agreement binding you to forget the mission and never to speak of it. Don't think this agreement is being generated only for you. Everyone in this room and anyone who knows about this mission is being required to sign it, also."

"I've never had to do that before," Tucker objected. "Is there some reason we're being asked to do this now?"

Bennett sighed. "Not my idea, Commander. Let's just say that this order came from way up high; way above our paygrades." He pointed up. "The good news is that they even forwarded the exact words to our legal officers to have you sign. It made the two of them very happy not to have to word it from scratch."

Tucker opened his mouth to object further, but closed it just as quickly. *Futile*. It wasn't the skipper. The skipper was as much a bit player in this masquerade of a mission as the four of them. Somewhere in Washington, a village was missing a fool, and it wouldn't surprise him if the asshole who did this wasn't some political appointee covering the administration. Then he thought of something. "Why don't we sign them before we go?" Bennett shook his head. The man's face scrunched up. Suddenly, Tucker didn't want to know the answer. "Sorry, sir. Belay my last."

Bennett held up his hand, palm out, for a moment. "No, you deserve to know, and if I knew for sure, I'd tell you, but I don't. Therefore, I'm going to give you my informal and personal observation."

Bennett held up one finger. "First, as you already know, this mission doesn't exist. It hasn't been officially approved. It didn't arrive through normal channels. I have nothing in writing, in either official message traffic or even informal emails, telling me to do this."

He pointed at Tucker. "Neither do you, nor the three volunteers who are going with you." Bennett waved his hand at Collins, Ricard, and Brute. "Therefore I would submit that if we sign these before you leave and something happens, and Congress, in its own *apolitical* way, demands an investigation, then those signed papers would be the bucket of blood for Washington sharks. If the mission goes well, then the papers bind you to silence under threat of criminal prosecution."

Tucker thought about this a moment. "So, basically, the papers are evidence if we get killed and insurance if we succeed."

Bennett smiled. "That's right, Commander."

Tucker nodded. "Nice to be trusted, isn't it, sir?"

"Yes, it is. Now, Commander, if we can get along with this briefing, I promise that Lieutenant Commander Portnoy, known for brevity—like most Intel officers—will keep it short. You're lifting off in less than an hour." Bennett pointed to the Navy-issue analog clock on the forward bulkhead. The clock showed ten o'clock.

Tucker glanced at the porthole. Still a little light outside. The ship's crew would still be working. Bennett had revised the work hours so the crew could stand down during the hottest of the afternoon hours and then do the remainder of the ship's work in the cooler early evening hours. *What cooler evening hours?*

"I think you'll want a fresh change of clothes before you depart. Our supply people are gathering the combat gear you'll need. Luckily, we have a depot of SEAL weapons here."

"That's good news."

Someone clearing his throat caught the two men's attention. "Sirs, if I may," Portnoy said.

Portnoy was a thin reed of man, but not much shorter nor thinner than Captain Bennett. Black hair ringed a small bald spot at the back of the intelligence officer's head, and Tucker noticed on the left side of the khaki uniform that the man had no warfare devices such as wings, submarine dolphins, or Surface Warfare insignia. That was expected for what the Navy called "unrestricted line officers" such as intelligence, cryptologic, and information professional officers.

"This is a photograph taken by satellite about two hours

ago," Portnoy said, his finger lightly touching an 8 x10 photograph on the table and pulling it forward so it rested in front of Tucker.

The photograph showed a dual runway with one tarmac running east to west and a second crossing it at a forty-five degree angle to run southeast to northwest.

"This is the French military airfield about twenty kilometers west of Seguela, Ivory Coast. According to our sources in the French military, this airfield doesn't exist. Never has. Naval Intelligence researched the archives of Office of Naval Intelligence when this mission rose. They discovered this airfield is less than five years old. Five years ago, this area was brush and rolling hills along the edge of the jungle. We don't know what they're using the airfield for, but . . ."

Tucker bent down to better examine the photograph. He wasn't an aviator, but he knew the numbers at the end of the runway were the compass bearing that aided pilots for visual landings. A large paved tarmac with several aircraft parked on it lay directly between a row of buildings and the taxiway to the airstrips. At the edge of each airstrip were circular aprons. He counted a total of eight. Four of them had multi-engine aircraft, of which any of those four could be the four-engine French Atlantique reconnaissance aircraft.

". . . you're going in with minimum intelligence . . ."

Which might not be too bad, considering some of the intelligence Tucker had received on other missions was found to be a myth.

". . . one of these four," Portnoy said, using a pencil to tap on the four multi-engine aircraft, one of which Tucker had already determined had to be their target, "is the Atlantique aircraft." Portnoy touched the pencil to the aircraft at the bottom-left side of the photograph. "This is the one we believe is the aircraft you seek. This one and this one," he continued, tapping two other circular parking spots, "have been confirmed as a C-130 and a French C-160 transport aircrafts. Most likely, these two provide logistic support in terms of transporting people and supplies to this isolated airfield. Reconnaissance photographs from two days ago show the aircraft we believe to be the Atlantique in this same location, and the C-130 and C-160 parking spots empty."

"So, we have a fifty-fifty chance of hitting the wrong aircraft?" Tucker asked, tapping the photograph in front of him.

Portnoy bit his lower lip, his eyes narrowing as if thinking of the proper answer to Tucker's question. Then the intelligence officer let out a deep audible breath. "I think it's less than fifty-fifty, Commander. The reason we believe this is the aircraft is that one of the times when we knew the aircraft was flying a mission, this spot was empty."

"Well, I would say that kind of seals the fact that this must the aircraft."

"Not exactly, Commander Raleigh. This other spot was empty also. What we've done is analyze the shadows of the aircraft at the time the imagery was taken. Both aircraft are within ten feet length of each other, but this aircraft is nearer the length of an Atlantique."

"Size isn't everything," a voice boomed out.

Everyone turned. It was Brute. The giant turned his head back and forth as if surprised at the attention. "Sorry, I thought I was thinking it."

"When we get out in the field, Petty Officer McIntosh, no thinking out loud."

"Sorry, sir. No, sir."

Portnoy reached over with his pencil, touched it lightly on a chart, and pulled it over in front of Tucker. He looked at the lieutenant commander standing beside Captain Bennett. "Steve, you want to take over here?"

The heavyset Navy officer wearing a Surface Warfare device stepped over to the table. "Evening, Commander Raleigh. My name is Steve Cutters. I am Captain Bennett's operations officer. Here is the operations plan for tonight's mission. Sunset occurred fifteen minutes ago. Complete darkness is expected by 2130 local hours—another thirty minutes. When darkness falls, you and your team will board a CH-53 Sea Stallion on the flight deck."

The operations officer took the pencil from Portnoy. "Lieutenant Commander Portnoy and his group of highly professional intelligence specialists have identified a small clearing about two kilometers from the edge of the French airfield."

"And we've identified what we think is a path that will take you directly to it," Portnoy interrupted.

"Thanks, Allen," Cutters said. "We are estimating one hour for you to get to the airfield and ninety minutes to do your job—which is to board the aircraft and recover the laser technology system. It should be latched onto the aircraft so you can flip a lever and pull it out. The French don't usually permanent-mount their prototypes. After you recover the system, you're to blow up the aircraft. The trip back I believe will take less time because of the great incentive the explosion will cause."

"Was that supposed to be a joke, Commander?" Tucker asked with a smile.

"A poor one, I see."

Tucker looked at Bennett. "I thought if we successfully recovered the technical boxes of our weapon inside the aircraft then we didn't have to blow it up."

"I did, too, but Admiral Holman called while you were with the Seabees and he passed on further directions from Washington."

Tucker sighed. "Should we warn the French before we blow it so they can move far enough away to avoid getting hurt?" he asked derisively.

"I think we both know this isn't being driven by our immediate bosses, Commander."

"Yes, sir, I know," he said softly.

"Departure time is 2130 hours. Arrival in drop zone—"

"Drop zone? By parachute!" Tucker said with disbelief.

He glanced quickly at the master chief, Brute, and Ricard. "Even if I thought we could jump, these three aren't quali- fied to jump in daylight, much less at night."

"I'm sorry, Commander. I thought drop zone was the right word for dropping you off—the helicopter is going to touch down—"

Tucker waved him off. As his beneficiary, his mother was going to be one rich woman the way things were look- ing with this mission.

Tucker kept his mouth shut as the operations officer continued the mission briefing. Two-hour flight time, two and a half hours on the ground, two hours back, and, after a warm shower, iced beer on the pier. Some reward should be there.

"That's it. Any questions?" Captain Bennett asked.

Tucker shook his head. "No. Let's hope it goes well."

"There is one 'by the way,' " said Portnoy. "The African National Army is operating west of your operations area. They have basically stayed away from contact with the French, focusing on an effort to clear out the missionaries and the Islamic schools. We don't know how they will react if you were to run into them."

"How big is this African National Army?" Tucker asked.

Portnoy shrugged. "Can't say for sure. They have a leader who is growing in popularity with the Africans all along the west coast. The older Africans like him because of the stability his forces bring, in this continent of chil- dren warriors. It's ironic because he's not getting rid of the children warriors. We have reports of some as young as eight carrying AK-47s, but somehow he appears to have them under control without the drugs and beatings other African warlords have used." Portnoy held his hands up in a questioning gesture. "Go figure. If you can, you're doing better than anyone else in Africa."

"Where is this African National Army right now? And, better yet, where do we think Abu Alhaul is?" Tucker asked. Tucker didn't have a bone to pick with this nationalist army and he was sure they had none with him. The newspapers said this mystery army was rounding up the Islamic Jihadists and killing them. He had no problem with that. He'd send his congratulations and a thank you card to this *whatever-his-name-was* who led them if they would get the Jihadist terrorist leader off his back.

"I don't think that Ojo," Portnoy answered, "will be where you're operating. As for Abu Alhaul, he was last located in the Ivory Coast, but I think he has his hands full avoiding Ojo, who has been reported to have said something about finishing his mission when Abu Alhaul's head is on a stake."

"What type of wood does he want?"

TUCKER PICKED UP THE M-4 CARBINE AND FOR THE umpteenth time checked the weapon. He hadn't fired it and wouldn't know the reliability of the weapon until he was in-country and traipsing through the bush and jungle of the Ivory Coast with three others who also had no way of knowing if every weapon would function properly. Collins, Brute, and Ricard were doing the same. Collins was putting his Carbine back together. It was that prior Army training that taught the master chief how to break a weapon to its bare bones and then slap it back together as if it had just come out of the factory. Master Chief Collins stood, propped his Carbine against the bulkhead of the forecastle, and disappeared inside the skin of the ship.

"The M-4 okay with you, Master Chief?"

"It's better than the M-16, but not as good as the AK-47."

"Why you say that?"

"I wish I could say the M-16 was as good as the AK-47 or the M-4 Carbine. You drop the AK-47 in a swamp, you can reach in, grab it, and come up shooting. You get a little dirt on the M-16 and she jams. You got to grease her like a pig to keep the dirt out, and all time you worry when she'll stop firing—not if, but when. The term 'piece of shit' springs to mind."

"I think you'll like the M-4. Lightweight, reliable, and, if we're lucky, you'll never have to discover how effective it is."

Tucker had offered Brute an M-50 machine gun only to discover neither he nor Ricard were familiar enough with the heavy weapon to ensure they could properly set it up and fire it. It wasn't as if they hadn't trained on it, just that the training was rudimentary, with just enough instruction so they could pass the Marine Corps defensive training course. The Seabees trained with the M-50 mounted on an anchored tripod so the weapon remained pointed in the right direction. SEAL training had the M-50 operator cradling the heavy weapon, firing it while on the move. If you haven't handled a free-wheeling M-50 cradled in your arms, spitting out hundreds of .50 caliber bullets a minute, it could be as dangerous for your friends as it was for the enemy.

Luckily, they did know how to operate the high-tech automatic grenade launcher mounted on the M-4 Carbine. He was pleased to discover the Seabees had used night vision devices so the PVS-14 technology, though vastly superior to the Seabee device, was familiar. The information technicians from the radio shack departed a few minutes ago after giving the three Seabees a brief training on the use of whisper microphones so the four of them could talk without shouting to each other. Tucker reached up and moved the mouthpiece away slightly. He had had the cams removed from the helmets. He wanted the mouthpieces removed also because he did not intend to use them. For this mission, he was going to keep the four of them close together; close enough that they wouldn't need the mouthpiece. The ITs explained it would take too long to remove the mouthpieces, but they showed Tucker how to turn them off.

The cameras were an unnecessary weight. There was no motherboard to watch their progress and no recording device to save anything they saw for posterity. He wished they could use the cams. *There's no substitute for evidence you weren't doing something wrong when you discover yourself standing in front of the green table of unsmiling investigators.*

Ricard squatted on the deck in front of an open box about the size of Admiral Holman's humidor. This was the C4 to blow the French aircraft. Tucker watched for a moment as the man ran his slender fingers across the top of the plastique. Tucker had already checked to ensure the contents of the box was the plastique explosives before he turned it over to Ricard. He had checked every item they were taking—he mentally crossed his fingers—or hoped he had. *What if I didn't check everything?* Then who would he complain to when they arrived at the mission area to discover something else in the C4 box, such as meals-ready-to-eat; MREs—which in their own way could be deadly. No, on this mission he checked everything as if he were going alone, which wasn't far from the truth. This checking and rechecking gave Tucker a little jump in confidence that they may actually have a chance of returning, but the roiling dragon of uncertainty never ceased reminding him of the odds stacked against them. How can you do a mission with less than twenty percent of the information you needed? A twenty-percent chance was what he would give a mission where they had no opportunity to prepare. *"Hey, you four! Yeah, you four! Here's a gun each. Now, get on that helicopter, fly into unknown jungle in the middle of the night, locate that damn enemy aircraft, and get yore asses back on board before morning. You hear? When you get back, we'll have some scrambled eggs waiting. By the way, here's telephone numbers for yellow cabs in the event we can't reach ya. Have a nice Navy day, Shipmates!"*

Brute reached up, grabbed the web gear on Ricard, and jerked the man back and forth. "Good job, Petty Officer Ricard," the giant said, his voice serious. "I think you might just be able to move at a fast walk with all that shit strapped to you."

Ricard slapped Brute's hands away good-naturedly.

"If you don't kill me first." He straightened the vest.

"You gonna sweat like a pig with that on, you know," Brute said with a smile. "And, it isn't as if you have a lot of body fat to sweat away."

Tucker smiled at the exchange. A little over two hours since they departed that gone-to-hell airfield the Seabees were repairing and improving. Hell! They improved it by moving into it. He'd say half their mission was done.

"What do you prefer? Petty Officer McIntosh or 'Brute'?"

The man shrugged. "Whatever the commander wants to call me is fine, sir," he drawled, "as long as he doesn't call me late for lunch."

Tucker detected a slight nasal twang of North Carolina in the man's voice. You had to live in the south to detect the various dialects of the overall Southern dialect. Trying to imitate a southern accent was something few did well.

Master Chief Collins stepped back onto the flight deck through the watertight door in the forecastle of the USS *Mesa Verde*. He reached behind him, swung the lever down sealing the door, and then started walking toward them.

"I'll call you Brute."

"Okay, sir. I'll call you Commander."

Tucker looked toward the approaching master chief. Beneath the bright glare of the flight deck lights, Tucker saw a slight smile on the man's face. He thought, *Collins is enjoying this too much.*

Without pausing, the master chief diverted slightly, reached down, and grabbed his Carbine with his right hand as he passed. Still heading their way, he shifted the weight of the weapon so the stock cradled in his right hand. *What's that?* Tucker asked himself silently? Across Collins's chest was a black strap with several grenades attached to it. *Where did he come up with that?* The master chief had a leather belt running from his right shoulder to his cammie belt line where it strapped to the web belt.

He started to say something, but instead kept quiet. Tucker made a mental note to advise the master chief to take that homemade thing off before they boarded the helicopter. All they'd need would be one of those grenades to have a pin jerked out. What was it that Marine Corps gunnery sergeant had told him? *"When the pin is out, Mr. Grenade is not your friend."* Tucker reached up and tugged on his own web gear. He did a quick visual inspection of the two sailors.

If nothing else, the four of them were dressed identically, wearing jungle camouflaged battle dress utilities. With the exception of the master chief, everyone else wore the Navy SEAL web gear designed to disperse the load of the various accessories they were carrying, such as canteen, flashlight, radio, ammo, and grenades.

Tucker turned his attention back to Brute and Ricard. Ricard squatted and shut the top on the C4. The explosive expert scooped up the blasting caps and jammed them into his pocket, causing Tucker to wince over the nonchalant way the man handled the miniature explosive devices. C4 exploded by being triggered through a smaller explosion. The blasting caps provided a small explosion slightly larger than the biggest firecracker.

Ricard stood, saw the expression on Tucker's face, and smiled. "Not to worry, sir," he said, patting the pocket jammed with blasting caps. "They're safe as long as you know what you're doing."

Tucker opened his mouth to protest, but Ricard held up his hand and continued, "And, sir, I know what I'm doing."

Tucker hoped he did. *"Hoping" isn't what I want to use for calibrating the success of a mission.* "Okay, gents, for this mission, you call me anything but Commander. Call me Raleigh. I'll call you Brute and you—"

"Stud," Ricard interrupted.

Tucker shook his head. "Stud? Don't you think it might be distracting for us in the middle of gunfight to be referring to you as 'Stud?' How about 'Turkey?' "

Brute laughed. "I think 'Turkey' captures Petty Officer Ricard's personality perfectly, sir."

Ricard's chin dropped. "Oh, sir—"

"I wouldn't insult the turkey that way, Commander. Benjamin Franklin always believed the turkey should've been our national bird. I wouldn't want to offend this father of our country," Master Chief Collins added.

"Master Chief—" Ricard said, shaking his head. "Turkey? I don't even eat turkey at Thanksgiving. Man, oh, man," he said with exaggerated shakes of his head from side to side.

"Just call him Ricard, sir," Collins added.

For the first time since the four had been thrown together to go on a mission that might determine the future of America as a superpower, they laughed together. Laughter is universal glue for a bonded team, but even the strongest bonded team had to have the right skills with an intrinsic appreciation of each member's capabilities. They didn't have that, and every one of them knew it.

"We could call you Horny," Brute said, smiling from ear to ear. "Because you've never gotten any."

"Oh, man, you don't know shit, do you?" Ricard laughed, putting his hand against Brute's shoulder and pushing hard. Brute didn't budge an inch. It was like shoving against a brick wall with the off-balance push nearly causing Ricard to fall before he caught his balance. "Shit man, why don't you lose some weight?"

The door swung open again and Captain Xavier Bennett emerged. The Marine Corps sentry, who accompanied the skipper of the *Mesa Verde* everywhere, closed the watertight door before quickly catching up and taking position to the left of his skipper. The presence of a Marine with the senior officer and with flag officers aboard major combatants of the United States Navy was a tradition bound in hundreds of years from when the presence of the Marine was to protect the "old man" from mutineers.

"Commander," Captain Bennett said as he approached.

"Attention on deck!" Collins shouted.

The four of them, along with the supply personnel inventorying the backpacks, snapped to attention.

"Stand at ease," Bennett said.

Behind them, the engines of the CH-53 Super Stallion began to turn, the engine noise rising in volume as the revolutions increased, drowning out normal conversation. A cloud of oily exhaust rolled across the deck, enveloping them for a moment, bringing tears to their eyes before the wind carried it off. Ricard coughed a couple of times before his coughing turned into a spasm.

Brute grabbed his shipmate by the shoulder. "Where is it?" he shouted above the noise. Ricard tapped a pocket on the top left sleeve of the cammie shirt. Brute unzipped it, pulled a breath applicator from it, and handed it to Ricard, who quickly uncapped it, shoved the open end into his mouth, and took several deep breaths from the fine mist into his lungs. The man turned away, his coughing easing, as the air cleared and the medicine worked its magic.

Tucker shut his eyes, thinking, *I hope my military insurance is up-to-date.*

Bennett leaned down to Tucker's ear. "Tucker, be careful out there!" he shouted.

Tucker opened his eyes and turned slightly toward Bennett, who continued, "You know the rules. I can't come with force to extract you. If I can't do it without some level of confidence of success, then you're going to have to make it to the sea or back into Liberia."

Tucker patted the top left-hand pocket of his cammies. "Yes, sir. I have a road map of Liberia." Then, he patted the radio pouch hanging from the waist strap of his web gear. "And, I have an M-bitter radio." "M-bitter" was slang for MBITR, which stood for multi-band inter/intra team radio; a radio designed for Special Forces–type operations. It weighed less than three pounds and operated in the low frequency ranges for distance and directivity. Tucker nodded at the other three members of his team. "Unfortunately, Captain, this is the only M-bitter we had on board. Let's hope it works."

An information technician standing nearby interrupted. "Commander, I personally tested the MBITR, and it works, sir. The battery is fully charged, and you should be good for forty-eight hours unless you decide to talk on it constantly."

"Should be good?"

"Will be good, sir."

Bennett's eyebrows bunched. After a couple of seconds he replied, "We could outfit the others with some of our aviation survival radios." He looked at the IT. "Sailor, you think you can scrounge up three survival radios for the other three?"

"Yes, sir," the sailor replied, taking off at a trot toward the forecastle.

"At least if something goes wrong the survival radios will pinpoint your location for rescue."

Tucker nodded. The last thing he wanted was for the three to have survival radios. Survival radios broadcast on the international search-and-rescue frequencies. Everyone monitored those mayday frequencies, including the French. He reminded himself to make sure those survival radios were ditched, disabled, or left behind before they reached their destination.

"Thanks, sir," Tucker said.

Tucker started his inspection tour, as he called it. Never go into combat confident you'd done everything you needed to do and that you had the proper gear to do it. Inspect, inventory, and then reinspect and double-check the inventory. Once in-country, it was too late to remember you forgot something.

Tucker was finishing with the master chief, leaning close and telling Collins to remove those grenades before they boarded the helicopter, when the information technician returned with three survival radios.

The sailor passed them out to Collins, Ricard, and McIntosh.

Bennett nodded at the sailor, who turned and quickly walked away, leaving the five of them alone.

"I think we're ready, Skipper," Tucker said. He glanced down at his web belt, checking again the radio, canteen, knife, ammo clips.

"That's very good, Commander." Bennett turned to the other three. "Master Chief, all the best. And I want you to know I feel better about this mission with you going along," Bennett said, shaking hands all around.

Bennett said a few inaudible words to the other two, while shaking hands. The deck vibrated slightly from the helicopter waiting to transport them to the unknown. Tucker felt the familiar tingle of excitement of heading into an operation. He welcomed it like an old friend in this jumble of a mission. The tingle would stay until they left the helo and started their mission. Until then, trepidation—a sense of foreboding—would accompany him. He shouted to the other three and motioned them toward the helicopter. If he had someone else readily available to replace Ricard he would. He knew why the young sailor was a Seabee explosive expert instead of an EOD—asthmatic conditions. *Can't very well dive beneath the waves or jump from aircraft if you're going to have a coughing fit every time you hit an environmental change.* EOD and Navy SEALs required good lungs.

It wasn't thought with malice, but as a fact of survival. There was no sympathy to the physical requirements of surviving a covert combat operation. He mentally crossed his fingers and speculated for a moment that they may actually do the mission and never encounter anyone; but in the back of his mind, he knew they would.

Tucker reached up, grabbed the sides of the helo doors, and hoisted himself inside the low fuselage of the CH-53. He bent around to look back toward Captain Bennett. Their eyes met and locked for several seconds before Tucker turned without either of them acknowledging the contact. In that moment, Tucker realized the Navy captain never expected them to return. *Must be the first time sending men into battle knowing you're sending them to their death?*

He shoved his backpack under the web seat. Sitting down, he balanced his Carbine for a moment as he strapped in. *Guess he'd never know how that felt, because when he sent warriors into harm's way he always sent them with the knowledge they had an overwhelming edge for success*, he thought. This was not the case this time.

Ten minutes later, the Super Stallion lifted off from the steady flight deck of the pier side of the USS *Mesa Verde*. It rocked side to side for several seconds as if the pilots were testing the flight controls, and then it began to rise. Moments later the black helicopter passed above the lighted flight deck and merged with the moonless African night, the noise of its engines the only indication of its presence. The noise faded as the helicopter turned north as if it intended to parallel the Liberia–Ivory Coast border. Inside, Tucker collected the survival radios, checked to make sure they were off, and pushed them under a nearby seat. Otherwise, they were one last thing to derail the mission.

ASHORE, IN THE SHADOWS OF A FAR WAREHOUSE, THE African porter laid his load down where it wouldn't be discovered until later. Walking swiftly, he exited the port through the broken gates shoved aside to allow traffic to enter and leave. Moments later he was behind the wheel of an old taxicab that at first glance looked as if years of rust was all that held it together. The port was terrible for cellular telephones, so he drove ten minutes before turning on a side road that climbed a nearby hillside. At the top, he reversed the car and pointed it downhill. He wanted to ensure when he left that if it didn't crank—and many times it didn't—he could coast downhill until sufficient speed jump-started it.

"Hello," said the voice on the other end.

"It is as he said," the man replied, pacing up and down alongside what had once been a bright-yellow car. "They are sending—"

"Who is this?"

The man stopped, pulled the cellular telephone away, and stared for a second at it before putting it back against his ear and mouth. "You know who this is, Charlie. It's yore brother-in-law. The man who married your sister."

"I know it's you, Charlie, but what are you supposed to say to show me you're who you are and you're not being held captive?"

"Okay. Let me think," he said. After several seconds, Charlie said, "It's Harper. That's the word; Harper."

"Okay, now I know it's you."

"You always knew it was me."

"What is it you want to pass to Ojo?"

"Tell him you were right. An American helicopter full of Marines or Special Forces has left the large American warship in the port. The Americans are not only flying reconnaissance missions from Monrovia, but I watched the soldiers jump into the helicopter before it took off.

"How long ago?"

"About thirty minutes. It was heading north, and you want to know something?"

"Charlie, tell me," the man replied, his voice betraying his irritation.

"I tell you. The helicopter turned its lights off. The helicopter is flying with no lights. Now, how about that?"

"How do you know they are coming toward us?"

For the next few minutes, Charlie told his wife's brother of overhearing conversations between American sailors who were having cigarettes near the warehouse. From other bits and snatches of conversation, the African pieced together that the helicopter was taking a team of warriors to search for the location of the African National Army and blow up their leader—Fela Azikiwe Ojo. Without him, the future unity of Africa would be endangered. Why America would want to do this, he had no idea, but it was enough that he knew. He didn't tell his brother-in-law that the sailors never mentioned the African National Army. Fact is they never mentioned anything other than a helicopter was preparing for a night flight.

Charlie let out a deep breath when he folded the telephone shut following his call. Tonight, he had saved the future of his continent. Tonight, the word would reach the African nationalist leader who was deep inside Ivory Coast.

Charlie didn't know what Ojo would do, but if he were Ojo, he would withdraw deeper into the jungle and turn north away from where the French were and where the Americans were headed.

His smile broadened as the taxicab cranked on the first try. Today had been his finest day. Even if he wasn't sure about the mission of the helicopter, his service wouldn't be forgotten, and, if he were correct, there would be much glory and honor for his family.

CHAPTER 8

FELA AZIKIWE OJO ROSE FROM THE FOLDING CHAIR IN front of his tent. With hands clasped behind his back, the commander of the African National Army walked around the fire, thinking, *Why would the Americans come after me?* Sure, he knew of the four-engine propeller reconnaissance aircraft flying out of Monrovia, and he knew they were trying to find him and his forces. But he had purposely avoided acts of violence against the Americans—and the French.

Ojo recalled how the Liberian president, who used to be an American general, routed Abu Alhaul's forces at Kingsville two years ago. Ojo had been there. He had led the Africans under Abu Alhaul—father of terror—and used the Arab name Mumar Kabir. *How foolish I was! To believe the mad terrorist would do anything but further enslave my people by wrapping the bonds of a warped religion around them!* The Western religions of Christianity and Judaism weren't much better, but generally they didn't kill you when you refused to convert.

Ojo kicked an edge of a piece of firewood half out of the fire, sending a shower of sparks flying into the air. The only Americans who could identify him as a former member of Abu Alhaul's Jihadists were the ones who nearly killed him above the arsenal at Kingsville. He had thrown himself into the bushes just in time—he smiled as he recalled the event. The hill hidden by the bushes into which he dove was a great surprise, and the rolling, tumbling trip down it had been painful. He had lost consciousness before he reached the bottom. When he woke up later, the smell of battle filled the air with the sound of gunfire silenced. He discovered his body covered by insect bites, his arms and legs bruised, and a great pain in the left side of his body with every breath. He realized later when he saw the dead rotting on the battleground how lucky he had been. The shooting of his two comrades, if you could call them that, and his own unfortunate fall down the hillside, had given Mumar Kabir the disappearance needed to return as Fela Azikiwe Ojo.

"General, you should move before they arrive," Niewu said. Niewu squatted at the edge of the flickering circle of light created by the large fire. Across the thin man's weathered legs rested the "stick," worn smooth from constant stroking. Ojo nodded in acknowledgment to the elder's advice and thought, *Niewu is only the general of the stick, and yet he wields more power than my other generals.*

Ojo's lower lip pushed against his upper. "Why do they come, brother Niewu?" Ojo asked, turning his head to the front as he continued circling the fire in his slow pace. "We have particularly avoided antagonizing the Americans."

The shadows hid the shrug of Niewu's shoulders. "It is enough to know they come. They send a team of four trained killers. The spy only identified a group of Americans lifting from the warship in the harbor, but others identified four men outfitted with automatic weapons. This is an American Navy warship, therefore those known as SEALs, who become one with the night, are coming this way, my General."

On the other side of the fire the voice of Feli Ezeji, his Nigerian General, added, "The American reconnaissance aircraft flew today along the north and east borders of Liberia, my General. Our telephone talkers tracked their flight path."

Ojo tried to make out the head of the large Nigerian, but only the man's huge legs—black as the African darkness—projected into the circle of light. Ezeji's body faded into the shadows of the moonless night and blended with the tree where he rested.

"It is hard to tell if they detect us or not," General Ezeji continued, "but the Americans must know our general area of operations or else they would be flying missions . . ." A hand appeared in the circle of light and waved clockwise several times. ". . . Constantly."

Ojo watched the thick, pudgy fingers on the hand as it moved in a circle. *Anyone who thinks those hands of Ezeji are weak have never seen him hold a man aloft with one hand and squeeze the neck until the spine popped.*

"Everywhere, searching for us," Ezeji continued. The hand disappeared back into the shadows. "No, they have located us and these daily missions have been probing our forces with their super technology. Now, they are ready and have dispatched assassins for you."

Ojo stopped pacing and walked to a small folding card table set up outside his tent. A card table that doubled as his place for explaining the army's operations and for eating the small amount of food he allowed himself every day. He would not become big and corpulent like those who through guile and deceit become leaders in Africa. Ojo failed to see a conflict between this belief and the size of Ezeji. Beneath his fervent desire to rid Africa of foreign influence lay this continuous, but slight, tug of hunger to always remind him of what his people suffered—for all of Africa were his people.

"Come here, everyone," he said, tapping his finger on a chart of the area. Ojo thought, *What if the Americans are after me? Maybe I should listen to those who would have us establish contact with them?*

The wizened Niewu braced the stick—his staff—on the

ground and used it to steady himself as he rose. On thin
legs and a back bowed from years of trying to pull a living
from a small patch of ground, the oldest of Ojo's inner circle shuffled forward to where Ojo stood.

To the right of Ojo's chair sat Darin, one leg spread out
in front and the other leg draped over the chair arm. Darin
was the youngest of the three generals who had led Ojo's
army. Ojo watched from the corner of his eye as Darin unwound as only young men can do and quickly stood. Ojo
thought, *It's true what the western press says about our
wars in Africa. We are the continent of child warriors.* He
shrugged his shoulder and turned his attention back to the
chart draped on top of the folding table. But what could
he do? When you have no one to help in your wars, then you
use whatever resources available; and, in Africa, children
were plentiful—more plentiful than healthy adults of fighting age. Ojo's finger traced their route from the north, down
along the border area of Liberia and Ivory Coast.

With little reluctance, Ojo used child warriors—some
as young as twelve—but in deference to his need for the
positive Western press he would need in the coming years,
he mandated the child warriors must all be taller than the
justice stick Niewu administered. Ojo enjoyed the belief
that he tempered his child warriors' immaturity with leaders of vision and discipline. Darin was less than twenty-
five and the most volatile of his generals. The young man,
whose body was crisscrossed with welts and wounds, knew
little else than fighting. Darin had been a warrior since kid-
napped at five. Ojo's attempt to discover more about his
young general revealed the young man had no idea where
he came from or who his parents were. The boy general
didn't know if they were alive or dead, if they searched for
him or not, or even if they cared whether he was alive or
dead. On the other hand, Darin couldn't care either, after
these years of warring. They were a faded memory of a
childhood that ended years ago.

Light reflected off permanent beads of sweat that blanketed the naked arms, legs, and head of General Darin.

Even Darin himself didn't know if *Darin* was his first name or last or even from which bit of West Africa—if he was from West Africa—the general came.

The grunting of General Fela Ezeji drew Ojo's attention as the huge Nigerian warrior placed two huge hands on the ground and pushed himself up, his large stomach rolling to the right. *I told Ezeji to use the folding chairs, but the man refused. It's because of pride. He knows he is very fat— corpulent—and he worries of losing face if he sits upon the folding chair and it collapses beneath him.*

Ojo turned back to the chart, his eyes searching for his army's next move while his mind thought about the Nigerian general. Ezeji was the only one with professional military experience. He had once been a member of the Nigerian military. Nigeria was the true regional power for upper West Africa, and like Liberia with its Americans, Ojo avoided the country. Nigeria would not hesitate to commit its army to wiping him from the face of Africa. The time for that conflict may never come, but if it should, it would be years into the future.

It was important not to engage those stronger than his own army, which were many in West Africa. *Someday,* he thought, *but not now.* Nigeria was a concern for the future.

At first, his trust for Ezeji had been tempered by the possibility that the man had been planted by the Nigerian intelligence service. Ezeji had arrived at their encampment in Guinea, bringing with him nearly fifty Nigerians. Ojo's skepticism and suspicions were of such depth that in the next few battles he put the Nigerians at the front and watched most of them die. Even with this willingness to die for a vision of a prosperous Africa led and controlled by Africans, it had taken a long time for Ojo to resolve his suspicion.

Ojo eventually reached the conclusion that if Ezeji were a Nigerian intelligence agent, he was a poor one, for the man failed to take numerous opportunities to betray Ojo and the African National Army; opportunities Ojo deliberately provided.

Ezeji stood, his heavy legs spread to hold the weight, the thick thighs touching through the khaki short-pants. The Nigerian saw Ojo looking at him and raised his right hand in a friendly salute.

Ezeji had killed a man whom Ojo had sent to ferret out the Nigerian's true allegiance. Ezeji had decapitated the deceiver and jammed the man's head so hard onto a stake that the sharpened end protruded several inches through the top of the skull. Then he had put the stake with its trophy in the center of the encampment. Ezeji had stood in front of the head, extolling for the growing crowd of African National Army soldiers the crime for those who betray Ojo.

Ojo was sad over the loss of such a close servant as the man who was killed, but he accepted the young man's death as necessary in determining the faithfulness of leaders who may be important for the success of the ANA.

Ojo shook his head as Ezeji approached, and his thoughts turned to the decapitated servant. He had yet to find a servant who could serve him as well as the one Ezeji killed; who knew how to think ahead and plan for whatever Ojo needed. *Yes, it was sad to lose him. But in return, he had discovered another loyal servant.*

Ezeji moved on heavy and unsteady legs toward the table. Unsteady from sitting cross-legged on the ground for hours. He'd regain his steadiness, Ojo thought, when the blood reached the sleeping parts of the legs. To comment on Ezeji's pain would be insulting. *Pride is such a fickle emotion.*

From the far side of the private oasis of Ojo's tent in the center of the jungle encampment of the army, the third general appeared, dancing one leg to the right and the other to the left as he zipped up his khaki shorts. Making remarks to the Enforcers guarding the perimeter about how lucky they were to be normally endowed and not have to do these strange antics to get their private parts to settle comfortably. The men laughed at General Kabaka's comments. Even Ojo smiled, thinking, *He is most congenial with the troops, as well as being the most dangerous one on my staff*.

Ojo had decided a month ago that he would have to remove—kill—Kabaka, for the man was a threat to Ojo and to the African National Army. *Kabaka must die, for he will come after me*.

Ojo recalled well when the epiphany of Kabaka's ambition soared through his mind. He had nearly fallen backward off his haunches, with Ezeji reaching out, placing his hand on Ojo's back, and steadying him. It is never one thing that causes an epiphany. Epiphanies spring forth when varied pieces of events collide suddenly within one's thoughts—coming together like a great puzzle. For Ojo's realization of the danger Kabaka represented had been a culmination of everything the man did, said, and left unsaid. Trust only requires suspicion, not facts, to destroy. The way Kabaka pandered to Ojo and the others when he wanted something; the way he ingratiated himself with soldiers not of his tribe; and the way he preferred the word "I" to "we." Then, there were the tantrums when Kabaka's will was thwarted, which wasn't often because no one wanted to confront the mercurial general.

Ojo's dreams were very important, for they revealed the future. In a dream that night of the epiphany, he saw Kabaka holding a machete to his throat as he lay in bed, unable to move his arms and hands to defend himself. In the dream, he could only watch helplessly as Kabaka laughed and began to saw through his throat with slow back-and-forth movements. He woke, soaked in sweat, with his own hands patting his neck to make sure his head was still attached to his body. The dream was confirmation for Ojo that Kabaka was not to be trusted, would one day oppose him, and when that day came, Kabaka would try to kill him. For now, being a leader within the army salved Kabaka's arrogance and pride. That was the problem with a rebel army. Too many join rebel movements—and terrorist groups—for the power they

can wield. Self-important people whose appreciation of
their own competence was only outweighed by the truth.
And this power was never freely given up and only lost
through violence.

Kabaka drew more laughter as he weaved his way
through the chairs, sleeping men, and Enforcers toward
the table where Ojo waited patiently. Ojo watched silently
as the boisterous Kabaka—tall, lithe, and richly black—
approached. He thought, *Kabaka is the very image of the
native African black man. You could put his photograph on
the cover of* National Geographic *with no words and
everyone would know immediately he was African.*

The firelight gleamed off Kabaka's good eye as he
smiled at Ojo. The left eye clouded long before Ojo accepted the warrior's offer to fight. Kabaka's humor hid his
cruelty from those who did not know him. The African
was known to laugh uproariously while telling hapless captives humorous stories as he slowly drew a razor down their
bodies, stripping their skin one inch at a time from their
frames. The screams of the captives only excited Kabaka to
even greater extremes. Ojo looked at the notorious woven
black belt wound through the loops to hold up his shorts.
Rumor reached him that Kabaka had taken two young boys'
skins to weave the belt. *Yes, I'll have to kill the man soon,
before Kabaka decides he needs a bigger belt.* Until then,
Ojo may not approve of torture, but in the path of libera-
tion, fear was as much a weapon as a warning.

"General Ezeji," Ojo said, turning his attention to the
wide one as he reached the table. "It appears we may have
company in the next couple of hours."

Ezeji wiped the sweat from his face. "I agree, my General. I don't know why the Americans come after you.
They should be sending money and arms for what we are
doing—clearing Africa of the Islamic killers."

"That's right," Darin echoed. "But, how do they know
what we're doing? They only hear what the press tells
them."

"To hell with the Americans," Kabaka added, stepping

up next to Ojo. "They're as bad as the Jihadists. Kill them, but kill them in such a way it strikes fear into their hearts!" Kabaka held up a clenched fist. "Kill them all."

The Nigerian nodded. "That would be good, if we had the bullets," Ezeji mocked. "And, if we had soldiers who would—"

"We have great soldiers," Ojo said, his voice soft as he intervened. *I may never have to make the decision as to when Kabaka will die. Kabaka is too arrogant to recognize the deadly consequences of antagonizing the Nigerian,* he thought.

Beneath Ezeji's corpulent rolls of fat were muscles capable of doing great harm. Further, hidden deep inside his Nigerian general was the discipline to know when death was a positive influence on an army.

"Gentlemen," Ojo said. For some reason, the thought that Ezeji might kill Kabaka made him want to laugh in gratitude, but he held it and continued. "What the Americans don't know is that Abu Alhaul is also somewhere along the Liberian border. We don't know where, but I hoped we could ease our way south, inside the border of Ivory Coast and find him." He moved his finger in a circle around the center of the chart. "We are here, and the last location of Abu Alhaul was in this area, but, unfortunately, our patrols and our questions to fellow Africans have yielded nothing. It is as if the man has disappeared into the jungle."

"Maybe he has left West Africa? Maybe he has returned to Egypt?" Darin asked. Suddenly, he slapped the side of his face and looked at his hand to see if he had killed whatever had bitten him. "Yes, maybe he has left," Darin mumbled as he wiped his hands on his khaki shorts.

Ojo shook his head. "No, I know this Abu Alhaul. I was with him when he led other Africans against the fort in Kingsville, Liberia. The battle where the Americans' arrival destroyed most of his forces and caused us to recognize that if we ever want true independence and a native Africa where a person may be born, grow up, raise a family, and

die of old age in a land of stability, then we must do it ourselves." *It was also where an American child warrior nearly
killed me,* he remembered suddenly.

"We should continue our search," Kabaka insisted.
"Once I have the Jihadists in my hands, we will find where
their leader is hidden. Everyone loves to talk to me," he
said, laughing at his own joke.

"We have two problems, my fellow generals," Ojo continued, ignoring Kabaka's boast. His finger moved to the
right. "About twenty kilometers to the west is Liberia. We
can turn back north, but we will lose this chance to rid Africa
of a major enemy. I think we should turn east, go deeper into
Ivory Coast; but we will have to be careful, for thirty kilometers east is a French military outpost. The one no one is
supposed to know about, but everyone does because of the
aircraft. Our patrols would scout ahead. Find what is out
there so we may avoid the French. While they aren't snakes
quick to react like the Americans, they still have a sting that
can hurt us deeply."

"We should take it," Kabaka added. "Overrun the airport; take the French. Show the world something to keep
them off our continent."

Ojo shook his head. "No. For the future, we will avoid
entanglements with the western powers." He looked at
Kabaka. "I, too, would like to drive the French, the Americans, and the Chinese from Africa, but we must be patient
and take one step at a time so we avoid alarming either the
French or the Americans until we are strong enough to do
so. There is a chance the opportunity to do this may not
arise until after we are long dead."

"Then, the Chinese are fair game?" Darin asked.

"Seems the Americans have already been alarmed,"
Kabaka said, laughing as he looked around the table.

"No," Ezeji snapped. "We must keep our focus as General Ojo merits. Clean our own house first." He held a
clasped fist over the table. "Consolidate our forces and
then surprise the Western world by beating them at their
own game. Force them with politics and guile." Ezeji

shook his head, huge jowls rolling back and forth. "We will never be strong enough to face Western powers with force, so we must wield the court of world opinion like a sword. We must show the world the strength in leadership they recognize."

"World opinion seldom works in Africa," Kabaka said. He turned his head to the side and spit, his eyes never leaving Ezeji.

"Thank you, General Ezeji," Ojo said. "Eloquently spoken." He sighed loudly. "I wish we had the luxury of avoiding the Western powers, but with the French controlling Ivory Coast and the Americans with their puppet general as president over my home country of Liberia, we walk through our own countries avoiding mine fields of confrontation."

"I think we should stay and fight the Americans. There are only four of them," Darin said.

"Four? Only four?" Kabaka asked, holding up his right hand with four fingers spread.

"Only four, but they're Americans," Ojo said. His gaze traveled around the small table. "According to our sources who watch the Americans, they are coming for me." Out of the corner of his eye, he detected a slight widening of Kabaka's eyes; a sharp twinkle in the good one. *The man enjoys the idea that Americans could be hurrying here to do his dirty work for him. The thought fuels an already dangerous ambition.*

"We will withdraw deeper into Ivory Coast. Turn east toward the French, but avoid contact with them," Ojo said. "Once the Americans leave, we will continue with our search. The Americans will come here to where we stand now. General Ezeji, you will provide the rear guard, and I would like to have our best trackers wait and follow the Americans. I want to know how their special forces operate. If the night does belong to them, I want to know how to make it work for us."

"I think I should stay behind to handle the Americans," Kabaka said sharply.

"No, I need you with me, General," Ojo said. *The Americans wouldn't even be out of their helicopter before you'd have shot them and brought the wrath of this power against me. No, keep your friends close, but your enemies closer. And right now, my friend, you are a friend in words only.*

The cellular telephone on the side of the table beeped several times. Ojo picked it up, instead of waiting for his sergeant to get it. He said hello and listened for several minutes before clicking the telephone shut.

A forced smile crossed his face. "They continue east toward the border and are headed this way. We must leave before they arrive."

"How long before they get here?"

"General Darin, I believe we have less than two hours. By then, we can be ten kilometers to the east, and as long we avoid the French, it will be too late for the Americans to do anything."

Within forty-five minutes of the telephone call warning Ojo of the American helicopter, the African National Army was moving east through the brush and jungle of Ivory Coast—a multitude of single-file columns weaving back and forth, moving in the same direction.

COMMANDER TUCKER RALEIGH'S STOMACH DROPPED for a moment as the Sea Stallion helicopter jerked suddenly, gaining altitude. He turned and looked out of the small round window on the left side of the helicopter. Africa was such a different battlefield from the desert sands of Aden and Iraq. Even different from the scratchy brush of Somalia. Down there, below them, was the jungle and brush of West Africa. Jungle and brush—friend to those we want to kill and to us special warfare types who want to kill them. Even in the pitch-blackness of a moonless night such as tonight, desert sands reflected starlight. You could see the ground. Over jungle, it was a different story. No lights shined to identify where the sky ended and the ground began. Nothing but darkness surrounded the helo as it flew toward their departure point. Nothing below to show signs of human life existed.

The door to the cockpit of the huge helicopter had been strapped open with a thin leather cord hooked to a bolt on the fuselage. Tucker could see the green glow of the cockpit instruments between the two pilots when the flight engineer leaned to the left. The gyrocompass showed a northerly direction, which meant they were still inside Liberia, paralleling the border. He lifted his cammie sleeve and twisted his wrist to see his watch. They had been airborne about forty-five minutes.

Across from him, the two petty officers sat. Ricard, the lanky Seabee explosive expert had the top open to the small ammo chest containing the C-4. The blasting caps had been shifted to a pocket halfway down his right leg. Brute—*Petty Officer McIntosh*—sat with his back against the bulkhead, his head tilted back. From the quiver of his lips when he exhaled, Brute seemed to be snoring. The noise of the engines drowned out the sound.

They say only two types of people are unafraid going into battle—the ignorant and the suicidal. He hoped Brute was the former. Tucker leaned back and shut his eyes. He thought, *This is the worst-planned operation I've ever gone on. I know nothing of these three, and they know even less about me. Special Ops is about having confidence in your fellow team members, not flying into danger with a bunch of strangers.* He glanced at Ricard—*one of them is an EOD dropout;* his eyes moved to Brute—*another is a barroom hero.* He stopped himself from glancing at the master chief, knowing the man would return his stare—*the master chief is ex-Army, has some combat training, and may have some idea of what combat is. None of them know what a firefight is like when it's dark and you're unsure where your teammates are.* He shut his eyes for a moment. Somewhere someone was crawling into a Washington bed, thinking what a great job he or she did sending an untrained, unqualified team into harm's way to do something he or she could deny any knowledge.

A tap on his shoulder caused him to open his eyes. The master chief leaned forward. "Commander, I know what you're thinking," he shouted into Tucker's ear over the roar of the engines. "I'm a little worried, too, but I think we can do what needs to be done."

The master chief turned his head forward so Tucker could speak into his ear. "Master Chief, I hope you're right."

The helicopter jerked again; a momentary feeling of weightlessness hit Tucker as the Super Stallion began descending.

The flight engineer rose from his fold-away seat near the cockpit. Tucker saw the young petty officer's hand cradling the push-to-talk switch on the cord that connected the earphones inside the helmet to the helicopter Internal Control System. After several seconds, the flight engineer disconnected the cord, pulled the loose end up, and held it so it wouldn't whirl around and hit someone. The sailor stepped back into the passenger area, the free hand braced against the side of the fuselage to keep his balance as he moved toward Tucker.

"Commander," he shouted. "Lieutenant Commander Maxwell said to tell you that we're clear of the trees. He's going to come down to three hundred feet. We'll be turning east in about thirty minutes, and unless the ground terrain radar shows more tall trees, we'll stay this altitude until we reach the landing area inside Ivory Coast."

Tucker couldn't hear every word the man said, but he caught enough of the shouting to understand that they were descending and would be heading east shortly. *I shouldn't feel nervous about this. The only dangerous spot is going to be when we get near the French. No one knows we're coming, so there should be no unexpected reception party.*

Ricard shut the C4 box and slid it under his web seat. Tucker grimaced involuntarily when the box jammed against one of the aluminum stanchions holding the webbing. Instead of pulling it out and sliding the box in at a different angle, Ricard used the back of his combat boot and kicked the box. Tucker slid forward, his fingers fumbling for the release on the seatbelt. Ricard kicked a couple of more times and the box bounced around the stanchion to stop against the inside bulkhead.

Tucker reconnected the seat belt and thought, *He's going to blow us up if this is how he handles explosives.* It mattered little to Tucker that C4 was harmless unless ignited. When ignited, though, like the grenade without a pin, Mr. C4 wasn't your friend. And just because they taught him that C4 was harmless until activated by the small explosion a blasting cap would bring, it didn't give him a warm fuzzy feeling knowing the instructor was right.

Tucker lifted his Carbine. His heart beat furiously as he ran his hand over the weapon, checking the safety, checking the clip to make sure it was secured tightly into the weapon.

The clip was firmly seated. He recalled Beau Pettigrew telling of how a clip fell out in the middle of a firefight when he was with Admiral Duncan James rescuing the president of Algeria. It was not only dangerous when that happens, but very embarrassing. If you lived, your fellow SEALs never let you forget the incident.

Tucker rested the Carbine between his legs and leaned his head back against the vibrating bulkhead of the helicopter. He took a deep breath, breathing in the combination of fumes, stale air, and body odors. He stared ahead and mentally went over the operational plan thrown together only hours ago for their mission. He knew to consider everything that could go wrong would take up the remaining minutes of flight time. Plus, there were so many possible pitfalls, none of which they had planned for. He glanced at his watch. Nearly eleven o'clock.

They should land in a slight clearing that the overhead satellite imagery had revealed. What those high-resolution photographs couldn't show was what was beneath that impassible canopy of trees that was between the landing zone and where the French reconnaissance aircraft waited for them. Five kilometers of unknowns. What if beneath those trees was a marsh or yard after yard of thorn-decked bushes? If they didn't drown or get sucked down by quicksand, then they could have their bodies ripped to shreds. *I can't dwell on the what-ifs and the multitude of other things that can go wrong. Some things I have no control over. Besides, you don't know what you don't know,* he told himself.

He would muster the team together at the drop zone and hurry to the edge of the jungle while the noise of the departing helicopter covered their movement. Get a GPS reading while still in the landing zone, and then use Geopositional Satellite readings to work their way to the target. *I will try to do what they want,* he thought, *but if that aircraft is too heavily guarded and/or I don't think we can get aboard without one of us getting killed, then I'm going to blow it up and they can just worry about whether this laser weapon survived or not.* He glanced at Ricard. *Unless we blow ourselves up first.*

OJO FOLLOWED THE FAINT TRAIL AHEAD OF THEM. EVEN IN the darkness of night, eyes became adjusted to the faint starlight interspersed with the cascading curtain of grays and blacks composed of the heavy growth of the African jungle. He didn't worry about the lions, tigers, or even the ornery wild pigs. His army was like the army ants of Africa weaving along various paths, sometimes separated by less than a meter and sometimes by kilometers, but always moving constantly toward a single point. Everything ahead of it scurried out of the way.

A slight murmur rode over the noise of thousands of fleeing feet. *Fleeing!* Ojo's eyes narrowed over the idea that he was fleeing from four Americans. Four Americans who his people said were coming to kill him. Americans who would support him if they only knew about his vision for Africa; but to talk to the Americans would violate the trust of his army. An army that believed Africa must be rid of all foreign influence; an Africa for Africans. *Why did they believe this? Because I told them this, that's why.*

The soft ring of a cellular telephone broke his battle rhythm, nearly causing him to trip on one of the many vines that crisscrossed the faint jungle trail. He caught the vague outline of a soldier stepping to the side of the path so he wouldn't block the movement of the army. The army moved, and it moved without stopping. Those who fell in front of it were marched over, for forward was the only direction.

As Ojo neared, he recognized that soldier as Darin, talking on the cellular telephone. He was young enough to understand the few items of western technology they carried. Ojo caught a few words of the conversation. A watcher along the border heard the noise of a helicopter as it crossed the Liberia–Ivory Coast border. The lights were off, but he saw the silhouette against the starry night as it passed, heading east into Cote d'Ivoire. So, the Americans were still coming. How could they know where he was? Ojo wasn't even sure where they were. Maybe they were going after Abu Alhaul, but if that was so, they would send many, for it would not only be the terrorist leader they would want to kill, but his followers also. *No, they're coming after me, for the vitality of this army is me. Without me, it will fade into the jungles like so many other movements.*

Darin had his hand cupped over the mouthpiece to muffle the noise. Ojo smiled as he marched past. The noise of the cellular telephone and Darin's conversation faded as Ojo moved onward, Darin's voice lost in the noise of the steady tramping of marching feet, one after the other, stepping to their own internal drum, as they continued eastward. Five kilometers, Ojo estimated, since they left the encampment. He followed the dark back in front of him, recognizing the man as a sergeant in the Enforcers. The Enforcers were Ojo's own security guards composed of fellow Liberians who would give their lives to protect him.

Darin would catch up and tell him what the watcher said. Regardless of what additional news he may bring, there was little Ojo could do. He could turn and fight; he'd win, but then the Americans would surely come after him. He could continue his attempt to avoid the incoming American Special Forces team and hope the Americans lose interest in him. If they would leave him alone for two years—even a year—he would rid Africa of Islamic influence. He would destroy the child bombers that the Madrassas trained to be martyrs, and he would impale, decapitate, and mount on stakes throughout West Africa the heads of the Arab mullahs who taught such ideas to the youth of Africa. As a side-effect his freeing of Africa would free America of some of its terrorists.

Ojo caught the sound of feet, out of step with the army's movement, approaching. He wanted to turn and be prepared, but if he believed everyone approaching him was intent on killing him, he would be hunched over with his arms spread, constantly ready to fight. He recognized the gait and knew it was Darin. *What now?* he asked himself.

Ojo felt a tap on his shoulder. "Yes, Darin," he said without turning.

The young man cleared his throat as he fell into step behind Ojo. "The telephone call?"

"Yes, I know. The Americans are still coming," he said, smiling slightly. Behind him, Darin's mind would be racing trying to figure out how the general knew without him telling.

"Yes, sir," he said with a trace of awe. "They're still coming."

"Maybe they'll tire and turn back to their ship."

Ahead of them, someone tripped and fell, cursing the parentage of whatever he fell over. Soft laughter broke the steady noise of the army before a harsh command stifled it. The pace never stopped. They kept moving forward, one step after the other, one trip after the other, but always forward.

"General," Darin said, his voice only loud enough to ride over the background noise of the army. "With your permission, I can take some men and we will meet the Americans."

"Where would you meet them, Darin? They're in a

helicopter. As it is, they can land behind us, beside us, in front of us, or even in the middle of us. We won't know until it's too late."

"Then we should stop and wait for them. Kill them. Kill them all."

A log blocked the trail in front of them. Like the others in front, Ojo kicked the log a couple of times, then lifted a leg high and stepped over the long-ago-fallen tree. It was best to warn whatever waited on the other side—snake, wild hog—that something was coming over. Give it a chance to move before you stepped over and stepped on it. Then, it was too late for both of you.

Ojo stopped for a moment as the young man leaped over the tree, then he turned and continued his march. "I don't want to engage the Americans now, just as I don't want to engage the French. We will focus on one enemy at a time, and the enemy is the one that is amongst us—Abu Alhaul. We'll destroy the Islamic Jihadist's strength, and from that we will push him and his religion away from West Africa, north to where it belongs, on the other side of the great Sahara. Then, we will confront the next threat to our independence."

Darin grunted as he tripped on a mess of vines, throwing his arms out and balancing himself on a nearby tree to stop from falling. "We can't run—"

"That is enough!" Ojo said, his anger riding the words. "The Americans won't come too far into Cote d'Ivoire. They and the French aren't the close friends they appear to the world to be. The Americans are paranoid about anything they fail to understand, and the French, as always, are just jealous of the Americans and barely understand themselves."

He recognized the huge shadow standing silently to the side of the path ahead. Once those legs began moving, no one could keep up with General Ezeji. When Ojo reached the huge man, Ezeji fell into step between him and Darin. "General Ojo, we have come about eight kilometers, I think."

"Eight? Maybe five or six; but, not eight, my friend."

"Yes, my General. My troops out front have found an open area where we can regroup. It's about five or six kilometers from the French airfield. I don't think we should go any closer."

The sound of a single gunshot caused Ojo to stop abruptly. The gunshot originated from ahead of them. He stood motionless with his head slowly turning as he assessed the surroundings. He became aware that the background noise created by hundreds of feet trying to move quietly through the brush had stopped, leaving only the faint noise of the night wind slightly shifting the dense canopy of leaves overhead.

CHAPTER 9

TUCKER RALEIGH SQUINTED, HIS HAND SHIELDING HIS
eyes from swirling debris as the helicopter, with lights off,
lifted and quickly disappeared into the night. He squatted
with the others until the noise faded and the jungle debris
stirred up by the props settled slightly. He had intended to
sprint to the jungle using the helicopter noise to mask their
run, but discovered that if the others don't know what you
want to do, then it's best to do nothing. *This was definitely
going to be the mission from hell.*

They couldn't stay here long. Anyone around the area
would have heard the helicopter and would be heading this
way to investigate.

"Okay, flip the 22 down," Tucker said, referring to the
monocle strapped to their helmets. The PVS-22 night vision
device. The PVS-14 was the favored night vision device of
Special Forces, but the newest generation of PVS-22s had
longer battery life. Tucker flipped the monocle down from
its strap around his head. He lifted his hat slightly so the
brim wouldn't cover the lens. The countryside burst into
television clarity with everything a highlight of varying
shades of green. The resolution of the next-generation

device was so fine—so minute—Tucker could discern individual leaves on the nearby bushes. Individual stalks of grass were distinct. He reached out and touched one of the nearby stalks. Tucker nodded, thinking, *The old depth-perception problem doesn't seem to be there.*

The tops of the trees above the jungle curtain at the edge of the clearing swayed back and forth from the slight night winds. Most believed night vision technology changed darkness into light, creating landscape as it would look during daylight. Nothing could be further from the truth. Night vision devices accented faint light signatures coming from the heat of the objects themselves, or highlighted by faint starlight.

Tucker watched as the others adjusted the single-lens device. He knew for the Seabees this would most likely be their first time with this type of SEAL technology. Brute pushed his lens up for a moment while the others adjusted theirs. The huge Seabee then pulled it down again. Tucker could see the man squinting the uncovered left eye closed.

"Listen, team," Tucker said, his voice intentionally low. "Keep both eyes open. The reason you only have one night vision lens is in the event we get into a firefight. You don't want to lose vision in both eyes." Tucker pointed briefly at the huge second class petty officer. "You okay?"

"It's like a gawldamn science fiction show!" Brute shouted.

"What the hell are you shouting for? Keep it down. We're all right here," Tucker said, his head twisting side to side, searching the edge of the clearing.

Master Chief Collins slapped Brute against the shoulder. "Don't make the Commander tell you again." Collins leaned toward Tucker. "Sir, I wouldn't point at him. Brute's got this thing where he believes he has to answer when someone points at him."

Tucker nodded, slightly confused about the "pointing" comment, but continued, "If we run into lights near the airfield, or we come under attack, flip that thing up as soon as you can. That way when you flip the PVS down again, your eye will be able to adjust to it immediately. Understand?"

The three Seabees acknowledged Tucker's directions.

"Listen to me, now." Tucker tapped the GPS reader on his wrist. "This is how we're going to get in and get out safely." The three looked at the small device strapped to each of their left wrists. "If we become separated, GPS is going to show you the way back." He tapped the device. "Push the red button on the upper right-hand side." He waited until they pushed the button. "You've just captured our current coordinates. If we become separated, hit the same button again and those coordinates will reappear. Then, press the button below it and hold it until you see a blinking arrow. That arrow will show you what direction to go to get back here." Tucker pointed to the ground. Brute was squinting his left eye shut again. The Seabee's head weaved back and forth as he stared at the GPS through his night vision device.

"You'll have to use your exposed eye—your left eye—if you're using the night vision device. The GPS will glow in the dark so you can see the readout and the arrow."

Brute opened his left eye. His head stopped rocking.

"You will also get compass bearings and ranges guiding you back to this place, so you'll know what direction you're traveling and how far you have to go. It's only a matter of following it. Got it?"

After the three acknowledged, Tucker stood looking at the group. He had intentionally omitted telling them how to use the device to move toward their target. *Why should I,* he thought. *If I'm killed or wounded, the mission is off. These makeshift SEALs the Navy has forced into harm's way aren't trained for this stuff. They build bridges, airfields, and barracks and do an outstanding job doing that. They're even trained to defend against an attacking force until help arrives; but blowing up an aircraft in enemy territory is a bit outside their job description.*

"Hold your left arms out," Tucker said. He held his out also, looking at their digital watches. The three had the same time as he. "We have to be back here by 0400 hours for pickup. We've got a little over three hours to do this mission."

He pressed another button on the GPS, got the readout he needed. He put his arm down. The others followed suit. *They don't even know how to move or what they should be doing. Without me, they're toast. All they bring to this is warm bodies with weapons. Somewhere in Washington, some asshole is having dinner unaware of what he's done.*

A dark swath wavered along the perimeter of the grassy area as if a gigantic impenetrable curtain marked the edges of the clearing. That swath was the edge of the jungle. To Tucker's right, the top of the grass leaned in the same direction. It meant a trail or a small body of water such as a stream had bent the grass. He motioned them to follow.

A few minutes later, they stepped onto a trail that stretched off to the west and continued onward east. It was a narrow trail, but even a narrow one was better than having to hack a new one out of years of old growth. Tucker glanced at the GPS readout. The trail headed off in the direction they needed to go. For the time being, they could use it. Tucker squatted for a moment, bracing his Carbine on the ground as he ran his hands along the trail bottom, looking for signs of shoes or feet. Several sets of small hoof prints pointed in the opposite direction. He figured they were from one of the several species of antelope that live in the Liberia and Ivory Coast border area. Satisfied, Tucker stood.

"Ricard, you got the C4?"

"The what?"

"C4; explosives?"

The man reached over his shoulder and patted his backpack twice. "Right in there. And, I've got the blasting caps to make it go boom in my front pocket." Ricard patted his right pocket. His smile disappeared. He quickly patted his left vest pocket. The smile left his face. "Wait a minute." He patted a pocket on his combat vest, then smiled. "Yep, they're right here. You show me what you want blowed up, Commander, and I'll make it so."

Tucker nodded. "Good." He let out a deep breath. "Well, team, it's truth or consequence time. With luck, we'll be back in three hours. Our helicopter will be here, and by the time the sun burns the morning fog away, we'll be eating breakfast on board the *Mesa Verde*." He started west, walking along the animal trail that led off in the direction of their target. Tucker continued to hold the M-4 Carbine across his chest, his right hand resting near the trigger guard, ready to swing the automatic weapon around and have it firing in one smooth motion. While the trail made their trek easier, it also increased, however slimly, the opportunity for them to be ambushed. Combat may seem to slow time as adrenaline rushed through the body, but it didn't change the speed of bullets.

Tucker searched the sides of the path ahead as he moved, looking for anything out of the ordinary. Anything that shouldn't be there. Then again, this was his first expedition into the West African jungles, and he doubted he had the full profile of what constituted ordinary and unordinary.

The thought made him do a quick 360 over the top of the grasses, stretching his neck, searching for unexplained heat signatures from anyone who might have heard the helicopter. Anyone who had decided to investigate and had arrived. He continued walking, glancing down periodically to avoid tripping on coarse vines that crisscrossed the trail as they moved toward the west side of the clearing where the jungle began.

Nothing—just faint movements of rustling leaves accompanying the humid night wind riding the heat currents along the edges of the jungle curtain. The wind carried the dank aroma of decaying humus from the jungle floor. He started to look down again when a quick movement behind them caught his attention. Several things moved rapidly through the top of the trees. His stomach fluttered for a moment until he reconciled the movement and figures as monkeys. He glanced down again, barely avoiding a vine that was a few inches off the trail floor. He wondered why the monkeys weren't shrieking like they usually do. He quickly attributed it to the helicopter's noisy landing and their presence, and kept moving, unaware the silence of the jungle was not entirely because of their presence.

"Man, I've got a bad feeling about this," Ricard said softly.

"Shut your trap," Master Chief Collins ordered from the rear where he had taken position. "You can have your bad feeling once we get back to camp."

Tucker sighed. *I agree. I, too, have a bad feeling.*

They reached the edge of the clearing. Tucker held up his hand and motioned them down, nearer him. They crouched, Collins and Ricard's heads a few inches from his. Tucker reached over, grabbed Brute's shoulder, and pulled him closer, so their four heads nearly touched.

"Okay, team, this is it," he whispered. "No talking. No bullshitting. Don't even pass gas—"

"That be you, Brute."

"Can the shit, Ricard."

"Yes, sir, Master Chief."

Tucker sighed. *We're going to die.*

"You heard the Commander," Master Chief Collins whispered, his voice hard. "You so much as cough, I'm going to wring your necks. Now cut the crap and listen to the man. He's the only one who's going to get us out of here."

Tucker saw Brute and Ricard nod. *Good,* he thought. *They realize that's true. I'm the only one with experience in this type of shit. Damn, why doesn't that make me feel good?*

"Let's go. Keep the man in front of you in sight. We'll stop if we need to reorient ourselves." He leaned forward to where his forehead nearly touched Brute and then did the same thing to Ricard. "We leave no one behind and we don't take off running if we come under attack. Everything is done calmly." He pointed at Ricard. "You understand?"

"Yes, sir."

"That's good, because you don't want someone putting a bullet in that pound of C4 on your back."

Tucker swung his finger toward Brute.

"Don't point—" Ricard warned.

"You understand?" Tucker asked, his finger pointing at the huge petty officer.

"Man, I'm scared shitless!" the giant shouted. Then he looked down for a moment and muttered quietly, "Sorry, sir."

Tucker jumped up, quickly scanned the area. His M-4 Carbine pointed up, his finger had moved to where he could flip off the safety and fire. He quickly squatted back down. "What the hell is this? You will get us all killed, if you don't hold your—" Tucker said, his voice angry but low.

"Commander, don't point at him," Ricard whispered, interrupting Tucker. The African-American's head weaved back and forth. "Man, oh, man, Brute, you one dumb shit. You gotta stop that."

"I can't help it," Brute whined.

"Can't help what?" Tucker asked quietly, not looking down at the three.

"It's some sort of quirk, sir. It's why I said, 'Don't point at him,'" Master Chief Collins added. He lightly backhanded Brute across the shoulder before looking at Tucker and tapping his own head. "It's what keeps getting him in trouble. You point at him and whatever he's thinking he's gotta say it out loud. Only he don't whisper it, he shouts it like some goddamn Marine."

Tucker shut his eyes for a moment and thought, *Just when I didn't think it could get worse.*

"Doctor says it's because—"

Master Chief Collins backhanded the giant's shoulder again. "I don't care what some shrink told you," Collins whispered, harshly accenting each word. "I don't want to get killed out here, in some God-forsaken jungle, because you can't stop yourself from shouting out whatever you're thinking when someone points at ya. You keep quiet or I'm going to sew those fucking lips together. When you get back, you can stand on a soapbox in the middle of that God-forsaken runway and shout to the world."

Tucker listened to the whispering as he searched the surrounding area, expecting any moment to detect movement heading toward them. *We've made more noise in this mission, than I've encountered in a whole career of covert operations.* Until Brute shouted, Tucker figured they'd manage to disappear into the jungle with some sort of confidence after they'd departed the clearing quietly.

He looked at them, nearly raising his hand to point. "Enough. Let's move in case someone heard that shout. Now listen to me. You follow me, you stay close, and for heaven's sake don't fire unless I do. And, if you have to fire, for Heaven's sake, don't shoot one of us."

Tucker turned, pushed aside a tree limb, and forced his way through the heavy concentration of grasses that blocked entrance into the jungle. He was pleased that the animal trail continued when the limb, bushes, and vines closed behind them. The green night vision darkened slightly as they entered the canopy of thick jungle trees; but within minutes, his eyes adjusted to the new low light, allowing him to follow the trail. The humidity increased within the jungle. Along the edges of the trail, heat signatures of a variety of animals appeared as the four of them walked; most remained stationary as the men passed. A few darted away, drawing their attention, startling them before they recognized them through the night vision devices. The animals avoided Tucker and the Seabees as he led them eastward, periodically checking GPS to make sure they were still on course.

The noise of their passage seemed louder to him than what a SEAL team would have made. The vines crisscrossing the trail grew in size the deeper they penetrated the heavy jungle. Tucker focused on each step, continuously searching the close-in surroundings. Here, in the thick of vegetation, any sign of an ambush or other humans would be seen in double-digit meters instead of a couple of hundred meters the open clearing had afforded. Thick bushes protruded over the trail like a low hanging canopy, forcing them to push limbs aside as they walked, and adding to the noise their passage was making.

Every calculated minute, Tucker glanced at the GPS, noting the distance traveled and distance to target. Seconds after glancing at the readout, Tucker would update his estimate of their rate of travel. His initial calculation showed they had slightly over an hour until they reached the target. If their progress remained on track, they'd have plenty of time to return to the clearing for their lift out of here.

Tucker estimated that the jungle limited his night vision effectiveness to about twenty meters. Not much distance for any kind of warning or any time for evasion. His finger slid along the Carbine, touching the safety lightly. Still on.

So many unknowns. So much to do. So much riding on their success—*at least that's what they say. How could one weapon change the superpower status of America?* He didn't know, but his wasn't to know; his was to do or die. With technology moving so fast, status in the world was being determined not so much by a country's size and strength, but by the ever-increasing discovery by individual minds.

Someone tripped. "Damn." Then a couple of seconds later, Tucker heard Ricard say, "Sorry."

"Do or die," he thought. *Looks as if "die" is the answer, if there's anyone worth a damn ahead of us.*

ABOUT TWENTY MINUTES AFTER THE FOUR ENTERED THE jungle edge of the landing zone, a lone African pushed his way through the jungle bush on the east side and cautiously entered the clearing. The man said something softly and then started along the same animal trail Tucker and the others used to leave the area on the other side. The man was quickly followed into the clearing by others growing in number. All along the edges of the clearing—some using other trails, others forging their own—men carrying weapons emerged from the jungle to tramp the grasses down as they moved into and started across the clearing.

One moment Ojo was surrounded by the wild of the Cote D'Ivoire jungle and the next he had stepped from it and into a huge clearing, lit only by the faint starlight overhead. *Where are the Americans?* he asked himself. *Have they given up trying to find me and returned to their ship in Harper?* The helicopter had flown over them and then disappeared farther to the north when it flew back. He didn't want a confrontation with the Americans. Since the terrorist attack on and collapse of the Twin Towers in September 2001, the world had learned quickly that Americans were unafraid to use their military might to remove threats to what they perceived to be their national security. He had intentionally avoided doing anything to draw their attention. Didn't he personally order his men to escort those stupid American missionaries to Liberia where he released them unharmed? Missionaries, regardless of their religion, were the bane of Africa. Western missionaries weren't so bad, it was just that they were over here. He countered this thought with the knowledge that they, at least, brought food and medicine with them. The mullahs brought with them enslavement and the promise for their children to die as martyrs.

Ojo had made sure the four American women missionaries understood the African National Army had nothing but the greatest respect for their country. When they departed his company, he had even allowed them to hold his hands as they prayed, knowing Americans would forgive most anything, if they believed someone to be a Christian. Dealing with American influence was better done in the court of world opinion than at the wrong end of the barrel of a gun.

Alongside the faint trail where he walked, his Enforcers flanked him, searching for any threat to the head of the African National Army. No, now was not the time to confront the Americans, even if they were sending assassins to kill him. The time would come for that.

The survival of his growing army was more important

than his life or his pride. Ojo had few illusions that his army would survive if he tried to engage the Americans . . . or even the French. It was not the French that scared him as much as it was their Foreign Legion, and most of the French warriors in Ivory Coast belonged to the dreaded Foreign Legion. His General Kabaka and the French Foreign Legion had much in common with their lack of compassion against an enemy.

The noise of the Enforcers drew his attention a few times as the rough terrain and thick grass kept causing them to trip and fall. They'd be better guards if they remained upright.

All along the eastern edge of the grassy clearing his African National Army continued to emerge, growing in size, the soldiers looking both ways before following the person in front who was tramping down the way, forging new manmade trails through the grasses. Like a line of black snakes, the army wormed its way into the clearing.

They couldn't stay here long. If the helicopter returned, it would have no problem seeing them even in the starlight. It could even be overhead now, for the Americans had those black helicopters that flew with no noise. He had seen them in an American movie. Even he knew the American military was notorious for its command of the night, with those small "thingies" they wore over their eyes so it turned the night into day. Ojo patted his left side, a sigh of relief escaping when his hands touched the two grenades that hung from his vest. If they should come under attack by the Americans, Ojo knew to throw a grenade or shoot toward wherever the Americans might be, because the blasts of light would destroy their vision, blind them. Blind them long enough for him to escape.

Ahead, several soldiers fell to the side of the trail. Ojo nearly dove for cover, believing the worst as to why they would be diving to the ground. Then, he saw they weren't taking cover. They were being pushed aside by someone working his way against the flow of soldiers.

The tall silhouette with shoulders level with most of the

heads of the soldiers being pushed to the side identified the approaching man as General Kabaka. Unconsciously, Ojo touched the pistol strapped to his belt on his right side and flipped open the flap. His finger flipped off the safety. He reminded himself, if he had to pull it, not to put his finger on the trigger until the pistol cleared the holster unless he wanted to risk accidentally shooting himself. Shooting oneself is not a good leadership trait.

Ojo stopped and waited, watching warily as Kabaka approached. The rifle Kabaka carried remained strapped across the mercurial general's back. That was fine, but Ojo knew the man carried grenades like every officer in his army. He watched the hands, ready to draw his pistol if they moved toward the grenades hanging from the leather webbing crisscrossing Kabaka's chest.

"General Ojo," Kabaka said when he was a couple of meters away. "The helicopter has been here. Maybe an hour ago." The man pointed toward the center of the clearing. "The grasses over there have been flattened. Flattened as if the American helicopter hovered over that spot for a few moments." He dropped the arm, lifted the other one, and pointed ahead, along the trail. "At least three, possibly more, were dropped off. They are heading west along this very trail upon which you stand."

Ojo inhaled a deep breath and let it out. *So, it was true. The Americans were here and somewhere ahead they waited for him. How could they know with such accuracy his position?* He turned his head as someone approached from behind. There was no mistaking the huge profile of his Nigerian—General Ezeji. He looked back at Kabaka. "A spy. A spy is the only way the Americans could have been so accurate."

Ojo had deliberately avoided using any communications device to avoid detection by the Americans. He had limited communications to incoming only or to landline telephones, though he usually preferred to use couriers. Couriers were slower, but more reliable.

"I heard," Ezeji said as he stopped behind and slightly to

the left of Ojo, "with the Americans, you never know if it is their technology or their CIA who is working the winds."

"What do you recommend?" Ojo asked, his head turning from Kabaka to Ezeji.

"We should hurry forward, find them, kill them, and leave them so when they are found"—Kabaka said, his voice tight with hatred—"they will know to leave the African National Army alone." He raised a clenched fist.

"Oh, yes," Ezeji retorted. "Tell that to Saddam Hussein or the Taliban! Or to the Indonesians who now control only a few small islands. They, too, said, *'Let's kill some Americans and they will leave us alone.'*"

Ojo could not see all of Kabaka's face in the dark, but he could tell that anger and hatred twisted it. Ezeji and Kabaka had been sparring constantly the past few weeks. Kabaka yelled for more action, more killings—or "examples" as he called them—while Ezeji, the Nigerian professional soldier, argued for consolidating gains and consistent planning—building the support of the people on whom they depended for food, clothing, and sustenance. Ezeji had killed three of Kabaka's tribesmen a month earlier for killing an innocent farmer and raping his wife and daughters. The incident had made Ezeji an enemy of this unpredictable killer.

"No, we will not hunt the Americans to kill them," Ojo said. "I want to turn the army north. Not only are the Americans ahead, but the French are, also." At the mention of the French, an idea welled up inside. A way out of being searched for by the Americans. A way to divert their attention.

"We will turn north. General Ezeji, have someone alert the French to the Americans' presence."

Ezeji pulled out a cellular telephone. "Easy to do, General Ojo." The corpulent Nigerian punched a redial function on the telephone. Ojo watched Ezeji for a few moments—a few moments too long before he changed his mind.

"No," Ojo said, the word trailing off as he heard Ezeji

speak to someone on the other end in the Nigerian Fulani dialect.

Ezeji nodded at Ojo, leading Ojo to believe that he must not have heard his "no" in time. It was too late now.

Ojo bit his lower lip as he listened to Ezeji pass instructions—instructions Ojo assumed were orders he had given. Two minutes later Ezeji flipped the cellular telephone closed. "Even as we speak, a friend is warning the French duty officer at Yamoussoukro, the capital of Cote d'Ivoire, where he will relay the information to the French at their 'secret' airstrip. We should turn north, my General." He lifted the cellular telephone. "Let's hope the Americans were not listening; but in the event they were, it will take time for them to translate my words."

"But it won't take long to locate the speaker," Ojo added.

"We should kill them," Kabaka said, stepping closer to the two men. He held up his right fist and shook it. "It will show Africans everywhere how powerful we are. It will increase our prestige among our people and rally them to us. Ezeji is wrong. America is spread too thin to come after every group who attacks them."

"No, we will let the French do our work," Ojo said. Kabaka may have been right, but it wasn't a decision to make without a lot of thought and discussion. When it came time to face the Americans, he must be sure they had a chance of victory. Victory didn't necessarily have to be achieved through fighting them.

"What if the French fail us? What if the Americans escape and are not killed? They will continue their quest for your head!"

"It doesn't matter whether the French kill them or not. The fact that the French will be looking for them will keep them distracted from finding us," Ojo said tensely, thinking, *From finding me.* For a moment, Ojo was back two years ago at the battle for the Liberian armory at Kingsville—tumbling down that steep bank to escape the Americans who had shot his fellow warriors. The next thing he recalled was waking to the bites of insects at the base of the steep incline, covered in cuts, scratches, and bruises from the fall. The nightmare shaped his fear of the Americans, for if American children warriors could do this to him, his own young Army would never stand a chance.

"Well, General Ojo?" Kabaka demanded.

Ojo's eyes narrowed as he stared at Kabaka, unaware in the dark that the man was unable to weigh Ojo's expression. His voice firm, he said, "We will turn north, because we don't want the French or the Americans to find us." He jerked his thumb at Ezeji. "And, though the Americans may fail to understand what General Ezeji has ordered, they may well have triangulated our location, so remaining here in this clearing should make us nervous. It does me."

That time two years ago, while he had been deciding what to do with American civilians, someone had open fire from the bushes, shooting the two Liberian rebels with him. It had only been the luck of Africa that he shifted his stance to the right as the shots were fired, otherwise he would have died that day, left alongside the trail for his body to be eaten. The hill was the last thing he remembered before awakening.

"I—" Kabaka started, the word a shout.

"Enough!" Ojo shouted. "You will follow my orders." He reached forward, his hands nearly to Kabaka's neck, before he dropped them by his sides. Now was not the time to create more animosity between him and Kabaka. Kabaka did have the loyalty of his tribesmen who made up most of his troops and one fourth of Ojo's army.

Kabaka nearly tripped, stepping back from Ojo's move. He touched his neck briefly, glanced at Ezeji, and back to Ojo. In a quiet voice, he said, "Yes, my General. I will return to my men."

Ojo watched as Kabaka walked away, the man's shoulders slumped, his gait slow as he headed down the trail in the direction from whence he came. He didn't believe what the man's body language showed. Kabaka was as good an actor as he was a killer.

"He is a dangerous man," Ezeji said softly.

Ojo opened his mouth to agree, thought against it, and instead said, "Our movement has need of warriors such as General Kabaka, my friend. We all bring unique talents to the table of African nationalism. Would you please pass the word"— he pointed to his left —"to turn north. We will move in that direction for the night. At dawn, we will rest before turning west to return to the border area between Liberia and Cote d'Ivoire. Somewhere out there is Abu Al-haul. If we deliver his head to the Americans, they will believe us to be on their side. Americans are great believers in taking sides."

"As they are great believers in those who profess to their God."

KABAKA SHOVED HIS WAY THROUGH THE COLUMN OF African soldiers who had slowed their progress forward. Someone at the head of the column had given the order to stop. At the far edge of the clearing, loyal tribesmen of Kabaka waited. They had stopped as Kabaka had ordered before he rushed to meet with Ojo.

"What did General Ojo say?" a tall, thin African asked as Kabaka pushed into the center of his lieutenants. The khaki short pants worn by the man blossomed around thin, sinewy legs common to a runner. Even in the faint moonlight, exposed kneecaps protruded from the legs like large tree knobs on wrenched, wrinkled limbs.

Kabaka stared at the speaker for a moment. Then he drew up to full height and laughed. "We are going to kill Americans."

"Americans?"

Kabaka pointed west toward where the animal trail disappeared into the jungle. "Out there—on this very trail where we stand—are Americans." He dropped his hand. "Senghor, you are the fastest. You are a great hunter. You will go with five of our best warriors. You will find them and you will kill them." He took several deep breaths, his head down.

Around him, his lieutenants exchanged glances. They had seen Kabaka's anger, and when he was this angry, you never knew upon whom or how his anger would fall. But, few lived who felt its brunt. It was better Kabaka's anger remain on the Americans, if there were Americans. Indeed, why would Americans be in the night jungles of Cote D'Ivoire?

Bright teeth reflected in the starlight as Senghor smiled, ignoring the signs of anger. "You must need new skins for your belts, my General," he joked.

The other lieutenants took a small step back, away from Senghor, thinking to themselves how foolish the man was to have spoken while Kabaka was in the throes of his anger. While the blood raced hot through their fellow tribesman's veins and Kabaka's brain was filled with the killing lust, even his own son and daughters weren't safe.

Kabaka looked up. Senghor felt the heat of a gaze hidden by the night and fueled by his own imagination. He stepped back, nearly falling over the vines growing over the faint trail. New beads of sweat broke across Senghor's forehead, and, without realizing it, he held his breath.

The others sidestepped away, leaving Senghor standing alone in the midst of them. Even they understood that Senghor might have overstepped his familiarity with the man known as the torturer of the camp. When Kabaka laughed, Senghor released his breath and laughed with him. The others joined in, even those who had no idea why Kabaka laughed. Not to do so may have brought unwanted attention upon them, so they laughed, trying to out-laugh Kabaka to show how close they were to their kinsman's ideas.

"New skins would be nice, Senghor. Along with the skins, bring me their heads. I will have use for American heads." He glanced back up the trail, toward where he had left Ojo and Ezeji standing, knowing in the dark they were too far away to see. Knowing in the dark they wouldn't be able to watch him either. He thought, *We will see how much you can avoid the Americans when I finish.*

Behind him came a shout, urging everyone to turn north. The march had begun again like a night host of army ants destroying everything in its path, but constantly, always, moving.

Kabaka turned to Senghor and patted the man twice on the shoulder, falsely believing the shaking was in admiration and gratefulness for the opportunity to serve him. He was truly blessed to have such loyal servants who loved and worshipped him. For what is a man in his own country, if his tribesmen and kin turn their backs upon him. "Go. Bring me their heads and," he paused, "their skins."

He watched quietly along with his lieutenants while Senghor grabbed others nearby and quickly disappeared through the jungle curtain, heading west, following the Americans. Kabaka turned left, leading his tribesmen, and headed north with the rest of the army. In time, this army would be his. Armies are people. Times and events change both. When the time was right, the event would happen. He mumbled quietly as he worshipped his ancestors and asked them for their guidance in this dance for leadership. In the back of his mind, he saw the American heads mounted on stakes, facing each other, and forming a macabre path to a giant chair upon which he would sit to greet petitioners. For what is power, if you are unable to use it? What would be the use of him possessing this power if he couldn't wield it for his own good? The sweetest virgins. The best cattle. Golden rings and crowns.

Near the northern edge of the clearing, he stopped, putting his hand out on the shoulder of the largest of his lieutenants, the Ghanaian, Yesuto. Yesuto crouched. You never bent down near Kabaka because to bend down was an insult.

"Yesuto, you will remain here. This is where the Americans were dropped off. This is where they will return if Senghor is unsuccessful."

"Yes, my master," Yesuto replied, his thick, bass voice easily heard by the other lieutenants.

"You know what you are to do, if the Americans return?"

"Yes, my master. I will kill them and bring to you their heads and their skins."

"Your ancestors smile upon you, Yesuto."

Kabaka turned and, with a tight smile hidden by the night, disappeared into the thick jungle.

Yesuto stopped four soldiers at the end of the column. Kabaka hadn't told him to keep the four, but moving through the night jungles of Cote d'Ivoire was better done when someone was with you. Otherwise, the devils of the night and the trees and even the ancestors of those who you have killed could come; one or all together. Wide-eyed, the huge Ghanaian searched the jungle night as they eased into the treeline to cover their presence.

CHAPTER 10

UPRIGHT, TUCKER SLID DOWN THE SLIGHT INCLINE, balancing with his left foot, as he worked his way quickly to the bottom where the others waited.

"See anything?" Master Chief Collins asked quietly.

"We're here," Tucker answered.

Ricard hoisted his canteen, the liquid sound of the swallowed gobs of water caught Tucker's attention.

"Whoa, Ricard," Tucker said. "Go slow with that. We won't have any more until we get back to the helo."

Ricard lowered the canteen and screwed the top back on. "Yes, sir, I know," Ricard gasped. "But, it shouldn't be as hard going back as coming in, sir. Fighting the brush this last mile was exhausting."

"Made me thirsty, too," Brute added.

Tucker balanced his Carbine between his legs, pushed his hat back on his head, and ran the back of his sleeve across his forehead, careful not to knock into the night vision device. He thought, *I hope you're right about working our way back. Going back, most likely, they're going to know someone is out here*. Rivulets of sweat ran down his body, soaking his cammies. His socks needed replacing.

Tucker had an extra pair in his pack, but for the time being he'd suffer the moisture.

Ricard was doing the right thing, just the wrong way. He was right to replace the water he's losing, but he needed to do it gradually, so the excess went through the pores and not out through the pecker. Tucker lifted his Carbine and, holding it by the stock, squatted with the three.

"So what'd you see, sir?" Collins asked.

"Up there about a hundred yards is the perimeter fence. It's chain link with razor wire on top. Should be able to cut it. I didn't see any motion sensors or any indication of it being wired," he said, referring to possible bolts of electricity surging through the fence. "The aircraft is about three hundred yards on the other side, parked on a concrete apron. We're going to shift further north, using the fence for guidance, so we can reduce the distance we have to go once we're inside the fence."

Collins stood. "Let's go, then."

"Ah, Master Chief, can't we take a break?"

"Ricard, you had a twelve-day break onboard ship. That's more than any self-respecting Seabee should have." Collins glanced at his watch. "Besides, if we don't get this over with, we may miss our ride to the ship and find ourselves eating insects instead of eggs for breakfast."

Tucker stood. He reached out and pushed Brute's night vision device up, away from the right eye. "The rest of you do the same. The French have enough security lights around the aircraft to light our way. We should be okay. There's a generator at the front of the aircraft. The noise from it will mask any we make, but that doesn't mean you can quit being quiet. Nor does it mean the noise is going to make us invisible. Stay down and keep alert. I didn't see any patrols, but again, that doesn't mean someone isn't on the other side watching."

"What kind of generator?" Collins asked.

Tucker shrugged. "I don't know. Just a generator." He held an arm out to his side and then over his head. "About this big, I guess. It's on wheels and its towing bar is lying on the tarmac, unconnected. It's powering the security lights around the aircraft by the looks of it."

"Yes, sir, it probably is, but do you know what type it is?"

Tucker shook his head. *Only a Seabee would care what type of generator it is. I hope they don't get professionally curious on how the tarmac and airfield are built.*

"Follow me, keep low, and keep quiet." With that instruction, Tucker turned and, leaning forward, scrambled up the incline, his left hand touching the ground for balance.

"You heard the man. Let's go. Ricard, you lead the way because *you da man* the commander needs." Collins reached over and pushed Brute. "Go ahead. Your turn now."

At the top, Tucker threw himself prone, raising his head cautiously so he could see over the rise. Never expect the landscape to be the same when you return, regardless of how short a period you were gone. This was landscape he and Ricard would have to cross. He worked his eyes from the nose of the aircraft, which was pointed toward the fence, past the two engines, along the fuselage, and then over the tail assembly.

The other three reached the rise and spread out alongside Tucker, seeing for the first time the French airfield built in the middle of the Ivory Coast jungle.

Left of their position was the Atlantique reconnaissance aircraft. The generator was about twenty feet from the nose, with heavy electrical cables running from it along the ground to huge metal tripods with bright lamps mounted on top, shining directly on the aircraft. Tucker thought, *They wouldn't do that unless they were watching from somewhere.*

Tucker finished his more detailed examination of the aircraft and the surroundings. "The door must be on the other side," he whispered to Master Chief Collins.

"Where's the guards?" Brute asked. "I would think they'd have someone guarding it."

"Maybe they feel safe way out here in the middle of

nowhere or they have a roving patrol," Tucker replied softly, wondering the same thing as Brute.

"That's an older generator they got there," Master Chief Collins said. He pointed. "Rust is about the only thing holding that generator together. Look around the openings."

"Let's hope it holds up."

He imagined them inside the aircraft and the security lights going off. The moment those lights go off, someone would be sent to investigate. On the other hand, if someone is holed up depending on the lights to reveal anyone around the aircraft, then they'd be easily spotted.

Collins shook his head. "We'll be okay if we know when they last filled the tank, which we don't. Those generators weren't meant to run on their own. This type of generator is built to support nighttime maintenance; that's why it's so bright. This type uses too much energy; it doesn't have the mechanical legs for an all-night run."

Tucker turned to look at the master chief, who met his stare.

"Commander, that generator can run for about six hours on a full tank of diesel," Collins told him. "If it was turned on when night fell about four hours ago, and if it had a full tank, then it has about two hours of fuel left. But, I wouldn't count on it."

"Why wouldn't you count on it?"

"Ain't something most people think of. They just run mobile engines like your lawnmower—until it runs dry. The condition of the generator tells me whoever is in charge of it doesn't have much pride in its upkeep."

Tucker turned his gaze forward. "Master Chief, that's great to know," he said seriously.

"These lights aren't for guarding the aircraft," Master Chief Collins continued. "They're there to make anyone approaching the aircraft think it's guarded."

"Let's hope you're right, Master Chief," Tucker replied. "We shouldn't waste time here. Let's try to finish our mission before the lights go out."

"If their roving patrol is like ours," Brute added, "it won't run on a regular basis. They'll just show up when they feel they have to."

Tucker nodded. He pointed to his left along the chain link fence. "We'll move along the fence, keeping ourselves low and on this side of the incline in the shadows. No one can hear us, and if we stay on this side of the rise, they shouldn't see us either."

Tucker rose to a crouching position and waited until the others followed suit. "Master Chief, make sure you have those wire cutters ready, cause we'll need them to snip our way in. Here's the plan, gents, once we get up there. Master Chief, you'll cut the fence as near to the ground as possible. Don't have to cut it away, just enough so you can pull it back to create an opening." He raised his hand and nearly pointed at Brute before quickly lowering it.

"Damn fast, Commander," Ricard said.

"Brute, you'll stay back from the fence and provide guard in the event we have to leave in a hurry. Ricard and I will be the only two going through." He reached out and touched the master chief on the shoulder. "Master Chief, once we're through, you take position with Brute and wait until we're heading back. Then, you'll pull the fence back so we can egress the site. Brute, you'll provide cover if we have to fight our way out. Everyone understand?"

The three nodded in unison.

"Good. Master Chief, you be ready to use those grenades slung around your neck. If, for some reason, we have to vacate before Petty Officer Ricard can get his C4 set, then the backup plan is to go with grenades. That should slow down anyone following long enough for us to put distance between them and us."

"I can do that, sir." Collins slapped the stock of his Carbine lightly.

"Why don't we just use grenades instead of sneaking on board and rigging it to blow up?" Ricard asked. "Sure would be safer for all of us."

"We could, but with you rigging it with a timed detonation, we'll have a little more time to put distance between us and the aircraft. With grenades, the attacking force tends to be nearby, and I don't want us nearby when that aircraft goes. Not to mention that C4 will do a hell of a lot more damage than a few grenades."

Ricard shifted on his haunches, a deep sigh escaping. "I wish we could just blow it up and hightail it out of here."

"Then we wouldn't know if the laser weapon is on board. All we would be able to say when we return was that the aircraft is now smoke and ruins." Tucker grinned. "I would prefer we do it that way, too, but our mission is to find the laser technology. At a minimum, if we can't recover it, we have to prove it was on there when we blew it."

"Sir, unless you have a camera to show those Intel weenies, they ain't gonna believe you," Brute said.

"Petty Officer McIntosh, you amaze me," Tucker said, smiling. He reached into his top right pocket and pulled out a small black-cased camera. "I just happen to have my favorite digital camera, approved for spy work by the Defense Intelligence Agency."

"Is that one of ours?"

"The DIA?"

"Yes, sir. Is that one of ours or the British?"

Tucker shook his head. "No, it's one of ours, Brute." Tucker motioned them forward. "Okay, keep low and let's move."

At a crouch, they moved quickly just below the top of the ridge. They were about fifty yards from where Tucker thought they ought to be when the generator coughed. The engine caught, ran a few seconds, and then began winding down as the lights faded simultaneously.

"Hurry," Tucker ordered, running the last few yards to where he wanted to stage their entry into the covert French airfield. A half-mile away, a light spilled out of a building as a door opened.

Tucker slid down the far side of the incline from the

fence. The others were close behind, diving down beside him. They all pulled on their night vision devices at Tucker's prompt.

"I think I see their guard shack," he said to the others.

"And I think they'll probably head this way to see what happened," Master Chief Collins offered.

"Think it ran out of diesel?"

Collins nodded. "Yep. That was the sound of a fuel-starved engine dying."

"Then we stay here, watch, and wait until they leave." Tucker glanced at his watch. They still had nearly an hour and forty-five minutes to do this mission and make it back to the clearing.

The door remained open at the guard shack, light spilling out into the night. The sound of a vehicle cranking reached their ears. At night, when background noises disappear or fade in volume, the slightly out-of-the-ordinary sounds ride the winds with little distraction.

It wasn't long before the sounds of an approaching vehicle increased in volume. Tucker and his team watched as its headlights lit up the aircraft for a moment before turning slightly to illuminate the generator. The earsplitting squeal of metal on metal, caused by brake shoes long gone, caused Tucker to shut his eyes for moment.

"Jesus Christ!" Ricard said. "Don't they take care of their trucks?"

"Quiet, fool," the master chief said. "You want them to hear you?"

"If they can hear anything over the noise they're making, they got better hearing than any human I know."

"Can it," Tucker said sharply.

Four soldiers in light-tan combat fatigues of the French Foreign Legion jumped out of the back of the topless four-wheeled military vehicle and ran to the four points of the compass, while the officer and the non-com in the front eased out of their seats. The driver stepped out, but stayed beside the military vehicle, one hand resting on the windshield. Tucker didn't recognize the type of vehicle, but it resembled a Humvee with its wide body and low profile. The officer had a holstered pistol while the non-com appeared to carry no weapon. The four others had automatic weapons with them, but Tucker couldn't identify the type. He couldn't use the night vision device because of the headlights, and the four armed Legionnaires had taken station around the aircraft, hidden by the night.

The French officer said something to the non-com beside him who ran around the side of the Humvee-like vehicle, slapped the driver on the shoulder, and the two of them hurried to the rear. Tucker watched as the two men off-loaded a couple of fuel containers. Then, walking heavily, the men worked their way to the generator where the non-com unscrewed the fuel cap and stood aside while the driver began filling the tank.

The driver set the last container down and wiped the sweat from his forehead with the back of his hand. The non-com said something in French, lifted the container for a moment before setting it down, and started beating a tattoo on the driver's chest with his forefinger. Tucker got the impression that the junior soldier hadn't used all the fuel in the container. Apparently satisfied having executed his military anger, the non-com reached over and pressed a button. The engine turned several times and then suddenly caught. Tucker could hear the generator working, but no lights—the man hit another switch and the flood lamps around the aircraft blazed to life. Tucker and his team kept low, shielding their eyes from the glare as their night vision turned to shit. They each flipped the devices away from their eyes.

"You hear that?" Tucker asked. It was a faint sound . . .

"That's a telephone ringing," Ricard said. "Yeah, man. That's a telephone."

The French officer heard it also and pointed toward the open door to the guard shack. He shouted something, waving his arm, punctuating the motion with the words *vite, vite, vite*. The four soldiers around the aircraft went back to the vehicle, two climbing into the back seat from the front doors and the other two jumping over the sides of the vehicle to take their seats in back. The non-com crawled into the front seat between the driver and officer. A minute later, the vehicle whipped around in a circle, its tires spinning, sending gravel and dirt into a stinging cloud behind it as it sped toward the guard shack a half-mile away.

"Master Chief, get that fence cut."

"Shouldn't we wait until they go back inside?"

"No. Don't have time, and when a telephone rings way out in the boonies, strangers like us should be nervous."

Collins pushed himself up and over, pulling a large set of wire cutters from a pocket along his right leg. Running at a crouch, the senior enlisted man reached the fence and went down on his knees.

"Ricard, you ready?" Tucker asked.

"Yes, sir."

"Good. Leave your Carbine here. You concentrate on getting the C4 ready and I'll carry my Carbine."

Ricard lifted the box of C4. "I'm as ready as I'm ever going to be."

They watched silently as the master chief quietly and quickly snipped wire after wire, connecting one clipped link to the next, hooking them as one up and out of the way. After a couple of minutes, the master chief leaned back on his legs.

"Okay!" Collins said in a loud whisper. "It's open."

Tucker and Ricard rushed toward the fence as the master chief pulled the cut portion back. Tucker hit the ground, pushed his Carbine through the opening, and scrambled after it. He grabbed the Carbine and was at a crouch, visibly searching the area around the aircraft, when the box of C4 tumbled by him. An unexpected chill rode up his back as he more leapt at than reached toward the explosives. Behind him, Ricard came running up. "Thanks, sir."

"Ricard, what are you doing?" Tucker said, his voice shaken.

Ricard smiled. "Sir, quit worrying. I know this stuff, and it ain't going to explode without something to help it."

"Quit throwing it around." Tucker stood, crouching, looking both ways. To his right, the revving engine of the French military vehicle still heading toward the guard shack helped the generator drown out any other sounds around them. A battalion of soldiers could march right up to them and they wouldn't be able to hear it.

Then it came again. This time, harder to hear; but it was the incessant ringing of a telephone. The decibel level of the telephone was high enough to ride over the sounds of the generator and the military vehicle. It must have a volume enhancer to be heard this far away. Tucker told himself it was probably a routine telephone check; something normal during guard duty. But his instincts warned him otherwise.

One of two things was going to happen—if the French failed to return in time to answer that telephone check and tell the sergeant of the guard that everything was okay, the main garrison would send someone out to check. It would piss the sergeant of the guard off if that happened. If, on the other hand, the telephone call was to warn the guards of Tucker and his team, then the French would be back here in a few minutes. Either way, he and Ricard needed to get aboard, take his pictures, let the Seabee explosive expert rig the explosives, and try to take something with them from whatever looked like a laser weapon.

Tucker took off at a trot, running behind the generator, noticing as he passed that the non-com and driver had left their fuel containers behind. He slowed for a second, shaking each of the containers, discovering one half-full. He grabbed the half-full one, twisted off the cap, and still trotting toward the aircraft poured the fuel from the generator to the front wheels. He told himself, *Pour the fuel between the generator and the aircraft and when the explosion happens there's a chance they'd blame the guards.*

A ladder ran from the tarmac to a closed door on the back of the fuselage. This would have been where the aircrew entered and left the aircraft. Tucker squatted at the bottom of the ladder, his left hand resting easily on the metal ladder. Ricard squatted on the other side of the ladder.

"Keep a good watch," Tucker said as he handed his M-4 Carbine to Ricard.

Ricard nodded.

Tucker stood, placed his left foot on the second rung, and dashed up the ladder. His combat boots jostled the ladder, drawing the sound of rattling metal as the ladder bounced slightly on the tarmac.

Hidden latches beneath the door held the ladder securely to the aircraft. Flush with the door and pushed into a recess was the lever to open it. Tucker pushed the catch beneath the lever, causing the lever to pop out of its storage position. He twisted the lever clockwise, glad that it turned easily. As he thought, *This is going too easy,* he heard the slight sound of suction popping as the lever unlocked the door. He tugged, but the door stayed put. It wouldn't open. Tucker looked along the edges of the hatch.

A steel-tempered padlock near the top secured the aircraft door to the fuselage. He shoved the lever back into position. They couldn't open the door until they cut the padlock. He put both feet along the edge of the ladder and slid down to where Ricard waited.

"Damn," he said. "I knew this was too easy." He looked down at Ricard. "It's locked."

"Why wouldn't it be?" Ricard asked. "I'd lock anything I left sitting around in the middle of nowhere; but then again, I'm from LA."

"I don't suppose we have a lock cutter?"

Ricard smiled. "Maybe we do, sir," Ricard said, handing the Carbine back to Tucker. The petty officer opened the box, turned one of the plastic-wrapped blocks of C4 end up, unwrapped it a little, and squeezed off a smidgeon between his forefinger and thumb. His smile widened. Ricard stood and, still holding the C4 between his thumb and forefinger, grabbed the ladder with his free hand.

Tucker put his hand on the petty officer's arm. "What are you going to do?"

"I'm going to open the door, sir," Ricard said. He glanced down at Tucker's hand.

Tucker dropped his hand. In three steps, the petty offi-cer was at the top of the ladder.

Tucker watched from below, his M-4 Carbine pointing up and toward the lighted guard shack. He alternated watch-ing the guard shack and Ricard, who was leaning against the door so he could reach the lock above his head. Tucker knew only a minute had passed, but it still seemed to be tak-ing a long time for Ricard to do whatever he was doing with the C4.

The entrance to the guard shack was still open. He couldn't see the vehicle. He could hear it. Tucker knew once the light disappeared, it meant the soldiers were back inside the shack. He'd be less apprehensive if the tele-phone hadn't started ringing five minutes ago.

"Watch out; I'm coming down," Ricard called softly from the top of the ladder.

Tucker stepped back and knelt on one knee, keeping an eye on the French guard shack. The sound of brakes squeaking to a stop pierced the night.

"We should move away, Commander," Ricard said, pointing back up to the door.

Tucker glanced up and saw the small timer stuck on the door near the lock. Barely discernible wires ran from the timer to the lock.

Ricard reached out and tugged on Tucker's shirtsleeve. "Commander, I'll be back there," he said, pointing toward the edge of the tarmac. The Seabee explosives expert took off, running, his back to the aircraft.

Tucker took off, following Ricard. When Ricard threw himself on the ground at the edge of the tarmac, Tucker dived also, figuring that Ricard had a better idea what was going to happen than he did.

Tucker spun around, staring back at the aircraft. "What did you—"

A small flash of light, accompanied by the sound of a small explosion, caught Tucker with his eyes open. The noise reminded him of those "cherry bomb" fireworks he used to buy when he was a kid.

"That should open the door," Ricard said, jumping up and running toward the aircraft. "Man, oh, man! Am I good or what!"

Tucker blinked several times as he followed, trying to get rid of that bright white spot in the center of his vision. He was supposed to be the professional for these types of missions, and here he goes doing something stupid like keeping his eyes open when he knew an explosion was going to go off.

In the few seconds it took to reach the aircraft, his eyes had readjusted to the security lights. The ladder was on the cement with Ricard standing over it. The top rungs were mangled and twisted. The clasps that secured the ladder to the aircraft had been sheared off.

Ricard scratched his head as he looked at the ladder and then glanced at the door. "Well, sir, the good news is the lock is gone."

Tucker was looking at the open entrance to the aircraft. The blast had caused the door to ricochet away from the blast and ride its hinges until the door slammed into the fuselage, wedging itself to the aircraft. Where the lock had been, a twenty-inch hole broke the symmetry of the opening.

Tucker bit his lower lip. How were they going to get inside the aircraft? The door was a good twelve feet off the ground.

Ricard lifted the damaged ladder and held it up. The twisted ladder was now a couple of feet too short to rest against the fuselage. Tucker looked at the wing, reached over, and tapped Ricard on the shoulder. "Let the ladder go." He pointed toward the wing where the flaps curled downward.

The ladder clanged on the tarmac as Ricard let it go. Tucker grimaced. "I didn't mean drop it," he said firmly. *I have to be more exact in my orders,* he told himself.

Tucker pointed at the wing again and explained to Ricard his idea as they ran toward it. Ricard cupped his hands together. Tucker strapped the M-4 Carbine across his back and, with a quick leap, using the petty officer's hands, he grabbed the open space between the flaps and the wing and pulled himself up. He raced along the wing toward the fuselage and pulled himself onto the top of the aircraft. Testing his balance for moment, Tucker then moved toward the tail, stepping carefully over the multitude of small antennas that jutted from the top of the reconnaissance aircraft and the two long wires running from the front of the aircraft near the cockpit to the top of the aircraft tail.

He crouched above the damaged door. Tucker looked behind him, saw the long wire, and hooked his shoe under it. Leaning precariously over the side—Ricard beneath, holding his hands out as if to catch him if he fell—Tucker was able to see inside the aircraft.

"How about that?" he said aloud. Using his foot, he pulled himself back onto the top of the aircraft. Crouching, he took the opportunity to glance toward the guard shack. The light was gone. It meant the French were inside and out of the way. By now, they should have called their sergeant of the guard and resolved the issue of the ringing telephone.

He turned back to the task. He grabbed the wire with his hands and eased his feet over the side of the fuselage.

"Be careful, Commander," Ricard whispered. "Your feet aren't exactly inside the door."

This isn't going to work, Tucker said to himself.

Tucker pulled himself back onto the top of the aircraft. He thought for a moment and then, with his boot hooked once again on the wire, slid his body over the side, holding the Carbine with his left hand. He tossed the rifle inside the aircraft. Tucker ran his fingers along the edge of the aircraft door, searching . . . After several seconds, his fingers touched what felt like a metal rod that ran along the top length of the door. Probably for the ripcord if the crew had to bail out.

Aircrews, unlike Special Forces who were trained to open their own parachutes during a jump, adhered to a mathematical equation that number of flights should equal number of landings. When that equation failed, it required nervous fortitude and mutual encouragement for them to bail out. Having the parachute open as they jumped relieved some frantic pressure off their shaking hands.

Tucker gripped the metal rod, running his hands around it a couple of times. Satisfied, he gripped the metal rod tightly and twisted his foot, freeing his boot from the antenna wire. Tucker slid, heading toward the earth. He tucked his head inside the door as his body came around and, with all his strength, jerked himself inside the aircraft. The metal bar came free, sending Tucker falling onto the deck of the aircraft, jarring him. The sound of metal ripping away from other metal like fingernails down a chalkboard echoed out and over the runway.

Red liquid ran across his hands. He rolled to the right on top of his Carbine. From the metal rod Tucker used to get inside the aircraft, thick, red fluid poured. It wasn't for ripcords; it was an exposed hydraulic line.

"You, okay, boss?" came a shout from below.

Tucker stood. He grabbed the hydraulic line and bent it so the fluid poured out of the door and onto the tarmac. Ricard had moved away several feet.

Tucker stood and ran his hand along the insides of the hatch, hoping this time his feel matched his instincts. A couple of seconds and near the top right-hand side of the door, his hands touched a thick plaster cover, held closed with Velcro strips. Tucker ripped it open. A rope ladder tumbled free.

"Here," he said to Ricard, tossing the rope ladder out.

Tucker reached over and bent the ruptured hydraulic line further to the right so the fluid avoided the rope ladder.

Ricard hoisted the small wooden crate containing the C4 explosives, tucked it under an arm, and put one foot on the rope ladder. As soon as he lifted the other leg, the ladder swung back and forth. Ricard jumped off.

"It ain't steady, sir."

Tucker started to tell him to toss the C4 up, but he had less confidence than Ricard did over the stuff not exploding from rough handling. Tucker grabbed the ladder and in two quick moves was on the tarmac beside Ricard. He grabbed the end of it. "Go ahead now."

Thirty seconds later, the Seabee was inside the aircraft. Tucker was quickly behind him.

"What do we do now?" Ricard asked.

"You get busy laying the C4. I'll see if I can match any of this equipment with this photograph."

"What does this weapon look like?" Ricard asked as he squatted next to the box and pulled out two sausage-looking blocks of C4 wrapped tightly in plastic. One block had the end already open from where Ricard had earlier broken off a piece.

"I don't know," Tucker said. He reached into a side pocket and pulled out a small military flashlight. He thought for a second on using the red lens, but their night vision had already been destroyed and the white light is always better.

He flipped it on. The light lit up the back end of the air-craft. Tucker glanced at Ricard, head down, unwrapping the explosives. On the deck beside the C4, Ricard had laid the timing devices and blasting caps. Tucker nodded to himself and left the expert to the job. He had his to do.

According to that intelligence officer on the *Mesa Verde,* the laser weapon would look more like physics and com-puters than like a normal shell-firing weapon. Tucker thought, *That's a lot of help, desk jockey.* The first few po-sitions Tucker passed along the starboard side of the air-craft he readily recognized as an Electronic Warfare suite. He had experience with electronic warfare from the vari-ous sea-going platforms Navy SEALs used. Most of theirs were automatic warning devices that only told you what the sensors picked up. Unlike the French Atlantique or the Navy EP-3E Aries II, the SEALs EW suites were un-manned most of the time and had a high incidence of false warnings.

He tripped, catching himself on the back of a nearby seat. In the center of the passageway, a huge bubble rose out of the deck. It didn't take the brightest crayon in the

box to realize this wasn't part of the normal installation of
a reconnaissance aircraft. At least, that was Tucker's initial
impression. When he couldn't find wires running from it to
one of the consoles, a doubt as to whether this was part of
the normal installation for a reconnaissance aircraft or not
rose in his thoughts.

He pulled the camera from his pocket and took a couple
of photographs of the plexiglass-enclosed opaque dome.
Then, he turned the camera toward the EW suite and took
another couple of photographs.

The camera held alongside his Carbine, Tucker moved
forward, keeping one hand free in the event he tripped again.
Behind him, he heard Ricard moving as the Seabee set the
explosives. *Hope to hell he knows what he's doing. Of
course, it's a little late in the mission to find out a little more
about the man.* He then heard the humming coming from
Ricard. It sounded like the Disney theme song from *Snow
White and the Seven Dwarfs*.

His flashlight gleamed over metal racks along the left
side of the aircraft. The fresh look of the racks and the new
bolts securing them to the deck convinced Tucker of a new
installation. "This has to be it," he said softly. He raised the
camera and took several photographs. This new stuff was
directly beside the communications suite and behind the
cockpit. Two seats had been bolted to the deck directly in
front of the new racks. Tucker pulled the photograph from
his pocket and tried to compare this French electronic suite
with the picture of the American laser weapon control console. He squinted at the photograph and then, running the
flashlight over the installation, tried to find something similar. Nothing matched.

Tucker sighed and stuffed the photograph back into his
pocket. *So much for intelligence,* he thought. He glanced at
Ricard. The petty officer was on the same side of the aircraft
as he. Meant the explosives had been set on the other side.

He looked at his watch. They would have to leave in
the next two to three minutes. They couldn't stay here
much longer. They were approaching the thirty-minute

mark from the time they reached the fence. It may only take an hour to return to where they were dropped off, but Tucker wanted an extra fifteen minutes. Coming in covertly is a hell of lot easier than leaving in a panic. Ricard was on his hands and knees about ten feet away, the Seabee's head hidden by a small foldaway table that ran along the EW suite.

The sudden sound of something hitting the back of the fuselage caused Tucker to lift his Carbine. He hurried toward the rear of the aircraft, stepping carefully over Ricard along the way. Tucker reached the door just as something hit the inside of the aircraft. A rock bounced a couple of times on the floor, coming to rest at his feet. He eased around the open door. Master Chief Collins stood out there on the tarmac, a hand full of small pebbles, throwing the rocks into the aircraft.

"Master Chief?"

"Commander, y'all get your asses out of there. The French are heading back and it don't look as if they're taking their time."

"How long—"

"Sir, you got two minutes," Master Chief Collins said, holding up two fingers. "Maybe, three," he added, holding up two fingers again.

"Okay, we're on our way." Tucker dashed back inside, hurrying toward the front. Ricard was on his knees near the front of the aircraft, near the suspected laser installation.

"What's going on, Commander?" he asked from beneath the console.

"Visitors on their way. We've got to go. You about done, or do you need more time?"

Ricard pulled himself out from under the console to a seated position. He shrugged and shook his head. "We can go down, sir. There's enough C4 on board this plane that when it goes, they'll be lucky to find a tire."

Tucker jerked his thumb toward the door. "Then get your ass out and head back to the fence with the master chief. I'll be a minute behind you."

Ricard pulled himself up, using a seat back. "You don't have to tell me twice, sir."

Tucker leaned to the side, his hands on the laser weapon installation, to give Ricard room to ease by him. He pushed himself upright once the man passed.

Ricard stopped at the door and looked back at him.

"Sir, I'm setting the timer now."

Tucker swallowed. "How long?"

"Five minutes, sir."

"Mark it four."

"Okay, sir, but you're knocking a minute—"

Tucker nodded. "Do it." He touched the stopwatch feature on his wristwatch and saw the glow of the second hand as it hurried on its circular path. *Not much time,* he thought, *but then I don't need much.*

When he looked up, Ricard was gone. He turned his attention to what he suspected was the laser installation. He moved the flashlight, starting at the top of the equipment, back and forth, moving lower each pass.

Gauges, scopes, radar, and readout devices decorated the front of the suite. They weren't the things that drove the weapon. The real weapon would be in one or two of the boxes that generated the data these readouts displayed. The boxes and displays were held in place much like American avionics, with small finger-bolts that could be twisted open or closed with a few turns of the fingers.

He stopped, lifted the camera, and took another couple of photographs as his mind raced over the decision on what to carry out of there. He couldn't take several pieces of gear. He'd never be able to carry the weight. He could carry one, *as long it didn't weigh too much.* Tucker squatted and ran the light beneath the console. Between the two chairs was a tall military-black computer server. He reached forward, touched the machine, and rocked it a couple of times. It was loose. He leaned under the table, pulling the flashlight closer to the server for a better view. If anything would tell the scientists back home whether this was the laser weapon or not, this should be it. The CD-ROM was missing, which meant the important data most likely were not on the machine, but it was something he could carry back. Let the experts decide what it holds.

He squatted and leaned forward, easing his head under the console. The black box was mounted on metal railings with a bar in front locking it in place. Tucker twisted around, lying down on his back.

The sound of multiple rocks coming through the back door drew his attention. He glanced at his watch. Two minutes before the explosions went, if Ricard was accurate. Tucker reached down and lifted the clasp that locked the server in place. He sat up and pulled the small server forward. It came several inches and then stopped.

He lay back down and slid under the seat. *Damn!* He let out a deep breath, a reflection from the flashlight glanced off his watch. He twisted his arm. Less than two minutes.

More rocks hurled through the door. He heard the master chief calling his name, but ignored it. Tucker reached behind the server and began to rip off connections. Two connections were screwed to the portals in back. Tucker sat up and pulled with all his strength. The connections ripped out of the server. He glanced at his watch. Nearing one minute. *Cutting it close, Tucker,* he thought. *And there's no prize for being close except in horseshoes. Why did he have to say "make it four minutes?"*

He lifted the server, estimated its weight at twenty pounds. *Risking our lives for a twenty-pound piece of avionics that someone thinks will change America's global power.* He tucked it under his right arm and with the Carbine grasped in his left hand, Tucker ran to the back door, careful to step over the plexiglass thing in the middle of the passageway. He glanced forward and saw the flashlight lying on the deck. Too late to go back.

"Commander, we gotta go!" Master Chief Collins shouted from below, his voice betraying his irritation. Ricard stood unarmed near him.

"Ricard," Tucker shouted. "Catch this. It's about twenty pounds." Without waiting for an answer, Tucker tossed the gear to Ricard who caught it, going to one knee, as he struggled to keep from dropping it.

"Shit! If that's twenty pounds, I'll eat your shorts," Ricard muttered as he stood up.

A second later Tucker stood beside them. Master Chief Collins pointed toward the short taxiway that ran to the tarmac. "Here they come, sir."

"And, here we go," Tucker said, pushing Ricard with the laser avionics toward the fence.

Spurts of concrete erupted behind Ricard.

"Goddamn!" Collins shouted. "They're firing at us." The master chief lifted his M-4 Carbine and fired a short semi-automatic burst at the French Humvee-like vehicle.

"Go!" Tucker shouted, firing his own burst at the French.

The French military vehicle veered off the road and into the bush alongside. Tucker didn't hear a crash, so they were still alive and would be headed this way.

"Sir!" Ricard shouted from the fence. "Thirty seconds! You've got thirty seconds!"

Tucker took off running, chasing the master chief toward the opening in the fence. On the other side, Brute held the fence back with his knee, his weapon pointed through one of the links of the fence. Ricard dropped and crawled through.

The master chief detoured to the right, stopped briefly in front of the generator, and hit a button. Tucker caught a glimpse of him turning toward the fence as the generator ran down; the lights dimmed and flickered for a moment, then went out. The night was theirs. Tucker kept heading toward where he recalled the opening in the fence was before the lights went out. He reached up and flipped the night vision device down. The master chief was crawling through the opening and taking the fence from Brute, sending the giant Seabee down the incline.

"Hurry, Commander!"

"Ten seconds!" shouted Ricard from the safety of the incline.

Tucker dove as he reached the opening, scrambled

through, felt the master chief grab him, and the next thing he knew he was sailing across the six feet between the fence and the incline. Brute grabbed him as he rolled over the incline.

The master chief took a couple of steps, jumped, and like a diver trying to get as much distance between himself and the shoreline, sailed over their heads just as the aircraft exploded. The concussion hit the master chief in midair and added several feet to the jump.

Tucker flipped up his night vision device and crawled quickly to the edge of the incline in time to see burning pieces of aircraft rain down on the tarmac and the nearby bush.

"Master Chief, you all right?" Tucker heard Brute ask from behind them. The cursing reply told him Collins was okay.

A loud crash to their right caused them to jump. They looked at the burning aircraft tire about fifty feet from them.

"Jesus Christ!" shouted Ricard.

"So much for them not finding a tire," Tucker added.

The four of them laughed. Nothing like danger to bond a military unit.

Fire engulfed the aircraft, the remaining fuel in the wing tanks blew, roiling flames and smoke leaped into the night sky. In the light of the burning aircraft, French soldiers eased out of the bushes, their weapons pointing toward the fence. Tucker rose to his knee, lifted his Carbine, and fired several bursts over their heads. They quickly disappeared back into the bushes, out of sight. He didn't want to kill anyone unless he had to.

"Everyone all right?" Tucker asked.

"I'm fine," said Ricard, "except I think I'm going to need a new set of skivvies."

"Brute, you okay?" Master Chief Collins asked as he brushed himself off from the tumble he had taken.

"Yeah, Master Chief. I'm okay, but I think I've decided being a Seabee is better than this shit."

"All right, guys," Tucker said. "Let's get out of here before they get up their nerve and come after us or reinforcement arrives."

They eased back along the edge of the jungle the way they came; only now the jungle was lit up by the flames on the other side of the fence. Just as they reached the trail that would take them away from the holocaust behind them, a volley of shots rang out, peppering the tree line above their heads. The four ducked, slid down the incline, and quickly disappeared along the trail at the bottom, heading back to a rendezvous with their only means of escape.

A hundred yards later, the sound of tracked vehicles rode over the sporadic, but smaller, explosions continuing from the burning aircraft. Tucker recognized the sound as armored personnel carriers—APCs they called them. Tanks would have been louder and more ominous. Tanks would have made the pucker factor go way up. APCs couldn't follow them into the jungle. Tanks, on the other hand, would view the jungle as a slight obstacle to be knocked aside, rolled over, and flattened.

"Stay close, gents, and keep those 22s ready to be flipped up," Tucker said as he picked up the pace. APCs may not be tanks, but they carry troops, and these troops would be French Foreign Legion. He had fought with Legionnaires a couple of years ago when he was staging anti-terrorist missions out of Djibouti, the small African country at the western end of the Gulf of Aden. The Legionnaires fought hard, fought dirty, and fought to win—much like their renowned nights on the town.

Legionnaires would follow them into the jungle. Not to do so would smack of failure. To fail would denigrate their reputation, and when a battle clears, a fighting organization's reputation is its legacy, and that legacy depends on honor, zeal, and tenacity in combat. Life and self were secondary. Especially to the Legion.

Rapid gunfire broke the silence behind them. Tucker knew the French were saturating the area beyond the fence with automatic fire. They wouldn't know how many of them there were. Then several explosions occurred.

"What the hell?"

"Relax," Tucker said, his voice failing to sound relaxed. He kept moving, keeping a steady but fast pace. "Mortars. They're making sure the place is clear before they move in."

"Well, at least we have a fence between us and them," Collins said.

The sound of an engine revving rode over the gunfire, then gears engaged and the engine was moving. A few seconds later, the noise of metal grinding upon itself filled the jungle.

"Uh, oh," Brute said. "There's no fence between us and them now."

He was right, thought Tucker. *They be Legionnaires in them thar hills, boys, and this ain't* Deliverance.

Tucker fought the urge to run. *Keep the pace brisk.* Those following would move slower, since they'd have no idea what they faced. They would be worried about ambush and booby traps. He, on the other hand, had no such worry; but they had to maintain their stamina to reach the rendezvous point.

Keep the pace brisk. If they could make the clearing in the next hour, their ride home would—*should*—be waiting; then the Legionnaires can have the jungle.

MINUTES LATER TUCKER GLANCED AGAIN AT THE GPS readout. He had been doing this every half minute or so. Trails look different when you're returning. If they took a wrong turn or lost the trail, they still had GPS to get them to the clearing. Two kilometers and forty-five minutes before pickup. Should be okay. He hadn't heard any sounds of pursuit, but that didn't mean anything. Legionnaires were quiet. They'd follow the tracks, and by now, Tucker figured, they would have determined that there were only four of them, which meant the pace of their pursuers would have increased. Plus the pursuers would have state-of-the-art reconnaissance hardware, such as night vision devices. Just because it was French didn't mean it was inferior.

It never occurred to Tucker to think they wouldn't be followed. It would have been nice if they could have had more time to make their exit. With the Legionnaires having night vision devices as surely they did, the situation could change severely if they caught up.

He looked ahead and caught a glimpse of someone peering from behind a tree. From the silhouette, it looked as if the figure was staring right at him. He held up his hand and motioned his team down. How could they have gotten ahead? Brute moved up beside him. Tucker touched him and pointed toward the person near the tree. The moment he pointed, Tucker wished he could have pulled his finger back.

Brute nodded in understanding. *Must only work when you point directly at him,* Tucker thought.

The Seabee tapped Tucker on the shoulder and pointed left. The night vision device highlighted two individuals standing alongside each other, their heads turning slowly back and forth. Tucker could tell the two men carried weapons, but the night vision didn't permit details such as what type of rifles the two carried. Ricard then tapped him and pulled his attention to the right of the trail ahead. A fourth man squatted on a small mound, his head moving slowly, back and forth, as if trying to decide where the noises they had heard were coming from. Those noises would be Tucker and his men. They weren't the quietest covert team in the world.

Tucker crouched motionless, with the exception of his head. He scanned the jungle through the night vision device to see how many faced them and where they were located. He counted four, possibly five ahead of them arrayed along both sides of the trail in ambush profile.

When things are going too easy, nothing can occur that doesn't make it harder. The trail had been a Godsend to their mission, and now it looked as if they were going to have to leave it.

Tucker turned to face the others. He held his finger to his lips for quiet and then pointed right. Tucker pushed a couple of bushes apart carefully, matching the soft noise of the wind through the leaves to his own movement. Following, the three Seabees eased off the trail with Tucker and moved as quietly as possible into the bush. To Tucker, they sounded like the Saint Paddy's Day parade down main street Savannah. Moving through the heavy brush got them off the trail, but meanwhile they were blind to what those waiting in ambush were doing. For all Tucker knew, the men ahead of them may be repositioning even as the four of them tried to put as much distance as possible from the trail.

He estimated eighty to one hundred full steps from the trail—roughly three hundred feet—when they emerged from the brush to find themselves in a small clearing. A clearing that may have been made by a large animal as it slept. Giant leaves intertwined overhead to form a weak roof, but an effective camouflage. Tucker hoped whatever pressed the brush down to make this depression was a vegetarian.

Tucker motioned his team nearer him. He pulled their heads close. In a real operation, he would never hold a conference in the middle of a combat situation, but three Seabees in the middle of an ambush without their bulldozers and graders are anything but a normal operation.

"Master Chief, you're it. I'm going to see just what we're up against so we can make up some kind of plan of attack. Wait here. Give me five minutes, then work north before cutting back toward the pickup area." He tapped the GPS receiver on the master chief's wrist. "You comfortable?"

Collins looked at the receiver. "I can work it, sir. But if I follow your directions, we'll miss our pickup."

"Master Chief, better to miss the pickup than die trying to make it."

Tucker lifted his M-4 and disappeared into the bush. As the vegetation closed around him, he heard faint German coming from behind them. *The Legionnaires have arrived,* he thought.

Minutes later, a stand of trees blocked his way. He stood, angling his body along the trunk of the nearest tree, blending with the nightscape. Tucker surveyed the jungle, and then focused his attention in the direction of the trail. The two ambushers on the right side of the trail were visible, their backs to him. Tucker thought about taking them out, but he knew it would take too much time and the Legionnaires would be here by the time he finished. The ambushers' heads turned slowly back and forth as they focused on the trail Tucker and his team had vacated.

Tucker smiled. He wanted to laugh at the irony of it. Sometimes the "Luck God" smiles on you, and this was one of those times. Tucker squatted for a moment, listening to his surroundings. Satisfied, he pushed his way under the brush and started working his way back to where he had left the others.

CHAPTER 11

CAPTAIN XAVIER BENNETT PLACED THE TELEPHONE RE-
ceiver back in its cradle, his hand remaining on it for a few
seconds. *I knew when I called Admiral Holman what his
response would be, but juniors keep seniors informed even
when they know what's expected of them. Same thing I will
expect when I relieve Admiral Holman next year.*

Xavier leaned back in his chair, his elbows resting on
the arms, hands interlocked with the two index fingers tapping his chin. Thoughts about the incident with the *Winston
Churchill* and the French reconnaissance aircraft mixed
with anxiety over Tucker Raleigh and the Seabees still
somewhere inside Ivory Coast.

He sighed. He had been doing that a lot lately. He
should be lying back, enjoying the African sun, and—*other
than watching sailors do ship's work*—listening to Seabees
complain about the screw-up with the airfield they were
sent to extend and improve. Couldn't extend something
that wasn't there. Tomorrow, he promised himself, he'd
take a Humvee out to the airfield and see for himself the
challenges Teddy Klein was bitching about. The Seabees
still had some off-loading to do from the *Mesa Verde,* but

with the recent oporder transmitted from Commander, Amphibious Group Two, the ship wasn't going anywhere soon. They were told to remain in Port Harper, Liberia, until further orders. He did give Commander Klein the use of a CH-53 Super Stallion helicopter to transport people and supplies between the port and the gone-to-hell airfield. That should help a little. He'd probably feel better about loaning the helicopter to the Seabees if the pilots hadn't been so damn happy about living off the ship. Tent life couldn't be that great, but then ice chests full of beer could temper most hardships.

Xavier intended to start Cinderella liberty with the buddy system for the crew tomorrow afternoon. Cinderella liberty was time given to sailors to enjoy the pleasures a port may offer, but around midnight the sailors had to be back onboard ship. The buddy system was just what it sounded like. You signed off the ship with a friend, and when you returned, you'd better have the same buddy with you.

Liberia was a lot more stable after the defeat of the Jihadists and the Africans who destroyed the government and started executing every American there.

Xavier reached out and flipped through the two-inch-thick report on his desk. Then his thoughts returned to Liberia. The president of Liberia, before he was killed by terrorists, had taken a lesson from the U.S. model for Israeli citizenship given to American citizens and had offered similar citizenship to African-Americans. The money earned through the issuance of Liberian passports provided Liberia with the necessary American dollars to improve its infrastructure and the standard of living for its citizens. What the president failed to foresee was the number of African-Americans who would emmigrate to Liberia. A small restriction in the passports forbade Liberian citizens not domiciled in Liberia from voting. Brilliant initiatives always adversely affect something, and while the money flowed into the Liberian coffers, American citizens flowed into Liberia.

Damn good thing, too, thought Xavier. He'd been at

the Pentagon doing his penance as the Division Chief for Network Interoperability in the J6 directorate at the time. He had weaseled his way into the National Command Center to watch the events unfold toward the end of the conflict. The rebels marched on a small American enclave named Kingsville, where a retired Army lieutenant general named Thomaston and a group of a hundred or so Americans holed up inside a small fenced-in armory. Outnumbered nearly twenty to one, they successfully fought off the terrorist horde for two days. The battle had become Liberia's Alamo. Video links from Unmanned Fighter Aerial Vehicles allowed everyone in the NCC to watch U.S. Marines join the defenders to rout the enemy during the final minutes of this battle. It probably helped that the retired general leading the Americans within the armory was also a former Ranger.

Now, this same Thomaston was the self-appointed president of Liberia, promising general elections this fall. Xavier hoped the man lived up to his word. Few would believe it, but even Americans were susceptible to the pleasures of power. No matter how hard someone argues that he wants to step down from a position of power, giving up the perks isn't easy. Power is a vice that beckons, cajoles, and contorts reality as it fights to retain its hold. Xavier figured a military flag officer would have a better chance of throwing off that chain than others.

Xavier glanced at his watch. The helicopter should be halfway to the pickup zone for Tucker and his Seabees. Wasn't a thing he could do until they returned. *Damn!* Wasn't a thing he could do if they didn't return. He was forbidden to even prepare a rescue mission. Right now, less than ten people on this ship were even aware that such a covert mission was occurring.

He reached down and thumbed through the hard copy of the investigating officer's report on the desk to his right, forcing his mind onto other things. He started to pick it up, but instead left it alone. He'd seen enough of it. Was becoming over-saturated with the events of the *Churchill*, the vanished fighter jets. Read it twice and then went through it a third time with a highlighter identifying what he considered pertinent portions. He had never seen an investigation that only captured the important things, events, times. Investigational reports were written objectively and chronologically—or so they were supposed to be. Statements by everyone involved gave varying perceptions of events, forcing the adjudicator to wade through the words to find his or her own perception of truth. This one had been put together quite well, considering it was written by a layman officer.

Two days ago, Xavier had emailed a copy of the report to Admiral Holman with no personal observation or comments other than a recommendation that they should talk once the admiral had had a chance to read it; digest it. Knowing Holman, the email had been forwarded to the Amphibious Group Two legal team for review. All Xavier had was a lieutenant commander and a couple of legal petty officers for that sort of task.

Xavier unfolded his hands, grabbed a bottle of water off the desk, and took a deep swig. The Navy wasn't all ships at sea and adventure ashore. The Navy also had tradition and expectations that must be observed or good order and discipline would decay.

What he had to do in the next forty-eight hours was something he dreaded; but something that was good for the Navy and good for the nation, he would do. It wasn't something he would do gladly. It was something he'd do with feelings of deep sadness, even though a fellow officer had violated the trust placed upon him. Harrison had violated trust in a position so that his peers and seniors must rid themselves of him much as a farmer would pluck a rotten apple from a basket, and Xavier hated it all.

Xavier had a strong idea what he was going to do, but in cases such as this, the process must be stringently followed. There must be no question of fairness when the results were announced. Legal rights must be protected.

Still, this was more complicated than your usual "relieve for cause" process. He was saddled with the challenge of doing what was right for the Navy and then, for the nation, keeping it quiet.

Admiral Holman and he believed the case had strong potential to gravely impact national security if the reason for discipline became known and was eventually linked to tonight's covert mission. Journalists were not fools when it came to putting together a full picture from a jumble of facts. Some would have said Captain Xavier Bennett had been left holding the bag, but within the Navy, no such thoughts would have occurred. With authority came responsibility, and the incident was his to handle. Those above could give *strong* advice, but the initial solution was always laid at the doorstep of the officer in charge. Xavier took another sip. One thing he had learned while serving with Admiral Holman was that the admiral expected his senior officers to resolve problems on their own. If a Navy captain couldn't resolve a problem at the 0-6 level, then how could he or she expect to solve them as an admiral?

Xavier recalled an older captain years ago teaching him a valuable lesson of command. At the time, Xavier had been a fresh-nose lieutenant suffering a supply problem in Norfolk, Virginia. The Close-in Weapons System—*his responsibility*—had been down for repairs for nearly two weeks. Despite continued requests for the needed spare part to restore it, the supply depots ashore hadn't seemed that helpful. Tired and exasperated one afternoon, he had bypassed everyone in the chain of command, knocked on the skipper's door, and a few minutes later was sharing this problem with him.

The captain had listened attentively, thanked him for the information, and asked him to come back when he had resolved it. The executive officer and his department head gave Xavier more leadership direction about the chain of command the next morning.

But then he solved it. He personally walked the request

chit through the supply depot and eight hours later—a full day—he walked up the gangplank with the spare part. It was years later during his first command that he realized what that captain had done. He had taught Xavier to depend on his own skills. Also taught the fresh-nose lieutenant that when you help someone solve a minor problem, the next thing you knew it became yours. Xavier smiled. He mentioned it to this captain when he ran across him a couple of years ago. Seemed Xavier had a better memory than the captain did, because this mentor had laughed and said it had nothing to do with teaching leadership; it had to do with him not wanting to inherit any additional work. After two ship commands and a tour at the Pentagon, Xavier understood what he meant.

A shout from a boatswain mate on the deck outside his porthole broke his reverie. Xavier stood, stretched, and took a deep breath. *Tomorrow, I'm going for a run regardless of what happens. Do it just before I go out to visit the Seabees.*

He lifted the telephone and dialed the quarterdeck, asking them to have the XO and the legal officer lay to his inport cabin. Shortly, a 1MC announcement broadcast his request through the ship.

While he waited, Bennett walked to the porthole and stared across the harbor at the lights along the far side. Every now and again, a person wandered out of the shadows to cross the lighted area and disappear into darkness on the other side. Reminded him of how each life is different, with people passing through along their own journey before disappearing from yours.

A soft knock on the door drew his attention.

"Enter."

The door opened and the XO, Commander Ellen Fulbright, and Xavier's legal officer, Lieutenant Commander Thomas Kilpatrick, entered the in-port cabin.

"Evening, Captain," Fulbright said. "We haven't heard anything yet, sir—from the team. Helicopter is about an hour away from pickup."

Bennett nodded. "No news is good news, they say," he replied languidly. It wasn't often in a skipper's career that he or she was blessed with two depressing orders simultaneously. He had the problem of the investigating officer's report on his desk, and he had a mission that was no mission ongoing in unfriendly territory.

Unlike most of his peers, he refused to think of the French as an enemy or hostile. The two countries still worked together when it was in their mutual interest. They were still two of the largest democracies in the world. He had had lunch on board the *Mesa Verde* the day after they arrived in Harper, Liberia, with the French commander in charge of the French forces along the nearby Liberia–Ivory Coast border. Friendly chap. Either the French man knew nothing about the missing F-16s and the French Atlantique reconnaissance aircraft, or he had great confidence.

"Let's pray you're right, sir," Kilpatrick said. "You never know about these things until they're over . . . then, that's where we legal types arrive *en masse* to tell you what laws you violated by doing it. As they say in my profession, 'Once we hear about it, it's too late to change your mind.'" He chuckled for a second until he saw the thin smile beneath Fulbright's arched eyebrows. The chuckle stopped abruptly.

Xavier forced a broader smile. "Well, Tom, I hope they come back okay, and I hope we don't need your services for a mission that never occurred."

"Yes, sir," Kilpatrick said. His smile fading altogether, he chewed his lower lip.

Xavier's smile widen. What he wouldn't give to play poker with Kilpatrick. He could feel the bulging wallet now. *Kilpatrick's lower lip must be bitten to pieces, the number of times he does that,* thought Xavier. *Just give him a little bit of worry and that lower lip disappears.* For a nice young man, it amazed Xavier that a future civilian lawyer in the great state of South Carolina failed to realize how goofy it made him look.

Xavier reached behind him and picked up the report.

"You both have had a chance to read this. And I know you did. Everyone reads an investigation; it's the seagoing equivalent to a daytime soap opera. Tom, what's your take on this? I know Commander Fulbright is to the right of Attila the Hun, so I know what she would say, and I think we stopped doing what she would propose sometime back in the nineteenth century."

Kilpatrick cleared his throat, took a deep breath, and started: "Sir, it appears Commander Harrison may have violated direct orders applicable to the standing rules of engagement. Further, if he did in fact order the executive officer to lock the fire control radar on the unarmed French reconnaissance aircraft, which was operating over international waters, then he violated international law—an act considered an act of war and, if known—*right now it is closely held*—could result in the United States being pulled before the International Court in Brussels by the French. Further, the Executive Officer—"

"Okay, okay, Tom. Take a breath," Xavier said, waving his hand at Kilpatrick a couple of times. He chuckled. "Tom, it's obvious you've given this some thought. What I want is to hear your comments on the report; and what I want from you, Tom, is an assessment of what I can and can't legally do. For now, I intend only to focus on the actions of the commanding officer. Tomorrow, I intend to hold a closed-door Admiral's Mast for Commander Harrison. He is the one ultimately responsible for everything that occurs on his ship. The XO and any others who may require disciplinary actions will have to wait until after I have decided disposition of this case."

"Yes, sir. You're right, because the disposition of their actions is directly tied to what is decided about the skipper."

"Correct," Xavier said. He motioned to the small circular table on the starboard side of the stateroom, and they all sat. "After the Admiral's Mast, if I decide to relieve Commander Harrison, XO, I want a helicopter standing by to immediately airlift him to Monrovia. He is not to return to his ship. His belongings will be gathered up and, if we have time, airlifted with him. Further, I don't want the results of the Admiral's Mast known. It would please me further if no one on the ship other than the three of us even knew it was going down."

Fulbright looked up as she sat down. "Captain, to do an Admiral's Mast, sir, you must have permission from the senior flag officer above you; that would be Admiral Holman."

"I know, Ellen. I spoke with the good admiral about thirty minutes ago. I have that authority, and they are faxing a copy of the signed letter sometime in the next few hours." Xavier nodded at Kilpatrick. "Tom, it will be coming to your office. I would prefer it be treated as something you expected and not something out of the ordinary. I know I don't need to say all this, but I want to ensure that you both understand that neither of you should leave this compartment with anything less than a clear understanding of my instructions."

"Yes, sir," the two officers said in conjunction.

Xavier looked at Kilpatrick. "Tom, you're the expert on what we can and can't do. Why don't you go ahead and run down what you see are my options, one at a time, so I can weigh the pros and cons."

"Yes, sir," Kilpatrick said, leaning forward and putting one arm on the table. "There is always an option of doing nothing. Of ignoring the incident—"

Xavier shook his head. "Sorry, I can't do that one." He thought, *If you only knew from how high up the direction to do something originated. For someone who wanted plausible denial—*

Kilpatrick bit his lower lip for a moment. "Then, sir, you have three primary options . . ."

XAVIER PUSHED THE CHAIR AWAY FROM THE TABLE. THE Navy-issued black clock on the bulkhead showed twenty minutes had passed since they sat down. He hated meetings and had little patience for any that exceeded thirty minutes. Fulbright and Kilpatrick stood, also.

"Thanks to both of you. Ellen, what time is the *Winston Churchill* due to dock tomorrow?"

"Around 1000 hours, sir."

Xavier nodded. "Please send an email to the skipper asking him to join me for lunch tomorrow." *I'll have to run in the morning and visit the Seabees before noon. But, by God, I'm going to work out!*

"Yes, sir, I'll do that. Captain, with respect, sir, do you intend to give him a heads-up about the Admiral's Mast?"

It would be the fair thing to do, but Xavier had given thought during the meeting of another way to resolve this issue. He shook his head. "No, XO. Not through informal email; he needs to hear it from me personally. Lunch provides a more relaxed setting for the news. Plus, as I said, I want to keep this as quiet as possible for the time being. Never put anything in an email you're not prepared to read about in the *Washington Post*."

Fulbright touched the doorknob at the same time a knock came from the other side. She opened the door. It was Lieutenant Embry.

"Lieutenant?" Fulbright asked.

"XO, Captain," Embry said.

"Come in, Lieutenant," Xavier said. He noticed the XO's face twist in displeasure. He knew what Fulbright was thinking. XOs hated information to reach the boss without them having had an opportunity to vet it. He knew from the watch bill that Embry was the command duty officer for the watch, and, as such, she had direct access to the skipper. Even though that was Navy tradition, that didn't mean XOs liked the idea any better.

"What've you got, Teresa?" he asked. Fulbright closed the door behind Embry.

"Sir, we received a message from Commander, Atlantic Fleet, sir. The USS *Denver,* LPD-9, Expeditionary Strike Group is being diverted to here. I checked blue force disposition before I came up, and the *Denver* is northwest of the Cape of Good Hope—"

"South Africa?" Fulbright asked.

"Yes, ma'am," Embry replied. "The Seventh Fleet ESG is making a round-the-world return to their home port of San Diego."

"It's a show of power thing, XO," Xavier added, crossing his arms. "With the number of failed states and the continuing rise of Islamic Jihadism, the Joint Chiefs of Staff thought it would be good to have battle groups and ESGs departing the Operation Indonesia Freedom to work their way back to their home port by hopscotch port calls along the way. There was a message from the Chief of Naval Operations, Admiral Yalvarez, informing flag and commanding officers of the deterrent operation. Good for our sailors, as they will see parts of the world most would never get an opportunity to see. A Royal Navy carrier strike force is to join it in the south Atlantic. Be quite an impressive sight."

"Kind of like the great white fleet of Teddy Roosevelt."

"Not as big as that, but still impressive, XO." He turned back to Embry. "You don't necessarily have to fire weapons to convince people you're a strong superpower. Port calls do that for our country. Ships sail into a port; sailors go ashore and spend money; the average citizen of that country sees our naval might and doesn't forget it. It sends a message that the United States is a better friend than foe." He swallowed. Xavier's throat was dry, so he took the several steps to his desk and grabbed his water bottle. "So, where is this message, Lieutenant?"

Embry lifted the folder from under her arm and handed it to Xavier. He quickly scanned the message and handed it back to her. "It's a secret message. Lieutenant, put it on my read board. I don't want to keep any classified material in my stateroom."

Embry took the message, tucked it under her arm, and looked at Xavier. "Skipper, any reply, sir?"

"Probably, Teresa, but it'll wait until tomorrow." The

challenges of command. He had already promised himself an intensive workout; visit the Seabees to see the challenges they were facing; lunch with the latest problem child, Commander Troy Harrison; and now he had another message on top of several others that required answering. And still out there on the end of the limb were Commander Tucker Raleigh and three Seabees trying to act like SEALs. He took a deep swallow. A cold beer and one of Holman's cigars would be nice about now.

Fulbright opened the door. "Thanks, Lieutenant."

Xavier glanced at Embry. "Good night, Lieutenant. Keep me informed if anything else comes in."

"Aye aye, sir," Embry said.

"Ellen, would you stay a moment?" Xavier said as Fulbright started to follow the command duty officer.

She stopped so suddenly that the legal officer nearly bumped into her.

"I can take a hint," said Kilpatrick, stepping back so she could step around him. He pulled the door shut as he left.

"The *Denver* is heading this way because it has a full SEAL team complement on board," Xavier said. "Once the ESG reaches airborne range, they'll fly the team to us. At the speed *Denver* is making, the ESG should be within air range in two days."

"Kind of late to help, isn't it? If this operation that's not an operation goes awry, we've been forbidden to try to rescue them."

Xavier nodded. "Wasn't it John Wayne in *The Sands of Iwo Jima* that said, 'Life's a bitch, and then you die'?"

Fulbright smiled, her eyes wide, eyebrows arched. "Sir—I don't understand, Skipper. What's so funny? This is very serious, I think."

"It's not only serious, Ellen, it's preposterous that we're sending untrained people to do a job that they will most likely fail. On top of that, we tell them that regardless of whether they're successful or not, they are acting without orders." He screwed the top back on the water and set the bottle on his desk. "I can't recall us ever having done this while I've been on active duty; but I do know that we military types are hung out to dry more times than we want to think by politicians more concerned with their power and spin."

"Politics is one profession that could use a higher unemployment rating."

He laughed. "Very good, Ellen."

A knock on the door interrupted them.

"Enter."

The door opened and it was Lieutenant Embry again. "Captain, we have contact with the helicopter. It's approaching the recovery area now, sir."

"XO, I can't stay here and wait. Let's go to Combat." He reached behind him and grabbed his water.

Three minutes later they were in Combat, waiting to hear good news. He pulled himself up into the captain's chair, his face half hidden by the blue lights. The air conditioning in the electronics-laden room was at least ten degrees cooler than his stateroom. To Xavier's right, the air traffic controller mumbled instructions into her mouthpiece. Without asking, he presumed she was talking over the internal communications system and not to the helicopter. He reached up to the speaker mounted directly forward on an overhead beam. Xavier touched the switch to make sure it was on broadcast. It was. If she had been talking to the helicopter, he would have heard the replies broadcast through the speaker.

Xavier settled back and tried to relax. A good thing about military life is it teaches patience. You hurry to wherever you have to go and once there you wait. It didn't matter if it was to mount an amphibious landing or stand in queue for your meal. "Hurry up and wait" was a military mantra.

He hoped he'd have a chance to visit with the skipper of the *Denver* when the ship reached their operational area. He smiled and looked down for a moment. It would be best for everyone involved if Tucker Raleigh and his Seabees were back onboard before the *Denver* arrived.

"Alpha Tango, Foxtrot Charlie; we're ten miles from zone; descending to cherubs two."

Two hundred feet, Xavier said to himself. *Some of those trees out there are that tall.*

"Roger, Foxtrot Charlie; notify when on final."

"I am on final, Alfa Tango." Two clicks followed.

Things are going too smoothly with this mission, Xavier thought, although he had no intelligence out there to even tell him if they had been successful. What little intelligence sources the United States had had been tied up around Indonesia. Because of the close-hold secrecy, he couldn't even ask European Command for Fleet Air Reconnaissance Squadron Two's EP-3E aircraft that sat on the apron at the Monrovian airport to fly a mission providing force protection for the team. *You never know how important information is until you lose it or it's unavailable.* If he even had some members of Naval Security Group Command on board, he'd feel better; but he had nothing but radar, electronic warfare—mostly useless in a low-tech war—and the eyes of the helicopter pilots. So, Xavier Bennett—future admiral and Commander, Amphibious Group Two—leaned forward listening to the soft chatter in the Combat Information Center and sorted through his thoughts of the paucity of alternatives he had if this mission failed. The problem was that he lacked options that did not conflict with his orders. Orders were obeyed, unless you wielded the power and influence so you could quasi-violate them, and then everyone would say what a great and wonderful person you were. He wasn't one of those people. He was Xavier Bennett, and in comparison to Admiral Dick Holman, he was a child in the game of high-stakes politics.

He leaned back and shut his eyes, thinking about tomorrow's lunch with Commander Troy Harrison.

"Alpha Tango, Foxtrot Charlie; we're descending for pickup."

"Any signs of your passengers, Foxtrot Charlie?"

"Not at this—" Static broke up the transmission.

The ATC called several times, attempting to reestablish

contact, before telling Lieutenant Embry that the helicopter had descended below radio contact altitude.

Xavier lifted his water and took another drink. He hoped the helicopter had just descended below radio line-of-sight communications. The cold air condensing on his sweaty T-shirt and skivvies chilled him slightly. There was nothing to do but wait.

CHAPTER 12

TUCKER GENTLY PUSHED ASIDE THE BUSHES, REVEALING A gun barrel six inches from his nose.

"Oh, it's you, sir," Brute said, lowering the barrel.

Tucker pulled himself into the small clearing. "Shhhh," he said, putting his finger to his lips.

He stood, forcing his way quietly through the leafy canopy that stretched over the small clearing. He reached up and adjusted the night vision device, which was jarred slightly by the brush. He blinked twice as his eyesight adjusted. Tucker scanned the back trail. Somewhere behind them were the Legionnaires. The voices heard earlier were no longer audible. That didn't mean much. They could be moving with no talk among themselves, or the wind may have changed, carrying the voices in another direction.

He ran his tongue over his lower lip and was rewarded with bits of vegetation. Tucker turned his head until he felt a change of wind across the wetness. He raised his left hand and glanced at the GPS readout. The light night wind was blowing southeast. It had changed direction slightly, so whispered words by the French would ride the wind away from them.

They were out there. He knew the Legion too well to think they wouldn't be. He'd heard them earlier, and, though he didn't speak German, he'd spent enough time with German forces in Afghanistan to recognize the language.

The French Foreign Legion was made up of foreigners who joined with a promise of a French passport when they finished their service obligation. The other attraction was its soldiers were never investigated to ascertain whether the name under which they enlisted was truly their own or not. Whatever their past, whatever their transgressions, everything was discarded, ignored, when they joined the French Foreign Legion. It was a chance to erase a life that had become too much to live and to start over. Many a Legionnaire finished his service to France and settled within its borders to start a new life. Conversely, many found the Legion the home they never had and grew to love the adventure and challenges of Legion life. They stayed and moved slowly up the enlisted ranks with no opportunity to become an officer. Officers within the Legion were French citizens. French military professionals, who, unlike draftees forbidden by French law to ever leave the country of France, were sometime during their career assigned overseas. The French army officer corps was much like the American in which to rise in rank you fought to get certain performance and duty blocks checked. Overseas duty was an important one if a French officer ever hoped to wear the trappings of General.

Tucker enjoyed working with the Legionnaires, even if the officers were for the most part pompous asses. The soldiers who made up the Legion were as ferocious in combat as they were in partying. He had conducted search-and-engagement operations with them in Somalia and Aden. This was his first time as an object of a Legionnaire search. He had little doubt that if the Legion caught up to them, it would become an engagement.

He glanced back at the ambushers. They had looked African to him. They were still in the same ambush profile alongside the trail. If it wasn't for the minute turn of their heads or the slight shuffle when they shifted their bodies, he might have thought they were dead—as if some sort of African warning you saw in some of the older movies. Probably some of Abu Alhaul's terrorists. This was another morsel to throw to the intelligence officers and let them try to figure out how Tucker and his team of Seabees came to be trapped between Abu Alhaul ahead and Legionnaires closing the gap behind them.

They were outnumbered. He had to do something to turn this situation to their advantage. Tucker turned his head slowly to the right, searching the terrain for any new presence. He'd be as blind as the Africans, if it weren't for these PVS monocles. How did Special Forces ever survive without these things?

Satisfied he had a picture of what confronted them, Tucker withdrew into the bush, a light rustle following as the branches closed over his head.

Ricard lay across the clearing, his M-4 pointing into the brush toward the trail as if expecting someone to follow them. Brute squatted on huge haunches on the far side, his weapon across his chest. The man never showed an expression, but Tucker knew all he had to do was point at him to discover what the Seabee was thinking. Unconsciously, Tucker tightened his hand around the stock of the Carbine and held the other hand close to his pants leg.

Master Chief Collins slid across brush, lifting himself slightly over Ricard's outstretched legs. "What now, sir?" he whispered.

Tucker reached over and tapped Ricard on the calf, motioning him over. The bushes shook slightly as Ricard shifted, pushing himself to a sitting position. He crossed his legs over his thighs. Brute dropped to his knees and knee-walked the few steps to where Tucker squatted. To Tucker, it sounded as if the bushes were rattling, screaming to the terrorists and Legionnaires their location.

He held his hand up and listened for a moment as everyone held their position and remained quiet. After a few seconds, he whispered his intentions, hoping they grasped his meaning. The wind blew toward the Legionnaires. When it was blowing his direction, he had caught their voices. He didn't want them to have the same luck.

Tucker gave them specific instructions as to what they were to do once the shooting started. He pointed west and told them they were to head in that direction for ten minutes and then cut left to recover the trail. Regardless of how much turmoil and confusion Tucker sowed, the only opportunity to reach the pickup point in time to catch their ride was to regain the trail. That meant circumventing the terrorists ahead and slowing down the Legionnaires behind them. Once the Legionnaires figured out how many they were chasing, they would pick up the pace, and there was little doubt they'd catch up with them. The question would be whether to fight and die, or suffer through the embarrassment and allow the Legionnaires to capture them.

TUCKER LEFT THEM IN THE CLEARING. HE CRAWLED BACK through the brush toward where they departed the trail. He pushed the last group of limbs apart, saw the trail, and quietly let the limbs close together, creating a hiding place close to, but out of sight of the trail. It was important for the Legionnaires to believe he was on the trail and this was close enough for it.

He turned and crawled several yards back along his path, certain now that he had his location mapped. Something bit him on the neck, but the slight pain was quick and gone. *Mosquito,* he thought. Experience kept him from slapping the annoying insect. He twitched his neck a couple of times as he moved and continued on, ignoring the momentary distraction. He glanced at his watch and the GPS readout. Thirty-five minutes to make the clearing if they hoped to fly out instead of walk. The GPS showed slightly over a mile to the landing zone. A mile was good as a foot, if they didn't start moving shortly.

He shut his eyes for a moment, concentrating on the

sounds of the jungle. Several seconds passed before Tucker recognized the quiet disturbance caused by people trying to move quietly. A lesser-experienced SEAL would even miss the sound. Boots weren't the greatest footwear for hiding movement. They make different sounds when crashing through grasses, running across sand, and scrambling up hills. Tucker heard the slight sounds of twigs breaking. Bushes sprung back as bodies passed—the noise told him the people making the noise were approaching. A grunt rode the wind for a moment. If he hadn't known the Legionnaires were there, he might have confused the man-made noise with one of the wild pigs in the area. He couldn't know for sure, but the cacophony of twigs breaking, bushes springing, and the occasional grunts caused him to estimate the number following to be at least twenty. There could be more, but twenty was more than enough to overrun Tucker and his team.

Tucker took a deep breath and started to switch the Carbine to automatic, but thought better of it because he still had to stand and expose himself; when he did, it meant crashing through the canopy of vines and leaves overhead. He'd be pissed with himself if the weapon discharged unexpectedly. Even more pissed if he accidentally shot himself. He'd never hear the end of it from his fellow SEALs, if he lived. If he didn't, he wouldn't be around to listen to their laughter, and the last thing he wanted was for his name to go down in history as a SEAL sea tale told during bouts of heavy drinking to entertain each other.

Estimating the distance to someone from you by sound only is extremely hard guesswork. It's even harder when those you're trying to locate are trying just as hard to hide their presence.

Once he crashed through the canopy above him, if the Legionnaires had night vision devices—and it would be a surprise if they didn't—they would see him. Maybe he'd just ease up through the canopy and take a looksee before jumping up and firing only to discover no one was there.

He intended to fire over their heads. Even when allies spied on each other, they didn't kill each other. So far, no deaths—and he wanted to keep it that way.

Tucker discounted the terrorists behind him. He knew from briefings at the ship that Abu Alhaul wasn't equipped with night vision devices. Here they were in the middle of the night in pitch-black jungle and the most valuable weapon in his arsenal was the night vision device. More valuable right now to him than knowing what weapons the two groups possessed. What he did know was that both the terrorists and the French were after his team. A team currently pinned between them. What he hoped was that neither the ambushers ahead nor the French coming up behind knew about the other. He eased through the bush overhead, using his left hand to push aside the foliage. His head broke through, and leaves and brush enveloped him, leaving only his shoulders and above exposed. He tugged his M-4 Carbine up until it cleared the brush.

Then he waited, glad he hadn't pulled a "John Wayne" and leaped up firing. It would have been more of a "Keystone Kops," if he had. The ambushers were still there, but he could see no sign of the French.

Each minute reduced their chances of making the rendezvous. Tucker was about to forego his plan, return to the others, and attempt to sneak by the terrorists. They must be terrorists. Terrorists would wait until the right opportunity to give their lives in pursuit of having their photograph plastered on some mud wall of a nondescript hut attesting to their martyrdom.

As he was beginning to ease himself back into the cover of the brush, an image of a pursuer flickered across his PVS. As if on cue, others quickly emerged into vision range. Tucker assessed those he saw, aware that their weapons were being held at the ready across their chests. He saw that none of the men had backpacks. That meant they didn't come prepared for a long chase, which meant if this ruse failed, there was a chance the Legionnaires would turn back. On the other hand, Tucker and the others had light backpacks, and with the exception of Brute, who carried the laser stuff, he and the others could discard theirs if they had to. They had an opportunity, if this worked, to outpace the Legionnaires, and with luck, the Legionnaires would take care of the terrorists. He believed they would stop anyway, if they engaged and killed what Tucker thought were terrorists. The Legionnaires would think the terrorists attacked the French airfield. Of course, eventually, the French would realize some of their technology was missing, but by then it would be too late.

He remained motionless, knowing his head would be easily visible to the French night vision devices, but moving it would bring immediate attention to him. His Carbine rested on top of the leaves surrounding him, pointed in the direction of the Legionnaires. Once the Legionnaires saw him, they would shoot. Legionnaires weren't known for warning their targets.

He wanted them to see him, but he didn't want them shooting him. Tucker figured the Legionnaires would also see the ambushers and presume Tucker was part of the group. That was what he wanted.

The lead Legionnaire held up his hand, fingers spread, and then he held the hand up again with two fingers. *Seven,* the man was telling those behind him.

Seven? Tucker's trigger finger tightened on the trigger. He casually lifted the Carbine without raising it so high that it separated from the bush. If the Legionnaire spotted the weapon, then shooting would start.

Seven? No way Tucker could have missed two. He wanted to turn his head and take his own count, but the lead Legionnaire pointed to the left side of the trail, marking the ambushers. Tucker counted with him. As the man pointed, Legionnaires began to melt into the surrounding brush. Tucker couldn't stay here long or they'd have him surrounded. How would the administration explain that when his lovely face appeared on television?

The hand continued moving, pointing out targets to his

fellow Legionnaires. No words passed between the officer in front and the Legionnaires spreading out to engage the threat. Then the finger pointed at Tucker, then continued left.

Left? There shouldn't be anyone to the left. He would have seen him.

He had no choice. Tucker turned. Where the Seabees were waiting, the upper torso of Brute broke the night vision landscape. He wanted to shout. Scream at the Seabee to get down. But it was too late. The finger of the Legionnaire pointed directly at Brute. Tucker saw the night vision device down over Brute's right eye.

"Jesus Christ! It's the Frogs!"

Tucker lifted his Carbine and fired a three-shot semi-automatic pattern over the heads of the Legionnaires on the trail. Numerous moving bodies broke the night vision pattern as more French troops dove for cover. "Get down!" he shouted, but Brute had already disappeared. Gunfire erupted behind, in front, and across the trail from him. The terrorists and the French were shooting at each other. *Time to get the hell out of here.* He looked toward the Legion one last time as he pulled himself down, aware of bullets hitting the bush around him. They were good. They were damn good. He caught a couple brief glimpses of Legionnaires, but the others had disappeared into the bush.

Firing continued to come from the terrorists ahead. That was good enough for Tucker.

Steady gunfire echoed through the jungle. Several times shouts in French seemed closer than Tucker would have liked. He was in the bush, nearly on all fours, working his way back to their hiding place. It mattered little if he made noise as he hurried back to the others. The bushes rustled with noise as the tempo of combat rose. An explosion behind him numbed his ears for a moment. Tucker wondered briefly if the French or the terrorists had used the grenade.

He broke into the clearing.

"What the hell are you still doing here?" he said angrily. "I told you when the shooting started—"

"The master chief—"

"My fault, sir. We heard people approaching and weren't sure if you heard them, too. Thought we'd better try to spot them and make sure—"

"Later," Tucker snapped. "Right now, we have three— maybe less—minutes to get back on the trail. Listen, because I'm only going to say this once. I'm leading, and when we hit the trail, I'm going to turn toward the clearing and I'm going to haul ass. If you want to ride back with me, then you better keep up. You hear?"

"Yes, sir," Master Chief Collins said.

"If we're lucky, there're nothing else between us and our ride out except jungle." Damn, he was pissed, even though he knew his anger should be directed at whatever asshole sent them into harm's way because of some political gambit.

"Let's go." Tucker ducked and drove into the brush. Behind him he heard the others following. He wasn't trying for quiet now, he was racing to gain separation and regain the trail. At the same time, they needed to keep low so their heat signature wouldn't be visible to the French. Firefights seldom lasted long. One side or the other would disengage, fall back, and either regroup or flee. Five minutes is what they teach in the schoolhouse. The average firefight is five minutes. It wouldn't be the French to fall back.

He glanced at his watch, nearly tripping in the process. Twenty minutes to cover about a mile. They could do it, if nothing else waited to impede them.

Someone to his right cried out in pain. Gunfire picked up in intensity. Like predators to a wounded animal, a cry of pain drew more gunfire in that direction. The few times he had been wounded, he had learned to bite back the urge to scream in pain. Keep it bottled up. Keep the knowledge you've been wounded to yourself.

The Legionnaires may make shorter work of those ambushers than Tucker needed. It wouldn't do to burst onto the trail to find themselves in the middle of a Legionnaire fire team. Scare the shit out of both of them. A limb whipped across his face, blinding him for a moment. He kept moving, blinking his eyes to clear them.

If these terrorists are any kind of terrorists they'll fight to the death. He'd shoot them himself if they didn't. All Tucker wanted from his unlikely ally in this firefight was for them to keep the French engaged for another few minutes. By then, he and his team would be on the trail and hauling ass eastward. He didn't want to discover the ambushers running alongside. How did that joke go about the two men stumbling across an enraged bear? One said to the other, "What do we do?" The other responded, "We run." "We'll never outrun that bear." "Don't have to. All I have to do is outrun you." All they had to do was outrun the terrorists if the ambushers decided to flee.

They were making an awful lot of noise when suddenly the gunfire slackened, then stopped. The terrorists or the Legionnaires may hear them, but it couldn't be helped. The sound of shouted French reached him. They were still back where he had seen the bulk of the column.

The French were shouting orders, and Tucker, who didn't speak French, figured the Legionnaires were maneuvering. Those who possess the maneuver advantage control the tempo—the pace of battle. They also control where the battle is fought, and, in the end, they achieve more combat successes than a superior-sized force.

Tucker turned left. Gunfire was behind and to their left. He had little choice. The trail was to their left too. The ambushers were amateurs compared to the French. But they had something. Whether that something was tenacity or stupidity, he didn't know. Sometimes there was little difference. *If the terrorists expect to live, they will break and run.* If they were smart, when Tucker fired the first salvo would have been an excellent indicator for amateurs to beat feet. Tucker had no way of knowing that those waiting in ambush believed they were fighting four or five Americans.

He broke through the bush, nearly falling onto the faint trail. He quickly regained his balance, turned right, and glanced just long enough to see Ricard fall onto the trail behind him. Brute nearly stepped on Ricard when he widened the access. They both looked at Tucker. Without a word, Tucker turned and started trotting down the trail. Behind him came the noise of the three Seabees as they ran to keep up with him. Gunfire erupted again for a few seconds.

Maybe he'd been too rough with them. All things considered, the Seabees had done well. He'd consider complimenting them, if they made the helo.

Once again, the sounds of gunfire broke the jungle. When, after a few seconds, it didn't stop, Tucker figured the terrorists and Legionnaires were engaged again. With every step, the gunfire faded. He didn't expect the firefight to last this long. He took time to glance at his watch and his GPS indicator. Fifteen minutes to pickup. They could expect the helicopter to wait a few minutes, to give them some margin of error. But, the helo wouldn't wait long, of that he was sure. Bennett's orders had been explicit. If Tucker and the Seabees weren't there within a minute— two at the most—after the helicopter landed, they'd have to hike home.

Tucker tripped on a vine, causing him to jump to keep from falling. He landed wrong, twisting his left knee slightly. A sharp jolt of pain ricocheted up his leg. This was his bad knee. Everyone has a bad knee, a bad arm, a bad eye—one of the many pairs of things on the human body that wasn't quite as good as its mate. He kept running, except now he nursed a slight limp with a sharp pain that rippled up his leg and across his back with each jarring step. *Hope it isn't that damn tendon again,* he thought.

"Come on, sir," Ricard gasped from behind him. "You okay?"

"Yep, I'm fine. I'm giving one of my legs a rest."

"Sure, you are, sir. We're all okay."

"Where are the others?" Tucker asked without turning around. He kept his eyes on the trail. He couldn't afford to trip again.

"They're right behind me, sir. I just outran the others."

A limb whipped back, caught the Seabee across the face. "Jesus!"

Tucker kept running. He glanced at the GPS. A quarter mile and ten minutes to make it. *Piece of cake.*

Overhanging brush and limbs pelted them as they ran. A jungle gauntlet was tearing at exposed skin, opening welts, and ripping their clothes, but they ran. Ahead was safety. Ahead was survival. Ahead was the promise of water, food, and rest. Vines entwined across the trail tripped them, caused them to stumble, and then they were up and running, moving forward, lured by the promise of safety ahead. Behind lay death, and death gave incentive to bodies unused to such physical exertion. Bodies that cried for their masters to slow down, take a break, take a breath; but still each foot moved in front of the other, and ahead of the three Seabees the lone Navy SEAL ran, urging them forward even with a limp that was slowing him down. Ricard muttered an obscenity.

Tucker heard the curse, but ignored it. The sound of feet running behind him was all the noise he wanted to hear. Several steps later, he realized Ricard had tried to drink water only to stumble and jam the canteen against his teeth.

He raised his head slightly, trying to hear the gunfire. It had disappeared, but he had no knowledge as to when it quit. It could have been right then or minutes ago. If any of the terrorists lived, they most likely were running pell-mell along the trail behind the four of them, unaware they were about to encounter the Americans. And behind the ambushers would be the French Foreign Legion, no longer concerned about stealth and guile.

Three bunches of people, all chasing someone or something ahead, and Tucker and his team the rabbit at the forefront. He only wanted to leap aboard a helicopter that maybe, just maybe, was already waiting for them. It would not be a pleasant experience if the CH-53 was late. In which case, he'd just keep running and hope the trail turned west and led to Liberia.

TUCKER BROKE THROUGH THE JUNGLE CURTAIN INTO THE clearing. His cammies were soaked, rivulets of sweat poured down his head and neck, forcing perspiration out of saturated undergarments further down his body. His boots felt as if they were full of water, his feet squishing with each step. He forcefully ignored the pain of the knee. Someone somewhere could always make it better, but it'd be hell trying to restore life if he gave in to the pain and got his ass shot.

Tucker ran thirty yards into the clearing before stopping. They were there. Ricard and Brute were close behind, but the master chief was nowhere in sight. He held up his hand.

"Where's the master chief?" he asked between gasps, continuing forward halfway between a walk and jog.

"He was right—"

Collins broke into the clearing. He waved. Tucker motioned him on. Even from here, tens of yards away, Tucker could hear the labored breathing of the master chief. Tucker turned and started running again. Not much further. He wanted to be in the center of the clearing, near enough the pickup point that when the helicopter touched down they could immediately leap aboard. As he looked around the clearing, it seemed to him the grasses that flowed like a fine carpet when they landed were laying haphazardly in different directions. Several large areas seemed flattened now. He didn't recall those areas when they landed.

He heard the noise of the rotors before he saw the CH-53. Moments like this in combat could bring tears to the eyes of the most seasoned veteran. This was the tenuous lifeline to home. It was the way out. It meant life until the next mission. It meant laying back, replenishing the body with water and food, and telling each other how brave they'd been. Sharing beers and basking in the excitement of the mission. It was the post-orgasm of combat.

He caught a glimpse of the darkened Super Stallion from the corner of his eye, turned his head, and there it was. Big, beautiful, and descending toward their location.

"Be ready to flip up the PVS, troops. He'll turn on his landing lights right before touchdown."

"Aye, sir," Ricard and Brute said in unison.

He glanced back. The master chief was behind them breathing heavily, bent over, his hands braced against the knees. He waved in acknowledgment to Tucker. *Damn good thing we don't have to go further,* he thought. *We'd have to carry the master chief or reduce the pace.* It's hard to increase speed across ground when you're outnumbered by pursuers. Tucker could have done it. He wasn't sure about Ricard or Brute, but they seemed in tiptop shape. The master chief would have been the linchpin if they had had to continue.

"Lift them, gents!" he shouted over the noise of the helicopter as it neared the ground. They all flipped their night vision up. The pilot must have seen them. The helo veered right, its nose aimed directly for them.

Gunfire joined the noise of the rotor. Tucker flipped the night vision device back down and looked north. Partially hidden by the descending helicopter, about thirty yards away, terrorists jumped up from where they had been hiding in the grasses and were firing at both the helo and at them.

"There!" Tucker shouted, pointing toward the attackers. He lowered his Carbine and fired. Ricard, Brute, and Collins moved alongside him, their guns quickly joining his. The landing lights of the helicopter came on. Tucker shut his eye, but knew it was too late. He should have listened to his own words, but he had to know who was shooting and where they were. The light blinded the attackers, also, who threw up their hands in a futile attempt to shield their eyes.

"ARGGGG!"

The cry startled Tucker, causing him to jerk his head to the right. It was Brute. The man was running, charging the terrorists. Brute's gun fired twice, hitting the African on the far right. The next three-volley round knocked the hat off the head of another terrorist who threw his gun down, turned, and started running toward the far tree line. A shot rang out, the man arched as if punched in the back.

"Scratch one for the good guys," Ricard said with a smile. He licked his finger and touched the far sight on the Carbine.

Brute was still screaming. *Arggg!* filled the area. The man turned slightly in his charge. Tucker couldn't shoot because the huge Seabee was in the way.

The helicopter lifted away. The lights blacked out.

Tucker opened his right eye, the vision device was still down. The heard the noise above them. The helo wasn't leaving the area. The pilots were probably watching the battle through their own night vision devices.

Brute reached the first African. He grabbed the soldier by the neck and lifted him in one sweeping motion. The man dropped his weapon. His feet kicking as he struggled against the grip. Tucker hadn't realized how gigantic the man's hands were. They were hands a proctologist would die for. Brute never ceased moving, the man turned toward the remaining terrorist, still holding the other one by the neck. The African brought his gun up. Several shots rang out, bright light arcing from the barrel. Tucker took off at a run, a chill in his stomach, moving obliquely to the right, trying to clear Brute from his aim. What the hell was he doing watching this one-man charge? Why wasn't he over there with him?

Footsteps beside him. Master Chief Collins had his Carbine pointed toward Brute, whose body blocked a full view of the remaining terrorist. Tucker saw the terrorist raise the gun again. At the same time, Brute brought the man in his grip around in front of him. Hands and legs jerked out from the side of Brute as bullets blasted into the human shield he had thrown up. And the Seabee never stopped running.

His *Arggg!* increased in intensity. Brute tossed the dying or dead man to the side as he reached the remaining terrorist. The giant stopped suddenly. The African was trying to swing his gun around again. Brute's right fist clipped the man under the chin. The African's gun went off, firing a burst into the ground before it fell from his hands. In the night vision device, Tucker watched small white specks shoot from the terrorist's mouth, followed by a long strand of what had to be a spurt of blood. The man fell. Brute stood over him, lifted both his arms, and screamed at the top of his lungs.

Tucker reached him. He waited a second and put his hand on the man's shoulder. "You all right?"

Brute's breathing came in rapid, quick gulps. He turned and nodded. "Yes, sir, but I ran out of bullets." Brute's hand rested flat on his right chest.

"Ran out of bullets?"

"Yes, sir. My magazine fell out, and that thing in my pack is sitting on top of my other magazines."

The sound of the helicopter descending caught their attention.

Ricard reached the two men. "Here, Brute. Here's your piece," he said, handing the M-4 Carbine to his fellow Seabee.

"Can you carry it for me? I'm kinda tired right now."

"Sure. No problem, bro."

The helicopter settled on the ground. The rotors never stopped. The flight engineer was leaning out of the open doors.

"Hurry up, y'all!" came a shout from the back of the helicopter.

More gunfire broke the night. From the trail, more terrorists were emerging. *Where in the hell are they coming from?* Tucker asked himself. He immediately answered the question with the realization that this group was the one that tried to ambush them. He fired several bursts toward the terrorists. They were easily a hundred yards away, and neither his nor their gunfire would be accurate. When bullets are in the air, you dive for cover.

"Go, go, go!" Tucker shouted at the three. Ricard and the master chief took off running toward the helo. Brute walked slowly to the open door and, using one hand, hoisted himself inside.

Gunfire stopped for only a few seconds before the ambushers started firing again. Tucker thought a bullet barely missed his ear—it seemed close. Had to be an accident; no one was that accurate with automatic weapons from that distance. Tucker fired another volley in the direction of the ambushers. Then he sprinted toward the open door of the helicopter. He leaped as the wheels of the helo left the ground. Hands grabbed his arms and pulled him inside.

The door slammed shut as the whooshing sound of the rotors increased and the helicopter tilted backward. It was up and moving. A bullet entered the back compartment, ripping along Ricard's leg before bouncing off the top of the compartment and rolling across the deck.

"Damn! I'm hit!"

"I think I am, too," Brute said, his voice barely audible over the noise of the helicopter.

The flight engineer stepped over Tucker. Tucker remained on the floor of the compartment. His knee burned with pain. A small compartment light, glowing red, came on.

The young flight engineer grabbed the first aid box off the bulkhead and tossed it to Master Chief Collins. "You take care of them," he said. "I have to be up front." He stepped over Tucker and disappeared into the darkness of the cockpit.

Flesh wound, Tucker thought, looking at Ricard's leg. Too much bitching and crying for it to be a serious wound. Anyone can live with a flesh wound. He should know, he had had enough of them. He looked at Brute.

A dark patch on the man's right side was growing. Tucker rolled over and scrambled to where the huge Seabee leaned against a row of web seats. Brute had his hand over the wound.

Tucker reached up and pulled the hand away. Bubbles appeared around the wound. "Brute, you've been shot."

The man nodded. "I figured it was something like that, sir," he said, his voice trailing off.

"Master Chief!" Tucker shouted. "Give me that kit."

"Sir, I need it for this—" Collins started, turning toward Tucker and Brute. He stopped talking when he saw Brute. "Jesus Christ! Here, Ricard. Press this over the wound!"

Brute's eyes shut, his head rolled to the side, and the huge body fell onto the deck of the pitching helicopter.

TUCKER ROLLED BRUTE'S HEAD BACK AND FORTH WITHOUT lifting it from the vibrating floor of the helo. Ricard was hunkered over Brute. His bandaged leg sticking out to the side.

Tucker thought, *Think yourself lucky Ricard; it could have been your balls.*

A moan came from Brute. *He'll live. He'll be laid up for a while recovering, but he'll live. I have seen worse wounded up and walking days after the doctors finished with them.*

While Brute moaned, Ricard rapid-fired to everyone how much pain he was in.

Master Chief Collins had pulled himself into one of the web seats, strapped in, and was chugging a water bottle. Tucker draped an arm over his eyes and rested. Somewhere, someone should be happy. He looked up on the web seat. Brute's backpack with the laser device leaned against the bulkhead, bouncing slightly with the jarring of the helicopter. He hoped the jarring didn't damage the item, but then again, that wasn't his problem. The mission they had assigned his team had been done. The French may later suspect them, but the presence of those terrorists would deflect suspicion from them.

He rested his head on the deck and started his breathing exercises to relax his body. Maybe the leg would quit aching by the time they recovered on the *Mesa Verde*.

Yep, somewhere, someone is happy and taking great credit for this fantastic idea.

CHAPTER 13

THE DOOR OPENED TO CAPTAIN XAVIER BENNETT'S IN-PORT cabin. Commander Harrison stepped out into the passageway. His eyes met Fulbright's. He nodded, his eyes slightly moist, and without a word stepped by her and Lieutenant Commander Tom Kilpatrick, the ship's JAG.

"Come in, XO!" Bennett shouted from where he sat. He leaned over and picked up the cloth napkin that had fallen from his lap onto the deck when he had stood to shake Harrison's hand.

The two stepped inside the in-port cabin as he wiped his lips. "Shut the door," he said, quietly. Many things in the Navy make life exciting—adventurous even—but along with anything good, there is an equal and less enjoyable counterpart. He just did one of them.

He tossed the napkin onto his plate and stood up. Pushing the dishes together, Bennett quickly stacked them. He set the first stack on the nearby food cart. Fulbright and Kilpatrick shifted forward and removed the remainder. No one spoke. These weren't moments for idle conversation. Combat pulled more nonsensical conversation than a lunch where a professional Navy officer's career had been jerked from him because of stupidity.

"Thanks," Bennett said. He lifted the silver plated coffee urn from the tray and held it toward them briefly before pouring himself a cup. "Want some?"

"Yes, sir, that would be fine," Fulbright said, taking the urn from him.

Bennett sat down and motioned the two officers to join him.

"It's done," he said. "It wasn't nice, but he knew it was coming. In a way, I think he was grateful for the honorable way out that was offered to him. Next time remind me not to do something like this over lunch. I realized halfway through that he would always think of this moment like a condemned man recalls his last meal."

"I take it I can tear up the court martial papers?" Kilpatrick asked.

Bennett nodded. "For the time being, we won't need them. He accepted my strong suggestion that he take his twenty-one years of active Navy service and retire. This way, I pointed out, he would have a pension for his family."

"How did he take it?"

"I think he expected me to relieve him. I suspect he was surprised at first when I didn't call you in, Tom, to make sure he knew his rights, and inform him to stand by for a court martial. As it is, voluntarily, he will ask to be relieved by fifteen hundred this afternoon." Xavier glanced at the clock on the bulkhead. "About three hours from now."

"I had him sign the document attesting he understood his rights, sir, before the investigation ever started."

Xavier nodded. "I know, Tom."

"Who's going to take his place?"

"You are, Ellen. Commander Harrison is going to relieve his XO before he requests to be relieved himself. He did recommend, and I accepted, that his operations officer, Lieutenant Kincaid, would fleet up to executive officer. Kincaid comes from a long line of Navy families. I knew his father."

"Aye, sir. When do I shift my stuff to the *Churchill?*"

"Later today. Plan for around dinner—between six and eight tonight. That should give him and the current XO, a Lieutenant Commander Richman, time to pack their seabags and report to the *Mesa Verde.*"

Fulbright refilled her cup, leaned left, and did the same for Kilpatrick. "They going to be staying with us long?" She set the urn down on the table.

Bennett shook his head. "Nope." He looked up at her. "Arrange for one of our helicopters to take them to Monrovia this afternoon."

"That should do it then, Skipper," Fulbright replied. She lifted the cup and held it lightly between both hands. "There's the early morning Air Force C-141 they can catch to the states."

Xavier nodded. It is never easy to deliver bad news, but it's doubly so when you're the reason for it. The lunch had been awkward for Harrison. The officer knew why he was here, but Xavier observed the niceties of lunch, discussing the incident informally after reminding the officer that he had had his rights read to him a while back. Harrison had sighed as if resigned to the fate he knew was coming his way.

Afterward, Xavier had told the commanding officer of the Arleigh Burke–class destroyer that there were several things working, and none of them looked good for Harrison. The initial investigation was complete and now the legal beagles would bubble to the top and start tearing it apart looking for loopholes to close and charges to bring. He opined to the shorter man sitting across the table from him that it would be another couple of months before that portion of the investigation was complete. Xavier noticed that the faint discoloration on the man's left cheek had turned a deep red. Harrison started to pick up the glass of water in front of him but quickly put it down when his nervous hand shook the glass, causing of the water to spill slightly over the top.

Bennett had looked away at the time, uncomfortable in

the presence of the man's fear. Someday—not now nor in the near future—Harrison would recall this moment and it would pass quickly through his thoughts to be discarded as one of life's moments; or would he forever remember this as some sort of last meal of the condemned?

On a positive note, Harrison had stepped up to the plate, acknowledged his responsibility for whatever happened on the *Winston Churchill* during the alleged lock-on of the ship's Anti-Air Warfare radar to the French maritime reconnaissance aircraft. The admission failed to earn any respect from Xavier, though, because every Navy officer knew that whether good or bad, intentionally or not, onboard or off the ship—it didn't matter: the commanding officer of a Navy vessel was always responsible for whatever happened on board his or her ship, and to state the obvious didn't change Xavier's opinion of the man earned over the two months the ships had sailed together.

But, Harrison was someone's golden boy, as evidenced by the Navy reaching down below the promotion zones and pulling him up to the next pay grade. If it hadn't been for this dumb error that may have cost the lives of those pilots, Harrison would have someday been wearing the stars of an admiral. Too bad. The Navy tolerates minor mistakes in learning the art of command, but some, such as this, are the kiss of death and the culprit might as well pack up, go home, hang up the uniform, and find a job cooking hamburgers.

"He seemed to have handled it well," Fulbright offered. She set her cup on the table and ran her hand across the soiled white tablecloth to get a few drops of coffee off her hand.

"Sir, are you going to call Admiral Holman?" Kilpatrick asked.

"Why do you ask, Tom?"

"Well, Captain, the legal officer at Commander, Amphibious Group Two asked me to call him once a decision was made, and I didn't want to call him and have him tell Admiral Holman—"

Bennett held up his hand and smiled weakly. "Tom, is this some sort of lawyerly thing where periods, commas, and breaths aren't taken when talking?"

"Sir?"

Bennett saw the look of confusion on his legal officer's face. "Sorry, Tom. Trying to lift the spirits in the compartment."

"Oh," Kilpatrick replied, his eyebrows arching deeper. "My spirits are fine, sir."

"Well, that makes at least one of us here. As for your question; no, I haven't called Admiral Holman yet. I will probably do it after we finish here. After I've talked with him, then you can start discussions with his legal department."

"So, what was the final decision, Captain?" Fulbright asked.

He shrugged his shoulders slightly. "Just what I said and nothing else. When Commander Harrison returns to *Mesa Verde* this afternoon, he will bring a request for immediate retirement. Tom," Xavier said, nodding toward the lawyer, "I need a note for him to sign promising on pain of court martial a promise he will never, ever speak of the incident on the *Churchill*."

Kilpatrick nodded. "Sir, I can do that, but time and higher authorities have in the past ignored such a document. Look at the USS *Liberty* back in 1967."

"I know, Tom, but I want to impress upon him as much as possible that the incident is classified and as such must be protected for the good of the country."

"What if—"

"Tom! Stop that," Xavier interrupted abruptly. "I hate 'what ifs.' He'll sign it. He'll sign anything right now." He pushed his chair back. "That's it. Ellen, go pack your bags and tell the Engineering officer he's the acting XO until you return."

They stood as Xavier stood.

"How long will I be on the *Churchill,* sir?"

Xavier shook his head. "I wouldn't suspect too long,

Ellen. I'm sure Admiral Holman already has someone standing in the wings with his or her seabag packed ready to take the next aircraft out here. I would be very surprised if he didn't." He walked over to the door and grabbed the knob. "The officers and sailors aboard the *Churchill* are what's important now. When something like this happens, it casts a dark cloud across the crew of a ship; a cloud that must be lifted as soon as possible." He opened the door for them. "Whoever Admiral Holman sends will be someone who has already had command and can take over for the months needed to divert or direct a new commanding officer to the destroyer."

He bit his upper lip for a moment, then looked at them. "I think as I get older and realize how much evil there is out there, the more emotional I become when good wins. When freedom to follow one's heart and mind is not dictated by the narrow constraints of zealots and cults. I may be in the minority, but I don't think the French are the adversary some of our fellow Americans believe. We make the French nervous with our might, which is too bad, because the real threat to both of our nations lies in the Jihadists who kill for no other reason than their arrogance."

He shut the door behind them. Moments latter he was speaking with Admiral Holman, who had been pacing the deck in his office at Amphibious Group Two—an office that would be Xavier's next summer.

"DUNCAN; DICK HOLMAN HERE, SHIPMATE," HOLMAN SAID when Admiral James answered the telephone.

"Okay, Dick. What's the story?"

"I wanted to bring you up to date on Tucker and the Seabee SEALs."

"Don't call the Seabees SEALs, Dick."

He laughed. "Look, Duncan, you had to declare Tucker a non-SEAL for this mission."

"I know, and it wasn't comfortable. Nothing about this mission has been comfortable. I have a message on my desk reassigning Commander Raleigh back to Washington in a SEAL billet. I was going to bring him back to Washington and let him do some admin shit for me for a while. The man needs a break, but he turned me down. Said he'd finish the mission he was sent to do; train the new Liberian Army."

"Doesn't surprise me. Somewhere deep down inside everyone of you snake eaters is—"

"Don't say it, Dick. We're as normal as any other Navy officer."

"If you say so, but I think you and your folk are the only ones who believe that. As for your ex-SEAL, Commander Tucker Raleigh, I expect to have his report on my desk later today."

"Wait a minute, Dick."

A few seconds passed before Rear Admiral Duncan James spoke again. "There! He's no longer an *ex*-SEAL. I've signed the papers returning him to full duty, so quit calling him an ex-SEAL."

Dick Holman chuckled.

"How about that asshole on the destroyer who started all this crap?" James interrupted.

"As I was saying, before you so rudely interrupted," Holman said humorously. "I will fax or email you a copy of the report as soon as I get it. As for the skipper, he has decided to retire and go off to some farm in Iowa."

"Iowa?"

"Well, some farm somewhere, I presume. That's what all fired Navy officers do. They go back to the land."

"And where in the hell does it say that, Dick? Is it some sort of Naval Academy lore that you have to become a farmer if you fail at sea?"

"Shouldn't be doing this, you know. Personally, if I'd had my way we would have court martialed the son of a bitch instead of letting him get off so easy."

"Someday, sometime, someone will discover all this, Dick."

"And they'll make millions exposing what will be

called a cover-up. And you can bet your bottom dollar it'll be us assholes in uniform who'll be blamed for it." James let out a deep breath on the other end.

"But, we have seen our duty and done it. It may not be something we enjoyed doing, knowing it could have blown up in our faces, but we did it, and thanks to Raleigh, it was a success."

James chuckled. "Yeah, a better success than we thought. According to the Daily Read board, the French have attributed an attack on one of their bases in the Ivory Coast to the African National Army we keep reading about, but no one seems to know anything."

"That's strange, too. According to Commander Raleigh and the debrief of the other three, they did have French Legionnaires chasing them, but were ambushed by Abu Alhaul terrorists."

"Could be, Dick. Maybe we'll know more later. So, what now?"

"Well, I have a full Expeditionary Strike Group approaching Liberia along the coast. They should arrive in the next few days. That will give me—"

"Two full SEAL teams."

"Yeah, but kind of late now. I still have the VQ-2 EP-3E reconnaissance aircraft in Monrovia. So, we're going to do some fleet reconnaissance missions to see if we can locate any Abu Alhaul elements first, and second, find out more about this growing African National Army. So far, the ANA hasn't done anything in Liberia, but they've been active all along the borders, including our French friends' Ivory Coast. What my intelligence officer tells me is that the ANA is as much an enemy of Abu Alhaul as we are. After all, this General Ojo, as he calls himself, freed some of our missionaries."

"He had them and let them go," James said, his voice low. "What a pity. *Missionaries*. Just what we need in America, more religious zealots."

"Ah, what a shame!"

"Oh, go screw yourself."

"That only happens when I've been to sea six months or longer."

"HALFPENNY" BAINES THREW DOWN THE CLIPBOARD. HE knew his face was turning red. It always did when he was pissed off, embarrassed, or frustrated; and right now, it was a combination of all three. He looked up at his director of the Joint Staff, Lieutenant General Winifred Hulley. "I should be happy, shouldn't I?" he nearly shouted. "Everything went well. The team brought back something that may be part of the French laser weapon, and the French are blaming the African National Army for attacking their airfield and blowing up the aircraft. Of course, as soon as they realize a piece of sensitive equipment is missing, they won't be thinking that."

"Yes, sir," Hulley said, his jowls bouncing with each word, his face expressionless. "I know I'm happy about it," he said unconvincingly. "I'm sure across the Potomac they're happy about it," he added in his monotone voice.

"Then, why don't you think I'm happy?"

Hulley shrugged. "Didn't get to kill anyone?"

"If I didn't know for a fact that you had no sense of humor, I might think you just tried to pull a joke."

"No, sir. Never would do that," Hulley said, a slight twinkle in his eyes. "What now, Chairman?"

Halfpenny braced his elbows on his desk and clasped his hands under his chin. He bit his lower lip as he stared at Hulley, who was standing in front of the desk. Finally, he took a deep breath and put his hands on the table. "Not a goddamn thing, Mr. Director. We can't court martial the skipper who was responsible for the deaths of four"— he held up four fingers—"Air Force pilots—one of whom is the son of an Academy classmate of mine. We can't tell anyone of our success in reclaiming our own technology because we can't let anyone know we ever lost it."

Hulley reached forward and lifted the clipboard. "Let me take this and make sure it's filed where you'll never have to see it again, sir."

Halfpenny stood. "There ought to be some way we can recognize this Navy Commander . . ."

"Raleigh, sir."

"Raleigh," Halfpenny finished, the anger gone from his voice. He chuckled. "That must have been something, using Seabees for a special operation such as this. You know, Win, the Navy may have more SEAL-type ops than they like to admit."

"Like their—"

"Yes, just like their claim of having only ten aircraft carriers. But those flattops they call amphibious ships carry more Harrier fighters than most other countries' *aircraft carriers* are capable of carrying." He came around the table, leaned back against the desk, and crossed his arms. "You know something, my fine Army friend, you gotta watch the Navy. If they had their way, they'd be in charge of the Space program also."

"The important thing is we regained the laser component, Chairman."

Halfpenny Baines nodded. "You know what we're witnessing, Win?"

"No, sir."

"In every era of human history, there is one weapon that determines an army's power and when that weapon rests with an adversary, only overwhelming might complemented with an overwhelming countermeasure will give you even a chance of victory."

Hulley agreed. "If a single weapon can clear the skies of fighter aircraft—"

"Then we may be witnessing the transformation from the information age to the age of physics warfare." He uncrossed his arms and pointed at the director. "We're even looking at particle beams as a ground weapon for our soldiers. Now, you tell me, Mr. Director, what is the impact of weapons of such profound battle damage; of weapons that can remove whole armies, navies, and air forces from the skies, on us old timers who are grounded in the physical components of what we think is modern warfare? It means we've come full circle."

"Full circle?"

"Full circle. In the early age of warfare, it was the ground pounder, the infantryman, who determined victory by taking an enemy's land. It was muddy boots slugging through the fog of battle, marching to the sound of gunfire. Then, we reached this technological era where information combined with military strength and operational superiority allowed us to win battles and wars with minimum casualties. Now, we're going to be faced in the next few years with weapons that exponentially use physics to defeat military strength and overcome operational superiority. How will we defeat those types of weapons that render our hardware— our weapons—meaningless? We'll have to defeat them by returning to the individual soldier." Halfpenny Baines pushed himself away from his desk and walked to the window overlooking North Parking. "Director, I'll talk with the Vice Chairman when he returns from Europe. Meanwhile, I want to put this question to our think tanks and to our best and brightest. How do we defeat weapons in the Age of Physics? What should be our strategy for national security? If ever there was an argument for transforming something other than North Parking, this is it."

The conversation passed on to several other Joint issues, including the war in Indonesia and a staff morale issue in one of the directorates. Twenty minutes passed before Hulley tucked the metal clipboard under his arm.

"Sir, I'll take care of those issues." He reached over and tapped the board. "About the mission, sir. Are you going to call across the Potomac and tell them?"

"I did, just before you came through the door. I put out a feeler to SecDef's office to see if he wanted to do it, but got a run around about their failing to fully understand what

I was talking about. How about that, Win. A fully successful mission no one wants to take credit for. What is our political leadership coming to?"

Hulley nodded. "You talk with our NSC friend, Ms. Alice Chatelain-Malpass?" he asked with irony.

"I did, and you want to know what she said?"

"If the Chairman wouldn't mind."

Halfpenny shook his head and laughed. "She told me she had no idea what I was talking about. She thanked me for calling, and assured me that we had never met, but she had heard a lot of nice things about me."

"Amazing how selective political appointees' memories are."

"They're definitely in a profession that would benefit from higher unemployment."

"At least we still have the Tank schedule that shows she was here."

"Not really, General. I thought about that a couple of days ago. I thought if the mission went to shit, what did we have that the inevitable congressional inquiry would want? The schedule was one. It doesn't reflect her by name nor as coming from the National Security Council. Just identifies someone from the administration receiving a brief on the current war in Indonesia."

"Who changed it?"

"No one did. Our administrative types enter attendees by their own identification. Apparently, she or her office just identified her as a staff representative coming here to receive a war brief. Never occurred—"

Baines waved him away. "Never mind, Win. Just get on with the tasks at hand and figure out a way to recognize Commander Raleigh and his Seabees without giving away the covert nature of the mission."

ALICE CHATELAIN-MALPASS GRINNED AS SHE GENTLY LAID the receiver back in the cradle. Conscientiously, she glanced at the digital readout to ensure the telephone was no longer securely connected to General Baines. Humming, she moved through the crowded spaces of the National Security Council, mumbling greetings to a couple of staffers who had just returned from the Hill. They were scheduled to debrief her later in the day.

She stopped at the Ladies' on the way down the hallway. Afterwards, she stood in front of the mirror and straightened her full-length dress so the seams rode down the sides of her body. She pulled up her pantyhose to tighten it against her legs. She wiggled her toes and looked down at her brown business shoes, made in America; she wouldn't have it any other way. The shoelaces fell over the top two eyes on both shoes. She opened her purse, pulled out a comb, and touched up the bangs across her forehead. Then she ran her hand over her ponytail, tightening the band, and flipping the hair up so it spread out, so it'd bounce when she walked into the head of the National Security Advisor's office and told him the good news. Satisfied she looked her best, she took a deep breath and exited the bathroom. Exactly ten steps later, she entered the outer office of her boss. Within the NSC, only he and she knew about the mission.

Alice Chatelain-Malpass was ushered into the man's office. Ten minutes later, she left, her mouth still open, feeling tears fighting to free themselves of her willpower. The man had thrown her out of his office. Told her he had no idea what she was talking about, but thanked her for telling him whatever it was the Defense Department had done. Furthermore he assured her that it had nothing whatsoever to do with him and, if by her words, she thought otherwise, she'd be wise to keep quiet and never mention this again. Especially if she enjoyed the job she had and the authority he entrusted to her in protecting our great nation.

She went back to her desk and sat down. For a long time she stared at the computer screen in front of her. Periodically a new email shifted the screen upward, boldfaced to remind her it hadn't been read. After a while, she pulled a 3.5-inch disc from her desk drawer and inserted it. Then, she began to download the information on this mission.

The mission had been a success. It had recovered the laser technology. It had blown up the aircraft, and it had managed to focus the blame on this African National Army; but successful missions have a way of going awry, if not immediately, then years from now. She raised her upper arms slightly, appalled to discover her armpits damp with a slight spreading stain beneath each arm.

Someday, someone would be searching for a fall guy on a mission that never was, and it sure as hell wasn't going to be Alice Chatelain-Malpass. She knew the Joint Staff could point at her; the navy could raise its finger in her direction; and, sitting down in Norfolk was that fat little Admiral whom she had instantly disliked at the Pentagon. She didn't know why she disliked him, but it mattered little to her why she did. Alice Chatelain-Malpass didn't need a reason to dislike someone, just because she disliked them was reason enough. She had worked too many years to reach this pinnacle in her political career. She glanced through the glass walls of her small office, watching to make sure no one was headed in her direction while she made copies. She took her time. For each item she called up from the archives of the server or within her own computer, she erased every classification, including individual paragraph classifications. She even removed the 'unclassified' classifications. Alice Chatelain-Malpass didn't get where she was today by being someone's patsy and she wasn't going to wake up tomorrow and find her name in the headlines of *The Washington Post*. If nothing ever happened, then this insurance would never be needed. She smiled as she downloaded the notes from the three meetings they had had on this one subject. The notes identified who was there, who made what comments, and the positions taken on the proposed mission that never was. The smile turned into a smirk as she read the one comment about making sure that if Special Forces were used, they had to be released from the Special Forces, because under the new Department of Defense guidelines approved by

Congress, only the President could authorize the use of Special Forces such as Navy SEALs.

The slight knock on her door startled her. She glanced at the door and then back at the computer. She glanced at her clock. It was the two from the Hill with their scheduled debrief. She was copying the last document on the fourth 3.5-inch disc. She could have copied all of them on a CD, but after the arrest of the spy in Arlington, periodic security inspections of CDs were occurring with more frequency.

"Come in," she said, popping the disc out.

The door opened. She looked at the clock on the wall. "It's already four o'clock?"

"Time flies fast when you're having fun," the young man said.

She popped the disc in a separate protective cover as she asked them to sit down. Alice Chatelain-Malpass was ready for whatever the future brought. She smiled. Minutes into the debriefing about the meeting, the two staffers saw Alice Chatelain-Malpass as her usual acidic self, full of questions, full of directions, and full of the first person pronoun.

Captain David E. Meadows, U.S. Navy, was recognized by *Writer's Digest* magazine as one of its twelve "First Success" authors for 2001 and profiled in the *Writer's Digest Guide to Writing, Fiction* (Fall 2001) yearbook. Captain Meadows is still on active duty serving as Deputy Commander, Naval Security Group Command.

FROM THE AUTHOR OF
THE SIXTH FLEET

DAVID E. MEADOWS

JOINT TASK FORCE:
LIBERIA

0-425-19206-7

A "VISIONARY" (JOE BUFF) IN THE
WORLD OF MILITARY FICTION,
PENTAGON STAFF MEMBER AND U.S. NAVY
CAPTAIN DAVID E. MEADOWS
PRESENTS A BOLD NEW SERIES THAT TAKES
AMERICA INTO THE NEXT ERA OF
MODERN WARFARE.

"ON PAR WITH TOM CLANCY."
—MILOS STANKOVIC

B135

DAVID E. MEADOWS

JOINT TASK FORCE:
AMERICA

Terrorist Abu Alhaul is bringing mass
destruction to America's east coast.
Alhaul says he is retaliating for the death of
his family, which he blames on one man:
U.S. Navy SEAL Commander Tucker Raleigh.

0-425-19482-5

"David Meadows is the real thing."
—Stephen Coonts

The SIXTH FLEET series
by David E. Meadows

★★★★★

The Sixth Fleet
0–425–18009–3

The Sixth Fleet #2: Seawolf
0–425–17249–X

The Sixth Fleet #3: Tomcat
0–425–18379–3

The Sixth Fleet #4: Cobra
0–425–18518–4

★★★★★

**Available wherever books are sold or at
www.penguin.com**

B032

P9-CAY-675

Thayer Memorial Library

P.O. Box 5 ❖ 717 Main Street ❖ Lancaster, Massachusetts 01523 ❖ (978)368-8928 ❖ Fax (978)368-8929

DONATION

Spencer Hill Press

Contact: Spence City, an imprint of Spencer Hill Press, PO Box 247, Contoocook, NH 03229, USA

Please visit our website at www.spencecity.com

First Edition: June 2013.
Jennifer Allis Provost
Copper Girl: a novel / by Jennifer Allis Provost – 1st ed.
p. cm.
Summary:
After a life spent avoiding magic, Sara finds herself pulled into the Otherworld and involved with a silver elf.

Cover design by Lisa Amowitz
Interior layout by Marie Romero

978-1-939392-02-2 (paperback)
978-1-939392-03-09 (e-book)

Printed in the United States of America

COPPER

GIRL

JENNIFER ALLIS PROVOST

SPENCE CITY

For those who never stopped believing in magic

chapter 1

It seemed like a good idea at the time.

My office, like most modern offices, cranked the air conditioning down to Arctic proportions during the summer months. Consequently, we workers arrived in the morning dressed in sandals and sleeveless tops, donned heavy sweaters upon reaching our desks, and ended up shivering by noon. Ironically, when our workday ended we were hit by a wall of oppressive heat the moment we stepped outside the main doors. No, this wasn't a flawed system in the slightest.

That day, I wasn't having it. I had the grand idea of spending my lunch hour outside, away from the icy wind stiffening my fingers and chilling my neck. After I unwound myself from the afghan I kept in my desk (and only used in the summer months), I gathered up my lunch and my phone and headed out for an impromptu picnic in my car.

What I hadn't considered was that the office runs the air conditioning so cold because it was, well, *hot* outside. Very hot, in fact. So hot that the cheese was melting in my sandwich and the lettuce looked like something that had washed ashore months, maybe even years, ago. I was parked in the shade and had taken down my car's convertible top, but I still couldn't manage to get comfortable. I'd already shed my sandals and cardigan, which left me wearing my sundress and…

Dare I?

I glanced around the parking lot of Real Estate Evaluation Services, the 'go-to firm for all your commercial real estate needs', according to the brochures. No one, human or drone, was taking a noontime stroll, and, by virtue of my being on the far side of the lot, no cars were near mine. Most of my coworkers didn't even have cars, so the lot was rarely more than half-full. What was more, from where I sat, I couldn't even see the office.

I dared.

I took a deep breath and channeled my inner wild woman, then leaned the seat back and slipped off my panties. Removing that small bit of cotton made an incredible difference, and the heat became somewhat bearable. Enjoyable, even. Was that a breeze?

Ignoring my decrepit sandwich, I fully reclined the seat, set the alarm on my phone, and closed my eyes. A nap. Now *that* would make today bearable.

Suddenly, he is there.

Here.

Kissing me, holding me.

I know I'm dreaming, because he's perfect. His lips are soft but insistent, his hands gentle. I glide my fingers across his back, feeling thick cords of muscle, before sinking my fingers into his hair. It's superfine, like cobwebs, and when I crack an eyelid, I learn that it's silver. Not gray or white, but the elegant hue of antique candlesticks and fine flatware. Cool.

I squeeze my eyes shut again, not wanting the dream to end any sooner than it has to. He kisses me once more, and I can't help melting against him. His hand travels up my leg, up past my hip... shit! No panties!

I try twisting away, but he already knows. I feel his mouth stretch into a smile, and he moves to nuzzle my neck. "What's your name?" he murmurs.

"Sara," I reply. "Yours?"

"Micah." By now, his hands have traveled to my waist, and he slides one around to stroke the small of my back. "Why did you summon me, Sara?"

"I didn't," I protest. "I don't know how." I would say more, but he nibbles a trail from my neck to my shoulder, and pushes my dress to the side. As for me, I let him.

Micah raises his head, and I get a good look at him for the first time. His eyes are large and dark gray, like thunderheads, his features chiseled into warm caramel skin, and his unruly mop of silver hair seems to float around his head. He wears an odd, buff-colored leather shirt, made all the odder in this heat, and matching leather pants and boots. Boots?

"You did summon me," he insists. "My Sara, you must tell me why."

"Does it matter?" I ask. I pull him back to me, kissing him with all the passion I've never felt with anyone during my waking hours. Micah kisses me back, fingers deftly unbuttoning my dress while his other hand rubs my lower back. I've never felt so free, so alive as I do in Micah's embrace, and I have no intention of rushing this. None at all.

My phone screamed for attention, thus ending the best dream that had ever been dreamed. Ever. I fumbled to silence it, then shook myself back to reality. I still felt warm and glowy from the dream, almost after-glowy. It wasn't until I stretched and got tangled in my clothing that I noticed anything was amiss.

The straps of my dress had slid down around my elbows, and the dress itself was unbuttoned to my waist. What's more, my bra was all askew and a nipple was dangerously close to freedom. I shot a quick glance around the parking lot as I fixed my clothing; luckily, there was no one around, either of the human or robotic drone persuasion. I hoped no one had gotten an eyeful of how I was apparently fondling myself in my sleep.

Some dream. Soon enough, I got the top half of my dress squared away and reached into the passenger seat, only to come up empty. My panties were gone.

Great. Either one of my coworkers had found me sleeping and stolen them, or a randy squirrel had absconded with my delicates. Hoping for the latter, I stuffed my feet back into my sandals and returned to the office and my ever-growing mountain of paperwork.

Speaking of the mountain, there was a fresh sheaf of reports on my desk, ready for sorting. My title, if it can be called that, is Quarterly Report Collator.

This impressive moniker meant that I had the ability—no, make that the responsibility—to place various documents and reports in their proper order, usually alphabetically. I've even been known to utilize ascending numbers when the occasion warrants, a feat those who got paid far more than I did could not seem to manage. As long as they kept paying me, I was fine with my place on the food chain, low though it was. It sure beat the alternative—a luxurious but caged life as a sellout government shill, performing spells on command as if they were parlor tricks. My family might have lost much, but we still have some pride left.

I dove right into the heap of reports, for once appreciating the mindless work since it gave me the mental space to dwell on my dream lover. Why would a man in my dream claim that I'd summoned him? And what was with his getup? Micah had looked like he should be playing the part of a swashbuckling hero in a trashy romance novel, not hanging around in the parking lot of a midsized corporation specializing in commercial real estate acquisitions and liquidations.

And his name: Micah. I was certain that I'd never heard it before, which puzzled me. If I were going to create a dream lover, wouldn't I give him a regular name like Tom or Joe? A name I was at least familiar with?

I swiveled in my chair and called up my search engine. We are not, under any circumstances, supposed to use this bit of technology that is standard issue with each and every one of our ergonomically correct workstations. I'm not quite sure what the punishment for internet usage is, but I've always imagined ninjas dropping out of the ceiling and hauling me off to their lair. After enduring a mild torture session, I'd be given a cup of hot sake and sent on my way.

I could have waited until I got home. I have a nicer computer and better, faster internet access than the office does, but I couldn't wait. Not while the image of Micah's thundercloud eyes still burned in my memory, inciting not-safe-for-work thoughts.

I typed in *Micah: define,* and the results page immediately listed a bunch of Biblical references. Mmm, not exactly helpful. I clicked around for a while until I found one of those sites that specialized in the meaning of names. It read thusly:

Micah (mī ' kə) he who resembles God.

Huh. My dream man was certainly attractive, but I didn't know if I'd go so far as to call him a god. Then I remembered that there was a type of stone called mica, which also seemed like an unlikely source for me to pull a name from. In the midst of typing *mica: stone*, I was interrupted.

"Hey, beautiful."

I glanced up and saw Floyd, the office sleaze, hovering at the edge of my cubicle. Better and better. I clicked off the browser and nonchalantly swiveled away from the keyboard. To throw the ninjas off my trail, of course. "You and Juliana heading over to The Room tonight?" he asked.

The Room is a local hangout, stocked with stale beer and watered-down liquor, not to mention a floor that has never, ever been mopped. Not. Even. Once. But it's cheap and close to the office, so we all go. Since I started working at REES, I've been a regular. "We haven't discussed it."

"Everyone's going," Floyd pressed. "C'mon, I'll buy you a drink. You like gin and tonic, right?"

I heaved the stack of reports from my lap to my desk and uncrossed my legs, squarely planting my feet in order to deliver the Keep Away From Me speech to Floyd yet again, when I remembered my lack of undergarments. Quickly, I snatched my afghan from where I'd tossed it before lunch and spread it across my lower body like a shield.

"Whatever," I mumbled, which Floyd counted as a victory.

"See you there," he drawled. *I hate him.*

I spent the rest of my shift with my thighs clamped together, having mild anxiety attacks whenever I stood. Or sat. Or reached for anything. Needless to say, by the end of the day I was more than ready for something eye-wateringly alcoholic. Juliana, my best friend and REES's office manager, was game, as she usually was, and we made it to The Room in time for happy hour. Normally, I feel like I'm in her shadow, what with her long, dark hair, matching eyes, and the body of a pre-war pinup girl, but tonight I didn't care. Right about now, a little overshadowing was just what the doctor ordered.

After a few bowls of pretzels, and more than a few cocktails, I confessed my *al fresco* state, to which Juliana and I clinked glasses and downed a few shots in honor of my missing panties. Floyd, the scum, welshed on his promise of gin and tonic. *I really do hate him.*

chapter 2

Happy hour turned into last call, and Juliana gladly accepted my offer of crashing on my couch. We were forever staying over at one another's apartments, since we lived on opposite sides of town. Not to mention that Juliana didn't own a car and public transportation was both expensive and unreliable. If you counted on the bus schedule, you might get caught out after curfew, and the Peacekeepers, our friendly neighborhood law enforcement goons, weren't known for their understanding natures. Since neither Juliana nor I wanted to pay the late penalty, whoever's place was closer to the side of town we ended up on invariably became our resting place for the evening. Since I lived closest to The Room, I played hostess more often.

While Juliana settled herself on the couch, I grabbed a quick shower, only to end up standing before my closet, dripping wet, overthinking what I would wear to bed. Like it mattered, right? Normally, I'm a tank top and shorts girl, but there was this cute, just sexy enough nightie that hung out in the back of my closet. Pale lavender silk, I'd bought it almost a year ago for a boyfriend who hadn't lasted long enough to see it. His loss, really.

I unceremoniously dropped my robe and slipped the nightie over my head. The lace bodice was so revealing I was practically topless, and the short skirt floated over my hips. As I pulled on the matching panties, I deliberately did not question why I'd decided on this outfit. Then I flipped off the air conditioner *(whenever it runs while I sleep, I get a headache)*, opened the window, and climbed into bed. In no time, I was asleep.

I felt him before I saw him, his firm body pressed against mine, his lips caressing the back of my neck. *Micah.* I rolled over to face him; even in the darkness of my room I could see he was still in that weird brown getup, boots and all, but I didn't care. Hopefully, it would be gone soon.

"Micah," I murmured, savoring his name on my tongue. "You're here."

"I heard your call, my Sara," he murmured. "You're wearing more here," he continued, tracing the edge of my panties, "but less here." His deft fingers danced across my lacy bodice.

"Do you like it?"

"I do." Micah hooked a finger inside my panties and drew them lower. "I most certainly do." We remained wrapped up in each other for long, blissful moments, until he spoke again. "I am so glad you called me again, my Sara."

"Why do you keep saying that?" I asked. *Yes, I argued with a dream. I am a psychology student's dream case study. Ha ha. Dream.* "You're not even real."

At that, Micah raised his head. "I am as real as you are," he replied, somewhat indignantly. "Twice now, you have called me to your dream."

What? No, no, no, no, that's not good. Not good, not good at all. "That's not possible," I whispered.

"It is more than possible, my Sara. It has come to pass." Serious now, Micah sat up and took my hands. "I have watched you often, gazing toward the entrance to my lands. I've always felt your power. Still, until earlier today, I had no idea that you were a Dreamwalker, as I am."

He said it. He just had to say it. "Don't say that!" Micah looked hurt and confused, so I amended, "If anyone hears you, there'll be questions." I glanced toward the open window, but I neither saw nor heard a drone whizzing by.

Micah nodded, but his brow remained furrowed. "As you wish."

"I still don't understand," I continued, moving to sit up. "You say I was looking toward your lands, but I don't even know where you're from."

"Where you put your mechanical for the day," he replied as he tucked a lock of hair behind my ear. "The trees you favor mark the entrance to my domain."

Once I figured out that "mechanical" meant "car", I considered where I parked in the office lot. I'd always chosen to leave my convertible in the back of the lot, mainly because it was a nice car and most of my coworkers, like most everyone else these days, were dirt poor. I didn't want to answer any questions about how I could afford such a nice vehicle if I didn't have to.

But Micah was right in that I'd always favored one particular spot. It was situated in front of two pine trees, their massive trunks wound together like a lovers' embrace. I'd never seen anything like it, certainly not in such big trees, and they'd captivated me from the moment I saw them. And yes, I gazed at them often.

"The pine trees?" I asked. Micah smiled when he nodded. But that didn't answer my questions, since they weren't in front of a door or path. There wasn't even anything behind them, except the electric fence separating REES from the property next door.

Suddenly, my eyes widened in shock and recognition, and I grabbed a handful of his silvery hair, exposing a set of pointed ears. "You're an elf!"

"Micah Silverstrand, Lord of the Whispering Dell," he replied, with a polite nod. Rubbing my temples, I considered my situation. I was in a dream that wasn't a dream, sitting in bed with a man whom I'd thought was a mere figment of my imagination, but who happened to be some sort of royal elf. And a Dreamwalker. Like me, though I had been oh, so careful to forget all that. Maybe—hopefully—I was just really drunk.

But... I can't explain it, but as I looked at this elf, with his silver eyes and fluffy hair, he was more real to me than anyone else I'd ever known.

"I'm sorry, Micah," I said at length. "I didn't know I could call anyone this way. Nothing like this has ever happened to me before."

At that, his pale brows nearly touched. "When you offered a token and lay nearly bare before me, I assumed you wanted me." Token? Oh, right, my panties. "And tonight, you have bathed for me, attired yourself as a queen, and have allowed me ingress to your chamber. What else was I to think?" I stared from the open window to my silk nightie. Why *had* I put this on? Had I been calling him, subconsciously? Could I even do that? I didn't know. But I couldn't do it again. Not unless I wanted to end up like Max.

Micah was still speaking, so I met his gaze. "When I learned that you are of metal, as I am, our attraction became clear." *Crap. He knows I'm an Elemental, too?*

13

Of metal. *There are two ways one can learn the workings of magic: years and years of rigorous study, or by simply being born to it. If you're born into a magical bloodline, you're said to be touched by an element, either earth, air, fire, water, or metal. The nature of your element is passed from father to child, just like a surname. Once in a while, someone is born touched by more than one element, but that's awfully rare.*

You also take on the characteristics of your chosen element, or rather, the element that's chosen you. For instance, those touched by fire tend to be quick to anger, and those of earth are stubborn but loyal. I've never met anyone who admitted to being touched by water, but I've always imagined them as cowardly. And air? Who knows what they're like? Flighty, perhaps?

I've always been glad that my family's line is of metal. It means I'm strong, both physically and mentally, and courageous. I'm loyal, like those of earth, but not quite so stubborn. And... and that's all I really know, because we haven't been allowed to speak of magic since the wars ended and magic was outlawed.

I was young when the wars began, but from what I remembered, the news reports all said that the wars had started when those who'd been born without magic became jealous of Elementals' innate abilities. So, the learned magicians got together with the Mundane humans and started up their own civil rights movement, claiming that, due to their own magic, they should be considered equal to the Elementals. The problem was, they weren't equal. They never, ever would be, being that it took months, or years, for a Mundane to learn even simple spells like the casting of a fey stone. When the Elementals brought up this small but important fact, all hell had broken loose. Literally.

Still, there had been no war or outright rebellion at that point. The learned magicians may have been collectively outraged, but they grudgingly accepted their place, and the Mundane humans—those who did not study magic—were content with things as they were. Then, a Fire Elemental conceived of a way to sell fey stones to the masses; normally, a fey stone will only burn in the presence of its caster, but this enterprising individual spent decades studying the spell and determined which materials would cause the light to burn for years. It was a brilliant invention, one that could save the average family hundreds, or maybe thousands, in electricity. Just imagine, a never-ending light bulb.

The Mundane CEO of the power company had not been pleased by this development.

The wars had lasted almost three years, but we hadn't been discouraged. We—the Elementals— knew that we were stronger, and we'd never had any doubt that we'd prevail. Then, the unthinkable happened. We lost.

To this day, no one knows how. Oh, there's lots of speculation, but the real reasons remain somewhat elusive. The schoolbooks say that many of the war mages realized the error of their ways and immolated themselves. Yes, they used the word "immolate", and that, right there, is a clue that it's all propaganda. Other sources claim that Elementals don't mesh well with those of opposing natures, and infighting was what did us in. That supposed infighting was also the impetus for creating the Peacekeepers, a squad of government goons specially outfitted to make Elemental lives miserable.

Well, no matter which version they hand out in their propaganda, the end result was the same—the Council of Elementals disappeared. Without their leadership, we lost.

My dad was on that council.

Once the Mundanes claimed victory, we assumed that life would pretty much return to normal, but we were so, so wrong. Instead of just declaring themselves equal to the Elementals, the learned magicians were also outlawed, along with all other 'unlicensed magic'. In essence, without a special dispensation from the government (which, I might add, tosses spells around like cheap confetti), you could be thrown in prison for something as innocuous as conjuring up a bit of heat to warm your coffee.

We never found out what happened to Dad.

I'd spent most of my life trying to pass for ordinary. I tried to act like a Mundane human, someone who didn't understand magic. I never talked about it, never thought about it, and never, ever practiced it. So, how did Micah know?

"Of metal?" I asked, tentatively.

"I was certain when I felt your mark." Huh. No one mentioned marks, either. I usually kept mine covered; those who saw it either thought it was a tramp stamp or refused to let on that they recognized the signs of magic. "Copper, yes?"

"Copper," I affirmed, my voice now hardly a whisper. "You could tell just by feeling it?"

"By your hair," he replied. I protested that I dyed my hair, but he looked pointedly at my hips. Oh, right. "May I see? Your mark, I mean."

I didn't see any reason why he couldn't, since he'd pretty much seen the rest of me. I turned around and lifted my nightie, exposing the mark across my lower back that forever named me as a member of the Raven clan, one of the most powerful bloodlines in history. Well, before magic was outlawed; now we were just... regular. And watched. My mark was copper-colored, and took the shape of a raven with its wings outstretched, the tips of the feathers reaching my sides. My sister, Sadie, bore a nearly identical mark. I didn't remember what Max's mark had looked like.

Micah traced the edges of the raven, his light touch sending shivers through my body. I remembered how he'd massaged my back during our earlier encounter, how I'd instantly become a molten heap of need. "Is everyone's mark so sensitive?" I asked.

"Some, but not all," he replied, his fingers now stroking my spine, near the raven's maw. "Fire marks may burn you if you touch them, and Elementals of stone feel hardly anything at all."

"Do you have a mark?" I asked, peeking over my shoulder. Again, Micah smiled at me.

"I do." He pulled off his leather shirt, revealing wiry muscle sheathed in warm, caramel skin. Before I could truly appreciate the most attractive male chest I'd ever encountered, he turned his back and I saw his mark. It was shining, metallic silver, just as mine was copper. It swept across his back like filigree wings emanating from his spine, arching over his shoulder blades in a graceful fall that reached below his waist.

"You... you're silver," I murmured, my eyes flitting from his mark to his hair. "Just like I'm copper, you're silver." Micah murmured some sort of an agreement, but I barely heard him. Hesitantly, I touched his back, his mark glinting in the near-dark. His flesh was warm and inviting, almost hot where it was incised with silver. "Oh, Micah. I've never seen anything like it."

"Many thanks, my Sara." His muscles tensed, and I wondered if touching his mark was having the same effect on him as when he'd touched mine. I dropped my hands, and he turned to face me. "Forgive me if I've misinterpreted your actions."

"I didn't know what I was doing, calling you," I admitted. "But I am glad that you came back to me." At that, he kissed me—hard—and pushed me onto my back. I didn't resist. Far from it, I welcomed him.

"Wait," I breathed. "Will I ever see you while we're awake?"

"You wish to?"

I nodded. "More than anything."

"Hold me tightly, my Sara." I did, and the air thickened and rippled around us. Once again, I heard street noises and the radio blaring one floor up, and I could smell the alley. I'd been so thoroughly enchanted by Micah, I hadn't noticed the lack of my usual annoyances. But now that I was awake, they had returned, and there was a half-naked man in my bed.

I screamed, my wakeful self having no idea who Micah was or why he was here. Ever practical, Micah kissed me, effectively smothering my cries and jogging my memory at the same time. He knew he'd succeeded when I stopped screaming and kissed him back.

"I'm sorry," I whispered, still trembling. "It was so sudden!"

"It is hard to pull yourself to wakefulness so quickly," he murmured. "You behaved much better than I did my first time."

"I did?" He nodded and wiped away tears I hadn't noticed. "Thank you."

"For what, my Sara?"

19

I didn't get to answer. My screams must have woken Juliana, and she was banging on my door. "I'm fine!" I yelled. "Just a nightmare."

"Open up!" Now she was jiggling the handle. Luckily, I always locked my door, a habit left over from sleeping in the dorms, but she was insistent. Once she had decided on doing something, nothing could stop her.

"She can't find you here," I whispered. "They'll kill you if they find you." Micah nodded, and in the next moment, he was gone. I don't mean he left by way of the window, which I assumed was how he had gotten in; he was here, and then he wasn't. I blinked, but was quickly dragged out of my amazement by Juliana's banging and yelling. I pulled on my robe and threw open the door.

"You're gonna wake the neighbors," I admonished her.

"The way you screamed, I thought one of them was murdering you," she countered.

"Aw. My Juliana in shining armor." She responded with an artful sneer, and we were back to normal.

"It's almost six, anyway. I'll make some coffee."

I nodded and shut the door to dress. Not only did I not want to explain my silk nightie to Juliana, but I figured I might as well get ready now. There wouldn't be any more sleep for me at the moment. After I picked out a pair of jeans and a shirt, I took off my robe and almost screamed again. He had taken my panties again!

chapter 3

A few hours later, I dropped Juliana off at REES's front door, and, being that it was my day off, peeled out of the parking lot like a teenage moron and cruised the streets for a while, intent upon securing a second (okay, third) caffeinated beverage. Thoughts I shouldn't be thinking—things I wasn't even supposed to know about—coursed through my mind, and I needed time to sort things out. Time, and maybe a bottle of tequila.

Not only had Micah known that I was of metal, he'd called me a Dreamwalker. Crap. Crap crap crap crap crap. Only the most powerful Elementals were able to enter other people's dreams, and I'd spent the bulk of my life pretending to be as unpowerful as possible. Hell, I hadn't even known I could dreamwalk, but I'd gone and done it twice now.

While this development wasn't wholly unexpected, it was still not good. Very, very not good.

You see, not only am I an Elemental, but my surname is Corbeau. I'm descended from the Raven clan, one of the most powerful lines of Elementals that have ever lived. Our collective hands have guided world events since before the time of the Merovingians. Of course, since the wars ended and magic has been outlawed, our influence has waned somewhat.

Pity. I'd make an awesome Elemental princess.

Despite the life-threatening risk of displaying my abilities, I'd always known that my power remained, coiled deep inside me, like a serpent waiting to strike, but I did my best to blend in with the Mundanes. I held down a menial office job, lived in an apartment building that wasn't in too nice of a neighborhood, and stayed away from anything even slightly supernatural. I didn't even own a deck of regular playing cards, for fear that someone would accuse me of performing readings, and all of my jewelry was plain, devoid of patterns as well as stones, lest I be accused of wearing spells about my person.

My lack of training made it easy for me to act ignorant, since I pretty much was. Max, my older brother, had tried to teach my sister, Sadie, and me the basics of our familial power, but that lark had ended when the Peacekeepers had barged into our home and apprehended him. That had been almost ten years ago, and we hadn't seen him since.

So, you can understand why this Dreamwalker label had me a wee bit anxious. While the government espoused a clear hatred of all things magic, rumor was that they used captured Dreamwalkers as spies. When you slip into someone's unconscious mind, all their hopes and dreams and fears lie bare before you. Everything they know, you can learn; whatever they fear, you can use against them. Secrets? Nonexistent. For an experienced Dreamwalker, subterfuge is easier than riding a bike, faster than reading a book or downloading files. It's evil at its diabolical, simplistic best.

Did Micah now know everything I knew?

"Thanks." I paid the drive-thru barista and took my latte; exotic caffeinated beverages were my one indulgence. Okay, my one indulgence along with my car—my 'mechanical' as Micah had called it. I wondered if he'd let me drive him around. I hated it when boys did all the driving.

As I sipped the hot, cinnamony beverage, I thought about Micah's silver eyes, his nearly-white hair, the mark that cascaded across his shoulders. I'd never seen anything like the rivulets of silver twirling and spiraling across his back, terrible and elegant as a raptor's wings. Despite the ban on magic, I'd seen a lot of marks in my day, though mostly on the preserved skins of government enemies that decorated our fine museums and town halls. None of those leathery bits had been half as amazing as Micah's warm, soft back.

After wasting an hour's worth of time and gas, I returned to REES's parking lot, waved at the oh–so–friendly drone, and found my usual spot in the back lot in front of the pine trees. *Micah had said that the trees marked the entrance to his lands, so I should be able to cross over with no difficulties. Right?*

As soon as the drone buzzed away, I gulped the remains of my latte, locked the car, and then stood staring at the entwined trees while my heart thudded away in my breast. It had been so long since I had entered the Otherworld that, for a moment, I wondered if I still could. And if I did, would the Peacekeepers know? Would Micah even want to see me?

You're being an idiot. Of course the Peacekeepers wouldn't know. I'd managed to cut out the tracker they'd implanted in my shoulder and set it in a watch, which was now neatly stowed in my glove compartment. I'd done the same with Sadie's tracker, though she'd placed hers in a locket. What was more, the cameras in the back lot had been off for more than a year on account of my boss being a tightwad. As long as no drones happened by during my entrance or exit, I was thoroughly incognito.

And, if last night was any indication, Micah would thoroughly enjoy a visit from me.

You're being an ass. I was stalling. And sweating, and having heart palpitations. I shook my head, since an anxiety attack was not going to give me any answers. I took a deep breath and stepped beyond the trees.

It had always struck me how ordinary the Otherworld seemed. Same trees, same birds, same sky; really, it was nearly identical to the Mundane World. In the midst of my musings about how the two worlds were so similar, a herd of miniature trolls galloped past me. They were tiny, green-skinned wonders, all knobby joints and funny grunts along with even funnier conical caps. Only through great force of will was I able to stifle my giggle. Even though I knew very little of the ways of magical beings, I knew better than to laugh at a pack of trolls.

Not so ordinary, then. Once the trolls passed, I took in my surroundings. Much like things on the Mundane side, I was in a dense pine forest. I examined a bundle of needles and found that there were three needles in each, which meant that these trees were red pine. *(White pine has five needles per bundle. Get it?)* The forest floor was littered with rusty orange needles, plump mushrooms, and the occasional bright wildflower, with shafts of sunlight breaking through the canopy here and there. I walked further into the wood, breathing deeply of the cool air, relishing that it was crisp and clear, surely more so than any air I'd encountered in the Mundane World. In short, the Otherworld was a lovely place.

It was also eerily quiet, devoid of the occasional sounds from a passing car, or people walking by on the street, or any of the background noise that I'd always taken for granted. Now that the trolls were gone, I couldn't hear anything other than the rustle of boughs. *How am I going to find Micah? I suppose I could wander around, but becoming lost in the Otherworld is not a fate the sensible among us strive for. I've read far too many fairy tales not to worry about what lurks around the bend. I debate calling out Micah's name, but that might also bring unwanted attention.*

Mind you, not that I know what I will say to Micah when I find him. Should I tell him to leave me alone, that it is far too risky for us to be found together, to stop stealing my underwear like a horny frat boy? I should say all these things, and more besides. This should be our last meeting. It will be our last meeting. Then, just as suddenly as he left my room, he stands before me.

"My Sara."

"Oh," I said, startled. "Hi."

Thanks to the sunny morning, I got my first good look at the elf who'd been haunting my dreams. His most striking feature was his silver hair, thick and impossibly fluffy like thistle down, and long enough to brush the tops of his shoulders. Micah's eyes were a matching hue, with hair and eyes set off by his rich, caramel skin. Add to that his chiseled cheekbones and knife-blade nose, and he was quite the impressive specimen.

Despite the warm morning, he was wearing another of those leather suits; now that I knew he was an elf, I didn't find his clothing quite so odd. Today, he was clad in a pale-blue tunic over gray leggings, along with gray knee boots. A black belt encircled his hips, replete with a wicked-looking blade. He smiled as he approached; when he was close enough, he took my hands. It is fair to say that, at Micah's touch, my resolve melted away.

"By coming to my lands, you have made me very happy," Micah murmured, bending to kiss the tips of my fingers. He looked so regal, so much like a lord, that I felt grubby in comparison. While my jeans were clean, they were just jeans, and my plain black sandals and white button-down shirt were decidedly casual. If Micah minded, however, he didn't mention it. "What good fortune has brought my Sara before me on this day?"

"I wanted to talk to you." I scuffed the ground with my toe. "You really shouldn't steal my underwear." *Yeah, nothing like just leaping right into the awkwardness.*

His brow furrowed. "I thought you were leaving me tokens."

"Tokens?"

"When two are promised, or if one seeks to know another, they will offer tokens," he explained.

"Wait. You mean to tell me that human women will give up their panties in exchange for—" My cheeks were on fire, and I looked away. "Is that what you thought I was doing?"

"Women have done so, yes," Micah replied. "I now know that you are too honorable to engage in such pursuits."

"It's illegal," I mumbled. I glanced up. "Have you gone to women like that before?"

"Only as a dream, never in flesh." Somehow, that admission comforted me. "Did you not want me last night?" As he spoke, Micah's eyes were soft, limpid things that told me so much more than his words. Gah. *Apparently, I am the sort of girl who falls for the fairy knight, hook, line, and virginity.*

"I didn't know you were real," I replied truthfully. "But I'm glad that you are," I added, enjoying how his face brightened. Then I was in his arms, and all the things I was going to tell him left me. Giving him up was suddenly not an option.

"Is this the Whispering Dell?" I asked, after he'd kissed me for a while. "I don't hear any whispering."

"Silly girl," he admonished, "this is only the upper ridge. Come." He led me away from where the parking lot would have been if I hadn't been traipsing about *in the Otherworld* and toward a break in the trees. The crest overlooked a wide, green valley, far prettier than any scene depicted in any storybook illustration. The rolling hills framed the vale, with the occasional sheep dotting the higher pastures. The lowlands were striped with sparkling waterways and what looked like manicured gardens, scattered with homes, here and there, along a main roadway. At the end of the roadway, there was a village, complete with thatched roofs and a few curls of smoke wafting up from chimneys. On a high point near the far end of the valley sat, predictably, a castle.

"Is that where you live?" I asked.

"I built it with my own hands," he replied, proudly. And well he should be. As we moved closer, I saw that, rather than a castle, Micah's home was shaped more like a traditional manor estate, and instead of the typical brown timbers and daubed white, it was gray. Light gray, that is, highly polished to an almost mirror-like sheen.

"Silver," I deduced. "Your home is silver." I looked at him, and asked very seriously, "Am I supposed to live in copper?"

Micah chuckled at my ignorance. "A copper abode would enhance your power, but any metal would do. Silver would do nicely."

I ignored that innuendo. "Micah, your home is beautiful."

"It is—" He opened his mouth to say more, then cocked his head to the side. "I regret to tell you, I am needed below. When may I see you again?"

"I came to tell you that I shouldn't see you again," I said. "It's just too dangerous. At least, that was what I decided this morning."

"And now?" he asked, hopefully.

"I..." I looked at him, this silver elf who had just thrust himself into my life, and uttered the very words I knew could be deadly. "Now, I don't think I mind the danger." Micah smiled, seeming content with that answer for now, and walked me back to the thin spot between worlds. We said a quick goodbye, since he had to respond to his mysterious summons, but when he turned to leave, I called for him to wait.

"Shouldn't you give me a token?" I dropped my eyes. "I mean, you have two from me. Shouldn't I have something from you?" I scuffed the pine-needle carpet with my toe. It was a foolish request, for many reasons. Not only was someone like Micah not likely to want to see an undereducated wretch like me again, I was seriously risking my life just by talking to him. Really, this couldn't go on.

Instead of telling me to go back where I came from, Micah pulled a chain over his head, and then stepped closer as he arranged it around my neck. On the chain was a pendant shaped like a silver oak leaf, along with a silver-capped acorn carved from amber.

"The oaks are my allies, and I take their leaf as my symbol," he murmured, fastening the clasp behind my neck. "Wear it, my Sara, and be guaranteed safe passage throughout my lands."

"Micah, it's too much!"

"It's not." He closed my fingers over the pendant. "Nothing is too much, my Sara."

"Should our tokens be of metal, since we are?"

"Traditionally, yes."

Hmm. He only had fabric from me. I dug in my pocket and retrieved a few pennies. "It's all the copper I have," I apologized.

"I will treasure them," he murmured. Micah slid the coins inside his tunic, close to his heart. "Just as

I treasure you." He kissed me then, softly, sweetly, almost respectfully. "And, I will see you again."

Yes. Yes, he would.

chapter 4

I stepped out of the Otherworld just as easily as I would have stepped from one room to the next. When I was a child, I'd thought walking from one reality to the next was amazingly cool, fodder for endless stories and Hollywood blockbusters. Now, it just made my hands shake and my stomach turn, the fear of discovery having replaced my childhood wonder.

I climbed back into my car and sat heavily behind the wheel, tracing the edges of Micah's token while I stared at the twisted pine trees. *If the trees are the same, why are the worlds different?* I squinted, trying to catch a glimpse of Micah or the Whispering Dell, but I only saw the fence separating the parking lot from the abandoned industrial park next door. I leaned to the side and saw the edge of a concrete building that, impossibly, occupied the same valley as Micah's silver castle.

Vaguely, I recall learning (from Max, not from any Mundane instructor) that the things we humans create only exist in our world, and the same holds true for beings of the Otherworld. Good thing, too, or there would be a lot of cities with awkwardly placed municipal buildings and sacred fountains. Despite this, the bones of the worlds are the same. This means that natural things, like trees, can exist in both places, but things like buildings can't. But humans and animals and elves are natural, and we only occupy one at a time, so the tree theory never did fully make sense to me. Then, I remembered that the Museum of Human Triumph exists simultaneously in both worlds, and my head drooped forward to rest on the steering wheel. I had no idea how magic worked, why trees could exist in whichever world they please, while buildings and people are confined to one at a time. I was certain, however, what my punishment would be if I were caught with an elfin artifact.

I missed Dad. I missed Max. They would know the answers.

They would know what to do.

The telltale hum of an approaching drone roused me. Missing Dad and Max wasn't going to get me any answers, so I tucked Micah's token inside my shirt and started the car. As the silver oak leaf warmed against my skin, I sped out of the parking lot, not caring if the drone slapped me with a fine for speeding or reckless disregard. Unlike my aimless morning drive, I knew where I was going, though my destination would probably lead to even more questions. I made a left out of the lot and headed toward the only magical place I had clearance to enter—my mother's house, the Raven Compound.

She'd been granted the estate in the hasty, unasked-for divorce, along with a generous government stipend that paid for the daily maintenance of the place, not to mention my and Sadie's living expenses. The estate itself was huge, boasting eleven bedrooms, fourteen baths, and not one, but two ballrooms. The house proper sat upon several acres of land, nestled between groves of oak and ash trees. *It was, as you (and the government) could well imagine, the ideal place for a clan of Elemental magicians to work spells unobserved.*

After Dad went missing during the third year of the wars, the government had wasted no time in declaring him an enemy of the state and divorcing him from my mother. You see, under the new regime political criminals couldn't enter into any contracts, of which marriage was definitely included; really, this was just another way to make us miserable. Mom hadn't wanted the divorce, and Dad had only been unaccounted for a few months when it happened, but then, she hadn't even known about any divorce proceedings until the papers were delivered. *By armed Peacekeepers, mind you.* Being that her husband was missing, magic had been declared illegal and she had three small children to care for, Mom had had other things on her mind instead of her newly-single status. However, she had put up enough of a fuss that we got to keep the house in exchange for turning over all our magical implements, spellbooks included. And once the house had been outfitted with cameras and listening devices, the checks had started rolling in.

Yeah. As if we were going to invite our Elemental buddies over for a magic party.

As I drove past the wrought-iron gates of the Compound, I nodded at the ravens standing guard along the weathered metal. On account of their presence, and our surname, we called the family home the Raven Compound, in honor of the birds who'd always seemed to flock to their namesake. Sometimes they were so still you could mistake them for statues, but the statues all had shiny glass eyes of green or blue. The living birds' eyes were black as a moonless night.

The leader of these silent sentries was the copper raven that sat alone atop the gable over the main entrance. Most probably thought he was nothing more than a weathervane, but Dad had always called him our watcher, an agent of The Raven; he was the one who made sure nothing bad got past our gate. When I was a kid, he'd gleamed as if we'd polished him daily, though to my knowledge no one ever had. Once Dad left for the wars, the patina slowly set in; I remember Max saying that the raven missed Dad.

Once the Peacekeepers came to serve Mom with the divorce papers, the green had taken over, engulfing him like so much kudzu.

I watched this raven, our so-called guardian, as I parked; even though he was well and truly blanketed by the thick, mottled patina, I still felt like he marked every move I made, for all the good it ever did us. I wanted to yell and scream at the metal bird, throw things at him, tell him that he'd failed in the worst way possible. He was no watcher, no guardian. Through his inattention, we'd lost both Dad and Max.

Shakily, I turned off the car. First, I was taking trips to the Otherworld and making dates with elves, now I was getting into fights with the decorations. Hoping I still had some time left before I totally lost my mind, I got out of the car. My feet crunched on the raked gravel driveway and, after a quick wave at the passing drone, I strode purposefully toward the door.

The foyer of the Raven Compound was ridiculously, over-the-top ostentatious. It was circular, the curved walls clad in gold-flecked marble and gilded plaster. The ceiling was a full three stories high, held aloft by eight pillars half as wide as I was tall. An enormous crystal chandelier, dripping with multicolored glass baubles, took up the top third of the room. Portraits and statues of significant ancestors had once encircled the foyer, but they had all been confiscated as evidence during the war trials. In an effort to brighten things up in their absence, Mom had placed some potted hydrangeas around the pillars. It was nice.

"Mom?"

After a moment, I called out again, a bit less softly, but Mom was nowhere in sight or earshot; the estate was so large you could easily go for several days without seeing another living soul. Once we had been allowed to move back in after Max's arrest, and it was just Mom, Sadie, and me, the three of us regularly had gone a week or more before all of us were in the same room. Now that Sadie and I had moved out, me to my tiny apartment and Sadie to the university dorm, Mom was all alone with her memories and a vegetable garden. *She doesn't even like vegetables.*

I sighed, unsurprised by Mom's lack of response, crossed the foyer, and entered the front parlor. It was my favorite room at the Compound, since it was the only one left unscathed during the war trials; the government, true to their "beneficent" nature, had deemed that nothing in it was spelled, so they had let us have one whole room of family memories. Mom refused to set foot in the parlor, since she's convinced that the Peacekeepers laid a trap in it and they're just waiting for her to slip up.

Hidden listening devices or no, the parlor was a nice room, if a bit outdated. Flocked red velvet covered the walls, and it was crammed full of dark wood furniture and tarnished silver bric-a-brac. A behemoth of a china cabinet graced the far wall, stuffed full of childhood drawings and lopsided plaster ashtrays, along with what was left of the eggshell-thin heirloom plates that Mom's ancestors had carried over from Ireland, and a set of crystal handed down by Dad's mother. The deal was that whichever girl married first would get her pick of the plates or glassware, with the other set going to the other, later-married sister. Since I'm a realist, I'd never had my heart set on either.

Despite the many familiar items, the aspect of the parlor I liked best was something intangible: its smell. The parlor held that distinctive odor of all rooms magic had been worked in: musk and brimstone, a touch of rot, sweet incense, and sour, bitter herbs. I breathed deeply of the smells of my youth, since they had been sanitized out of the rest of the house.

A few deep breaths later, I flopped down on the mustard-yellow divan and looked at the tiny framed photograph resting on the end table. It was of me, Max, and Sadie. We were out back under the big oak tree, which was where Max had taught us spells. Max would tell us a story, or give us bitter herbs to chew, then he would have Sadie and me stare upward and squint until we could see the fairies frolicking in high branches. When I got older, I had assumed the fairies were one of Max's illusions, but after meeting Micah I was not so sure.

Ironically, with all the effort the government had expended on removing every iota of magic from the Raven Compound, they had left the stately oak intact. When we moved back in after Dad had been declared dead, we'd expected to find it little more than a pile of sawdust, but there it was, welcoming us back to our home. Max had laughed and said that this oversight was further evidence of how clueless the Peacekeepers really were; normally, we ignored Max's rants, but he'd had a point. The oak tree had been the hub of magical activities for hundreds of years, which was one of the reasons the Raven Compound had been built nearby. You didn't need to be an Elemental to feel the tinge of magic covering its bark, hear it rustle in its leaves, and yet the Peacekeepers hadn't given it a second look. They were so busy hauling off badly composed portraits of long-dead Corbeaus that they had left behind a veritable fountain of power.

The first day we moved back, we had tried to have a picnic in front of the oak, just like old times. That hadn't turned out to be the best idea, since before long Mom was weeping for the loss of Dad, Sadie was terrified that a Peacekeeper would leap down from the branches and get her, and Max was yelling at them both to keep it together. Me, I had just concentrated on my sandwich and hoped it was all just one long, terrible nightmare.

That had been the last time the four of us had visited the oak; sometimes, I wondered if the tree missed us, or if he was glad not to have three rambunctious children snapping off his twigs and leaves. My hand strayed to the pendant Micah had given me that morning, and I traced the edge of the oak leaf, felt the amber acorn warm in my hand. Was it a sign that Micah was allied with the oaks, just as the Corbeau children had been?

Micah… I shoved his image from my mind, for all the good it did. I wondered if he'd enchanted me, if that was why I couldn't stop thinking about him. I mean, I had gone to the Otherworld to tell him to leave me be, and ended up practically begging to wear his token. Yesterday, I hadn't known what a token was. Today, one dangled against my breast like a supernatural calling card.

Of metal… Micah had just known that I was of metal, as surely as if I'd hung a sign around my neck. I'm not ashamed to admit that, after a lifetime pretending to be nothing more than ordinary, it rattled me that he had keyed into my true nature almost instantly. I wondered if anyone else could divine my Elemental nature just by looking at me. No, probably not while I still dyed my copper hair a dark, earthy brown. Micah's…astuteness had been just the result of a wardrobe malfunction.

Yeah. That had to be it.

Max had had copper hair too, and freckles, just like Sadie. Sadie hated her speckled nose, but I've been jealous of her freckles for as far back as I can remember; a face without freckles is like a sky without stars, as Meme Corbeau used to say. It was something Sadie shared with Max that I never would.

Then they took Max, and now Sadie's freckles are all alone. It just isn't fair.

"Hey, baby."

I looked up and saw Mom in the doorway. She was muddy from the garden, still wearing thick gloves, with her blonde hair tucked under a hat; Mom's skin, freckle-free and smooth and white as a porcelain doll, burned something fierce at the mere mention of the sun. Her blue eyes were tired and sad, as they'd been every day since Dad had gone. She hefted a basket, multicolored produce spilling over the sides. Food grown in the ground, as opposed to a hydroponic greenhouse, is a rare treat in the post-war world.

I set the frame back on the table and joined Mom in the hall. "Tomatoes?"

"Eggplant," she replied. "I have zucchini, too."

I followed her into the kitchen, which was full of granite counters and state of the art appliances, all thanks to the government's magnanimous nature, and watched my mother bag up the assorted vegetables. When I was younger I couldn't understand her rampant need for gardening, since she always grew ten times what we could eat. Now that I had worked at REES, I got it; the routine tasks completed by her hands allowed her mind time to roam.

"I know you didn't come here for vegetables," she said once the last bag was full. "What's on your mind?"

Oh, so many things. "Do you ever think about Max?"

We weren't supposed to say his name. Hell, we weren't even supposed to have any pictures of him, either, but the goons had missed the one in the parlor. Usually, Mom scolded us for being careless, but today, she only sighed.

"Every day," she murmured. "Every blessed day."

chapter 5

After I left Mom and the creepy birds behind, I did some more aimless driving. I didn't want to go back to my empty apartment, and I absolutely did not want to go into the office on my day off. Now *that* would be pathetic. Far, far more pathetic than mooning over an elf lord from the Otherworld, whose very presence in my life could mean imprisonment and/or death.

Yes. Wouldn't want to be caught with a work ethic, now, would we?

Since I was already on the wealthier side of town, I parked my mechanical next to the Promenade and headed over to the open-air market. Great. Now, I was even *thinking* like Micah. There, in booths ranging from little more than mildewed cardboard held together with dental floss, to palatial tents of multicolored silk fit for a king, you could purchase anything, or anyone—a maid, a handyman, maybe even a bride—your heart desired. Well, as long as you had the money to burn or an item to trade.

For instance, you can obtain clothing (both elegant and utilitarian), government-approved (and unapproved) reading material, exotic pets, exotic foods, exotic pets made into exotic food…you name it, it is sold along the Promenade, though some wares only make appearances during that magical time between dusk and curfew. There's even a booth selling milk so fresh the cow is tethered behind the counter. All can be had, and once the sun goes down, it usually is.

It was a mostly legal market (except for the after-hours trades, not that I had *any* firsthand knowledge of such things), but savvy shopkeepers had ways of getting the Peacekeepers to overlook their varied indiscretions. A charred booth or puffy lip served to signify when someone had let their bill languish too long unpaid.

Despite the somewhat illegal nature of certain transactions, this market was a necessary evil of modern life, or rather, of what our lives had become. Since the Magic Wars had ended, there was a dearth of viable storefronts, being that every property with a smidgen of technology had been seized by Peacekeepers and slowly sold back to corporations, once those corporations had been proven to be magic-free. But the farmers and butchers still had crops and meat to bring to market, and the craftspeople had stoneware and cheeses and cloth to sell. So, since there was no place else for them to go, and the crops and goods couldn't very well be left to rot on the vine (or crack in the kiln), the Promenade Market had sprung up amidst the unused office blocks. Really, compared to the concrete wasteland it had been before, it was an improvement.

Still, I hadn't really started frequenting the Promenade until high school. My mom grew her vegetables, and we had an apple tree, so we'd never really wanted for fresh produce. Also, my family was one of the few left with money, both old and new, so we could have almost anything we wanted delivered to our doorstep. Not to mention that Mom was convinced that the market was run by evil imps just waiting to drag off unsuspecting children to their lairs.

Then tenth grade rolled around and Juliana and I had been faced with third period study hall, followed by lunch, then fourth period science. Since the study hall took place in an auditorium of hundreds of kids, attendance was never taken, and our science teacher had been little more than an experiment in reanimating corpses, we'd felt the immediate and pressing need to take a break from campus.

As for lunch...that was an evil that must not be named.

I was chicken at first, since the government-implanted trackers in our arms would alert the Peacekeepers to our truancy, but Juliana helped me remove mine. (She'd taken her own out years before.) I also balked at her plan of leaving them in our lockers, since wouldn't they notice that we hadn't moved, at all, for more than three hours? Again, Juliana was confident, and explained that the Peacekeepers only looked for people being where they were not supposed to be. As long as our signals registered as being on school grounds, it was all good.

So, armed with a camping knife and a filched bottle of wine (which functioned to sterilize the instrument *and* anesthetize the patient), we cut my tracker out. Make no mistake, it had hurt like hell, and I had a mid-grade infection brewing for a few weeks afterward, but the feeling of freedom had been well worth it. That, and the real food we got to enjoy at the Market instead of the slop we were used to getting for school lunches, made the lingering numbness all worthwhile.

Remembering those excursions with Juliana made me smile as I wandered amidst the nicer booths. Unlike in my younger days, when I had wanted everything but had to be careful what I brought home in order to keep both Mom and Sadie in the dark about my whereabouts, today I saw lots of interesting things but wanted nothing. I mean, my apartment was small, so I didn't need any knickknacks or lamps or what have you, and my fridge was stocked, though I could always stuff the cupboards with more dry goods.

And now I was contemplating stocking up on pasta. More evidence of my exciting life.

I sighed and considered stopping by the wine sellers' tent when I came across a jeweler. I'd never been much interested in jewelry, but something about her booth, maybe the way the sun glinted off the stones and polished metals, drew me in. Her wares were comprised of what seemed to be found objects, like skeleton keys and pebbles, and all were wrapped with wires and shiny beads. Almost without realizing it, I withdrew Micah's token from my shirt and traced the edges of the oak leaf. It was a perfect, albeit tiny, replica, as was the warm amber acorn. I found myself wondering if they'd fallen from a miniature silver tree that grew in a silver wood.

I bet he made this. Somehow, I could feel the residue of Micah's magic, a signature that was uniquely him, and I understood that he'd manipulated the silver into the likeness of a leaf. Maybe it was my own magic recognizing his, or maybe it was just my strong attraction to him. Maybe I was just going crazy and reading too much into it.

"That's a lovely pendant," the jeweler complimented. She was a middle-aged woman, her brown hair pulled back in a ponytail. The silver streaks at her temples matched my token. "Did you make it yourself?"

"No. It was a gift."

"Quite a fine gift." I nodded; it was a fine gift, wasn't it? And I had given Micah pennies in return. Beat-up, grungy old pennies.

"Do you also sell supplies?" I asked, suddenly.

"Of course," she said, smiling ear to ear. Money had that effect on the merchants of the Market. "What were you looking for? I have silver chains, and charms, and—"

"Copper." I took a deep breath, since the step I was about to take couldn't be undone. "The metal needs to be copper."

A short while and a small fortune later, I was the proud owner of a few hundred yards of copper wire in varying thicknesses and finishes, as well as a wide assortment of natural stone beads. Oh, and tools; lots and lots of tiny pliers and wrenches and snippy things with which to create my masterpiece. I'd gone straight to my car after leaving the jeweler's booth and called Sadie.

"Hey," was how she answered the phone. She sounded only mildly annoyed, so I figured there wasn't an exam or paper due in the near future.

"I met a boy," I said, in lieu of a proper greeting. "He gave me jewelry."

"When did you meet him?"

"Yesterday."

"Jewelry already?" Sadie whistled. "Must have been some night."

"Yeah. It was." I swore, not at Sadie, but at the dumbass who had cut me off. People seriously needed to learn how to merge.

"Are you driving?" Sadie accused. Before I could defend myself, she continued, "Listen, if you crack up that overpriced piece of metal Mom is gonna freak. Again. Call me later."

With that, she hung up. I made a face at my phone and tossed it into the passenger seat, then carefully drove the few remaining blocks to my apartment. Not that I was being careful because of Sadie. Once I was inside my apartment, I dumped all the bits and baubles out on the kitchen counter.

Wow. That's...that's a lot of stuff. I stared, dumbfounded, at the heap of metal and stone. I'd never made jewelry before, not even a friendship bracelet when I was a kid, and the sheer amount of what I'd purchased was overwhelming. Overwhelming, and ridiculous, and...and stupid. *If there was anything I was not, it was creative.* There was no way I could take these spools of wire and heaps of beads and turn them into anything other than wire and beads, no matter how many tools I bought.

This was a mistake. I'll never make anything good enough for Micah. Despondent, I grabbed the trash bin and moved to sweep the mess of it out of my sight when a bit of copper wire brushed against the back of my hand. Its coolness was strangely calming, almost centering. Intrigued, I traced the smooth edge of the wire, feeling the pull of the metal...*my* metal.

Trash bin forgotten, I set to work twisting and braiding and weaving until the metal strands became a wide cuff. It was amazingly intricate, not only due to the odd sizes of the wire, but also because of the stones I'd added to the overall design. In the center of the cuff, I placed a large piece of malachite and surrounded it with smaller bits of amber; the amber was to mirror the acorn Micah had given me, the malachite meant to pay homage to the green dell he lived in. And the copper…the copper was all me. I hoped Micah would like it.

He'll love it. I stood and stretched, achy and exhausted from the last few hours spent hunched over the counter. I wanted to show Micah the token immediately, but I still didn't understand how to call him with my dreamself. Not to mention that it was close to midnight, which meant that curfew had been in effect for the past hour; once the government had decided that most magic was done close to the proverbial witching hour, they'd enacted a curfew and begun releasing unmanned drones to patrol the streets at night. All the curfew had managed to do was piss off the bar owners and patrons, and to my knowledge all the drones ever caught were a few drunks stumbling their way home. Still, our government wasn't one to admit when it had done something wrong, so we kept our eleven o'clock curfew and got the added bonus of daytime drone patrols.

And, since I only knew of two places where the veil was thin, and since neither place was in my apartment building, this curfew meant no visiting the Otherworld on foot, either.

Since it had worked once before, I opened my bedroom window, hoping that Micah would somehow find his way inside. After a moment's hesitation, I placed the cuff on the sill, and then lay down on my bed for a short nap. As I drifted off, I wondered if Micah would come to me as a dream, or in the flesh. *Flesh. Hopefully, flesh.*

chapter 6

When I woke, my first thought was to wonder why my alarm hadn't gone off. Slowly, my muddy brain remembered that I hadn't set it. I had assumed Micah would wake me once he got here, and I hadn't intended to sleep all night. Well, morning light was streaming into the room, though a quick glance at the clock told me that it was still a bit too early to get up for work. I sighed, assuming that displaying a copper cuff on the windowsill wasn't the proper way to call a silver elf, and moved to shut the window. When I saw the empty sill, I froze.

The cuff was gone.

My eyes flew to the floor below the window, but the cuff wasn't there. I dropped to my hands and knees and crawled under my bed, then looked in my closet and in my dresser drawers; I even went so far as to look under the couch in the living room. No cuff. I went to the kitchen and picked through the leavings from its creation yesterday; there was nothing but the leftover bits of wire.

I ran out of my apartment, down the stairs, and to the alley outside my window, in case the cuff had fallen outside. The asphalt was pristinely scrubbed, which made it easy to see that the cuff wasn't on the sidewalk, nor in the road, nor had it rolled under the communal dumpster. Briefly, I wondered if it had been stolen, when a cold knot formed in my stomach. I'd gone to bed after curfew, which meant that only drones had been left patrolling the streets. A dumb robot would have no more use for a piece of jewelry than a kitten.

The cuff was gone, and Micah wasn't here.

I ran back to my apartment, snatched my keys, and flew back out the door, a hundred scenarios playing across my mind, each worse than the last. Mom was convinced that the three of us were constantly being watched, but Sadie and I had always told her she was paranoid. But the drones…

The drones, motorized robots that hovered about on the pretense of safety, patrolled all public areas during the day, but they came out in force after curfew. Even Peacekeepers weren't allowed outside after curfew fell, unless they were apprehending some ne'er-do-well. The drones were theoretically harmless, being that they supposedly didn't carry any weaponry, but they all carried cameras and voice recorders in order to document and punish the guilty. What if one had happened by my window just as Micah had arrived? What if there was official government documentation of an elf hopping through my bedroom window? Would the Peacekeepers punish only me, or Mom and Sadie, too?

What if they'd taken Micah, just like they'd taken Max?

I clutched the wheel, white-knuckled, as my car careened across town. The rational part of my mind was somewhat amazed I wasn't stopped for speeding, or reckless driving, or operating a mechanical under the influence of magic. When I turned onto Real Estate Row, the street REES was located on, I almost had a heart attack.

There was a full squadron of Peacekeepers blocking the street.

I skidded to a halt, since mowing down the men with guns would not improve my situation in the slightest. While I tried to get my breathing under control, I searched for a way around them. The sidewalks were blocked too, and I saw a separate squad in my rearview mirror blocking off the adjoining street. For a moment, I entertained the notion of leaving the car and making a run for the Otherworld, but then I noticed the drones overhead. Like a swarm of metal mosquitos, they buzzed away, recording everything with their state of the art surveillance equipment.

Yeah. I wasn't going anywhere.

And a Peacekeeper was walking toward me.

They know! They have Micah, and now they're here for me! Sweat bloomed across my back and neck, and my stomach plummeted to the floorboards. Why else would they be here, if not to apprehend me? Why would a *full squadron* of Peacekeepers be blocking the entrance to my employer, unless they were lying in wait to capture me?

The tiny, rational voice in the back of my head said that I was freaking out over nothing. If the Peacekeepers had wanted me, they would have barged into my apartment and taken me from my bed. They wouldn't have let me have access to my car, with which I could potentially make my escape. Unless they wanted to hunt me down…

No, no, that would be silly. That would be a waste of resources. Still, they were here, and Micah wasn't in my room when I woke, and…and…

Gods. I hoped Micah was okay.

Finally, the Peacekeeper reached my car. Being the dutiful citizen that I am, I promptly rolled down my window and handed over my paperwork.

"What's your name?" he asked, even though it was printed on the card in front of him.

"Sara Corbeau."

"What's the E. stand for?"

Oh, so he can read. "Elizabeth."

"Is that your mother's name?"

Yeah, that's also listed on the card. "No. Her name is Maeve Connor Corbeau. I don't know how she came up with Elizabeth."

The goon smiled at that. "I feel ya. My middle name's pretty horrible." He lowered his sunglasses, and met my eyes. "Jerome."

"That's not so bad."

"That's not my middle name. You need to earn that." Then the creep winked at me. All at once, I was shocked, disgusted, and scared in a whole new way. My emotions must have been plain, because Jerome straightened up and handed me back my identification.

"You came around that corner pretty fast, Sara," he stated.

"I know. I'm sorry about that." He looked at me expectantly, so I elaborated, "I work right over there, at Real Estate Evaluation Services. I wanted to get in early, for overtime. The end of the month's coming, you know."

Peacekeeper Jerome nodded at that. The last day of the month was when our tax payments were due, and everyone paid the same amount, regardless of their income. Yeah, it was unfair to make the poor pay the same price as the rich, but the government did not see it that way. After all, we all had access to the same government services, so shouldn't we all pay the same share? So, in the name of fairness, we all scrambled to work as much as possible to make these unwieldy payments by the end of the month, and were dirt poor the following week, or at least until our next paychecks came in.

From the set of Jerome's jaw, I guessed that Peacekeepers were not exempt from taxes, either. He leaned closer, whether to share financial advice or hit on me further I couldn't tell, but he was interrupted by a commotion down the street. A man I vaguely recognized as working at one of the other real estate firms was being forcibly escorted to a waiting transport. The side of his face was bruised, and he was bleeding pretty badly from the shoulder.

"W-what did he do?" I asked.

"Something he shouldn't have," Jerome replied. He stepped away as a second Peacekeeper approached and briefed him on the capture. It seemed that the prisoner in question, one Malcolm Hernandez, had been selling charms. They didn't know how long it had been going on, but being that he'd gotten bold enough to sell them in the office cafeteria, Jerome said that they were going to assume that the illegal activity had gone on for over five years, and their commander would recommend the maximum sentence. Death.

The second Peacekeeper went off to relay Jerome's orders, and Jerome sauntered back to me. "We'll have all this cleaned up in no time," he murmured, leaning on my door. "I won't keep you from work much longer, little lady."

Really? Little lady? I forced a smile and hoped Jerome would think I was nervous rather than disgusted. "Thank you. I appreciate it."

"So, what time do you get off?"

"Eight," I lied. My workday ends at five, and I hardly ever stay for overtime. I wouldn't want happy hour to think I didn't love it anymore.

"That's an awfully long day."

"Overtime, you know," I said quickly. "Taxes and all."

"Well, maybe I'll swing by around then," Jerome suggested. I smiled a bit wider, so much so that my cheeks ached. Thankfully, another Peacekeeper shouted to Jerome that they were ready to transport the prisoner. "Till then," he said, patting the hood of my car.

"Till then," I echoed. I kept the ridiculous clown smile plastered across my face as they drove off, Jerome waving and nudging his buddies. Once they were out of sight I exhaled heavily and rested my forehead against the steering wheel. First, I was going to wash his slimy handprints off my car. Second, I was never, ever going to stay at work until eight ever again, overtime be damned. It wasn't like I needed the money, anyway, and—

And my token chose that moment to fall out of my shirt, reminding me why I was here so early in the first place.

I started the car, threw it into gear, and practically flew down the street toward REES. I pulled into the parking lot so fast I caught air on the speed bumps, and then screeched to a halt in my usual spot before the Lovers' Pine. I was so rattled it took me three tries to cross into the Otherworld; for a moment, I didn't realize I'd made the jump. It appeared as serene as it had yesterday when Micah had offered me his token, tranquil and lovely and totally at odds with my frazzled state. Clutching the silver token, I ran toward Micah's home, shouting his name.

Suddenly, he was there. "My Sara," Micah called in greeting, then looked me over from head to foot. "Again, you've come to me dressed like a man." Speechless, I looked down at my jeans. Here I was, terrified for his safety, and all he could say was that I was wearing pants?

"Where have you been?" I yelled. Micah, wearing his usual buff leather gear and a slightly bemused expression, was obviously fine. I, however, had by now well and truly lost it.

"Here," he replied. "Should I be elsewhere?"

Now that I was certain of his safety, I really wanted to beat him. "I thought you'd been captured!"

Micah cocked his head to the side, as if capture was an utterly foreign concept here in the Otherworld. "Who would attempt to capture me?"

"Anyone!" I shrieked. "Peacekeepers, spies, someone who thought they could cut your ears off and sell them at the goddamned Promenade!" His eyes widened at that last bit, and he absently touched his ears. As he did, his sleeve slipped, and I saw the copper cuff about his wrist. Faltering, I stammered, "You're wearing it?"

"Is it not for me?" he asked.

"It is. I…" I turned away and covered my face with my hands. Micah was obviously fine, and I'd freaked out over nothing. "Why didn't you wake me?" I whispered. "Or… or dreamwalk to me?"

"You looked so exhausted. I couldn't bear to disturb you." Then Micah's hands were on my shoulders, and I leaned against him. He was warm. Solid. Safe. "Forgive me, my Sara. I meant no offense."

"You didn't *offend*. It's just…" I gulped some air, and started again. "They took Max."

"Max?"

"My brother. They just took him." Micah shifted so we faced each other and wrapped his arms around me, and for a moment I just enjoyed being in his arms. Never mind that I'd known him for less than a week, or that his presence in my life only meant danger. I'd never been as happy and relieved as I was in that moment, knowing that the Peacekeepers hadn't taken him.

"Come," he said suddenly, drawing me lower into the valley. When I asked where he was taking me, he replied, "To my home."

"I need to get to work," I protested. Everyone at Real Estate Evaluation Services started their workday promptly at nine, lunched at noon, and left at five. It was much easier for the drones to keep track of everyone if we all kept the same basic schedule and, since overtime hours were input to an official database, there were no stragglers. This also meant that, if I showed up more than ten minutes late, there would be an official report. More than four hours late meant my job would be forfeit.

"No," Micah said, firmly. "Not until you have told me all you know of those who have taken your brother, who may also attack me."

"They've taken others," I mumbled. Micah's only response was to squeeze my hand, but it was enough.

It was only a short walk across the dell to Micah's little castle. "Castle" really wasn't the proper term for his home, but it was full of turrets and arched windows, and I couldn't bring myself to call such a grand structure a house. It was so much, much more than what that simple word conveyed. But then, it did not have a drawbridge, and thus no moat and no moat monster. Pity.

As we approached, I caught sight of two figures lurking on the far ridge. I was still pretty shaken up from my run-in with Peacekeeper Jerome, and my first thought was that they were an Otherworldly police force. "Who are they?"

"Iron warriors," Micah replied.

"Will they…is it safe for them to be here?"

Micah tightened his arm about my shoulders. "Of course," he murmured. "I would never let anything harm you, my Sara."

Gods. I hope he means that.

The whole of Micah's home was a reflective gray, oddly bluish in the morning light, and as we drew nearer I finally appreciated the beauty of the silver structure. I suppose it was only natural for Micah Silverstrand to reside in a silver abode, but I was awed nonetheless. The metal walls and roof were brushed in offsetting squares, mimicking shingles. It was pristinely maintained, save for a bit of tarnish close to the ground, but that was only on the exterior. Inside, the walls gleamed as though they had just been polished. To spare our eyes, the glare of the white metal was broken up by many thick rugs in claret and burgundy hues, and the walls were adorned with intricate tapestries.

"You really live here?" I murmured, staring up a silver staircase. The risers and banister were studded with opals, and a massive ruby sat atop the newel post.

"I do," Micah replied, his bemused smile having returned.

"Does your family live here, too?"

"No. There is only me." He guided me past the staircase and into an elfin version of a front parlor. Portraits, both full-size and miniatures, graced the walls, and there was even a mantle that held what looked to be mementos. Family heirlooms, maybe? I found myself wondering what sort of family lurked in Micah's past. Surely, they were tamer than mine.

My elf led me toward the far wall, which was all but overtaken by a massive knot of tree roots, gnarled and knobby. A thick expanse of cushions in varying hues of blue lay atop the woody ledge. I gladly sank onto the Otherworldly couch, perhaps the most comfortable seat I'd ever experienced. In a soft voice, Micah asked, "Now, tell me of these abductors."

I dropped my eyes, at once full of irrational fear and shame. "Do you know about the Magic Wars?" He nodded. "Ever since, magic has been illegal. I mean, the government still uses it, but they say it's too dangerous for the public."

"Dangerous?" Micah echoed, his brow furrowed. "For one such as you, wielding magic is as natural as a bird taking to the wind."

"That's what Dad thought," I murmured. "My father fought for magic with the war mages, but he went missing during the wars. We still don't know if he's alive or dead." My voice trailed off, and I was silent until Micah pressed something into my hand. It was a silver chalice, large and heavy, like the grail of legend.

"It will calm you," he replied to my unasked question.

"Where'd you get this?"

"One of the servants brought it," he replied.

"No one's been in here!" My voice was a bit too shrill, but Micah only chuckled.

"You can see them, if you know how to look," he soothed.

I squinted and looked around the room. I saw nothing, not a person or gnome or field mouse…but then, something shimmered. That something slowly took the shape of a being, not male or female, but a being, nonetheless. It was about three feet tall, pale, and slightly shiny.

"The metal!" I exclaimed. "The metal does your bidding!"

"It does," he confirmed, obviously pleased with my reasoning. "I call them the silverkin."

"Silverkin," I murmured. "I thought you were all alone here."

"As long as I have silver, I am never alone," he stated. "Now, tell me of Max."

Instead of speaking, I stared at the contents of the goblet. "What is this?"

"Chamomile," Micah replied. "Along with a bit of brandy."

"I shouldn't have this," I said, pushing it toward him. "They say, if you consume food or drink in the Otherworld, you're trapped here for eternity."

Micah laughed. "What nonsense you humans believe! I have consumed your food and drink on many occasions, yet I am not trapped in the Mundane World. And," he murmured, pressing the rim to my lips, "would it be so terrible to be trapped with me?" His silver eyes held me fast, almost daring me to answer him.

"I guess not," I murmured, then took a sip to placate him. Despite what he'd said, it seemed to be mostly brandy with a touch of chamomile, but it was good, and it did calm me. When I lowered the goblet, Micah was still looking at me expectantly, so I launched into the tale of two girls who'd lost a boy.

"Do you... how much do you remember about the Magic Wars?"

"A bit," he replied. "I try not to involve myself in the affairs of men."

Smart idea. "The wars came out of nowhere. We're taught in school that there was unrest for years between the Elementals and the Mundane leaders, but I don't remember it that way. I mean, I was young, but I was old enough to understand what was going on around me." I fell silent for a moment, once again lying under the fairy tree behind the Raven Compound, Max and Sadie beside me. Mom and Dad were off in the meadow, laying out sandwiches and fried chicken for a picnic lunch. Life was simple then, simple and good.

My life was neither of those things now. "Then, all the radio and television stations went black, and for a few days, no one knew what had happened," I continued. "We were cut off. After almost a week of isolation, Dad received a summons. It was from the war mages. He never came back."

"Was he killed?" Micah asked gently.

"We don't know. Yeah. Probably." Micah pulled me against him, and I rested my head on his strong shoulder. "I mean, why else wouldn't he come back? Unless he thought we were dead; no, even then, he'd have come back to the house." He would have had to return to the Raven Compound, since one just didn't abandon more than a thousand years of family legacy. Even if one thought that family had died.

"When I was younger, I imagined that he was in hiding, and that someday he'd just come walking through the front door," I continued in a small voice. "But that hasn't happened."

The few times I'd told this story, people usually told me to keep my chin up, that I should never give up hope that Dad might come home. Juliana, my confidante in all things, had always gone out of her way to assure me that Dad would find his way home, somehow, some way. Micah didn't do that; he just gave me the space to speak. "You were very small?" he asked at length.

I nodded. "I was seven, and my little sister, Sadie, was three. Almost four." I wondered if Sadie would be able to recognize Dad. My own memory of him was hazy; I remembered strong arms and bright copper hair, and riding on his shoulders. I remembered laughter and happiness.

"Your brother, Max is his name?" Micah prompted, rousing me from my memories. I nodded, and he continued, "He is older than you?"

"Yes. He's two years older than me." I took a deep breath, and burrowed further into Micah's arms. "After the war ended, the government outlawed all magic. No leniency was given; if you were caught practicing, you were taken by the Peacekeepers. If you came from a known magical clan, you were put under guard." I was silent for a moment. "We were watched, me and Max and Sadie and Mom. The three of us still are. As soon as Dad disappeared, before the war even ended, Peacekeepers served Mom with papers dissolving her marriage. They said that Dad was a political criminal, so the government just divorced them and put everything in Mom's name. Max didn't like that."

"A good man never lets an insult to his mother pass," Micah observed.

"He wouldn't stop practicing. No matter how much we begged, no matter how much Mom yelled and Sadie cried, he just wouldn't stop." I pushed up Micah's sleeve and traced the edge of the copper cuff. "So they took him. They just walked in uninvited, went into his room, and took him. He was only fifteen."

I babbled on for a while about my mother's repeated attempts to find out where Max was being held, as she had asked all over again how the government could act so heinously against a child, what the specific charges were, if we would ever see him again. I hadn't openly spoken of Max in so long, it was like ripping open a wound, and a waterfall of pain and anger came rushing forth. Throughout it all, Micah just listened.

"So, when you weren't there this morning, I thought the Peacekeepers had taken you," I finished at last. "I didn't see them take Max. I just woke up and he was gone." Micah smoothed back my hair.

"Max's metal is copper, as yours is?"

"I'm not sure. All three of us have the same coloring. So yeah, probably." He was still messing with my hair, picking through it like a monkey searching for lice. "What are you doing?"

"Looking at your true color." Oh, roots. "Why cover such loveliness?" Micah murmured, as he stroked my dark brown tresses.

"After Max was taken, Mom started dyeing my hair, and Sadie's," I replied. "She said we looked too much like Max and Dad." At that, Micah became serious again, and took my hands in his.

"Then Max must be like you, of copper. If he lives, the Iron Queen should be able to find him."

"What?" I nearly choked on my disbelief. After all this time, to finally be able to learn what had happened to my brother. "Dad, too?"

"Since his power is of metal, then it is quite possible," Micah replied. "Especially if one or both have taken shelter nearby."

"Can you take me to her? Can we ask her now?" I gasped.

"I will request an audience. Be warned, my Sara, this request may not be granted. My queen is a subtle woman, most fickle in her temperaments."

I couldn't believe it. Awed beyond words, I slipped my arms around Micah's neck. "Thank you,"

I whispered. "You don't know what you've given me. Thank you. Thank you so much."

"You are very welcome, my Sara." He stood and drew me to my feet. "I will go at once, and advise my mistress that my consort requires an audience with her."

"Consort?" I repeated. "Why did you call me that?"

"What else am I to call you?" he countered, tracing the silver chain around my neck. "We have exchanged tokens, I have been to your bed." He kissed me, softly. "As long as you wear my token, I belong to you, my Sara."

Well, I hadn't known that *that* was what these tokens meant. "Is being a consort like being married?"

"Somewhat. Once you give me an heir, you will be named Lady Silverstrand."

"Heir?" I still held the chalice and gulped the rest of the brandy, which wasn't the best idea, since my head was already a bit fuzzy. "You mean, a *baby*?"

"Of course."

I swayed a bit on my feet, then looked accusingly at the now empty goblet.

"What was in here?" I slurred. Micah caught me about the waist and lowered us against the cushions.

"It was meant to calm you," he replied. Well, I wasn't just calm, I was positively languid. I pressed my face against Micah's chest; his leather shirt was so stiff and rough compared to his skin, and to get it out of the way, I fumbled with the buttons. I didn't look up, but I imagined his bemused smile as he shrugged out of the shirt and nestled me against his bare torso. The last thing I remember was one of the silverkin tucking a blanket around our waists.

Some time later, I stretched, rolled over, and nearly suffocated myself. After a bit of wheezing, I opened my eyes and discovered that I'd rolled toward the back of the couch, inadvertently pressing my nose against the soft cushions. Impressed that I could manage to be so clumsy even while sleeping, I turned over and found myself faced with a sleeping elf.

He really was a beautiful, albeit unusual-looking, man. Micah's most notable feature was his fluffy silver mane, but even that dramatic hair couldn't detract from his fine-boned features, nor his rich, caramel skin. It didn't seem to be a tan, either, since his neck and chest bore the same deep tone as his face and arms. Unless Lord Silverstrand spent a good deal of his time shirtless…

I grazed my fingertips across his cheekbones, then down his lips, then took the time to trace his jawline. His chin was baby-smooth, and I found myself wondering if elves grew beards. Trolls have beards, everyone knows that, and so do gnomes…but elves? Honestly, I had no idea, but what I did know was that any human male attempting to pass as a non-magical (so really, any modern) man went about clean-shaven. There was an old folk tale that claimed magical beings couldn't bear the touch of iron, or stainless steel razors, against their skin, hence all those bearded trolls. My father had worn his beard proudly; the only time I'd ever seen him shaven had been the day he'd left for the wars.

But Micah was certainly a creature born of magic, and his chin was as smooth as mine. This meant one of two things: the folk tale was wrong (no surprise there), or elves just weren't that hirsute to begin with. I made a mental note to check Micah's bathroom for a shaving kit.

Putting aside the question of elfin facial hair, at least for the moment, I continued learning Micah's topography. I stroked a path down his neck, across his collarbones and southward along his chest, my fingers at last coming to rest upon his belly. His leather pants were laced up with rawhide cords, and, after a few less than appropriate thoughts, I considered his strange attire. As Micah's consort, would I be expected to wear leather suits and run through the forest?

Probably not, since Micah hates it when I wear pants. Dressing like a man, he'd called it. Well, if he thought that I was going to sit around all day and buff my nails just because he put a necklace on me—

Micah opened his eyes and smiled, and suddenly sitting around looking pretty didn't seem like such a bad idea. "My Sara," he murmured after he kissed me. "You've awakened."

72

"How are your eyes silver?" I mumbled. "Like little bits of metal. Mine don't look like copper."

"When copper is left to its own devices, it acquires a most pleasing green patina," he replied. "Perhaps if I polish them a bit…" He made a wiping motion, and I ducked against his chest.

"You're silly," I retorted. I was smiling with him, mumbling about silliness and the brandy having gone to my head, when I sat bolt upright. "What time is it?"

"It is not yet noon," he replied, completely misunderstanding my agitation. "Worry not. I've plenty of time to petition the Iron Queen for your audience."

"I need to get to work!" I tried to vault over him, but his arms held me fast.

"Work? What sort of work?" I sighed, knowing he wasn't about to relax his hold any time soon, so I gave him a high-level explanation of my occupation as a Quarterly Report Sorter. As expected, Micah was unimpressed.

"There is no reason for you to so demean yourself," Micah stated. "I beg you to not suffer this… this *job* again."

He said 'job' as if it were a curse. While I certainly wasn't on the fast track to any career goals, my job at REES wasn't demeaning. Mind-numbingly boring, yes, but not demeaning. "I have to work," I insisted. "It's how I pay for my apartment, and the heating bill, and buy food. It's what people do." I didn't bother mentioning that the only real reason I was working was to blend in with the non-Elementals. That, I was certain, Micah wouldn't understand.

"My Sara, I will care for you," he murmured as he kissed my jaw, "your every need," and trailed his lips across my throat, "your every want," his fingers plucked open the buttons of my blouse, "I will see to." Micah pressed his lips against the thin skin over my breastbone, lingering for a moment. Suddenly, he moved so his face was directly over mine. "Do you doubt me?"

My voice having fled, I merely stared at him. Before he noticed—or at least, before he mentioned—my newly mute state, one of the silverkin appeared beside us. While I fastened my blouse, Micah and the tiny silver creature communicated in their own language. By the time they were through, I was properly covered and winding my hair into a ponytail.

"If I don't show up soon, I'll get fired," I let out in a rush, before his eyes or lips could influence me.

"They will burn you?" he demanded, aghast.

"No, I'll lose my job, which would be bad." I took his hand and tried to impress upon him my need to spend time in a dingy office with overzealous air conditioning and no natural light. "And, if I'm fired, there will be an official report that will follow me for the rest of my life. It will hurt my chances of ever getting a job again. And," I said over his 'I'll care for you' spiel, "it will adversely affect my mother and sister, too."

"Your family is welcome in my home," he said, but his soft eyes betrayed that I'd already won.

"Didn't you say that you'd petition the Iron Queen for me?"

"Very well," he conceded. "Will you be waiting for me tonight?"

"I will," I promised. There was no place I'd rather be than with Micah tonight.

chapter 7

Micah led me back through the trees to where the veil between my world and his was thin. After a goodbye kiss that left me feeling that this consort situation was workable, except for the whole heir aspect, I stumbled out of the Otherworld. And into my car. *Just call me Grace.*

Apparently, that brandy Micah had given me was lingering in my system, since I thought it was a great idea to head directly from the Otherworld into the office. Luckily, I hadn't lost as much time as I'd feared while napping my morning away in Micah's silver castle, and it was long before lunch, and firing, time.

"I had car trouble," I explained to my boss, hoping he'd buy my admittedly lame excuse. I was still wearing the clothes I'd slept in, twice now, which bore evidence of my walk through the woods. Between my rumpled blouse and the pine needles sticking out from the cuffs of my jeans, I certainly looked like I'd been struggling with something all morning. I smiled brightly, and hoped my heretofore-spotless attendance record counted for something.

Luckily, my boss was the owner of a cantankerous old jalopy, and he sympathized. "Make it up by the end of the week," he grumbled. I nodded and left his office quickly, before I could say anything (else) foolish.

No sooner was I at my desk than my coworkers arrived in droves, wanting to know what had happened, and, more importantly, what had *really* happened. In a culture where everyone scrimped and saved merely to eat every day, no one came to work late for any reason short of death. What's more, the fact that I'd had car trouble and been able to get it fixed without having to wait for a paycheck or two was unheard of. Since the wars ended, jobs were still scarce, and money scarcer, unless you worked for the government and, let's face it, your average desk jockey isn't exactly Peacekeeper material. Over the past few months of my employment at REES, I'd gotten pretty good at pretending to be poor.

You see, when the government had dissolved Mom and Dad's marriage, they'd also made her the sole beneficiary of the Raven clan's vast fortune. That, coupled with the government stipend that was wired directly into our bank accounts every Friday, meant that the remaining Corbeaus wanted for nothing. Hush money, she called it, but they claimed they were only doing right by her. As far as anyone knew, Dad had married a Mundane woman with no magical abilities to speak of, and his children were too young to be trained. So, as a show of good faith, they'd given her the means to live her life in the fashion she and her children had become accustomed to.

Yeah. Hush money.

So, I lived in a tiny apartment, worked at a low-paying office job, and had a closet filled with thrift store finds. I'd explained away my new car by inventing an uncle who worked at an auction house and detailing the many tricks he'd used to make an old heap look new and shiny. My coworkers had grumbled in solidarity, each recalling a car they'd gotten taken on in the past. When I told the horde of gossipmongers crowded around my desk that a mechanic near my apartment owed me, so he'd gotten the work done fast and cheap, the lies just rolled off my tongue. Well, with everyone except Juliana, who lingered long after the rest had wandered away.

"Your car broke down?" she repeated with a raised brow. She was one of the few who knew how I babied it. We'd never missed regular maintenance, my car and I; I hardly ever let the wiper fluid get low.

I tried to play it cool. "Turned out to be a loose wire," I replied. "I guess it wasn't hooked up properly during the last tune-up."

"Mmm." She let that one go, but only to start a new line of inquiry.

"I tried to call you this morning," she said. "About five times."

My hands flew to my pockets, only to come up empty. I'd been in such a panic this morning I'd only grabbed my keys, leaving behind my phone, my purse, and all my other daily necessities. I didn't even have money for lunch.

And…I'd left the watch that held my tracking device in my car. Crap.

"I was in a hurry, and I forgot it," I mumbled. Distracted as I searched my desk for food, I stood and rummaged in my file cabinet. As I did, Juliana's eyes fixated on my neck.

"Where'd you get that?" she asked, eyeing the silver chain.

"From a boy," I replied, fluttering my eyes. I pulled it out of my shirt to show her the oak leaf and acorn. "Isn't it nice?" Juliana leaned forward to get a better view, and caught a whiff of my breath.

"Have you been drinking?" she accused.

No point in adding to the lies. "Keep it down," I hissed. "I had a late night."

"You were out all night with this mysterious man, you show up late for work smelling like a brewery, and now you've got a fortune in silver hanging around your neck." She lowered her voice and asked, "Is he a pimp?"

"What? No!" Her accusation wasn't completely out of the blue; lots of girls we knew turned to streetwalking in order to make ends meet. I, however, would never, ever be one of them, even if that Raven-funded bank account dried up this instant. "He's just well-off. I think his family has money."

Juliana straightened up, still giving me that appraising eye. "You didn't have any car trouble, did you?"

"No," I replied sheepishly. "It was the first excuse I could think of."

"Well, tonight, at The Room, you can tell me all about your man."

"I can't go tonight. I'm meeting up with him."

"Bring him."

Oh, that would just be awesome. Hey, Juliana, meet my elfin consort. He lives in a silver palace, you know, with gem-encrusted hallways and tiny silver servants. "Maybe after a few more dates," I replied. "Why bother introducing him if he won't be sticking around?"

Juliana nodded, then rolled a chair over and made herself at home in my cubicle. "So, tell me about him now."

"Well," I began, playing coy while my brain desperately tried to filter out inappropriate content. "What would you like to know?"

"A name, for starters."

"Mi—Mike," I said. "His name is Mike Silver."

"And he gives silver jewelry." Juliana rolled her eyes, but I didn't mind. Although, if Micah really had been a human, a name like Mike Silver would have been pretty lame.

"And he's tall, and super sweet, and—"

"And do you have that same dumb grin on your face when you talk to him?"

My hands flew to my face; yep, I was grinning like a fool. "I can't help it. I really like him."

"All the more reason you should bring him tonight," Juliana said. "We need to properly evaluate him, to know if he's a keeper."

"Oh, he's a keeper," I said, "but we have plans."

Juliana cajoled for a bit longer, but I was adamant in my refusals. It was easy, since showing up with an elf would be an automatic death sentence for Micah, and me, and possibly everyone else at The Room. After Juliana extracted a promise from me to tell her everything over breakfast the next morning, she finally returned to her desk. I turned to my own heap of work, but I couldn't concentrate, couldn't even see the reports in front of me. I couldn't stop thinking about Micah's silver eyes.

chapter 8

I struggled through the rest of the day, though I only managed to accomplish an embarrassingly small amount of work. A few times, I considered shoving those reports into the shredder and pretending that I'd never seen them. Stupid, pointless wastes of paper, that's all they really were. As soon as I organized and logged one folder's worth, Floyd dropped off a new stack, along with a few comments about how I'd paid for the work on my car. I seriously considered stapling his mouth shut.

What was worse than both the endless mound of paper and Floyd's continued existence was avoiding Juliana. I didn't like lying to my best friend, but I really didn't have a choice in the matter. I couldn't exactly tell her that I'd spent the morning with an elf and had asked him to petition a magical queen for help in finding my missing brother and father—*you know, that missing dad I told you about, the patriarch of the Raven clan? Yep, those Ravens, the ones we read about in the history books, who made a final, fruitless stand against the government.*

I spent the afternoon walking reports here and there across the office, repeatedly declining Juliana's invitations to head over to The Room. Finally, I insisted that I would be staying late to make up the hours I'd missed that morning; she didn't like that excuse, but it was one she couldn't argue with.

Before I knew it, the clock struck five, and all my dedicated coworkers made a beeline toward the door. From my vantage point by the file cabinets, I watched as they practically ran toward the parking lot, pairing up in twos and threes as they piled into cars and departed. As soon as the lot was empty, I abandoned my pointless paperwork and drove home.

I burst through my apartment door, relieved that I'd remembered to lock it, doubly relieved to find my purse in its usual spot on the side table. I plunked the watch/illegally-removed tracker on the table, and I wondered if—no, make that *when*—I'd be questioned about today. Since I had been at REES, the government had known exactly where I had been all day, my presence having been verified by several drones and our ancient, cranky time clock, not to mention extra-thorough Peacekeeper Jerome. I still needed to wash those handprints off my car.

I sighed and shoved the watch into the depths of my purse. Would they ever really know where I had been that morning? Did they bother to check time clock reports against tracker coordinates? I couldn't imagine why they would bother, unless Mom was right and we really were always being watched. *Gods. Please, don't let Mom's paranoias come true.*

If the Peacekeepers did choose to question me as to my whereabouts, I'd have the not so small problem of my tracker being outside my body. And, no, there was no suitable explanation for this; they'd even started leaving trackers in corpses, since a group of mages had faked their own deaths a few years ago. I didn't want to re-implant the tracker in my shoulder, but what else could I do? If Peacekeepers chose to examine me and it wasn't there, I'd probably be locked up. The only excuse I could think of was a malfunction of my powers; no, that definitely wouldn't work, since I was not supposed to be able to use them. Not to mention that a fresh wound on my shoulder would be a dead giveaway.

Great. Looked like I'd finally find Max, after all.

Since there was nothing I could do about the tracker, I left it and grabbed my phone. As I unwound the charging cable, I checked the call log. Yep, Juliana had called me five times before lunch, and twice since she'd left work. I appreciated her concern, but really, if she didn't start paying less attention to me, and more to her own life, I wouldn't be the only terminally single girl.

Phone comfortably charging, I headed toward the bathroom. As I stood in the shower, letting the steaming water soothe my aching muscles and rinse away the lingering scents of pine and alcohol and toner cartridges, evidence of both my morning in the Otherworld and my afternoon in the office, I couldn't help thinking about Micah. 'Consort.' He'd called me his consort and seemed to have no problem becoming instantly serious with a woman he hardly knew. It hadn't even been a week since he'd showed up in my dream (or rather, since I'd pulled him into it), and he was already discussing heirs. Which was a fancy word for children! Sometimes, I didn't feel like much more than a child myself.

Not that any of this heir and consort nonsense mattered. The few men who'd ever been serious about me hadn't stayed that way for long, as evidenced by my unworn lingerie and single occupancy apartment. As much as I wanted Micah to be different, past experience had me a bit too jaded to be picking out baby names just yet.

The water ran cold, as sure a sign as any that my shower time was over. After I toweled off and ran a comb through my hair, I pulled on a pair of shorts and a T-shirt, and then padded barefoot to the kitchen in search of food. I hadn't eaten all day, except for a few stale pretzels I'd found stashed in my desk, and my rumbling stomach refused to be ignored any longer. I'd hardly made any headway when I heard a knock at my door.

Who could that be? All my friends were at The Room, my rent was paid up, Mom never came over without calling first, and Sadie was in the middle of a semester. I squinted through the peephole, and to my utter horror saw Micah standing in the corridor.

"Did anyone see you?" I whispered, after I threw open the door.

"Of course not," was Micah's indignant reply. "I thought you would prefer it if I knocked."

He looked hurt, and I felt like an ass. "I'm sorry. I shouldn't have greeted you that way. Start over?" Micah nodded, then I shut the door. Playing along, he knocked again.

"Micah," I said with a smile, as I opened the door. "I am so glad to see you."

"My Sara," he greeted me, his bemused smile having returned.

"Was that better?" I asked.

"Much." As I invited him inside, I noticed his clothing. Instead of his usual suit of pale leather he wore a soft ivory shirt that laced up the front, tailored black breeches, and tall black boots. His puff of silvery hair was neatly restrained at the nape of his neck, and an ornate sword hung at his side. Yeah, my elf was pretty hot. "You are dressed very nicely."

"And you are dressed like a man, yet again," Micah observed. I sat cross-legged on the couch beside him, something else he clearly didn't approve of.

"I can dress however I like in my house," I declared. "Did you pull out the formal attire for me?"

"You are worthy of far more than a few bits of fabric," he said, catching my hand and pressing it to his lips. "I am dressed so for my audience with my mistress, the Iron Queen."

"What did she say?" I gasped.

"She will hear your petition." Relief washed over me, and I flopped back against the couch. "She did not guarantee aid," he warned.

"I know." I sat up, and looked into his silver-gray eyes. "For nearly half of my life, I've tried to find out what happened to Max and Dad. Even though this is only a step, it's still the closest I've ever come." I leaned forward and took his hands. "Micah, I don't know how I will ever thank you."

"You are most welcome, my Sara," he murmured, squeezing my hand.

"We should celebrate." I sprang up from the couch and returned to the kitchen. In my world, good news was best served with a side dish of alcohol and food. I emerged in a few moments with two glasses of wine, balanced on a tray, alongside a block of cheese, some crackers, and a few apples. I set everything down, realized I had forgotten a knife, and returned to the kitchen, swiping the bottle of wine and some honey on the way.

"Eat," I ordered, once the apples and cheese were sliced. "And put honey on it; it's so much better that way." Micah sampled a bit of cheese, and nearly spit it out.

"You eat this on purpose?" he demanded, after a big gulp of wine.

"It's the only cheese I can get right now," I said apologetically. Real cheese was contraband, though it sometimes showed up at the Promenade bearing outrageous price tags. Food was highly regulated in this day and age, and almost everything we ate had to be inspected by Peacekeepers. Since the government no longer trusted natural items, this meant a lot of factory-processed foods and tasteless vegetables grown without soil or fresh air. Ironically, we still had full access to harmful things, such as alcohol and cigarettes, but possessing too much sun-ripened fruit could put you on the watch list. "I know, it's not as good as real cheese."

"You are a woman of contradictions," Micah said, shaking his head as he assembled slices of cheese atop the apple. I leaned forward and liberally doused them with honey, hoping to mask the rubbery flavor.

"Contradictions? How is that?" I asked, licking honey from where it had dripped onto my wrist.

"You live in a hovel, eating this slop your elders force upon you. You have more power than ten mages, yet you pretend to be a weak girl." Silver eyes narrowed over the rim of his wineglass, taking in all that was me. "No one truly knows the depth of you, is that right?"

"I don't live in a hovel," I protested. My apartment was small, but it was nice. And very clean.

"I meant no insult," he amended. "I only believe you worthy of a far more comfortable abode." I smiled, since how could I argue with that? Micah caught a lock of my hair between his long fingers. "I wish you hadn't made your hair the color of mud."

I grinned wickedly, drained my wineglass in a very unladylike manner, and balanced the stem between the soles of my feet. Micah either understood what I was about to do or was content to wait, since he said nothing as I flipped my hair forward and began running my fingers through it. After a moment, a single drop of brown goo splashed into the bowl of the wineglass, and then another. It was slow to start, but in a short time I'd squeezed the dye from my hair like so much water.

"One of the few tricks I can do," I explained, as Micah wrinkled his nose at the ammonia-scented chocolate liquid. Laughing, I set the wineglass on the coffee table. One of the many things the Mundane World has forgotten about Elementals is that we can wield many forms of magic, not just the spells linked to our elements. I still remembered, all too vividly, the time I'd accidentally dyed my hair green and willed the offending color as far away from me as possible; it turned out that the farthest I could send it was splattering onto my mother's white tile floor. At first, I had been amazed that I could accomplish such a feat, then I had feared for my life if Mom ever walked in on such a mess. After an afternoon spent on my hands and knees, using harsh bleach to scrub away the evidence before Mom—or tattletale Sadie—caught me, I was always careful to keep a bowl nearby.

"My true Sara is at last revealed," Micah approved. "Never obscure this lovely shade again." My cheeks warmed; as I ducked my head, I caught sight of something on his face.

"You have honey on your chin," I explained, as I leaned forward to wipe it away.

"Do I?" He dipped a finger in the jar and quickly dabbed honey on my lower lip. "So do you. Here, let me." Then, I was in Micah's arms as he gently licked the sweet, sticky stuff from my lips. "I wonder if there's any more." He explored my chin, my neck, and the sensitive spot behind my ears, before returning to claim my lips. I must admit, he was quite thorough.

I pulled his shirt up and over his head, feeling those amazing silver streaks and curls across his shoulders and broad back, and was rewarded with more fervent kisses. Micah's mouth traveled down my neck to the edge of my shirt and snaked down my body to caress my belly. He inched the thin cotton upward, taking the time to thoroughly acquaint himself with all he revealed. Slowly, as if asking permission, his hand traveled around to stroke my mark. When I arched my back he smiled, and I felt a gentle tug at my waist.

For the second time that evening, a knock sounded at my door. "Ignore it," Micah all but commanded, his voice muffled by my breasts. Then the unmistakable voice of Juliana H. Armstrong wafted through the reinforced steel, and I sighed.

"I can't. She's persistent." I sat up and wound my hair into a messy knot, then pointed toward the bathroom. "You. Hide."

"I do not hide," he said, with a peevish tone worthy of having been asked to empty a litter box.

"Micah—"

"She will not know me for what I am," Micah stated as he pulled his shirt over his head. Juliana's pounding grew more insistent, so I had to trust him.

"Yes, dear?" I asked, as I opened the door.

"The Room was lame, so I thought I'd see what you're up to." I resisted the urge to point out that The Room was always lame, just as the grass is always greener in your neighbor's yard, and the sky always bluest while you're working. Then my heart was in my throat as Juliana walked past me, only to halt when she saw Micah. I followed her gaze, but I didn't see an elfin lord. Instead, there was a man with close-cropped brown hair and round human ears seated on my couch. His billowy ivory tunic and dark breeches were gone, replaced by a white button-down shirt and jeans. But the features were still his, and the twinkle in his suddenly brown eyes as he raised his glass in greeting was undeniably Micah's.

"The boy?" Juliana asked, with a sidelong glance.

"The boy," I confirmed. "Juliana, this is Mike."

They exchanged nominal pleasantries, and then Juliana's gaze swept to the table. Her brow wrinkled when she saw the wineglass full of dye, but she didn't ask about it. Thank. Freaking. God. Taking a hint for perhaps the first time in her life, she apologized for barging in unannounced. As she turned to leave, she snatched a lock of my hair.

"Love the color," she said. "When did you do it?"

"After work," I said. It wasn't a lie, so it came easily. "Mike asked about my natural color, and here it is."

"Mmm. Well, talk to you later." With that she was gone, and I slumped against the closed door. Cold sweat broke out across my body, and my heart beat in an irregular tattoo.

"That was the most nerve-wracking two minutes I've ever spent," I mumbled. I looked up and saw Micah, once again in all his elfin glory.

"She is not your friend," he stated.

"What? Juliana is the best friend I've ever had!"

"She lies to you. The deceit swirls about her, black, like poison." I considered Juliana's earlier interrogation after my late arrival at work, and now she'd just popped up here. She'd never dropped in before, no matter what she was out doing. Not to mention the way she'd tried to barge into my room after my dream with Micah. I know, I screamed, but my life has given me ample fodder for nightmares. Based on the hundred or so times she'd slept over, there was no way that had been the first time she'd heard me call out in my sleep.

Worst of all, her weird behavior had started a few days ago, the day after I'd met Micah.

I shook my head, unwilling to deal with such implications at the present moment. I had more important matters before me, specifically the matters of Max and Dad. "When can we see this queen?" I asked.

Micah cocked his head to the side, as if listening to a chime in the distance. "If we leave now, we will arrive in time for her next audience."

"All right." I pushed myself up from the door, at once determined and terrified. And I was grateful, both for Micah's help and his calm, reassuring presence. "Let's go."

chapter 9

After a long, tedious discussion centered upon what was and was not appropriate attire for a woman *(basically, Micah disapproved of my entire wardrobe, using such words and phrases as "mannish" and "not worthy of my consort")*, Micah and I climbed into my car and drove toward my employer's parking lot, the closest location where the veil was thin. I was wearing the nicest dress I owned, an emerald-green sheath that had made occasional appearances at weddings and other formal events. The neckline was much lower than I usually dared, and it showcased Micah's token against my décolletage, which were both factors in his approval. I'd decided to wear my hair up, and ever-helpful Micah had worked the bits of copper wire and malachite left over from his cuff into elegant combs. A girl could get used to this.

What I could not get used to was Micah's human illusion, Mike. Every time I glanced toward the passenger seat I was startled by the sight of a strange man in my car. Of course, he really was still a stranger to me, wasn't he? Why was I letting him call me his consort? Of all the things I wanted in my life, a husband, no matter what he was called, wasn't one of them, and neither were children. Was I only going along with him to find out what had happened to Max and Dad? If so, then I was a terrible person. A terrible person who needed to end this now, before it spiraled further out of control.

As if he knew I was thinking about him, Micah slid his hand onto my knee and squeezed. Instantly, I felt his heat slowly spread throughout my leg. The attraction between us was strong and undeniable, but I still couldn't let myself trust in it. Blame my past if you will, but I kept expecting to find out that Micah was using me.

These fears of mine weren't entirely irrational, and neither were they without precedent. Past boyfriends, employers, and even one of my college professors had tried to influence me, a Raven fledgling. Neither my identity nor my parentage has ever been a secret—I mean, my last name *is* Corbeau—though it's not something I usually brought up. Still, many had sought to gain my favor, only to be disappointed when I'd informed them that I *had* no power to speak of. Invariably they left me, apparently having forgotten the heartfelt promises they'd made a short time before.

"You have nothing natural in your world," Micah murmured, rousing me from thoughts of past betrayals. I glanced toward him and saw his temporarily brown eyes tracking a drone as it hummed across the horizon. "Everything is a machine."

I laid my hand on top of Micah's and grazed my thumb across his knuckles; all too often, I'd felt cut off from nature, imprisoned in a life dominated by timers and alarms. "The government told us machines were safer than nature, and we believed them," I explained.

He harrumphed at this, and I smiled in spite of myself. Micah just might be different than all the rest. He hadn't known about my family when he'd sought me out. He'd wanted me for me.

No, he'd just wanted to get some.

"When we met," I began. "In the parking lot. Do you do that a lot?"

"Dreamwalk?"

"Hop into cars with strange women."

Micah chuckled. "No."

"Then, why me?"

He leaned closer, caressing his fingers down my neck. "I couldn't help myself."

I downshifted, and Micah moved aside to allow me room; the action also hid the shiver that radiated from where his fingertips had just rested. I pulled onto a street that bordered the office lot and parked behind a decrepit hardware store. Only fools went there expecting to purchase hammers and nails; the place was really a front for an herbal tincture supply ring. In the modern world, midwives and Peacekeepers didn't exactly get along.

"Why are you leaving the mechanical here?" Micah inquired.

"The office lot has cameras," I explained. "If they see me pulling in with someone who isn't an employee, I'll have some explaining to do." We got out and, when I looked across the roof, Mike was gone and my Micah once again stood before me. I felt a surge of warmth, as if the missing part of my soul had been returned to me after a long absence. He looked quizzically at me, but I just shook my head. I wasn't quite ready to admit what I was feeling, consort or no. Then he took my hand, and after a short walk through the trees, we stepped out of my world and into his.

In a far shorter time than I needed to mentally prepare myself, we stood before a towering iron edifice. Maybe it was just the color, but the sight of the cruel spires and jagged, toothy gates chilled me to my core. It was a metal palace like Micah's home, but the similarities ended there. Micah's silver palace radiated warmth and happiness, but the structure before us was cold and gray, as if cold had transitioned from a sensation to one of the more tangible elements. I wanted to run and hide from the emotions stirred up by this iron palace, but I couldn't. My way to Max and Dad lay within.

"Is it always like this?" My earlier uncertainties forgotten, at least for the moment, I laced my fingers with Micah's. His flesh was warm, and likely the only bit of comfort I'd find here.

"Yes." He squeezed my fingers as he led me through the massive gray archway. It reminded me of the entrance to a fairyland dungeon, replete with grotesques and gargoyles set about the roofline and a wickedly pointed iron gateway poised to impale any trespassers below. On either side of the entrance stood iron footmen, a bit rusty about the lower joints but formidable nonetheless. The sight of their gnarled, pointed teeth was enough to stop my heart.

"Ignore them," Micah muttered as they leered at me. The footman to my right leaned closer, whispering the many things he'd do to my fragile form once Micah was distracted. I did as I was told and tried to ignore him, but this only made him mad. Saying he'd teach me a lesson, the footman's hand shot out, quick as a snake, and grabbed at my wrist. Before I could scream, Micah's hands were around his neck, and the footman's head was rolling away from me.

"Sara!" I blinked, realizing that Micah was repeating my name. I tore my eyes from the severed head and looked at Micah. "Did he harm you?"

"N-no." I looked at my wrist; Micah had moved so quickly that the footman hadn't even touched me. "Is he dead?"

"Ferra will repair him, or not," Micah said flatly as he ushered me inside the iron palace. I could hardly believe that Micah had so easily separated an iron guard's head from his body, or that the guard wasn't permanently dead—and wait, was Ferra seriously the Iron Queen's name?

But then we were in the atrium of the Iron Queen's palace, and I thought it best to leave off such musings. The interior gleamed with polished iron, accented here and there with ornate gold scrollwork supporting fat candles; it seemed like, if I looked closely, I could make out what appeared to be bones set amidst the gold, so I didn't. As I glanced away, another vision caught me, this time the opening to an oubliette. A stench wafted upward along with pleas for clemency, and I wondered what they'd done to be thrown down the forgotten hole.

"Why does she get to use gold?" I mumbled, trying to make out the symbols etched into the golden ring edging the oubliette. Micah's home was floor to ceiling silver, without so much as a speck of any other metals. Well, none except for me.

"She once captured a number of Gold Elementals, and stripped them," Micah responded, startling me. For one, I'd been asking a rhetorical question, and two, what, exactly, did he mean by 'stripped?'

"You mean, she took whatever metal they carried," I said, a bit desperately. Micah's grim eyes told me otherwise, and he nodded toward the oubliette. "Weapons and jewelry."

"Everything that was of their element, she took," he said. I clenched his arm so tightly I knew I'd leave a mark. Even I, intentionally kept ignorant of my power, knew that stripping one's element left one a pathetic shell of one's former self: powerless, hopeless, less than Mundane.

"Why didn't the gold king—the gold queen! Why didn't they stop her?" I demanded.

"Whose essence do you think decorates Ferra's throne?" Micah countered. "Who do you think calls to us from the oubliette?" The room was warm and humid, but I shivered.

"What is this place?" I gasped, my eyes sweeping around the room, again coming to rest upon the oubliette.

"My queen's home." I must have looked well and truly panicked, because Micah leaned close and whispered against my ear, "Be strong. Your audience will be over quickly, and then we will leave at once."

I nodded and offered him a reassuring smile; I knew it was weak, but what else could I do? I would try my best to remain aloof and ignore the obvious corruption pervading the Iron Queen's palace. There was none of the softness of Micah's home, no colorful tapestries or silky cushions. Even the floor was bare metal, but it was scuffed until it was little more than a murky puddle. I hated being here, hated everything about this horrible, wretched place. If it weren't for the slim chance of learning vital information about Max and Dad, I would have turned and fled.

We pressed on and, upon reaching a massive set of rusty doors, Micah murmured a set of instructions to a footman. Quickly, he hurried off, and a few moments later he escorted us to the front of the atrium with alacrity, all the while referring to Micah as Lord Silverstrand.

"Why are we moving past the rest?" I wondered aloud.

"My name carries some clout," Micah replied, with a wry grin.

Silverstrand. His surname was Silverstrand, he lived in a silver castle…

"Are you the lord of *all silver*?" I blurted in an almost reverential tone.

"I am," he confirmed. "Though other metals are compliant as well," he added, lightly touching the copper combs in my hair.

"I had no idea." Micah looked as if he would say more, but another of the metal attendants stepped forth, this one rust-free. After a few curt instructions, we were ushered before the Iron Queen.

The queen's hall was polished metal, not all scuffed and dull like the outer rooms,, though it had a long way to go before it would reach the reflective sheen of Micah's home. Or maybe iron just doesn't reflect as nicely as silver. Not to mention that the hall was packed shoulder to shoulder with, I don't know, supplicants. Or petitioners, or whatever you call people who hang out in a glorified dungeon. There was every sort of beastie imaginable, from the innocuous gnome to what appeared to be the mythical

Cyclops. Of all the critters to turn out to be real, it just had to be him.

Micah was unmoved by the press of bodies, and he strode purposefully toward the Elemental monarch. A gleaming gold pathway snaked through the hall like a ribbon, leading us toward a raised golden dais. There were four shallow steps, atop which Ferra, the Iron Queen, sat on a golden throne.

My breath caught in my throat at the sight of the metal queen. I'd never been in the presence of royalty before, and she carried herself as if she'd been born to her position. While she wasn't beautiful, she sure wasn't ugly. The queen's jaw was square and her brow wide, her long steel-colored hair restrained by a narrow gold fillet before cascading down her shoulders. I wondered if that fillet was all that was left of the Gold Queen's hair.

As my eyes traveled down her form, I gasped again; perhaps it was due to her status as Iron Queen, but whatever the reason, her upper body was clad in a rather sheer chain mail shirt. Then, she shifted and my suspicion was confirmed: there was nothing beneath the mail. She also wore a mail skirt, though thankfully she was seated so I could at least pretend her lower half was covered, and a long crimson cloak shielded her back. My cheeks grew hot as I struggled to maintain my composure, and I hoped Micah would be called upon to speak first. I didn't know if I could converse with half-naked royalty while maintaining a straight face.

"Lord Silverstrand," the queen greeted. "Twice in one day you grace my hall. To what do we owe the honor?"

"As I advised my liege during my prior audience, my consort desires a boon," he replied, his voice low and sonorous. The queen shifted her gaze to me and laughed softly. I could not imagine what was more amusing than her attire.

"You call this girl your consort? There is no silver upon her!" A chuckle bubbled up around us, but Micah kept his face impassive. I almost told the queen that she was wrong, that I was wearing Micah's silver token, when the full meaning of her barb dawned upon me.

"You see, she blushes like a maid!" Ferra laughed at Micah's expense. "What sort of consort have you dredged up, Micah? You'll never get an heir if you only call children to your bed!"

His ears pinked, but his tone remained respectful. "Our situation is unusual, yes," Micah allowed. "About the boon, my lady?"

"Yes, yes." The queen waved her hand, and all laughter in the hall ceased. "What would you like to know, child?"

"My brother," I squeaked; Mom would be furious if she knew I had let this woman intimidate me, queen or no. I took a deep breath and squared my shoulders, and was still a little shocked that my voice held steady. "He was taken away by my government ten years ago. I want to know if he's still alive."

"And he is an Elemental?"

"Yes, ma'am. He is of copper, as I am."

The Iron Queen regarded me in silence for long, arduous moments. "If I am to determine whether he is live or dead, I must first hear his name."

"Maximillien Corbeau," I replied readily. "Maximillien Laurent Corbeau."

The queen's brows peaked in interest. "Should I know of your family?"

"My father was—is—Baudoin Corbeau." When I said my father's name, a palpable hush rolled across the hall. Those who'd laughed at Micah and me now looked at us with a measure of respect. Yes, I silently told them all, my father is the patriarch of the Raven clan and yes, in my brother's absence, I am the heir apparent. No one was laughing now.

The queen rose and descended from her dais, and my hope that the lower half of her wore somewhat more than a chain mail skirt was dashed. It was more of a loincloth, leaving her legs bare nearly to her waist. There was, thankfully, a strategically placed belt. She stood before me and placed her fingertips on my temples; Micah mumbled a protest, but we both ignored him. Her fingers were hard, hard as iron, and I swear they poked through my skull and directly into my brain. After a small eternity, she spoke.

"I could tell you many things, little Raven," the queen began. "I could tell you that in every generation there is a singularly gifted wielder of each element, an Inheritor of Power. I could tell you that all such Elementals of this generation are known, save metal. But I won't." Her steely eyes glinted, cold and foreboding like a winter's dawn. "What I will tell you is that your brother lives, though I cannot bring him to you." She pressed her fingers harder into my brain, and frowned. "You father I cannot sense, but then, that was always his way. Likely, Baudoin still breathes as well. I certainly cannot imagine him allowing death to have its way with him."

Relief flooded me. Max was alive, Dad was probably alive. "Thank you, mistress." She graced me with a cold, calculating smile before sweeping back to her throne; at least the cloak covered the back of her.

There was a bit of ceremony as Micah and I were dismissed from the Iron Queen's presence, but I hardly heard it. The fact that Max and Dad were alive had me so elated my feet barely touched the floor. My head swam, drunk with my newfound knowledge, and I wondered what I should do next. I needed to call Sadie and get her to come home from college so I could tell her and Mom together. Then, we'd go into the old basement, the one the Peacekeepers hadn't found…

"This was a mistake," Micah said, suddenly. "We should not have come."

I grabbed his hand, walking backward as I led him out of the dour iron hall and into the fresh air. "But she helped me, just like you said she would. Max is alive!" Micah yanked me toward him, trapping me between a metal wall and his similarly unyielding body.

"Why didn't you tell me who your father is?" he demanded.

"I… I didn't think it mattered," I mumbled. Micah's silver eyes blazed, and he pressed closer to me, so close I could feel the cold of the wall seep through my thin dress. He opened his mouth to say more, but one of the iron guards tapped him on the shoulder. After a few lewd comments about what we were doing pressed up against the wall, he sent us on our way. Micah remained sullenly silent until we were out of sight of the queen's palace.

"It matters," he said, his voice quiet. "You father is a powerful man."

"I know," I mumbled.

"And why did you let Ferra touch you?" he continued. "Gods, first she humiliates me before the whole of her court, then you let her place her hands upon your flesh!" He rounded on me, his anger blazing. "You should not have done that!"

"Why not?" I countered. His humiliation was the least of my concerns. "How else was I to get answers?"

"She didn't need to touch you to learn them." I tried to keep walking, but Micah grabbed my arms, effectively halting me. "Sara, she is a very dangerous woman."

"Then why did you bring me here?" I demanded. "You said she could help!"

"That was before I knew that you are a Raven." He spat the word, as if it had dirtied his mouth. "She learned much when she touched you. Too much! I believe she was looking for your father."

"Of course she was! It's what I asked her to do, remember?" I twisted free and started walking again, but Micah wasn't through with his lecture. He grabbed my shoulders and forcibly dragged me against a tree.

"Sara, listen to me," he said, his voice so low it was almost a growl. "You must not return to the Mortal World! I cannot protect you there."

"What about my mother, and Sadie? I can't just disappear on them!"

"After you have been in hiding for a time, I will retrieve them. Now, it will be too dangerous."

"After a time," I repeated. "Where will I be hiding?"

"At my home," he replied, as if the answer was obvious. "I can best protect you where my power is strongest."

"And get silver on me?" I sneered. His eyes widened in shock, then narrowed.

"I'm trying to keep you alive, not take you to bed," he hissed.

"Bullshit," I countered. "You've been trying to get into my pants from the moment you met me! That's all this is about to you! And now you want to separate me from my family, 'protect' me in your home! Is that what elves call it?" I wrenched myself free and stalked away. He caught me yet again, this time grabbing my forearm and whipping me around to face him.

"If all I wanted was an afternoon's frolic in your garden, I'd have had it by now," Micah growled. His grip on my arms was so tight it brought tears to my eyes, but I held his gaze. "I've made you my consort."

"I don't want to be your consort." He released me so suddenly I stumbled, but he steadied me with a hand at the small of my back. My mark flared, making me want him again, but I tamped down my desire like it was an unwanted campfire. "You knew that I didn't know what all this meant. Tokens! All you've done is try to trick me into having sex with you. I never want to see you again!"

"Sara," he began, but I turned and walked away. "My Sara!"

"Not *your* Sara!" I shot back. "We're done, Micah!"

I managed to make it all the way to the car before I broke down in sobs.

chapter 10

I cried during the drive home. I cried as I walked up the stairs to my apartment. I cried while I engaged in apartment-cleaning therapy. I cried while I showered and combed my hair. And I cried while I searched for my favorite bathrobe to wallow in. Micah's loss reverberated to my core, so much so that my breath was ragged and my hands shook. Clumsily, I pawed through my closet until my jittery movements caused the rod to give way. I stood there, shivering and wet as I stared at this latest betrayal, then turned away and left everything in a giant heap. It wasn't like I needed to find anything nice to wear for Micah, anyway.

As I stumbled to the couch and wrapped myself in a fleece blanket, I couldn't recall ever being so heartbroken, not when Max had been taken or even when Dad had disappeared. With the former I'd just been mad, so mad that I was going to give the Peacekeepers a piece of my mind as soon as they brought my brother back, and with the latter I'd been too young to understand what had happened. By the time I was old enough to realize that my father might be forever lost to me, the pain had dulled to an occasional ache.

Not this. This was constant, with sharp spikes of pain tearing at my heart.

Knowing that I'd be useless at work, I called the operator and told her I was feeling sick. Normally, Violet screamed a blue streak at anyone who dared call out of work, especially since tomorrow was a government holiday (Tax Day!) followed by the weekend, but my snuffling must have touched her craggy old heart. "You take care, sugar," was all she said.

And I did, if lying on the couch and eating everything in the kitchen counted as caring for myself. Shortly after noon, there was a knock at my door. My heart leapt, assuming Micah had come to apologize, but it was only Juliana, bearing cartons of takeout. She took one look at my swollen, tear-streaked face, dumped the cartons on the side table, and dragged me right back to the couch.

"Was it as bad as Bill?" she asked.

Oh, she would just have to go there, wouldn't she? Bill was the one I'd bought the nightie for. We'd met shortly after I got the job at REES, on one of the rare occasions when Juliana and I had gone to a bar other than The Room. He was a carpenter who tended toward high-end finish work; his hands were always rough, and he smelled like sawdust. He'd had a rugged masculinity that I'd loved, so much so that I'd told him about my family, and that I was an Elemental. The very next day, he had told me he didn't think we'd work out, and I had been devastated.

I missed Micah so much more than I'd ever missed Bill.

"Worse," I mumbled, sinking into my robe. "Way worse."

That admission prompted Juliana to get the wine, and we sipped chardonnay while we watched bad pre-war monster movies on the Picture Vision. I noticed that she'd swiped one of the good bottles I had been saving for a special occasion, but I didn't call her on it. I supposed today *was* special, if you considered being miserable and wanting to stick your head in the garbage disposal as special.

"I need to head out," Juliana said after the second movie. It was about a shark and an electric eel who had put aside their aquatic differences to keep the ocean safe. Not one of my favorites. "Mom's working, and I need to get dinner together for Corey."

Corey was Juliana's much younger brother. Since their father died, Juliana had become his second mother. She was good at taking care of people, myself included.

"I'll be fine," I said decisively. "He was just a guy." Juliana gave me that look, so I elaborated.

"Really. We'd only known each other for a week. Go. Handle the brother."

I ushered her toward the door, repeatedly affirming my rock-like mental state. As soon as the latch clicked behind her, I was sobbing again.

Only now I was mad as well as sad. Micah had said that Juliana wasn't my friend, but who was here with me? Her, not him. Of course, he had probably only said those things so I'd sleep with him. Jerk.

Once this latest round of sobs had calmed to a somewhat steady flow of tears, I called Sadie. She'd been away at college for a few years now, pursuing an advanced degree in library sciences. Me, I'd studied for two years, grabbed my degree and run, but not Sadie. She had figured that, after all we'd gone through to get into college, she was staying until she either earned her PhD or they kicked her out. Being that she was brilliant, I was betting on the former. In a few years, we'd all be calling her Dr. Corbeau.

I told her as much as I could about Micah over the phone, leaving out the obvious supernatural bits. Since all of the school phones are tapped, I also couldn't tell her what I'd learned about Max and Dad; we'd tried using a code word once, just to see what would happen, and Sadie's entire dorm had gotten searched. All the Peacekeepers had ended up finding was some contraband chocolate.

So I began the call by telling my little sister about Mike, how I liked his gray eyes and his silly smile, how happy he made me; before you knew it, Sadie liked Mike almost as much as I did. Then I told her about our fight, substituting the Iron Queen's dungeonesque palace for a wedding reception, and even the phone monitor expressed her disapproval over how he'd treated me. College lines tended to be tapped by volunteers.

"And you just left him there?" Sadie asked, once the monitor had finished her piece.

"Yeah," I choked out around a sob. I stroked the bruises his fingers had left on my forearm. "I think it's for the best. He's a jerk."

"He doesn't sound like a jerk," Sadie said. "Maybe you should call him."

"And say what? 'Hey, still want that roll in the hay? Come on by!'" Sadie was silent, but I could feel her disapproval through the phone. "No. I can't."

"He's done an awful lot for you over the past few days," Sadie pointed out.

"I know." My hand found his token, and I traced the edge of the oak leaf. I should have given it back to him (or flung it in his face), but at the time I'd forgotten about it. Now, I couldn't bear to take it off, my last connection to him. "I was too mean. He won't want to see me again."

"You might be surprised," Sadie murmured. I uttered a few noncommittal words, trying to ignore the spark of hope that flared in my breast.

Our call ended soon after that, leaving me well and truly alone in my empty apartment. Normally, being on my own didn't bother me, but I had to do something to take my mind off Micah. Unfortunately, my options were limited. I could go to the office and bury myself in work, but it was close to curfew. If the buzzer sounded and I was still at work, I'd be sleeping under my desk. I'd launched into a cleaning frenzy when I'd first gotten back from the Otherworld, and my apartment was so tiny it hadn't taken long to reach hospital levels of sanitation. I tried to read, listen to music, but my mind kept wandering back to the Otherworld. I needed a distraction, one that didn't involve me going out and showing the world my red, puffy eyes. Being that Juliana had brother duty, and that there was no way I could make it to Mom's before curfew, for the time being, it seemed that I was stuck.

Wait. I could dreamwalk. I bet I'd been dreamwalking for years, and just hadn't realized that my realistic dreams were, um, real. In my dreams, I could go anywhere. Lie on a beach in the tropics, scale a mountain, visit friends and family...

I could dreamwalk to Max.

I'd never tried to find a specific person in my dreams; then again, I hadn't known I was a Dreamwalker until Micah had appeared in my car, and then my bed, and then...

Stop. I gulped a lungful of air and willed myself to be calm. *I'm thinking about Max, not Micah. For so long, I've just been waiting for my brother to be found or rescued, but things are different now. Now I know that Max is alive, and I don't need anyone's help to find him.*

I ran into my bedroom and dove into the mess on the closet floor, quickly fishing out jeans, a black tank top, and a black sweater; one thing Micah had impressed upon me was that my dreamself wore whatever my physical body did, so I was trying to be practical. After all, Max could be anywhere, and it was always smart to dress in layers.

As I laced up my sneakers, I spied the hem of the lavender nightie I'd worn the other night, and the waterworks started all over again. I rubbed the soft silk against my cheek, and contemplated reaching out to Micah. Just to talk. Just to see him one more time.

No. This is for the best.

I threw the tearstained silk back into the depths of my closet and lay flat on my bed. I pictured Max as I'd last seen him, a gawky, freckled teenager, and tried to imagine what he'd look like today. In no time, I was asleep.

chapter 11

The gray mist slowly dissipated, and I realized that I was inside a building of some kind. More specifically, I was walking down a painted concrete hallway that reminded me of both a hospital and a jail. The walls were institutional green, the floor that colorless linoleum that hid splatters of all sorts. There were no windows; set into the wall, behind breakaway glass, waited an emergency alarm and tools. On closer inspection, I saw that, instead of a fire extinguisher and hatchet, the emergency box held a vial of holy water and a handful of rowan twigs bound with red thread.

This isn't a hospital, it's a prison. A prison for rogue Elementals.

Shivering with a chill that wasn't physical and thankful for my invisible dreamself, I continued down the hallway, noticing the faintly glowing orbs set at regular intervals where the walls met the floor, bathing everything in a bluish light...This place was illuminated with fey stones?

Fey stones, which were really nothing more than plain old rocks that gave off light and had nothing to do with fairies, had been nevertheless credited as the impetus behind the Magic Wars. Obviously, if you knew how to create a fey stone, you had no need for electric lighting, but since most people weren't Elementals, entities like the power company just shrugged off the loss of a few customers. Then, about thirty, thirty-five years ago, an enterprising young mage had figured out how to set a charged stone into a lamp base, so Mundane users could also take advantage of lighting that would never set the drapes on fire or need replacement bulbs. Suddenly, homes all across the land were lit by fey stones that would last centuries, each one of them costing less than a dozen donuts. The power company was not pleased by their abrupt drop in revenue, and neither were the politicians they donated to.

Harmless fey stones conveniently became one of the excuses the government had used for declaring its war on magic, why my father had disappeared, and why my brother had been abducted. Stupid things. I'd rather carry a flashlight. And now, adding insult to injury, I was walking through a Mundane building lit by the bane of my existence. If hypocrisy were a virus, all these Peacekeepers would have keeled over a long time ago.

I reached a set of metal doors, the sort found in public school hallways. I leaned on the push bar to no effect; right, dreamself. Having no other options, I took a deep breath and slipped through the doors.

Once the weirdness of passing through a solid object had worn off, I took a good look at the room I'd entered. It was huge, like an auditorium, with blindingly white walls and a black and white checkerboard floor. It was filled with tables and shelves and what looked like gym equipment, all made of clear plastic, giving it the appearance of a bad science fiction movie. Suspended tunnels full of right angles and curlicues dangled from the ceiling, and a central area was filled with dangling ropes and gymnastic mats. For a moment, I wondered if I had discovered a training camp for gigantic hamsters. Then I saw him.

Max.

I was surprised that he was older, which was silly. It had been almost ten years since his arrest, and time had marched on, making my teenaged brother into a man. Despite the years, he was still skinny, and his hair, a shade or two darker than my own coppery hue, was just as unkempt as ever. He looked to be unconscious, and he was held upright inside a clear plastic cylinder with tubes and wires stuck all over him. The cylinder held a clear, greenish liquid that reached his chest, and lights embedded in the cylinder's walls blinked in a halo around him. They, whoever his captors were, appeared to be monitoring his vital signs, but for what purpose I couldn't guess.

I was at his side in the instant way of dreams, and stepped through the plastic wall. The liquid was warm and thick, almost comfortable. "Max," I whispered. "Max! I'm going to get you out of here."

"Sadie?" he rasped, without opening his eyes. I noticed his lips were cracked and dry. He was probably being fed through one of these tubes and hadn't had real food or drink in who knows how long.

"Sara," I corrected. "The older one."

Max cracked an eyelid, then gave me a weak grin. "Pest," he murmured. Suddenly serious, he realized that I wasn't a mere figment of his imagination; really, what brother dreams about his sister? "Sara, you shouldn't be here."

"They won't know," I soothed. "I'm dreamwalking."

"Here, they know." Both of his eyes were now open, wide and terrified. "They know if you dreamwalk, and they will punish you for it. Look!"

I followed his gaze, and saw a control room separated from the auditorium by a large, clear plastic panel. Inside the room, people in lab coats looked over various monitors and readouts, most likely the information gleaned from the many wires stuck in my brother's body. Despite Max's warning, I was still confident in my anonymity, until one of the labcoats turned around.

Shit.

Juliana was in the control room.

I saw the badge around her neck, and my hope that she was also a prisoner died. My best friend was a Peacekeeper. Just as my heart skipped a beat, she looked directly at me. Shit. Shit shit shit.

"They know," Max repeated. "Get out now, before they find out who you are!"

I tore my eyes away from Juliana and back to my weakened brother. "I'm coming back for you," I promised. I found Max's hand in the viscous liquid and squeezed, then melted out through the plastic. The labcoats were busy watching Max and their readouts, none of them noticing my noncorporeal form as I crossed the room right in front of the clear panel. They actually looked rather foolish, all bustling about as they made minute adjustments to their forest of knobs and toggles. All I had to do was relax, and then gently wake myself up. In a few heartbeats, I'd be safe in my apartment.

"There!" one of them yelled, pointing directly at me while his eyes remained fixed on a computer screen. Any hopes I had of his meaning anything other than me were dashed as a team of Peacekeepers burst into the room behind me and leveled the strangest weapon I'd ever seen in my direction. It looked like it was made of high-density white plastic, with tiny green lights blinking across the barrel. I did not want to learn what it was or what it could do, so I ran across the room and through the wall, past the scientists with all their strange equipment. I didn't stop until I was back in the corridor. I was still my dreamself, and still confident that they hadn't actually seen me. But how had they known I was there?

Then a group of labcoats burst into the hallway, and I left off my wonderings. I ran as fast as I could, until my lungs burned and I wondered why I needed oxygen in a dream. I also wondered why I wasn't waking up, why this hallway was so long, and what the hell were they doing to my brother? Finally, I turned a corner and saw another set of double doors limned in light. Freedom was close at last, or so I thought.

A Peacekeeper shoved the doors open and stepped into the hallway, not pausing before he fired his odd weapon at me. It hit me square in the chest with a bolt of green energy, and I was there. I mean, I was *there*.

The bolt from the Peacekeeper's gun had pulled my physical body to my dreamself, and now the situation was a great deal more dire. I was stunned, my body still in the throes of waking, and I could hardly raise my arm to shield myself against the Peacekeeper. He grabbed my shoulders and pushed me against the wall, lifting me up until my feet dangled above the floor.

"A pretty one," he leered, groping me through my sweater. I whimpered in protest, so he slammed my head against the wall. "Quiet," he growled, raising his arm to backhand me.

Instead, he jerked and fell unconscious, taking me down with him. I struggled out of his now-limp grip and into a crouch, dimly aware of the labcoats rushing down the hall behind me, their sensible shoes click-clacking on the linoleum. A second and then a third Peacekeeper flew past me, both striking the wall with sickening thuds. I pressed my back against the concrete, steeling myself against whatever this new threat was. Then I felt a hand on my shoulder, and I assumed it was over.

"Come, my Sara."

I whipped my head around, not believing the voice I was hearing. He stood over me like a silver statue, hair floating about his ears like storm clouds. Micah.

"You're here?" I gasped.

He responded by jerking me to my feet and dragging me behind him at a breakneck run. A Peacekeeper barreled toward us, but Micah didn't slow his pace, waiting until the last moment before releasing my hand and striking the Peacekeeper in the center of his breastplate. The black-armored man flew back into the wall, but I didn't look to see if he was still alive. I only wanted to escape.

We skidded around a sharp corner, only to halt. The corridor ended abruptly at a plate-glass window. Micah grabbed something from a pouch hidden in the folds of his cloak and flung it at the glass; in the next instant the glass shattered, a deadly and beautiful spray of diamonds. Micah pulled me into his arms, and we jumped through the window.

As luck would have it, we were only on the second level, and a few ragged shrubs cushioned our landing. Micah sprang up instantly, hauling me to my feet as we hurtled toward the cinderblock wall topped with barbed wire that encircled the building. Micah flung another handful from his pouch, and a heartbeat later there was a hole in the concrete fence. It was such a perfect circle it was almost comical, the edges black and smoking, as if a gunpowder charge had just gone off, though there hadn't been a noise or flash of light.

We leaped through the hole and fled into the trees. The wood was dark and damp and looked like a scene from a bad horror movie, but behind me I heard sirens and voices over loudspeakers. Whatever lay ahead had to be better than what we'd just escaped. Once we'd made it a few hundred yards into the trees, I caught my sneaker on a root and fell to my knees.

"We must keep moving," Micah panted. Despite his words, he knelt beside me. "This land is not good for those like you and me."

"Wh-what…mean?" I choked out.

"There is no metal," Micah explained. "Not in that edifice, not in the ground. The guards wield plastic guns." He looked skyward just as I felt cold droplets. "Rain is good. Rain will obscure our trail."

It didn't feel good as it ran down my neck, but I kept quiet. I must have shivered a bit, since Micah drew me into the folds of his cloak, rubbing my arms. When my breath had calmed, I asked, "Were you following me?"

"Yes." He didn't elaborate, and I didn't think it was the right time to question his motives.

"Micah," I began, but he touched my lips. Then, he cursed.

"Dogs," he hissed, again pulling me to my feet. "Can you run?"

He didn't wait for my response, since our only options were to run or become dog food. Now I really was glad for the rain, but it didn't do much to dissuade our pursuers. At times, I swore I heard the dogs' teeth gnashing, could feel their hot breath on my neck. There were Peacekeepers out there too, and... and men of metal, like the footmen who guarded the Iron Court. I heard them more than saw them, their limbs grating with rust.

Before I had a chance to wonder if the metal men were there to help or hinder us, the Peacekeepers began firing blindly into the trees. At least, I assumed it was Peacekeepers; I didn't exactly turn around to check. I kept hoping they'd hit one of the dogs and lessen at least one of our problems, but they were better shots than that.

After we had run for a small eternity, Micah halted so abruptly I collided with his back. We were in the midst of a clearing and Micah was staring straight ahead, slowly turning in a circle. The rain had become a torrential downpour, and I could hardly see the trees through the sheets of rain. I could not fathom why we weren't moving, or what he was looking for, but I was panting so hard I couldn't ask. And I didn't think Micah would be pleased if I told him that I thought I was about to pass out from exhaustion.

"There!" He pointed at a massive oak, grabbed my shoulders, and shoved me through a crack in the bark. Only, I didn't end up in the center of a tree, but something more like a cave. The interior was vast and quiet, with a packed dirt floor, and walls comprised of living wood. Those wood walls stretched far overhead into darkness. Most importantly, it was dry as a bone.

"What is this place?" I murmured.

"A hiding spot," Micah replied. "Remember, the oaks are my allies." He quickly shed his cloak and set about collecting twigs and leaves, making a heap of them in the center of the chamber. Once my eyes adjusted to the dusky interior, I realized he was gathering kindling.

"Wouldn't a fey stone be faster?" I ventured.

"Yes, but fire is warmer." As I watched Micah arrange the bits of wood and detritus, soaked to the skin, with his silver hair hanging in clumps around his face, I wanted to kick myself. I'd insulted him so gravely, yet he had come for me. No one had ever rescued me before. Sure, there were the times Max had gotten me away from the neighborhood bullies, and Mom could scream a blue streak at whoever was doing us wrong at the moment, but for the most part, the only one who'd ever looked out for me had been me.

Micah had put his life on the line for me, even after I'd treated him like dirt. Even though we'd been apart less than a day, I'd been despondent without him. I never wanted to feel like that again.

I never wanted to be away from Micah again.

My hands shook, whether from nerves or the cold I couldn't tell, and I knelt in front of him. "Micah," I began, but he didn't look up or pause in his intricate arrangement of twigs. "Micah, are you angry with me?"

"Is there cause for my anger?" he asked levelly. Well, I had nothing to say to that. My head drooped forward, and a fat drop of water fell from my hair to the kindling. Micah must have thought it was a tear, because he abruptly put down the wood. After another heartbeat, he tilted my chin upward.

"I understand that my ways are foreign to you," he said softly, "just as yours are to me. But please, have faith in me. I would never do anything to harm you, or those you hold dear."

"I know." I reached up and threaded my fingers through his. "Micah, I'm so sorry. I was angry, and confused, and—and I shouldn't have said those things." His eyes softened, and he leaned over the wood to kiss me. It was soft and gentle, just the way I'd worried he'd never kiss me again.

"I was angry as well," he conceded, "but not with you."

"The Iron Queen?" I asked, surprised by my deduction.

"She is a woman of questionable loyalties," Micah stated. "And she is your father's enemy."

We were sitting on the ground, but my stomach felt like we had just plummeted down an elevator shaft. "Do you think she had something to do with his disappearance?"

"Nothing about her would surprise me."

I tried to say more, but was overcome with shivering.

"Get out of those wet clothes. I will have the fire started soon."

I nodded and stood stiffly, the cold rain having reduced my muscles into hard, stony lumps, and proceeded to struggle out of my clothing. The sweater wasn't too difficult, but the laces on my sneakers had swelled to twice their normal size. I yanked them off, followed by socks that now held enough water to turn a desert into an oasis. My sodden jeans were the worst, the rain and dirt having rendered the denim rather argumentative.

As my clothing landed in a shapeless heap of wet on the dirt floor, I heard a strange squeaking noise close to my ear. Apparently, the oaks hadn't shown me all of their tricks, at least not yet, because I was shocked to find a mouse sitting on a thin branch. He (or she) gestured wildly, and I gradually realized that the branches were meant for me to hang up my clothes while they dried. When Micah had claimed that the oaks were his allies, he hadn't mentioned this concierge service. When I had stripped down to my tank top and underwear, having dutifully hung up the rest of my clothing, I turned back to Micah. I'd meant to ask if he'd like me to hang up his gear as well, but the sight of him before the fire nearly made me forget my name.

The fire was, indeed, blazing away and my naked elfin consort lounged before it, his cloak spread atop the dirt floor. While I understood that elves, like all Otherworldly beings, weren't big on modesty, I was more than a little shocked. I tried not to stare at the fire licking across his caramel skin as I sat beside him, and though Micah raised an eyebrow at my undergarments, he said nothing. Instead, he wrapped his arm around my shoulders and I huddled against him.

"I missed you last night," I mumbled.

"Then you shouldn't have walked away from me," he countered.

"You were yelling at me."

"I was not yelling," he bit off. "I only wish I had known all of the facts before we arrived."

"I don't even know all the facts," I pointed out. He kissed the top of my head.

"I should have known, when you showed me your mark," he murmured. "How many bloodlines bear a copper raven as evidence of their power? I wasn't thinking clearly."

"You weren't?"

"You have that sort of effect on me." He stroked a long line from my temple to my cheek, down my neck, his fingers at last coming to rest on my shoulder. Then he flicked aside the strap of my tank top and kissed the flesh beneath. "May I see your mark again, my Sara?"

I knew why he wanted to see it, but I leaned forward anyway and drew up my tank top. Just as before, Micah began by tracing the outline of the raven, his fingers moving from its crest over my spine to the tiny pinfeathers that hovered above my hips, and then he slowly stroked each and every feather. His touch was light and delicate, like a ghost against my flesh; nevertheless, my mark heated up. By the time he'd reached the raven's maw I wondered if I could burn him.

A strangled, desperate noise, one that I would have been thoroughly embarrassed by in any other circumstance, issued from my throat. Micah's arm snaked around my waist, and I leaned back to kiss him. Somehow, I twisted around without breaking the kiss, and in another moment I was pressed against him, my legs wound around his hips. Then my clothes were gone, and Micah laid me beneath him, settling himself between my thighs. His caresses were gentle, but I didn't want gentle any longer. I wanted him. Now. In the next moment he pushed forward, and… There. No going back now.

Abruptly, he stopped. "Sara," he murmured, his face a mask of concern. Oh, right. I'd forgotten to tell him I was still a virgin.

chapter 12

I know, you probably think it's a little weird to still be a virgin in your mid-twenties, especially well after your college days; not so long ago, it would have been. Sadly, in that day and age it was more the norm, especially when one bore a magical sigil emblazoned across one's back. The Peacekeepers maintained fairly close tabs on all of us young people, espousing the virtues of abstinence and monogamy, until you thought you'd puke if you heard another "wait for your mate" commercial. And since they'd pretty much eradicated all religion after the wars, theirs was the only voice you heard.

In today's world there were no counseling services for unwed mothers, and birth control in all but its most basic forms was a thing of the past. If you were foolish enough to bear a child out of wedlock, it was confiscated and sent to a more appropriate (read: married in nothing less than a fully sanctioned government ceremony) couple for a proper upbringing. But fear of an unplanned pregnancy was only one of the tools the government used against its youth; far more effective was a college education.

As it has always been, college is an expensive, yet necessary, evil, unless you enjoy flipping burgers for an indecently small paycheck. No one had had any money after the wars, what with the new tax increases and general expenses associated with launching a new republic, and as a result, within a few semesters the colleges were nearly vacant. Mind you, the government didn't care a whit about our standards of living, but they did need a somewhat regular supply of educated people in order to keep the basic infrastructure up and running. So the government, in all its devious glory, came up with an ingenious plan: prove your virginity, and you could attend college for free.

Sounds like a good deal, right? For a time, I wavered on the fence about taking the government up on their offer, since the Corbeau bank account could easily fund ten doctoral degrees, if not more. But when someone paid for his or her own education, it seemed that everyone else found out, and no matter what your circumstances were, you were labeled a whore. Slut. Easy.

Not aspiring for any of those labels, Sadie and I had gone to our college entrance examinations together.

Mind you, these were not written examinations. Oh, for the days when good grades and a halfway-decent essay were all that mattered. As you could imagine, it was a bit difficult to prove a boy's virginity, but a girl's was pretty straightforward. I had assumed we'd be in and out in a few minutes. Was I ever wrong.

When we'd arrived, we were given standard-issue hospital gowns that split down the front, left in a rather ordinary room, and told to wait our turn. I thought we'd be guided into a private doctor's office for the examination, but when the time came, I was led into an auditorium before at least a hundred spectators. Before I could really register what was happening, my arms had been strapped down to an exam table, and my legs buckled into stirrups and pushed so far apart my hips had nearly dislocated. The doctor had proceeded to completely open my gown, baring me from neck to knee, and I lay there, naked and humiliated, for the next twenty minutes while he prodded the most intimate parts of my body. He had been so thorough that, once the exam was over, I questioned whether I was still a virgin, but after the ordeal I had been presented with my papers, and thus enjoyed a free education.

If I ever see the bastard again, I'll shove my degree down his throat.

After the exam, I had tried to give it away whenever I could, but that had been an impossible feat. No respectable boy would have me, and even drunks at college keggers had turned me down.

Per regulations, you needed to file with your local Peacekeeper when you were deflowered, being sure to include the identity of said deflowerer, and no man was willing to take on such a daunting task. If he slipped up and got you pregnant, he could be forced into marriage; if the girl in question was an Elemental from a family the government had deemed not fit to breed, he could possibly face prison. No man had ever found me worth the risk. No man, that was, until Micah.

My Micah, my wonderful Micah, the man who now gazed at me with tender eyes. "Sara," he repeated as he withdrew.

No, not after all this! I stroked the silver tendrils of his mark, arousing him much the same way he'd done to me a few moments earlier. His mark grew warm and he arched his back, then Micah tensed above me, resisting the desire that I knew pooled in his belly. Deviously, I leaned up and nipped his throat. Finally, he could take it no more, and thrust forward.

I yelped, more in surprise than anything else. While I'd been on display at my examination, the doctor in charge had taken it upon himself to regale us with a short lecture on how unpleasant sex was for a woman, and the pain that I, in particular, could expect. The doctor had been kind enough to indicate the various parts of my anatomy that would be sore, and maybe even bruised, afterward. He'd been fondling my breast while he spoke, and his other hand was doing... other things. Later, when he had handed me my papers, he leaned close and whispered that he'd been trying to bring me to orgasm, and the fact that he hadn't meant that I was one of the girls who would find sex especially nasty. The good doctor had painted a picture of a horrible, excruciatingly painful act, one I didn't exactly want to try.

It wasn't like that, at all, with Micah. It was perfect.

Afterward, Micah held me close, gently stroking my hair, his cheek pressed against my neck. I mumbled that I wanted to lie inside that tree with him forever, and he laughed deep in his chest. It felt so...so comfortable, snuggled in his arms with his warm breath and the gentle rumbles of his voice. "Eventually, we'll need to eat."

"Have your oaky friends toss us some acorns." I felt his face stretch into a smile, then he propped himself up on an elbow and I saw it in the flesh. I liked his smile.

"Why didn't you tell me?" he asked.

"I didn't want you to say no." Micah laughed again, and drew my face close to his.

"There was very little chance of that happening," he informed me. "What fools human males are, to have let you slip through their fingers." I sighed and told him about the examinations, of the careful rosters kept of who had bedded—and impregnated—whom, of all the men who hadn't thought me worth the bother. The thunderheads returned to Micah's eyes as I spoke.

"To treat a woman so poorly is the vilest of acts," he murmured, smoothing my hair back from my brow. "My Sara, you have given me a gift without equal. I only regret the circumstances."

"Maybe I've always wanted to make love in a tree, next to a fire," I quipped.

"Then I will dispense with all my furniture, and have dirt floors installed where the beds once stood," Micah declared. "I do not know if I can coax a tree to grow around my home, but I will try, for you."

He would, wouldn't he? I nestled closer, kissing him in order to fully express my gratitude. He moved against me, intending to do a bit more than kiss me in return, but recent memories distracted me.

"Max," I said, in response to his quizzical face. "I saw Max."

"He is alive, then?" Micah asked, and I nodded. "That explains why there is no metal around that facility. His captors do not want your brother to draw upon his power and free himself."

"How can there be none?" I murmured. "What about the computers, the monitors? Don't they have wires?"

"A small amount," he replied, once I explained what a computer was, "too small to make a difference for your brother." I nodded, but another memory came forth, this one easily as awful as Max's plastic prison.

"Micah, there's more." I squeezed my eyes shut, replaying the scene one more time, hoping I was wrong. Instead of being wrong, I saw my best friend's dark hair, the distinctive way she carried herself; hell, I thought she'd been wearing the sweater she had picked up when we had gone shopping last week. "Juliana—the one you said wasn't my friend—she's there, too."

"She is also a prisoner?"

"No."

He could have said so many things—I told you so; listen to me next time; you're a stupid, naïve girl—and he would have been right about all of them. Instead, Micah tucked my head against his neck and held me, sharing in my pain.

"Did she see you?" he asked at length.

"I don't think so. I was my dreamself." I straightened, remembering what Max had said. "But that doesn't seem to matter there. Max said that they know when you dreamwalk. I thought he was just scared for me, but he was right. They knew I was there. Then one of the guards shot something at me, and I was awake."

"*Shot* you?" Micah got to his knees and pulled me to a sitting position. "Where? Are you injured?"

"My chest," I replied. I looked down, but there wasn't a bruise. "I don't remember it hurting. I was just awake."

Micah scrubbed his face with his hands, and blew out an exasperated breath. "Please, do not ever attempt such a thing on your own again," he said. "I know we fought, but you still could have called upon me."

"I could have?" I asked, startled.

"Of course," he murmured, tracing the silver chain about my neck. "Even if you had removed my token, I still would have come."

"I couldn't. Remove it, I mean." I looked down, busying myself with rubbing a nonexistent mark off his cloak. "I cried the whole night." Micah's arms were around me then, and if another hot tear or two escaped my lashes, he was kind enough not to mention them.

"What are we going to do?" I asked, once I was calm again.

"For right now, we are going to remain here and wait for the storm to cease," he replied. "Then, we shall retreat to my home and consider how we will retrieve your brother."

"Is the veil thin nearby?"

His brows peaked. "We are not in the Mundane World," Micah said, carefully.

"You mean humans are holding Max in the Otherworld?" I gasped. "They… they should not be here. Peacekeepers setting up a base in the Otherworld totally goes against everything the government stands for, everything they fought for!" Why was my dad gone and my brother a science experiment if the Peacekeepers just wanted to dabble in magic behind our backs? Couldn't they have done whatever they were doing without ripping my family apart?

"I know not what to make of your race," Micah said bitterly. "In the space of two decades, humans have managed to undo most of the good they'd wrought over these past centuries. And to shun magic, as if a part of one's spirit can be amputated like a frostbitten toe. Fools. I wonder if this government of yours shouldn't be overthrown."

"They should be," I agreed, "but who would do it?"

Micah shot me a mischievous glance. "Perhaps *we* shall do it. But first, let's free your brother."

chapter 13

Shortly after dawn the storm abated, and once the sun was shining Micah and I reluctantly put on our lumpy, somewhat dry clothing and left our wooden sanctuary. Once we were outside the oak, I marveled that its trunk seemed no larger than what Micah and I could wrap our arms around and still have our fingers touch, yet its interior had been large enough for both of us to stretch out next to a small fire. Micah had called the oaks his allies, and I was now in firm agreement.

"Thank you, old friend," Micah murmured, patting the rough bark. "As ever, I am indebted to you."

Micah took my hand, and we set off through the dense forest. There wasn't a path, or even a game trail to follow, and the ground bore a thick blanket of wet, slippery leaves.

"How will we get to your home?" I caught my foot on a rock, but Micah steadied me with a hand on my back. My mark flared at his touch; I wondered if he could feel its heat through my sweater. "I can't even tell where we are or what direction we're headed."

"You must learn to read the signs around you," Micah replied. "The Whispering Dell is to the west and south."

"We're going to walk there?"

"Unless my Sara knows how to fly." I tried to swat his shoulder, but he caught my hand and tucked it into the crook of his arm.

So, we walked. And what a walk it was, beginning with the two of us bashing our own trail through the underbrush like intrepid explorers searching for treasure. It wasn't too long before the trees thinned a bit, and we could comfortably walk side by side. Micah kept a leisurely pace, likely for my benefit, and I thought I'd take the opportunity to address a few lingering questions.

"How do you appear and disappear?" I asked. "Like that time you were in my room, and Juliana was banging on the door." Bile rose in my throat at the mention of her name, but I tamped it down. I'd use that emotion later.

"Metal," he replied, cryptically. After a bit of cajoling, and letting him steal a kiss or three, he elaborated. "If there is sufficient metal nearby, I may travel along it. Think of it like sledding down a hill, only on metal instead of snow. It's quite easy in your world, what with your many mechanical devices."

"Does this traveling only work with refined metal?" I asked.

"Refined, as in pure?"

"Can you also travel on natural metal, like an ore?" I clarified.

"Most definitely. I frequently travel along the veins of silver that run beneath the Whispering Dell."

"Huh." I wondered if I could do that, too. Goodbye, car insurance and overpriced fuel. "But you said there was no metal where you found me."

"There isn't. I sent my dreamself after yours, and when I felt you wake, I followed you with my earthly form."

"Micah, they could have killed you!"

"You were in far more danger than I." He hugged me to him, and as much as I hated the thought of Micah in danger, I was so glad he'd followed me. It was all I could do to keep the image of Max, imprisoned in his plastic and electrode coffin, out of my mind, but if Micah hadn't arrived when he had, I'd likely be sharing that coffin with my brother.

In far less time than I'd feared, we crested the ridge above Micah's sparkling silver home. Even though I'd seen it a few times already, the sight of his highly polished chateau-like manor took my breath away. But now I thought it could be much improved with a copper roof.

Our approach took us to the back of the house, and I walked through Micah's gardens for the first time. They were an orderly affair, reminding me of the knot gardens that had once graced stately English manor homes. Short, trim hedges of boxwood and rosemary made a labyrinth of tight corners and spiraling circles, and lush carpets of flowering herbs filled the tiny green rooms. Arm in arm, Micah indulged me by leading me through the twisting paths; we must have been a sight, the two of us navigating amidst hedges that scarcely reached our knees. The diminutive maze ultimately terminated at the stone statue of a woman, set high atop a marble base and surrounded by white roses. The base was inscribed with what I assumed to be her name: Selene.

"It's beautiful," I murmured. "Is she an ancestor of yours?"

"My mother," Micah replied. He didn't elaborate, and I didn't ask. I had brought more than enough family drama to the party, so if he wanted to leave his out that was fine with me. There would be enough time to ask him about it later.

We kept on through the maze, and a few strides past his mother's statue we emerged before his home, to be met promptly by a bevy of silverkin, Micah's energetic, insanely devoted servants. As they ushered us inside, Micah quickly apprised their leader of what had happened since last night, including the aid offered by the mighty oaks. After a bit of discussion, they decided to send a tribute of blessed rainclouds to the copse, so the noble trees need never go thirsty.

"My consort will also require clothing," Micah continued. As he had made clear many times, jeans and sneakers were not befitting a lady of my stature. We would just see about that. "What else do you need, my Sara?"

"Maybe a shower," I said, dragging a hand through my hair. After running through the rain and lying on dirt all night, it had seen better days. "And breakfast?" I added, hopefully.

"Food is being prepared," he said, to my relief. "As for bathing, I do not possess an indoor waterfall such as you humans crave. I hope you will find my primitive accommodations acceptable."

Micah offered a shallow bow along with an outstretched hand, and I giggled as I accepted. He pulled me into his arms and kissed me, banishing the proper butler image he'd so carefully crafted, and led me along several halls full of twists and turns. Each passage was as spectacular as the last, what with the shining silver walls and jewel-colored tapestries, but after a time, all the lovely sights blurred together. I wondered if I'd ever be able to find my way around Micah's home without a map and sunglasses.

Eventually, we entered a corridor that was different than the rest, being that its centerpiece was a painting comprised, not of jewel tones, but actual jewels. It depicted a woman with pale golden hair and blue eyes; I assumed the colors had been rendered with citrine and sapphire. She was lovely, but with sad, sad eyes. I wondered if I was looking at a jeweled representation of Micah's mother.

The corridor ended with a massive wooden door (I wondered if it was a relative of the oak that had sheltered us), which opened onto yet another courtyard. In contrast to the orderly knot garden, this space was filled to bursting with flowering and fruiting trees in every variety and color imaginable, and many I could never have conceived of. Delicately carved marble benches and statues wound among the trees, but they were not what made the courtyard grand. The undeniable centerpiece was a wide pool, so still that, for a moment, I thought it might be quicksilver or glass.

"This is where you bathe?" I breathed.

"It is," Micah replied, already pulling his tunic up and over his shoulders. I spied movement on the far side of the pool, and caught Micah's arm.

"Micah, there's a woman in there," I whispered loudly.

"Of course," he replied, now unlacing his breeches. "This is her pool. If she favors you, she may let you borrow a comb," he added with a wink.

I was momentarily stunned. Micah really expected me to bathe with...her? Whoever—whatever—she was? I tilted my head to the side, trying to get a better look at this creature inhabiting Micah's bathwater. She was obviously some sort of water being, and as she was naked, I knew without a doubt she was a she.

Still, she didn't look like any mermaid or undine or naiad I'd ever heard of. Her long hair was the palest blue, and it flowed like a gentle stream over her pale pink shoulders and breasts. Those blue tresses also did a very poor job of covering her as she lounged on the pool's bank, with only her feet dangling beneath the water's surface, not that she seemed to notice. In fact, she was thoroughly preoccupied with combing out her hair, and had a selection of combs and mirrors laid out beside her.

Why is everyone in the Otherworld always naked? Micah was already wading into the pool, either oblivious or uncaring with regard to her—and his—unclothed state. With a pang, I remembered my college examination, and the hundred or so strange onlookers. *Well, at least it's only one.*

My clothing, stiff with dried rainwater and mud, soon made an untidy heap at my feet. I dipped a toe in the pool and found it pleasantly warm. Since I didn't really have a reason not to, I followed Micah's example and waded in, then ducked my head. When I surfaced, I felt instantly clean and refreshed, and the notion of soap just seemed frivolous.

As I stretched my sparklingly clean limbs, I spied Micah's tangled silver hair and decided that now was as good a time as any to make nice with his supernatural neighbors. Both Micah and the woman watched intently as I made my way through the water, Micah with his bemused smile and her with a look of calm indifference.

"Excuse me," I said to our poolmate, "may I please borrow a comb?"

"Will you use it with good intent, and return it to me unscathed?" she countered.

"Of course," I replied. She smiled, and handed me a fine silver implement. The handle was carved abalone, with tiny pearls set along the edge of the shell. Reassured by my simple victory, I murmured my thanks, and returned to Micah's side. He had taken a seat on a rock set beneath the surface, and the water reached his chest. I stood behind him and began to comb out his hair.

"She allowed you use of her comb?" he asked.

"She did," I replied. "What's her name?"

"I call her Bright Lady of the Clear Pool," Micah replied. Well, that was cumbersome.

"I don't like your hair wet," I mumbled, tugging the comb through a nasty tangle. Sleeping on the ground in a tree was not good for your hair, Elemental or not. "I like it when it's puffy, like a dandelion." Micah shot me a glance, and the Bright Lady might have laughed. Sensing that I'd broached a touchy subject, I shifted topics by tracing the uppermost edge of his mark. "Is this real silver in your skin?"

"Silver flows throughout my body," he replied. "I call upon it when I'm in need." I remembered the great force he'd struck the guards with, how his bones hadn't broken when we'd jumped from the window, and that he'd twisted so he could hit the ground first, sheltering me in his arms. I wondered if I could do the same. As if he'd read my mind, Micah flexed his hand into a fist, and I watched as it took on a pale, reflective sheen. When I touched his flesh, it had the cool hardness of metal. A quick glance at his back confirmed my suspicion.

"You called the silver to your hand," I murmured, stroking the abrupt line on his wrist where the warm flesh gave way to hard metal. "My raven is real copper?" I asked, and he affirmed it. "So, that's why I weigh so much. All this time, I just thought I was fat."

At that, he shook the silver from his hand, just as a Mundane man would shake off a bit of rain, then twisted around and snatched me in his arms. "I'll not hear you insulting yourself," he warned. "The beauty of my consort is not in question." Ignoring my warm cheeks, I perched on his knee and began combing out the front of his hair.

"If I was an Air Elemental, would I have a... a windy mark?" I ventured.

"Your element would be represented upon your flesh in some manner," Micah stated. "The air marks I've seen appear as blue or gray brushstrokes, like paintings of the wind. But then, I've seen very few marks that are not metal. Those whose magic is beholden to different elements do not usually commingle."

Huh. We really *didn't* all get along. The government had actually been right about something. "Like how fire makes water evaporate, or water makes metal rust?" At that, I glanced at the water we lounged in, hoping that our bath hadn't just doomed Micah and me to a few creaky joints.

Micah laughed. "In a way, yes. Fear not, my love, for neither silver nor copper succumbs to rust."

My eyes traveled to the Bright Lady, and I sneakily examined her creamy skin, looking for a mark, but I had no idea what a watery sigil would be. A wave, or a fish scale, maybe? I even craned my neck to check hers for gills. She felt my scrutiny and boldly met my eyes, at which I blushed and looked away.

"She's quite lovely, isn't she?" Micah murmured against my ear. "But you, my Sara, are lovelier yet." He took the comb from my hand and settled it safely on the bank, then wrapped his arms around me and kissed my shoulder.

"Micah," I protested, "this doesn't feel right."

"And this?" he murmured, as his lips teased the hollow of my throat.

"That's not what I meant!" I was interrupted by a haughty splash; the Bright Lady had come to reclaim her comb. Only a truly miffed water being could manage a splash that sounded like a huff. After waggling her finger at Micah for leaving so precious an item on the ground, she took my hand.

"You kept your promise to me," she said, seductively; I could see waves crashing in her blue eyes. "You, I favor." The Bright Lady held out her finger, and a single droplet of water coalesced into a multifaceted jewel. She pressed the jewel into my palm; after a brief but sharp moment of pain, it lodged beneath my flesh. She graced me with a coy smile, then the Bright Lady resumed her place on the far side of the pool, and Micah resumed his nibbling.

"I mean, it isn't right that we're here, enjoying each other, while Max is still a captive," I explained, flexing my palm around the sparkly jewel. "Shouldn't we be doing something?"

"I know little of human ways," Micah began, once again serious, "but I am well-versed in the ways of battle and intrigue. Perhaps too well-versed." A cloud moved across his face, but before I could ask, he continued, "The stone fortress where your brother is held is difficult to enter, even for those with our abilities. His captors will have doubled, perhaps tripled, his guards after last night's events. His captors may relocate him, though that is unlikely, but no matter where Max is held, he will be surrounded so densely that we'll have no hope of reaching him." He paused and tucked a lock of hair behind my ear. "If the humans have kept him alive for all this time, they need him. Max is safer, for the moment, if we leave him be. Our best course of action is to wait and speak to our allies. We shall research, and we shall plan. Once we have learned all we can, we shall act."

"I don't have any allies," I mumbled. I was useless, a copper girl who couldn't bend a penny, surrounded by government operatives and powerful Elementals.

"Not so," Micah corrected. "You have me. My allies are yours, my love."

That was the second time he'd called me that. "Can we go to the Iron Queen?" I asked. Surely, she was powerful enough to help Max, and even though she was Dad's enemy, the Peacekeepers were the greater foe. Enemy of my enemy and all that.

Micah made a noise somewhere between a laugh and a snort. "Her help is unlikely, especially now that you are my consort." Call it woman's—or consort's— intuition, but I heard what he'd left unsaid.

"You have a history with her, don't you?" He looked away, but I poked his chest. "Don't you?"

"I have never laid a finger on her," Micah said indignantly. "She, however, had other notions." I ducked around to meet his eyes, and he blew out a slightly frustrated breath. "She desired me as her consort."

"And you turned her down?" I asked, in amazement.

"Immediately."

"So, that's why she received us in her chain mail bikini," I mused.

"Bi...kee...nee?" Micah repeated.

"She was almost naked when we arrived. I think she wanted to show you what you were missing." I laid my head on his shoulder, full of satisfaction over Micah spurning the Iron Queen's advances. "You turned down a queen, yet you want me."

"You and I are far more suited to one another," Micah said, dragging his fingers through my hair.

"She is so... I cannot imagine why anyone would desire that woman."

I stifled a laugh, only to feel its echo in Micah's chest. "Are we an alloy?" I asked, suddenly. In response to his raised eyebrow, I added, "You know, like bronze or something."

"In a way," he murmured. "We are much stronger together than apart."

I liked that. However, if I was going to alloy myself with Micah, I needed a few more answers. "Why do you hate my father?"

"What?" His brow furrowed, and he pushed back my tangled hair. "I have always had the utmost respect for Baudoin Corbeau."

"Then why were you mad when you found out about my relationship to him?"

Micah exhaled, and stared at the clouds for a few moments. "You must admit that—No, you are probably too young to remember." He shook his head, and started over. "Your father is more than an Elemental, more than a Raven, even. He is an amazing man, gifted in the arts of magic as well as leadership. Many flocked to him, both for protection and guidance."

"I know," I said, a bit peeved. I mean, he *was* my father, after all.

"When Baudoin disappeared, it was a blow to Elementals. All Elementals, not just human Elementals." He fell silent for a moment, his hand stroking my mark. "Without a rallying point, we faltered. Then the Gold Queen fell, and Ferra came to power. It... nothing has been the same, since your father went missing."

"So, you'd like to find him?" I ventured.

"More than anything," Micah affirmed. "We of metal are in dire need of a leader such as he."

Before I could truly appreciate the mental image of Dad as Copper King, we were distracted by laughter from the opposite side of the pool. A group of pixies had arrived and were shedding their diaphanous, many-colored dresses as they readied themselves for a swim. Before entering the pool, they formed a circle and grasped hands, glittering wings poised, dancing about while the Bright Lady clapped. Then a few fauns burst forth from the trees, their bare phalluses announcing that they were after a different sort of dance.

"Perhaps it's time we went inside," Micah murmured. He held my arm as we left the cool water, and I gladly leaned against him. I saw that the silverkin had thoughtfully left a pair of neatly folded robes on a nearby bench, our filthy clothing having been whisked away to some magical washing machine. Or maybe they'd burned them, who knew? As Micah held one of the robes open for me, I peeked over my shoulder and saw the Bright Lady handing out combs and mirrors to the pixies. I guessed that they wanted to look nice for the fauns.

"Come along, my love," Micah said, drawing my attention. "We will eat, and rest, and then we shall plan. In the space of a few sunrises, we shall better understand how to combat this foe."

"That's the third time you've called me that."

"Called you what, exactly?"

"My love."

"So I did." Micah wrapped his arm around my shoulders and kissed my hair. "So I did."

chapter 14

"I do *not* like this," Micah said for the millionth time.

"Well, I don't, either," I snapped back. I did not like that my best friend since middle school now appeared to be nothing more than a filthy Peacekeeper, in my life for no other reason than to keep tabs on me and my family. Really, if I looked at my and Juliana's history objectively, there were more than a few odd points, beginning with how she had just *appeared* at my school shortly after Max had been dragged off by the Peacekeepers. Juliana and I had become fast friends, mostly because she was the only one who hadn't shunned me for having a brother who'd openly practiced magic; in that respect, I had been a captive audience. After graduation, we'd gone to separate colleges—I had studied liberal arts, while

Juliana had apparently gone to spy school—but, lo and behold, there she'd been the day I'd walked into REES for my interview.

Really, there's no such thing as coincidence.

I'd been lied to for half a lifetime by Peacekeepers. Since the wars had ended, Peacekeepers hadn't allowed me and mine a moment's rest, and now I knew that Juliana was one of them. I never wanted to see her again, much less interact with her. I wanted to scream and tear out my hair; better, I wanted to tear out *her* hair. No. I just wanted to hide.

I wanted to stop taking out my frustrations on Micah.

"I'm sorry. It's just…" I clenched my fists, frustrated and mad and feeling just so damn stupid for never seeing her for whom she really was. "I just wish you had been wrong about her."

"I know. I wish the same." Then his arms were around me, and I was in that cocoon of Micah-ness, that safe harbor that was uniquely him. It was in this safe harbor I'd come up with my grand plan, and Micah hadn't liked it any better at the outset.

After we'd donned the robes the silverkin had so thoughtfully left by the pool, Micah had led me to his—well, *our*—dining room. The centerpiece was a long, highly polished table of dark wood, topped with covered dishes and platters and pitchers of everything I could ever want to eat or drink. I'd never seen such delicacies before (items such as sugared jasmine blossoms and roasted swan had never even made appearances at the Corbeau holiday table), but there were also Mundane items such as grilled cheese sandwiches and tomato soup. I gave the silverkin a few brief instructions, and soon a plate of steaming, salty fries lay before me. Yes, I could certainly get used to being Lady Silverstrand.

When our meal was complete (I knew the exact moment, since I'd eaten so much I could hardly move), a bevy of silverkin had whisked me away to a dressing room of sorts. There, in massive wardrobes larger than my apartment's bathroom, hung gowns in every color and fabric and style imaginable, as long as your taste tended toward 'damsel in distress.'

If the silverkin understood my preference toward more casual attire, they didn't show it. Instead, they chattered away while they showed me one garment after another, extolling the virtues of this blue silk frock or those cream suede slippers. When I asked what had become of my jeans and sneakers, the little silver devils feigned ignorance.

"Wait." Suddenly, the silverkin stopped their mad bustle and stared at me. "You have seen me, what, three times by now?" That got a cheery chorus of nods. "During any of those times, was I dressed like this?"

Silence. Well, silence and fidgeting. I took a deep breath, and continued, "These dresses are all very nice. You did a very good job. However, I *like* jeans. I like sneakers and sweaters with hoods. Can you make me some of those?" They anxiously looked from one to the other; obviously, my request contradicted their orders. I crouched down and said, with a conspiratorial smile, "Oh, don't worry about *him*. I'll tell him it was all my idea."

At that, their chatter resumed, mostly because they were relieved that they weren't going to get in trouble. This time. Since my jeans wouldn't be ready for some time, I settled upon a simple ivory and rose-colored dress that laced up the bodice, despite their continued insistence that I wear one of the more formal gowns. *Hadn't we just had a discussion about that?*

"It's not that I don't like them," I insisted, "I just have no idea of how to wear all of…this." By "this," I meant the petticoats, corsets, and other bric-a-brac that came with such ensembles. The dress I ended up wearing had a straight skirt, no petticoats or other god-awful undergarments, and long sleeves that came to a point over the back of each of my hands. While the silverkin piled my hair atop my head, I tried on shoes; none of them got my joke about glass slippers. Much to their chagrin, I selected plain slippers of ivory suede and made my return to the hall.

I found that Micah had also changed out of his robe, and was resplendent in a burgundy velvet tunic edged with silver, chocolate leather breeches, and tall boots. If I'd seen any other man in such a getup I'd have laughed, but Micah looked like a king. And his reaction to my dress… Well, let's just say that looking like Rapunzel had a definite upside.

A long, happy time later, I'd brought up my latest plan, which was only a little bit likely to get us killed. We'd probably just be captured.

"I should go talk to Juliana," I'd said suddenly. We'd been ensconced in Micah's enormous bed; I'd worried that it would be some sort of metal contraption, but it had turned out to be a real bed, complete with four posts and a feather mattress. Everything in Micah's bedroom was a brilliant shade of blue, from the rich teal wall tapestries to silken sheets dyed the color of the sky. Even the floor fit the overall theme, a tile mosaic of blue accented with ochre, topped with a white fur rug, lest our toes be chilled. The Otherworld certainly didn't lack for luxury. "Maybe I can learn a few things from her, like how Max is guarded."

"He is guarded by armored men who shot at you," Micah stated. "I need no more information."

"No, I mean maybe I can find out about a weak spot. Like the rotation of the guards."

"They change every two hours. I saw that myself, while I was waiting for your dreamself to be done with that place." He was stubborn, yes, but I'm Irish on my mother's side. We're not known for being pushovers.

"Maybe I can find out if they saw me, and if Sadie and Mom are in danger." Micah was uncharacteristically silent on that; he valued family, and would hear out any plan that involved protecting mine. I hoped. I moved so I was lying on his chest,

159

my nose almost touching his. "What if they really are in danger? What will we do?"

"If they are so endangered, we will bring them here, where your government of fools cannot harm them," Micah replied.

"Those fools are already here," I said softly. He pursed his lips and looked away. "Micah, I know it's risky, but I need to know if the Peacekeepers have plans concerning my family."

"You want to learn if she was ever your friend," he countered.

It was my turn to look away. Was it so wrong to want to know that? To find out if we'd hit it off in school, only to have Juliana's loyalties bought later on? I hoped that wasn't the case. I hoped she'd been a spy from day one. The betrayal would be somehow less devastating that way.

"I do," I whispered. Micah admitted that he understood, albeit only in theory, and now we were sitting in my mechanical in my usual spot in front of the Lovers' Pine. Since this was the last time I was ever going to set foot in Real Estate Evaluation Services, I didn't care if my parking privileges were revoked for letting unauthorized individuals into the lot.

The plan was simple: I would go to work and behave as if nothing unusual, or magical, had happened over the long weekend. I would engage the enemy—Juliana—in conversation, hopefully learn something useful, and somehow keep myself from calling her out as a government spy. Micah, my over-protective consort, would follow me as his dreamself, and if I appeared to be in any sort of danger he would yank me out of the office and we'd retreat to the Otherworld. Really, what could go wrong?

Well, in spite of the many flaws in the plan we were doing it, anyway. Or at least I was; Micah still wavered somewhere between being my unwilling accomplice and my potential abductor.

"If things go awry, you will leave," Micah ordered, as I took the key from the ignition.

"And what does 'awry' encompass?" I asked lightly.

"Anything out of the ordinary." He squeezed my hand. "Anything."

"Like fresh coffee?" He frowned; I wondered if he knew what coffee was. I made a mental note to speak to the silverkin about the virtues of espresso and frothed milk. "I will. I promise. If anything looks weird, I'll leave."

"Mmm. 'Weird.'" Micah eyed me appraisingly, then put his hand on the nape of my neck. "And if *I* think there's anything weird, I will be at your side in a moment."

"I'm counting on it."

Micah lowered the passenger seat as a drone flitted by, but the metal beast gave no indication of having seen him. After a short follow-up lecture on the inherent dangers he was willing to rescue me from, Micah allowed me to exit the mechanical and go to work.

It turned out that my office was the same as ever, so boring that I wanted to claw my eyes out. I nodded a few hellos as I walked to my desk, terrified that someone would sense something new about me, something magical or…Other. Then Floyd made a crack about where I'd been wearing my high heels when I wasn't at The Room last Friday night; in his meager defense, it was tradition to go out for a much-needed drink on Tax Day. I rolled my eyes, relieved that everything appeared normal, and sat down to work.

As you know, my official title was Quarterly Report Sorter. *I know, glamorous.* But I was assured that mine was a vital occupation, and that without these many sheets of paper properly sorted and filed in the correct folders, chaos would ensue, so I sorted. In fact, I sorted so fast that I had no idea what the reports were about, which was a good thing. My employment contract specifically forbade me from reading them due to their sensitive, confidential nature.

Now don't get me wrong, I'm no goody-two-shoes like my sister. I read a few in the beginning, and after learning everything I never wanted to know about easements and accessibility, I realized exactly why these reports needed to remain confidential. Can't have the workers nodding off at their desks, can we?

So I sorted in ignorance, only keeping my eye on the prize, which was, in this case, a clear inbox.

Since I didn't really care about this job anymore, I gave in to my rebellious streak. After a quick glance, I peeled away the title page and read the top report. It went thusly:

Report A: The Care and Feeding of Hamsters
A hamster is an excellent first pet, and can do much in the way of teaching a child responsibility...

And it went on for fourteen pages.

Well, that can't be right, I mused, still searching for the rational needle in the insane haystack. REES dealt with commercial real estate procurement, not disposable pets. I flipped to Report B, which was all about carnivorous houseplants, then on to C, a treatise on natural furniture polish. Apparently, lemon oil could do wonders for your grand piano.

Somewhere around the fifteenth report I found another copy of the hamster information; by the time I made it to the very last report, which was also the *third* hamster summary, a cold knot had formed in my gut. All of these 'vital reports' were nothing more than lame articles, reprinted and plopped on my desk to keep me busy. I'd been wasting my time sorting garbage.

Why am I sorting nonsense? I remembered how hard it had been for me to find a job after graduation, how I'd chalked it up to a bad economy and dim prospects. Then an ad for a Quarterly Report Sorter at Real Estate Evaluation Services had suddenly been plastered all over the local paper, and they'd hired me after the shortest interview I'd ever endured. I remembered how excited I was to have work, and at the added bonus of working with my old friend, Juliana. I'd always been grateful to her, assuming that she'd put in a good word for me.

I now understood that that was not quite what had happened.

That cold lump in my belly had grown into a boulder of ice. I pushed the worthless reports aside and called up the search engine on my computer. I wasn't supposed to use it, which was also duly noted in my employment contract. Whatever. Since I'd gotten away unscathed last time, I waited for the company's internal search field to populate, and took a deep breath. Then, I typed in Max's name.

I didn't really expect to find anything, except maybe a security guard appearing at my elbow, waiting to escort me away from my desk. Instead, I got incident reports that detailed Max's rampant magic usage, grainy surveillance photos of my family at the Raven Compound, and a link to a video of my family having a picnic in the side yard. Dad was in the video, which meant that whoever had been spying on my family had begun their mission even before the wars.

Before the wars?

Another page held a detailed account of Max's capture and subsequent trial as an enemy of the state. I had never known about a trial, and I sure as hell didn't think Mom had, either. While perusing the details of his sentence, I clicked a link and was rewarded with schematics of his prison, the ironically named Institute for Elemental Research.

They wanted me to find this. They've all been waiting me out. It was obviously bait for a trap, me being the mouse in question, but I had faith that Micah wouldn't let REES spring it. I hit print, then tried to look inconspicuous as the ancient machine whirred to life. I hoped it wouldn't run out of ink. I did *not* want to call the help desk, especially since I was pretty much committing treason.

"Whatcha doin'?"

I managed to complete those few short steps to the printer, despite the icy sweat that broke out over my entire body. Calmly, I gathered up my papers and turned to face Juliana.

"I needed to reprint a report."

"Really?" Her surprise was understandable, for who really needed a better copy of a sham report?

"Yeah. First time I've ever had to." I resumed my seat and shuffled the newly printed papers in with the dissertations on house pets and gardening tools, then turned to face her. My best friend. "So, are we on for The Room tonight? I talked Mike into meeting me there."

"I thought you two were done."

"Not quite," I said. "I called him after you left, and we worked it out. We spent the weekend together."

"He was with you all weekend, and now he wants to hang out with your friends? He must be into you," Juliana said with a pointed look. *Of course he's into me,* I wanted to shout. *He's not a government spy, he wasn't paid to like me! He wants me for me!*

I took a deep breath, and mustered my slyest gaze. "Oh, he's into me."

Juliana laughed at that, attracting the attention of half the office with her high-pitched cackle. As she made her way back to her desk I was left wondering if her laugh, which had frazzled my nerves on more than one occasion, was some sort of signal to the rest, maybe code for 'the jig is up, she knows', but no one paid me any mind. Then again, they'd never paid me any mind, had they? Their indifference to me must have been part of the master plan.

Bastards.

I shuffled through my fake reports, sorting and filing them as I'd done countless times before. After half an hour of this, I surreptitiously nudged the printouts about Max and his prison into my bag. Fifteen minutes after that, Juliana finally headed to the ladies' room; she has a bladder like a frickin' camel. With a sigh of relief, I grabbed my bag and headed for the door. Almost as an afterthought, I turned and ripped down a picture of Sadie and me, the one personal item I'd kept at work, from my filing cabinet. Now, I could leave and be done with this place once and for all. Unbeknownst to me, a stinking river of slime was poised to block my escape.

"Hey, beautiful," Floyd purred. "Where ya headed?"

"I need to run an errand," I replied. "I'll use it as my lunch."

"Want me to come along?"

"Actually, I do." He was almost as shocked to hear the words as I was saying them, but I didn't give him time to think. "Yes, please join me for lunch." I grabbed Floyd by the elbow and dragged him into the elevator. Luckily, it was a quick ride, and Floyd didn't manage to regain the shreds of his composure until after the doors opened on the ground floor.

"Where ya takin' me, baby?" he oozed. "Your place?"

"Yours is likely infested," I muttered as I stalked out of the building. I was walking too quickly for his stubby legs to keep up, and he was doing this weird little skip-hop while he panted like a dog. Unfortunately, neither of these activities interfered with his voice. While he was describing the many disgusting things we could do while still in the parking lot, Micah appeared before us.

"What is this creature?" Lord Silverstrand demanded, his voice booming. Floyd blanched, and possibly wet himself.

"A pathetic worm, not worthy of your notice," I replied, ignoring Floyd's feeble protests. "This company is a sham. They were set up to spy on my family."

Micah's eyes flamed, and he grabbed the front of Floyd's shirt. "Were you sent to harm my Sara?"

Amidst the babbling froth that erupted from Floyd, we deduced that he was little more than a hired thug. The operation, whatever this operation truly was, hadn't entrusted him with more than the basic info needed to complete his job. Floyd's mission was to hit on me constantly, and act as a filter to deter any men who approached me in public; it seemed that those in charge wanted me to stay single. With a pang, I wondered what had really happened with Bill.

"Would you like me to kill him?" Micah asked, once Floyd was done. Floyd, tough guy that he was, promptly fainted.

"I don't think he's worth the effort," I murmured. I almost felt sorry for Floyd as Micah pushed his unconscious form into the Otherworld; he was just a man trying to earn enough to survive. Then I remembered a few of Floyd's past comments, the drunken groping at The Room and sober groping in the break room, the never-ending propositions and innuendos, and all those sympathetic thoughts dried up and blew away. The Otherworld was a far better sentence than the creep deserved. After all, who knew what manner of beastie might beset him when he woke up? I hoped for a dragon. With talons. Long, shiny talons.

"Where are we going?" Micah asked.

"The Raven Compound," I replied. "If we want to spring Max, we need real magic." And I knew just where to get it.

chapter 15

Tires squealed and gravel flew as I hooked a tight corner into the Raven Compound's driveway. Micah said nothing but clutched the dashboard in a white-knuckled grip, and he'd gone an unflattering shade of green.

"You okay?" I ventured. I parked my mechanical alongside the main house, and Micah gave an audible sigh of relief.

"I am now," he muttered, leaping from the passenger seat onto solid ground. "Madwoman." He said it affectionately, so I ignored the implication that my driving was less than perfect.

"My mother can be kind of intense," I warned for the umpteenth time. By now, Micah probably thought I'd been borne by a hellbeast. "Just try to not let her get to you."

"Is she also an Elemental?" Micah asked.

"Most definitely. I think she might be of gold," I added, considering her blonde hair.

"Should I appear as a human?"

"No," I said, without thinking. Then I considered, and elaborated, "No. I want her to see you as you are." I reached for his hand. "As I see you."

Micah squeezed my fingers, and I felt the strength of our togetherness. Perhaps we really were an alloy, and therefore enjoyed the strengths of both and the weaknesses of neither. Together, we walked toward the front door in search of the only human I'd ever known to take on the Peacekeepers with a modicum of success: my mother.

Despite the fact that I'd grown up in these marble-lined halls, the opulence of the Raven Compound usually distracted me, not to mention newcomers; once, a pizza boy had let the pie fall with a splat as he stared into the foyer, oblivious to the hot sauce that splashed his ankles. Micah, steeped in Otherwordly glamour as he was, hardly batted an eyelash at the gilt trim, and I didn't even pause to assess whether the hydrangeas were in bloom. I was intent on finding Mom.

Not that she was to be easily found. We searched the kitchen, both parlors, and a good portion of the second floor. While I descended to the foyer, I groaned; was she really not home, today of all days? She was always home, being that she could hardly bear the outside world now that Dad and Max were gone. Then I looked through one of the oriel windows and spied a bit of movement in the backyard; there she was, weeding the vegetable patch. I felt foolish for not checking her favorite place earlier, but no matter. I'd found her.

I took Micah's hand and led him across the expansive, manicured yard to the only place Mom felt at home. There was something calming about working the soil, or so she always claimed, and on any passable day she could be found wearing her floppy sun hat, up to her elbows in compost. After the events of the last week I understood, more than ever, what she saw in gardening; truly, it's the little things that get us by.

She looked up at our approach and smiled when she saw me, that smile fading as her gaze moved to Micah. Wordlessly, she stood. Micah and I followed her to the kitchen. She flipped on the light over the sink while I started the dishwasher.

"The light obscures the camera," I explained to Micah, who was staring at the dishwasher in mingled amazement and horror, "and we're pretty sure the only bug is by the washer. Well, the only bug in the kitchen." Mom joined us in front of the washer, pulling off her gloves. "Mom, this is—"

"An elf," she finished, rather loudly, tossing her muddy gloves into the sink.

"Micah Silverstrand," he said with his most gracious bow. Mom looked unimpressed as she pulled off her hat, but Micah's own face was cast in wonder as her golden hair fell about her shoulders. "Is it truly you?" Mom only pursed her lips, so he asked me the same question.

"Mom, what does he mean?" I asked, but Micah answered.

"Queen Maeve," he said, his voice flat, certain. After another awestruck moment of staring at my mother, Micah turned to me. "Not only is your father Baudoin Corbeau, your mother is the Queen of the Seelie Court. Small wonder you possess such power."

"That was a long time ago," Mom said softly. "I haven't been to the Otherworld since—"

"Since you dragged Sadie and me out, that time we got lost," I finished. "The first time we went without Max." Mom nodded, remembering the grief-tinged fury of that last, unplanned trip abroad.

Then we were all staring at each other: my elf-man, the Lord of all Silver; my mother, Queen of the Seelie Court; and me. You'd think those two could have held it together, but they seemed to have been struck dumb. I sucked in a deep breath, and took charge.

"Okay. My mother is a fairy queen. I'm consort to a silver elf." Mom's eyes bulged at 'consort," but I kept going. "We'll deal with all this tomorrow. Mom, I've seen Max."

The color drained from her face. "He's alive?"

"Barely," I replied, and went on to detail his captive state, the human research facility smack in the middle of the Otherworld, and Juliana's involvement with the Peacekeepers. Her eyes went hard as stone—hard as metal, even—and she set her jaw like a warrior about to enter battle. Once my tale was complete, she turned on her heel and walked toward the front parlor. Wordlessly, I beckoned Micah to follow. He stared at the abrupt transition from the austere granite and polished steel of the kitchen to the cozy, inviting room, but we didn't allow him the opportunity for questions. Mom grabbed one side of the china cabinet as I latched on to the other, and we dragged the mahogany behemoth away from the wall.

At first glance, it looked like we'd revealed nothing more than slightly less faded wallpaper, until Mom tapped her fingers in a few vital locations. The wallpaper disappeared, revealing a staircase that descended into blackness. Very horror movie-esque. Mom immediately plunged forward into the murky, spiderwebbed darkness; after a moment, Micah and I followed, his hand protectively hovering over my mark. The faint glow of fey stones at the bottom showed the way, brightening as we descended.

No one had been down these stairs in years, probably more than a decade. When Dad had first gotten the call to war, he'd rounded up most of the family artifacts and stashed them here in the old basement, so named because it mirrored the footprint of the original house. When the house had been rebuilt around a century ago, the basement—then a humble wine cellar—was no longer convenient to the kitchen, so a new one had been dug. That left the original as little more than a receptacle for odds and ends—that is, until the war had begun.

Now the old basement housed my family's history. The government had confiscated a great deal, but if they'd only known what treasures lay beneath their feet, well, they probably would have gotten in a lot of trouble for missing such a trove. There were ancient spellbooks of every class, some little more than runes scratched onto badly cured hides. Others were priceless works of art, richly illuminated with gold leaf, inscribed on vellum; however, I'd learned the hard way that a spell's potency had little to do with the way in which it had been recorded. Each of these books was powerful, and each could blast your brains to bits if you weren't careful.

There were also more traditional works of art scattered about—well, traditional for the Corbeaus. There were paintings that held captured beings, still running about and pleading for release; enchanted rings and necklaces and, um, handcuffs; and a crumbling granite statue that was, in reality, a troll unlucky enough to have been caught out in the sun. Micah looked over the heaps of magical artifacts, pausing to admire a cut crystal decanter. He picked it up to watch the light dance off the facets, only to nearly drop it when he saw the remains of a sprite crumpled in the bottom.

"Oh, that. Unfortunate," Mom said, glancing over toward the dull thud of crystal on wood. "Poor thing couldn't breathe, once we replaced the stopper."

"Indeed," Micah murmured, respectfully setting the crystal coffin back upon the shelf. Mom, oblivious to the sprite's plight, plunged farther into the room and I followed, the fey stones coming to life with a quiet, brimstone-scented puff wherever we walked. She didn't have to tell me where she was going, because I could feel it. It was in my blood.

She was taking us to visit The Raven.

The Raven had died long, long ago, and an ancestor of mine had had it embalmed. *Well, the legend is a bit more colorful than that. It claims that my ancestor was a wizard without equal, and his pet raven accompanied him in all things, magical and otherwise. After a time, my ancestor learned that his faithful companion was the source of his magic. Eventually the bird had died, as all things do, but as my ancestor was preparing to bury his dear friend, the dead bird offered a bargain: take my name, keep my memory alive forever, and I'll bestow upon you untold power.*

Since we're all here, you can imagine that the wizard accepted. Now, whenever there's a moment of strife or a family member needs a magical boost, we speak to The Raven. That first Raven had not only shared his name with my family, but we bore his image across our flesh. Sure, there are other clans who have magical totems—the Coyote of Southwestern America, for instance—but none have quite the affinity, or power, of the Corbeaus.

Mom stopped abruptly before The Raven's tomb, a leaded glass coffin that I suddenly found eerily akin to Max's current resting place. After a brief moment, she stepped aside. "Sara, you must ask," she said, turning to face us. "The Raven and I, we've never really gotten along. Different sorts of magic, you see."

I nodded and looked beseechingly at Micah. "No, my Sara, it is not for me to petition your ancestor," he said, obviously having divined our purpose.

"I can't," I mumbled. "I can't even handle the little magic I have. If he gives me more, I won't know what to do with it."

"You're a powerful girl," Mom said, tucking a stray lock of hair behind my ear. "You always have been. When you were a baby, you'd make your dolls dance on their own, create working zoos with only your stuffed animals. Once, you conjured a genie to do your bidding. Then Max was gone, and it was all I could do to hold on to you and Sadie." She swallowed, her voice catching as she continued, "And The Raven is a part of you. He won't give you anything that would hurt you, Beau's daughter. He will only offer guidance." Mom gripped my hands. "The Raven will help you save Max."

I stared from Mom to Micah, terrified that they both thought I could do this. "Your mother will not let anything harm you," Micah said softly. "If I recall, Maeve was always one to kill her enemies rather than capture them. I cannot imagine that the Seelie Queen would lead her daughter into danger." My mother smiled wryly. "And," Micah continued, sliding his hand across my lower back, "I stand beside you."

My mark flared, whether from his touch or his words I could not tell, and confidence rushed through my veins. For the first time in my life, I was more than a Corbeau, more than a member of the Raven clan, more than Max's little sister.

I may be all those things, but I'm also so much more.

I smiled at Micah, then took my place before the glass tomb. "Raven," I began, "please grant me wisdom."

chapter 16

Twilight came, and under cover of darkness Micah and I left the relative safety of the Raven Compound and my fairy mother behind. I would definitely be asking her a few questions about *that* when we had the time. Now, we were hiding in the woods that encircled the stone prison that, in turn, encircled my brother.

As we crouched in the damp, decaying leaves, I considered how much my life had changed in such a short time. Only a week ago, I had been an office drone whose only indulgences had been caffeinated beverages and fast driving. I had pretended to know nothing of the ways of magic, had hidden my mark from anyone who might glimpse it. I had never hung out at a beach or even sunbathed in the park, never joined a gym, never worn any of the cute, fashionable shirts that might have ridden up and revealed my secret. I had been gifted with one of the strongest bloodlines in history, yet I'd spent much of my life wishing for the magic to just leave me alone.

No more would I hide. I was a Corbeau by birthright, and the daughter of a fairy queen.

I am a force to be reckoned with.

I slid my hand into Micah's, seeking a bit of warmth for my cold fingers. He squeezed reassuringly but didn't look away from the prison. And well he shouldn't, since we'd been waiting for the guards to change for the better part of an hour.

"Do you think it will work?" I'd asked back at the Compound. The Raven had given me one of its feathers, still glossy and black despite the many centuries since his death, along with the assurance that we would be able to leave the prison with Max in tow, unseen and unstopped by the guards. Of course, like all things magical, it had come with a hefty catch: our dreamselves could not carry the feather, thus making this rescue all the more dangerous.

"What does your heart tell you?" Micah countered.

"It's rather silent on the matter," I replied, though, in truth, it beat a quick tattoo against my breastbone. "But I do know that The Raven has never failed my family, not once, when we needed him."

Micah had smiled at that; in the Otherworld, the integrity of a long-dead bird was as good as gold.

Once we'd returned to the Otherworld, the rest of our preparations had been simple. First, we'd spent a good amount of time placing small pieces of metal in various pockets and pouches about our bodies, retrievable at a moment's notice, in case we needed to wield them either to strike a foe with added force or even build a wall. Well, in case Micah needed to wield it, since I was still limited to gently bending small portions of copper.

At first I didn't understand why the metal we secreted in our clothing was mostly iron. Micah had a quantity of silver within his body to call upon, and I'd assumed he would stay true to his metal. When I asked, he explained that it was far more effective to strike someone with iron than silver.

"Is that why Ferra's a queen?" I'd asked when he pointed that out. "Because iron is a stronger metal?"

"In a way. You don't find her to be the picture of royalty?"

I made one of those unladylike sounds that Micah so disapproved of. Really, he was just going to have to accept the fact that I was not very refined. "I always imagined a queen as a kind woman, who cared for her people more than anything. Ferra is not that sort of woman." An image of my mother appeared in my mind's eye; while I hadn't known she was a queen, Mom would move mountains for her family. I couldn't imagine her behaving like the despicable Iron Queen, not one bit. "And shouldn't the queen be a precious metal, like gold or platinum?"

He smiled ruefully. "Things are not always as they should be." I caught the sadness in his tone, and remembered the gold gaudily displayed in Ferra's palace, and the gold-lined oubliette. I also remembered that silver is a precious metal too, surely worthier of the throne than ugly old iron. But Micah didn't want to talk about it, and he turned his attention to the far more pressing task of breaking Max out of prison. As for me, I let him get away with his distraction technique. For now.

"It is getting inside that requires stealth," Micah murmured as we watched the guards. "Leaving shall be simplicity itself."

By simplicity, Micah meant that he intended to take Max and me along one of the metal pathways he used for traveling, much as he did in the Mundane World. In order to accomplish this, he'd tasked the silverkin with placing sufficient metal at short intervals between the prison and his home, almost like a trail of silvery breadcrumbs, to guide us to safety. Since the prison proper contained only a small amount of metal in the various electronic devices, and all metal had been removed from the soil underneath it, that was the best we could do.

I nodded, deliberately not speaking, or even thinking, about our impending escape. Micah was confident, and that was all that mattered. Never mind that it was a foolish, risky plan that centered on a dead bird's feather and a few pounds of iron filings. Never mind that it could very well end with Micah and me either dead or sharing Max's cell. Nope, not thinking about that at all.

Micah lightly touched my arm and jerked his chin toward the prison. The guard had finally retreated to a small side building the size of a garden shed; through the window, I could see him munching on a sandwich. Carefully, we rose and Micah wrapped his cloak around both of our shoulders.

"You're sure this will work?" I asked.

"It worked the last time," he replied. "They never saw who breached their puny wall."

"I thought you were your dreamself then."

"I woke as soon as I sensed you in danger." Huh. So Micah, in his wakeful body, had charged through a stone fortress full of enemies armed with terrible, terrible weapons, enemies with a special taste for Dreamwalkers at that, all for me.

I stood on my toes and stretched to kiss his jaw. He touched my hair but said nothing, not that I'd expected him to. He had to concentrate on blending in.

Micah referred to his cloak as his chameleon skin, but it wasn't really a lizard's hide. As near as I could tell, the fabric was woven from various plants with magical properties; close to the hem I could make out something like mandrake leaves, and the clasp was a curl of belladonna, complete with dark, shiny berries. The sum total of these plants meant that the cloak would keep Micah either warm or cool as needed, lend him speed if he were pursued, and hide him from his enemies. It was not like a cloak of invisibility, he'd cautioned me. Some things were quite rare, even in the Otherworld. No, this cloak worked more like a pencil eraser, blurring itself along the edges, so it was hard to tell where the cloak ended and the surrounding landscape began. If one looked directly at Micah one would see him, clear as day, but who looks directly at something that isn't there? This chameleon skin was a most useful garment indeed.

Gingerly, we made our way across the open space toward the imposing cinderblock wall encircling the prison. Unlike Micah's last visit, when he had rushed into an unknown environment hoping his illusion would hold, we were trying to be subtle. Conveniently, there was no door or fence, just an opening wide enough to drive a truck through, flanked by cameras and plastic spike strips poised to be flung under any uninvited tires. I wondered how well plastic fared against rubber.

My heart pounded so loudly I thought the guard would surely hear it, but he didn't look up from his lunch as we walked by the shed or as we stepped beyond the wall. A few steps later, Micah opened the door to the facility, and, as anticlimactic as it was, that was it.

We were in.

The halls, all of them an identical shade of elementary-school green, made me feel like a rat in a maze. I couldn't imagine how the labcoats managed to navigate the place without a map, but Micah strode purposefully ahead, making sure to drop a tiny speck of iron every few paces. When we reached the doors to the auditorium that held Max, Micah put another piece of our plan into play.

After I'd spoken to The Raven, my mother had rummaged around the dusty, morbid artifacts and produced a special gift of her own: a wolfhound's tooth. Similarly to the desiccated sprite, it was encased in a stoppered crystal decanter, the tooth's enamel long since cracked and yellowed with age. When I'd questioned her, she'd smiled wickedly and said that we would need a diversion. And, she'd added, she'd greatly prefer a diversion that would kill a few of her son's captors.

So we'd tossed the tooth near the hole in the wall that Micah had left during our last visit and taken up our vigil on the other side of the facility. Now that we were standing before the auditorium door, Micah smashed the glass jar, and we heard the monstrous wolfhound burst into being, the bloodcurdling screams as it launched itself at the nearest guard, its sharp Otherworldly teeth making short work of the plastic guns. Wrapped in Micah's cloak, we pressed flat against the wall as alarms sounded and the control booth emptied. The scientists rushed away, whether to help or hide, I didn't know. After the last labcoat had fled, Micah grinned.

"Come, love," he murmured, as he opened the door for me. "It's time for me to meet your brother."

At the sight of Max's pathetic form, my gut clenched. He looked far worse than the last time I'd seen him, which, I reminded myself, had only been a few days ago. He was still in that plastic cylinder attached to tubes and wires, but the green, viscous liquid had been drained away, leaving him naked save for the electronics wrapped about his limbs. I think the liquid had been keeping him warm, since he was now covered in gooseflesh. He was freezing but too tired to shiver.

Also, without the liquid I could see how gaunt he really was; his ribs jutted out painfully, and the pasty skin hung in loose folds from his joints and abdomen. How long had Max been kept in this science experiment gone wrong? How long had it been since he'd eaten real food or seen the sun? Too long; far, far too long.

I hoped we weren't too late to save him.

"I will kill whoever is responsible for this."

I hadn't realized I'd spoken aloud until Micah nodded. "We will."

Micah popped the flimsy latch on Max's plastic shell, but as I reached in to rip the electrodes from Max's skin, Micah stayed my hand. "Careful," Micah warned. "His dreamself may be held elsewhere."

What? How is that even possible? I swallowed and tried to keep from screaming. "What should we do?" My voice was hoarse, my arms trembling; we were so close to freeing Max, and now there was *one more fricking obstacle!* Micah, of course, remained as calm as ever.

"I shall call him back." Micah gently nudged Max's shoulder, then placed a hand on his forehead. Max cracked an eyelid, only to squeeze it shut again.

"He's here," Micah proclaimed, and we plucked away the feeder tubes and wires and other torments attached to my brother. Even without them, the evidence of his imprisonment was obvious, from the small circles crusted over with blood that patterned across his torso, to the greenish bruises where plastic bars had held him in place for—how long? Weeks, surely. Perhaps months, or even years.

Yes. I would like to kill every last one of these Peacekeepers.

When we removed the last bar, Max slumped forward into me, his flesh so cold I gasped. My fingers flew to his neck, and I sighed in relief when I found his pulse. Micah hefted Max's limp form and wrapped him in the chameleon skin cloak. Luckily, we wouldn't need to worry about blending in for our escape. "The feather," Micah murmured.

I pulled out The Raven's gift and placed it where Max had stood, still unsure what a feather was supposed to do for us, but I didn't have to wonder for long. As soon as the feather was out of my hands it began to shimmer and melt, its mass increasing, changing color and shape. In the space of a few heartbeats, it had grown into a perfect replica of Max, with all the assorted tubes and wires properly attached.

"Oh," I mumbled, too stunned to do more than stare; the replica was perfect, right down to the bruises and gooseflesh. Micah, apparently used to such magical occurrences, grabbed my hand and pulled me toward the door and out into the corridor, Max slung over his shoulder. We could still hear shouts and growls from the far side of the prison. I imagined the wolfhound was ripping the guards to shreds. Good.

We walked out of the Institute for Elemental Research just as easily as we'd walked in and made our way to the nearby tree line. When we reached the first few scraps of metal, I asked Micah the fateful question.

"Are you sure you can do this?" I gasped. While we had been planning at the Raven Compound, and in front of my mother, Micah had been confident that he could travel along the metal path carrying both Max and me. Later, when we were alone, he'd admitted that he'd never done so with a single companion, let alone two.

"I should be able to," he replied, settling Max more comfortably across his shoulders.

"Should?" Should was just a nice way of admitting that he had no idea. Should was *not* acceptable. I grabbed his shirt and pulled his ear to my mouth. "Listen, if you have to leave someone behind, leave me. Just get Max out of here!"

Micah touched my cheek, the sun breaking behind the thunderclouds in his eyes. "My Sara, I will never leave you."

Before I could respond, there was a commotion in front of the Institute's main entrance. Micah didn't turn to see what it was. Instead, he threw an arm around my shoulders and we leaped into the metal.

Traveling via metal is…weird. As near as I can tell, the molecules of your body separate and merge with the metal, passing you along, slipping and sliding between protons and dodging electrons as they whizz by in their orbits. Remember chemistry class, and how they talked about covalent bonds? Well, imagine taking a covalent bond, instead of a bus. I know. Weird.

The beginning of the journey was the worst; we were sucked into a piece of metal, then forcibly thrown into the next piece. More than once, I thought I'd be sick, and I might have been if not for Micah. He expertly steered us from one metallic island to the next, his calm never wavering, his arm around me never loosening.

Once we'd made our way into the woods surrounding the prison, the metal breadcrumbs lay closer together; Micah, who'd recently freaked over my driving, took off at a breakneck pace. When we finally arrived before Micah's silver house, I had the distinct feeling that my stomach was still a few feet behind me. Micah, in order to set down Max, unwound his arm from my shoulders, which turned out to be a bad idea. Still off-balance from our swift travels, I tumbled to the ground.

I hadn't realized that any time had passed when I opened my eyes, my first sight Micah's concerned silver gaze. "Where's Max?" I mumbled. I looked around and wondered why we were in the knot garden.

"The silverkin have brought him indoors." Micah gathered me to his chest, and I felt him shudder. "My Sara, don't ever frighten me in such a way again."

"What happened?" I dimly recalled our journey, but we were here—Max was here—so everything must have worked out.

"Once we leapt free of the metal, you fainted. It has taken me more than an hour to revive you." His embrace tightened, and I had to admit that it felt good to have him worry about me. No one but my mother had worried about me like that for over ten years.

"I'm okay," I murmured. "Really." I got to my feet only a bit unsteadily. "Let's go see Max."

With Micah's arm about my waist, we went indoors and found my newly-freed brother lying upon a makeshift bed of cushions on the hall's main floor. He was still out cold, but the silverkin attended their strange guest as if he were a prince. They had washed his raw, tender skin, and dressed the many puncture wounds. Now they gently chafed his limbs, warming him to a normal temperature, and had tucked a myriad of shawls and blankets, along with the coverlet from Micah's own bed, about him. A bowl of steaming broth waited on a side table, ready for him when he woke.

I sank to my knees next to him and took his hand. "Hey," I murmured. I couldn't believe he was here, alive and (mostly) whole. I'd dreamed of finding him since the moment he'd been arrested. Weird. What girl's dream come true was her older brother?

Maybe I had been his dream too, because Max opened his eyes. "Sara?" he rasped. I smiled, and he blinked. "Sara, where are we?"

"We're still in the Otherworld, at Micah's home." Micah came to stand beside me. Max's eyes flicked over to him for the barest second, widening in shock and terror.

"He's a freakin' elf!" Max sat bolt upright and grabbed my shoulders. "Sara, it's not safe! You have to get away from him!" That outburst brought on a fit of coughing; once his hacking subsided, I continued.

"Don't worry, I'm his consort!" Wow, that sounded stupid.

"You're his *what*?" Max, weakened by his many years of captivity, still managed a disapproving tone. Mom would be proud—at least, if I told her about it. "Never mind," he grunted. "Why are we here? I'm supposed to be at the Institute!"

"Max, we rescued you," I soothed. "You're safe here. They won't hurt you anymore."

"I went there on purpose!" Max, far past exhaustion, leaned forward and propped his elbows on his knees, resting the weight of his head in his hands. "I was distracting them," he muttered.

"What the hell from?" I demanded.

He blew out a deep breath. "All magic is governed by one of the elements. You know how we're metal?" I nodded. "Every generation, there's one really powerful member of each element born. An Inheritor of Power, they're called. The Peacekeepers thought it was me."

"It *is* you," I said. "Isn't it?"

"No." He raised his head, eyes wide and jaw trembling. I'd never seen Max scared before. "It's Sadie."

chapter 17

"Well, this has gone from bad to worse," I grumbled. Shortly after Max's revelation that Sadie was the true metal Inheritor, and that he'd gone willingly to the Peacekeepers in order to keep her (and me) safe, he had succumbed to his mingled fatigue and anxiety. He'd only managed a few spoonfuls of broth before leaning back and closing his eyes; ironically, just before he fell asleep, Max had been ranting away about the regimens of drugs that had been pumped directly into his bloodstream. Some had kept him in a REM state for extended lengths of time, for days or even weeks, while others had held him on the edge of deep sleep so he was unconscious for hours, but never actually rested—then, they had added stimulants to his pharmaceutical cocktail and kept him awake until his eyes were like sandpaper. All of this had been done to study the effect of dreamwalking on various areas of the brain. Yeah, it would probably be some time before those poisons worked their way out of his system.

Micah draped an arm across my shoulders and kissed my temple. "You did not know," he murmured against my skin. "Would you describe wanting your brother returned to you, whole and safe, as a fault?"

My ignorance of the facts didn't make the present situation one bit more appealing. I glanced over at the bed where Max slept fitfully; after the unsuccessful feeding, the silverkin had moved him to a bedroom close to the kitchen, apparently so they could rectify his lack of a proper meal as soon as he woke. As I watched Max's eyes move to and fro behind his lids, the small, jerky movements of his arms and chin, I wondered if my brother would ever again sleep peacefully.

Probably not, not after what I've done. After Max's initial freak-out, we'd calmed him down and convinced him to eat something. While he'd spooned the thin broth past his cracked lips, he had enlightened me as to my stupidity.

"They always knew it was one of us," he'd mumbled.

"Who're they?" I asked. He shot me a knowing glance, and my curiosity deflated like a balloon. Yeah. The Peacekeepers.

"The Inheritor of Metal hadn't been located in any of the other families," said Max. I must have looked utterly befuddled, because he explained, "You can track where the heir is likely to appear, based on the strongest bloodlines. There are charts."

Of course. Charts. "What makes you think it's Sadie?"

"I don't *think*. I *know*." Cocky, cocky Max. He slurped some more of the broth before he continued. "I never thought my first meal when I got out would be chicken soup."

"Really?" Max had never been picky about food, but then, his diet at home hadn't been nutrients pushed through a tube. "Want a steak or something?"

He grinned. "Only if it's rare and bloody."

I wrinkled my nose; he'd always eaten his meat extra rare to gross me out. I explained what steak was to the silverkin, and asked for a side of mashed potatoes and asparagus for good measure. As they scurried off, Max resumed his tale.

"They'd gotten to the rest of the families before us," Max continued. "Then Dad told me—"

"*Wait*." Max dropped his spoon, and Micah, who'd been lurking about the doorway while I spent time with my brother, rushed to my side. I think my commanding tone might have sounded a bit like Mom. "Dad?"

Max didn't pretend to misunderstand me. "Yeah. Dad and I stayed in contact for a few years after the wars."

Ever take an elevator up to the top level of a skyscraper only to let it plummet back to the ground floor? "What about Mom?"

"I don't know. I never asked." Great. I gestured for him to continue; clearly, this bit of family drama wasn't getting sorted out today, and possibly not within my lifetime.

"He said that when Sadie was born he'd felt it, the huge swell of her power. He was able to mask it while he was home, but then he got called up by the war mages. She remained hidden for a while, but then the old Inheritor died."

"Olquin," Micah said. "A good man, he was."

Max glared at Micah but kept his tone civil. Barely. "Once Olquin was gone, the Peacekeepers started turning things upside down looking for the new Inheritor. Dad had told me it was Sadie, but she was just a kid!" He shook his head, raking a hand through his shaggy hair. "How's she doing?"

"Good. She's in school, going for a master's degree. She wants to be a research librarian."

Max laughed soundlessly. "Sounds like Sadie. Always with her books and stories." He fell silent for a time, fingering the ornate handle of the spoon. I wondered if Micah had made it. "I couldn't let them take Sadie. They would have broken her."

"A noble sacrifice, but foolish," Micah stated. Max's head snapped up, but Micah continued, "No matter what you had done, eventually it would have become apparent that you are not the Inheritor. In fact, if one sensitive to magic is in close proximity to either of your sisters, they would be able to feel her powers."

"Sadie doesn't even know how to use her power!" Max defended. "She was never trained!"

"Neither was I, but Micah found me," I said quietly. "He knew that I'm an Elemental and a Dreamwalker."

"Sara's power is quite remarkable. It washes off her in waves, no less strong than the sea," Micah said, a gleam in his eye not unlike pride. "Her strength went so far as to make the Iron Queen uneasy."

"Ferra?" Max asked. My recently captive brother was on a first-name basis with the Iron Queen? "Sara, you've got to stay clear of her! She hates our family!"

"Really? Why?" I remembered Micah telling me that Ferra was Dad's enemy, but I'd never asked why. Ferra seemed like the kind of woman who cultivated enemies the way others tended roses. "Is that why those iron warriors were following us after the first time we escaped the Institute?"

Micah and Max shouted in unison, both demanding why this particular bit of information was late to the party. "I was distracted," I mumbled, remembering rainy escapes and accommodating oak trees. "So, what's her deal?"

"I don't know," Max replied. "What I do know is that, after the war ended, Ferra acted like she was an ally to the remaining Elementals. Then she got pissed, and then Dad was gone…"

His voice trailed off, so I finished for him. "Then, you took matters into your own hands." Max only nodded, looking so despondent I couldn't stay mad at him. Shortly thereafter, the Peacekeeper drugs knocking around his system had sent him back to sleep, a luxury I didn't think I'd have for some time yet. It was all right; Max had done the best he could. He'd been a fifteen-year-old kid desperate to protect what was left of his family. It was time for me to handle things.

Now, as Micah and I watched Max sleep, his steak gone cold and his potatoes a congealed lump of glue on the bedside table, we planned our next move.

"Should we get Sadie from college?' I asked.

"Yes," Micah murmured. "She and Maeve should be brought here to safety."

Micah didn't mention Dad. Max had claimed to have lost touch with Dad a few years after the wars had ended, but a girl could hope. "Then what will we do?"

"Then, we wait. We will let our enemies move first, and we will watch. We will learn. When we know all that they can teach us, we will strike." That speech was similar to the one he'd given me while we had been hidden in the oak after I'd dreamwalked my way to Max. I wondered if Micah was some sort of elfin warlord, experienced in rallying spirits. I hoped so, since I felt like we were in need of someone who'd seen more than a few battles.

I rested my head against Micah's shoulder. "Have I told you that I love you, Lord Silverstrand?"

"You haven't."

I reached across his body and laced my fingers with his, the words he'd spoken in the Clear Pool echoing in my mind: *we are much stronger together than apart*. "Consider it done."

chapter 18

By the time Max woke, as cranky as a wet cat, Micah and I had prioritized our next tasks:

1. Get Sadie
2. Get Mom
3. Determine what the Peacekeepers are doing with Dreamwalkers (and all Elementals)
4. Try not to get killed

Numbers One and Two would be relatively easy, and we already knew part of the answer to Number Three. The trick would be adhering to Number Four. Of course, both Micah and I wanted to leave Max in the Otherworld while we completed Numbers One and Two. My darling brother, true to form, wasn't having any of it. I was remembering that he was definitely the stubborn one.

"Max, you can*not* go," I said. Again. "You're too weak from being cooped up in that plastic box for so long!"

"Am I?" he demanded. To prove his point he glared at a metal bowl, and we watched it crumple like so much paper.

"Your body is what's weak," I bit off. "Small wonder, after ten years as a lab rat."

"I wasn't always in the tube," he pointed out. "In the beginning, they were good to me."

"Were they?" I sneered.

"Yeah, they were. Besides, unlike *you*, I know how to use my power!"

"Then why didn't you escape?" I demanded. "Why weren't you ruling the Otherworld, O Great and Powerful Max?"

"There wasn't enough metal," Micah said quietly. Our sibling rivalry was getting on his delicate elfin nerves. "They hobbled him. Or perhaps it was a punishment." Micah turned to Max and fixed him with his silver gaze. "What had you done to displease them?"

Max's eyes narrowed, but he answered, "You're right; they kept only the bare minimum of metal in the Institute. I couldn't have broken out if my life depended on it." He was quiet for a moment, fingering the edge of his sleeve. "One day, a few years into it, I found a piece of metal in the exercise yard. It was nothing really, just a scrap. So I took it, and made a little sculpture for one of the techs. It was a lily; she liked the lilies that grew near the fence." He was silent for a moment, staring at his hands. "I thought she liked me."

"Perhaps she did," Micah murmured. He regarded Max for another moment, then turned back to me. "We should bring your brother."

"What?" I demanded, while Max snapped, "Don't talk about me like I'm not here!"

"Maeve is unlikely to accompany us without good reason," Micah explained. "What better reason than her long-lost son, returned? Also, once Max's disappearance is discovered, your government will likely begin monitoring the known portals, as well as your family. Therefore, it would be foolish to retrieve your sister and bring her here only to make a second journey between worlds in order to bring your brother to the Raven Compound."

I chewed the inside of my mouth; between the two of them, I was mad enough to spit. Micah's logic was sound, but that didn't mean I had to like it. "Fine," I grumbled, glaring while Max smirked. "But if you die, don't bitch to me!"

With that I stalked out of the room, not slowing until I reached the knot garden behind Micah's palace. Exhausted, exasperated, and all other sorts of "ex"-emotions, I sat heavily on one of the stone benches near the bathing pool. I heard Micah and Max follow, then stop while they argued in hushed tones. A few moments later, only one set of footsteps approached me. Surprisingly, it was Max.

"Hey," Max murmured. I ignored his voice, so he stood in front of me. *Jerk.* "You know we're right."

"Max, you can barely stand. You can't even eat anything!" After he had woken, he'd made a valiant effort to consume his steak dinner, but that had ended… badly. He'd joked about just how spectacularly he had vomited, downplaying our concerns, and asked for more broth. "I didn't get you out of there just to let the Peacekeepers kill you in some other way." My voice caught on the last word, and I covered my face with my hands.

"They won't kill me." His voice was hard as nails, and that was the Max I remembered. I hazarded a glance at him, and his eyes burned like hot coals. "They hurt me, but that was because I let them. They needed me too much to kill me." He dropped his eyes. "I'd do anything to keep you and Mom and Sadie safe. I thought I was doing the right thing, biding my time, waiting for them to slip up, but now… now, all bets are off." He flexed his fingers, wincing when his knuckles cracked. Yeah, he was really fit to strike terror into the hearts of millions. My thoughts must have been written across my face, because he sat beside me and draped a gaunt arm around my shoulders. "Listen, I don't need to stand. I'm just as powerful sitting down. And I don't need to eat, either. For now, I can get by just fine on chicken soup and coffee. Before you know it, I'll be eating peanut butter and bologna sandwiches. With pickles!"

I laughed, remembering all the gross concoctions we used to make each other eat. Whoever didn't puke was declared the winner, inasmuch as one could win that kind of event. "Yours were always the worst," I said, remembering an unfortunate incident with chocolate frosting and sardines.

"I am the master." Max grabbed my hand, his flesh baby-soft. I guess that green liquid had had some benefits. "C'mon. Let's get the little one."

Now, let's get one thing straight: Sadie is not *like me. She's always gotten straight As, and she's been on the dean's list since her first semester at college. She never got in trouble, never made Mom roll her eyes and pray to the old gods for guidance, never practiced magic after we were told to stop. From the day she was born, she was always the perfect baby sister, and we all loved her for it. She was sweet, and kind, and saw the good in every person and situation.*

Like I said, we're not all that similar.

What's more, I was about to waltz into her life and turn it upside down. More than anything, Sadie loved school. All her life, she'd wanted to be either a college student or a librarian; now she was a college student studying to be a librarian. And after today's visit, she wouldn't be either.

I'd say that Micah somehow sensed how horrible I felt about this, but the way I was dragging my feet made it pretty obvious. "It is for the best," he murmured.

"I know." I glanced at him and somehow managed not to do a double take. He'd once again altered his appearance to look human, but the close-cropped brown hair and round ears just didn't seem normal to me, not anymore. His voice was the same, though, so I looked around at the crumbling, pre-war architecture and imagined that he still looked like an elf. My elf.

"This is a lovely spot," Micah murmured. We were crossing the center of the campus, a carefully tended lawn called the Old Green. It was about half an acre of grass dotted with majestic old oaks; I wondered if Micah knew any of them. Surrounding the Green stood stately red brick buildings, which had been covered in a few centuries' worth of ivy until last fall, when it had become known that a local coven was using the vine in their full moon rituals. The ivy had been hauled off and burned, and eleven students had never been heard from again. "Why are there so few natural places among your people?"

I sighed and took his hand. At least he still felt like my Micah. "Natural places are full of herbs and flowers, the very things used for spells. The Peacekeepers don't want anyone to have access to such contraband. Even our food is grown in greenhouses, hydroponically. Without sunlight or soil," I explained, in response to his raised brow. "My mom had to get a special permit for her vegetable patch."

Micah pulled me against him, wrapping his arm around me as he kissed my hair. "With such restrictions, how am I to collect flowers for my consort?"

"I don't need flowers." I cast my eyes downward, suddenly warm-cheeked and shy.

"You do." Micah halted and turned me to face him. "You deserve flowers and jewels, and everything that is sweet, soft, and beautiful. I seek only to please you."

"You do please me," I said, my voice husky. I glided my fingers across his jaw; somehow, he was taller in his human guise. When our skin made contact, Micah assumed an invitation and kissed me hard, right there in front of half of the student body. I whacked his shoulder but he refused to release me, even when the catcalls grew too loud. Then we heard the warning bleep from a drone, and our romantic interlude was done. Public displays of affection were frowned upon these days, especially at an institute of higher learning.

"I'm glad," he murmured, a spark of silver glowing in those temporarily brown eyes. I tugged him toward Sadie's dorm, and he fell into step alongside me. "Perhaps, once this matter with your sister is sorted out, I shall please you further."

I gave him my best seductive look. "Oh?"

"I'm considering overthrowing your government."

I stopped so abruptly I almost fell on my face. My heart pounded and I broke out in a cold sweat, but a quick glance didn't reveal any Peacekeepers within earshot. "Why... Why would you do that? What makes you think you even *could* do that?"

"I know something of exchanging one regime for another." He pulled me close and whispered, "Why do you think we Elementals are ruled by metal and not stone?"

His eyes had completely reverted to silver, his gaze as hard as metal. Sure, I wanted the Peacekeepers gone—who didn't?—but that was in the same category as wishing away the twin devils of cold weather and the heating bill. I never really thought they'd go away, I just didn't want to deal with them.

I licked my lips, suddenly parched under Micah's intense gaze. He parted his lips, whether to utter more treasonous ideas or kiss me, I never knew. More catcalls caused him to release me; we were quite the attraction that morning. Since we couldn't really talk about such matters out in the open at a government-run university, I twisted free of his embrace and entered Sadie's dorm. Silently, we traversed the halls and two staircases; Sadie lived in a tiny single room shoved in the far corner of the building. After a not-at-all nervous knock later, Sadie opened her door and found me standing next to Micah. Or rather, she saw Mike.

"Sadie!" I said, a little too loudly. For the cameras, you know. "This is the guy I told you about."

"Mike?" she asked, blinking. "The one you said was a jerk?"

"Yep." I pushed inside her dorm room, Micah following me.

"Jerk?" he questioned, frowning.

"I was mad." Sadie shut the door, and I mustered my widest grin. Ironically, grinning like fools was the only signal we had. I mean, we couldn't very well wink, or use a secret handshake, those being the clichés of the spy world. We'd long ago agreed that whenever one of us needed to signal the other, a shit-eating grin was the way to do it. "So, are you all packed for our weekend with Mom? I bet she's already cooking!"

Her brow wrinkled; Mom might have grown exotic and heirloom vegetables, but her cooking was limited to opening and reheating. Sadie, trouper that she was, played along anyway. "Not yet. Help me?" Sadie grabbed a tote bag, but I shook my head ever so slightly. Hesitantly, she yanked one of her suitcases from under her bed. Still acting like the ever-helpful big sister, I took out the other suitcase and began tossing in the contents of her dresser drawers. Wow, she owned a lot of socks.

"We're not coming back," I breathed in her ear. Her jaw tightened, her sole betrayal of how she felt, and I felt her disappointment like a stab in my gut. Sadie loved school, and getting her master's degree meant the world to her. Suddenly, I was the jerk.

"What does Mom have planned for us?" Sadie asked, just a shade bitter. Despite her worldly university lifestyle, Sadie hated change of any sort.

She'd lived in this tiny dorm room since freshman year and still used the blankets from her childhood bed.

"Oh, you know," I demurred. "Just things for the trio."

Her hands froze, clutching a sweater in mid-fold. "Trio?"

Ah. She remembered. "Yep, all sorts of things for the Trio of Destruction. Kitchen mishaps, small fires, maybe we'll even round up a few stray cats." I absently scratched my elbow, recalling a time we'd done just that and had ended up with a flea-infested house.

Sadie grabbed my wrist, effectively ending my rambling. "Truly?"

"In the car." Relief washed over Sadie's features. "Yeah, let's get these bags in the car. Mike?"

A slightly peeved Micah grabbed the suitcases and set them by the door while I surveyed the rest of the room. Sadie owned so many books she could open her own library, degree or no. "Which books are we taking?"

Sadie grabbed a few and stuffed them into her tote bag. Reading material secured, she ducked into the bathroom, emerging a moment later with a robe slung over her shoulder and clutching a toothbrush. "I'm ready."

Another trek across the Old Green later, during which Micah and I got an encore of catcalls, we stood at my mechanical. While Micah stowed the bags in the trunk, Sadie climbed into the back seat and saw our gaunt, disheveled, but alive brother.

"Hey, kid," Max mumbled. "Tell me about school."

chapter 19

While Sadie's reunion with Max was somewhat restrained *(you just never know when a drone or flesh-and-blood Peacekeeper will happen by and peek inside your car)*, Mom was long past attempting to curry the government's favor. After a tearful, sappy, not-at-all-awkward for Micah family reunion, the topic turned to what we should do next.

"We all need to go to the Otherworld," I said. We were in the front parlor, since it was the only way to get to the old basement, which was, in turn, the only place we could hide. We knew the Peacekeepers would come looking for Max eventually, and while we'd had this last hour to ourselves, our time was quickly running out. Max, Mom, and Sadie were crammed onto the mustard-colored loveseat, while

Micah and I snuggled in the matching chair. "At Micah's, we'll be safe."

"I still don't think I'm the Inheritor," Sadie murmured, staring at the flocked velvet wallpaper. The Rococo pattern had an oddly hypnotic effect. "Wouldn't I know?"

"You have always known," Micah stated. He was back to his natural elfin appearance, all sinewy arms and poufy hair. "For your transactions, you prefer to deal in coin rather than paper?"

"Uh, yes."

"Your bed is brass. In fact, all of your furniture and shelves are metal, without any wood or stone. The implement used to maintain your teeth is stainless steel, as is your comb." Sadie, along with the rest of us, stared at Micah in mingled amazement and horror; we'd spent less than five minutes in her dorm room, yet everything he'd said was true. Micah was a metal elf in every sense of the term to have noticed such details. "You surround yourself with metal, because it soothes you. Metal does your bidding. It yearns to please you."

Sadie dropped her eyes, the first hint that she'd intentionally surrounded with metal. Maybe she'd even used her power on some of the objects, intentionally or not. Good for her. "But I don't know enough to be the Inheritor. I-I just want to work in a library."

"You already know everything you will ever need," Micah said firmly. "Your gift is born of your heart and resides in your soul, not in a dusty book." He leaned forward, now speaking to Sadie alone. "You will be an excellent Inheritor, easily as great as Olquin was. Perhaps you will be greater. You will do well by your family. Of this, I am certain."

Sadie blinked and hid her face, more than a bit overwhelmed by Micah's impromptu speech. "And you called him a jerk," she muttered.

"I was wrong," I said, gazing into his silver eyes. "He's wonderful."

"All right, you two," Max interrupted as he got to his feet. "We need to move. Now. I'd rather not be here when the drones come knocking."

"But what about the Corbeau artifacts?" After all the trouble we'd gone through to keep the old basement a secret, the thought of Peacekeepers getting their greasy paws on my family heirlooms made my skin crawl. "We can't just leave them here. And what about The Raven?"

"I'll cast the wards," Mom said, calmly. "Beau and I set them up a long time ago. As for The Raven, he will accompany us to the Otherworld."

"Almost like a homecoming," Sadie murmured. I wondered what, exactly, she'd been reading about in these library-themed courses.

Mom held out her hand to Sadie, claiming only the two of them were needed to activate the wards. Good thing, since I knew absolutely nothing about wardsmithing; it must have been one of the perks of being the metal Inheritor, or maybe it had to do with being the youngest Raven. Anyway, Mom went on to explain that the wards would not only obscure the old basement from anyone not of Corbeau blood, they would also push the room ever so slightly into the Otherworld. That way, our family history need never be unavailable to us, no matter which world we inhabited.

"You sure we can't help?" Max asked again. He was a bit miffed at being left out of the first magic worked at the Raven Compound in years.

"Only two of us are required to see to the wards and collect The Raven," Mom affirmed. "You three go on. Sadie and I will be along directly."

Mom and Sadie descended the dark basement steps as Micah, Max, and I turned to leave. Max swiped the picture of the three of us as kids, lounging under the fairy tree, but I didn't call him on the theft. I was glad someone had remembered it.

Once we were outside, Micah wrapped his arm around my waist and Max threw some daggers with his eyes. This overprotective brother crap was getting real old, real fast, but I knew better than to confront him directly. Instead, I shocked him into silence.

"Mom's a fairy queen," I mentioned, ever so casually.

Max stopped dead in his tracks. "*What?*"

Finally, I wasn't the last to know something.

chapter 20

The Corbeau family's return to the Otherworld was, thankfully, uneventful. Sadie, cradling the well-swaddled Raven against her breast, gazed about in barely concealed wonder, and well she should. It was the first time she'd returned since we were kids and had attempted to rescue Max, and her wide eyes made it apparent that she, like myself, had come to believe that the Otherworld was little more than a half-remembered dream. I laughed to myself; here I was, pretending to be the jaded older sister, when I'd only made my own return to the Otherworld about a week ago.

My musings were interrupted when we happened upon a tree that looked similar to a magnolia, only the leaves were shiny and metallic, like enameled brass, and the blossoms sparkled like pink sapphires.

"It's beautiful," I murmured, my aloof façade forgotten as I stared at the tree that seemed, impossibly, to be made of metal and jewels. Micah, again wearing his bemused smile, caught my hand and pressed it to his lips.

"My eyes rest upon a far lovelier sight." Wow. Cheesy, yes, but my heart did a little somersault at his endearment. Sadie, however, was unimpressed.

"You two are horrible," she commented, adding an eye roll for extra effect. My darling baby sister.

Micah, however, was unperturbed by her outburst. "What makes us so horrible? Is it because we both freely admire beauty wherever we find it, or because I can hardly let a moment pass without my Sara's touch?" Before she could respond, we turned a corner and entered the lush gardens behind Micah's home. I heard Sadie's breath catch in her throat, and I smiled. It seemed that she freely admired beauty, too.

Max, for his part, was quite taken with the Bright Lady of the Clear Pool. "She's always just hanging out in your backyard?" Max asked Micah, after we'd explained why a naked woman lounged by the water. After a short explanation to Micah as to what a backyard was, he affirmed (to Max's utter joy) that he'd never known the Bright Lady to leave her pool.

"You humans never should have turned your backs upon magic," Micah continued. "Without magic, you deny yourselves untold wonders."

"We didn't turn our backs on anything," Max grumbled. "It was taken away from us. Stolen! Everything worth—"

"Max. Enough." Mom's voice was soft, but he fell silent nonetheless. More than a decade apart from her son hadn't diminished Mom's authority in the slightest.

However, her authority over me seemed to have waned. I touched her elbow, and we fell back behind the others. "You knew?"

Mom pursed her lips and looked away. I understood that she didn't want to talk, but we deserved some answers. I *needed* answers. "The day Sadie was born, we knew. You should have seen Beau." She closed her eyes for a moment, remembering a time when we had been a happy, whole family. "He was proud of all of you, but to have the Inheritor of Metal in our own family was an untold honor. Sadie's the first to be born into the Raven clan."

"Why didn't you ever tell her?" I pressed.

"I'd already lost my mate by the time she would be able to understand, and then I lost my son. I couldn't bear losing one—or both—of my girls." She opened her eyes then, her clear blue eyes that I'd always wondered about. Her gold hair could have marked her as metal, but her seawater gaze could have been the manifestation of a water affinity. Now I knew the truth: my mother was not wholly human.

Hmm. If she wasn't, then, neither was I. Had Micah somehow sensed my fairy blood?

Forget that, and all the accompanying questions. I was mad: mad at Mom, and Dad, and *especially* Max, even though he'd paid for whatever deceit he'd used against us many times over in his imprisonment. I mean, I was used to the government lying to me, but I never thought my own family—my own *mother*—would keep such vital information from me. I turned back to Mom, ready to tell her how wrong she had been, that we should have been told the whole truth from the beginning, but one look at her and my anger fizzled away. Her gaze, resting on the back of Max's head, was mingled relief at the return of her son, as well as longing. It was then that I saw it: Max's bright, coppery hair, his short, lean build, the nimble way his feet and hands moved. Add a full beard, and Max could be Dad's twin.

Her husband is still missing, I remembered with a pang. *Dad.*

That my parents had adored each other had never been in question. I remembered how they used to look at one another, the stolen kisses when they thought we weren't watching, the lazy days when the two of them had cuddled on the couch while we watched movies or on the lawn chairs in the backyard while the three of us made our own trouble. Dad had been gone a long time, yet Mom had never looked for another companion, never even gone on a date; once, Sadie had suggested it, and from Mom's reaction you would have thought she'd suggested stuffing The Raven and roasting him for dinner.

As I remembered my parents' strong, loving bond, my eyes traveled to Micah. Instantly, he felt my gaze, turned around, and smiled. After we'd fought, I'd been lost without him, even though we'd been apart for less than a day. I couldn't imagine how Mom had managed without Dad for all these years, the pain and loneliness she must have endured.

We needed to find Dad. I hooked my arm into Mom's and rested my head on her shoulder. I still felt a bit betrayed, but at least I understood why she had kept things from us. I couldn't say I wouldn't have done the same.

"I've only known him a week," I mumbled.

"That's how it is with Elementals," Mom soothed. "When you find your mate, you know, and no one else will ever compare."

The five of us had crossed nearly the whole of the garden, and we now approached the edge of the bathing pool. As always, the Bright Lady reclined on its bank, gloriously naked and busily tending her hair. Now that we were only a few paces from the pool, Max was unashamedly staring at her, until he stumbled and nearly face-planted. It occurred to me that he had only been fifteen when he'd been arrested, and I wondered if he was still as innocent as I'd been only a short time ago. He'd said that he hadn't always been held in that medical device, but I couldn't imagine Max dating one of the labcoats. Not to mention that Peacekeeper-prisoner relationships were probably frowned upon.

Still, from the way Max blatantly ogled the Bright Lady, I wondered if he'd ever seen a naked woman before. "You should ask to borrow her comb," I suggested.

"Why would I need her comb?"

"If she likes you, she'll let you use it. Don't you want to know if she likes you?" Mom shot me a look as Micah tried not to laugh. Yes, the Otherworld was truly a strange and wondrous place.

Once we were inside Micah's silver chateau, Max remaining sadly comb-free, the silverkin immediately presented themselves, seeing to our every comfort. They swiftly herded us into the front sitting room, and we settled on the vine- and cushion-covered settees, with The Raven perched upon his own special cushion. The 'kin were in the midst of passing around a steaming beverage, the Otherworld's version of hot buttered rum, when my consort turned to my brother.

"Max, I believe it is time for you to tell us what you know." Max looked as if he might decline, but Micah's tone made it clear that he wasn't making a request.

"What do you want to hear?" Max mumbled. "That I'm an idiot, or that the Peacekeepers are going to win?"

"Haven't they already won?" I said, while Mom exclaimed, "You're not an idiot!" Mom and I stared at each other, then she reached over and grabbed Max's hand.

"You only tried to help your family. That is the most noble act one can attempt," Mom soothed.

"Maeve is correct," Micah stated. "There is nothing, not in this world nor the Mundane, more important than one's family. You did an admirable thing by taking your sister's place." Mom whispered something in Max's ear, and he nodded. After another gentle prompt from Micah, Max continued.

"Funny thing is, fey stones really did start the war. It was the head of the power company who started all the fuss, saying that a few enterprising Elementals were stealing the food right from his children's mouths. After a few years of no one paying enough attention to him, he changed his tune and claimed that those born of the elements were less than human, and that all we did was fight with other Elementals. He claimed that we were a danger to everyone else. To the *real* humans." Max exhaled heavily and supported his head in his hands. "What always got me, got Dad, was that they said we were less than them. I mean, aren't we all just people?" Max fell silent again, but only for a moment. "After a while, the 'real' people started to listen."

Max went on, occasionally supported by Mom's affirmations, and told a story of bigotry and xenophobia. In the space of a decade, Elemental and Mundane humans had gone from a peaceful coexistence to one filled with animosity and distrust, at least on the Mundane side of things. The Elementals hadn't seemed to care what the Mundanes thought—about them or anything else.

"See, that was the real problem," Max said. "The Elemental-born—us—we thought we were untouchable. After all, when you can wield fire and stone and metal with just a thought, how could a Mundane really hurt you?" He fell silent, shaking his head. "We were wrong. We were so wrong."

His voice shaking just a bit, Max went on to detail the weapons the Mundanes had developed to capture and torture us, the plastic guns and manacles and holding cells specially engineered to render Elementals powerless. Simultaneously with the stockpiling of such vile objects, anti-Elemental factions had spread across the country with a religious-like fervor.

"I do remember the factions," Micah interrupted. "But they had existed for many decades. Centuries, perhaps. As I recall, most of the world ignored them. What occurred to change that?"

"You mean what rang the bell that started the fight?" Max leaned back in his chair and shot Mom a glance. "The President's son was born with a mark, and his nanny ratted him out to the media."

"What?" Sadie and I gasped in unison. Sadie continued, "The Law states that the ruling body is always made up of Mundanes! That was recorded when our country was first founded, so Mundane and Elemental could live together in peace. The checks and balances were meant to keep both sides equal, regardless of ability." Sadie left off that, before the days of the Law, rogue Elementals had been known to enslave Mundanes, not that the Mundanes who spent the time to learn magic handling treated us any better; there were plenty of cautionary tales about Elementals being taken captive by Mundane magic users. I guess you could say it was the never-ending war that had preceded this war, which, despite all the government propaganda, was far from over. At least we'd had a few calm centuries in between.

"I know," Max agreed. "It was a mess."

"Wait," Micah interjected. "Even if the woman had been Elemental-born, an Elemental mark is only passed down from the father. Either she had lain with one other than her mate, or your President was false."

"They tried to hide the baby's ability, but word got out quickly," Mom said. "First, the President's wife claimed she'd been raped by an Elemental. Of course, there was no report of the incident, and no one quite believed her. I mean, if a woman in her position had found herself in such an undesirable state, there were things she could have done. Adoption, erasure…"

"So, what was done?" I prompted. I'd never been so attentive in school, and with good reason. This was the true history of my people we were learning, not the recycled garbage we'd been taught in history class.

"The President was hauled before the Senate and publicly stripped," Mom said. "It was on live television. We all saw his mark; it was air, as I recall. Then everything went to hell."

Mom was silent for a moment, the images of that long-ago scandal flitting behind her eyes. When she continued, she relayed the ensuing fallout from the President's secrets. "Those factions—the ones everyone had brushed off as bigots and fools—started up again," Mom continued. "They were louder than they'd ever been, only this time far more people were paying attention."

"They said the President was a spy," Max grumbled. "As if an Elemental needs to go through all the trouble of infiltrating the government to spy on Mundanes when we could just dreamwalk!"

"You mean, to learn what they know," I said. That made Max, Micah, and Mom look at me as if I'd sprouted another head.

"I'm not sure what you mean, love," Micah murmured.

"The government," I said. I looked to Sadie for support, but she was as confused as the rest. "They say that the government takes Dreamwalkers to use as spies. That if you dreamwalk inside a person's head, you instantly know everything they know."

I don't know what emotion was greater, my mortification at Max and Micah's laughter, or relief that Micah hadn't been reading my mind. "That's not exactly how it works," Micah said, his eyes still twinkling.

"Yeah, sis," Max chimed in. "Worried your boyfriend knows all your secrets?"

Ignoring the hot blood seeping up my neck, I motioned for Max to get on with his story. "Despite what Sara thinks she knows about dreamwalking," he said with a pointed look toward me, "we didn't do any spying. We should have, but we were busy proving that we were nobler than the Mundanes."

Micah nodded, then asked, "Is this when the Inheritors began disappearing?"

Disappearing? "Yes," Mom replied. "Fire—Soledad—was the first to go. She was a crotchety old girl, never one to compromise, never one to take a bribe. Beau was certain she'd been killed."

"Then Air disappeared," Max continued. "What was his name? I remember him being called Avatar—"

"Heh. Avat-air!" Four sets of eyes glared at me, and I slunk down in my chair.

"Jorge, I believe," Mom murmured. "He was a good man. They were all good people. The war mages didn't want to fight, but what else could they do? Elementals were being picked off. It was either join up or be put to the sword."

"'Join?'" Sadie blinked rapidly. "Join what, exactly?"

When Mom and Max's only reply was a nervous glance, Micah spoke. "Please. I, myself, have wondered what the Mundanes have been up to for far too long."

"The Peacekeepers aren't against magic," Max said. "They're all for it. Problem is, they don't want just anyone wielding it. They want it all for themselves."

"Then the President wasn't a spy," I murmured. "He was a plant."

Max nodded. "Been that way since the Compacts were signed. Only, the last President never let his personal staff know that he was an Elemental."

"Foolish woman, that nanny was," Mom spat. "That fame-grubbing harlot's bigoted view of her charge's nature ruined the lives of many children and tore my family apart."

Max leaned across the table and grabbed Sadie's hand. "This is why we didn't tell you, kid," Max murmured. "They would have hauled you off to the Institute. They *did* take me, thinking I was the Inheritor."

"And you let them," Sadie bit off, her face like stone. "My life has been a lie, all because you thought I couldn't handle the truth!"

"No, baby, no," Mom murmured. "Your life has been safe because we shielded you. I intended to tell you once you were done with school."

"Really?" she snapped. "Interesting claim, since I'll never know if you're telling the truth."

"Believe what you wish," Mom retorted. She would have said more, but fell silent when the silverkin's leader approached Micah. He reminded me of a shepherd, herding his little shiny flock about the chateau, so I'd started calling him Shep.

Now, Shep chattered away to Micah in the lilting tones all the silverkin used. Even though their language was still difficult for me to follow, Shep was clearly upset about something.

"It seems that the Mundane humans have assembled some sort of a war council at the Institute for Elemental Research," Micah explained for the benefit of those of us not fluent in silver-speak. "They've accused the Iron Queen of absconding with their prisoner," he added, with a nod to Max.

"Ferra?" Mom spat. "What would she want with Max?"

"She's tried to capture me before," Max mumbled. "Or at least, that's what they told me." Max sat heavily, rubbing the back of his neck. "In the beginning, it wasn't so bad. In the Institute, I mean. I had my own apartment; I could go outside…" He fell silent, memories of the beginning of his incarceration playing behind his eyes. An incarceration he'd willingly gone to, to keep Sadie and me safe.

"The Institute was attacked six, maybe seven years ago," he continued abruptly. "They said it was Ferra. I never really knew if it was her, but there were iron warriors. I guess it must have been her."

"What did they do you after the attack?" Mom asked, gently.

"At first, nothing much. I couldn't go outside alone, but that didn't really matter. Even before the attack, I wasn't allowed to leave the courtyard. Then, they caught me messing with a leftover bit of metal from the iron warriors, and everyone freaked. Said I was planning something with Ferra, but that wasn't true."

"The sculpture for a girl," I murmured.

Max laughed mirthlessly. "It was a lily, about the size of my thumb. That's all it was, yet they insisted it was a tool to destroy them."

"They wouldn't listen to reason," Mom said. Slowly, Max shook his head.

"No. They sure didn't," Max mumbled. "They didn't listen, not at all."

We all fell silent, awed and humbled by Max's experiences. It was Micah who spoke next. "When was the metal removed from the facility?"

"The piece I had?" Max asked. "For all I know, it's still there."

"Impossible." Micah stood and paced, rubbing his chin. "There is effectively no metal at all in the building, not in the walls, ceilings, or floors; their blinking devices only have the barest amount. The guards wield plastic weaponry. There is no metal in the ground, not even a trace amount, not even in the bedrock below. It is at least a half mile in all directions before one encounters a sizeable portion of metal again."

"Are you sure?" Max demanded.

Micah's face was grave. "Yes. I am certain."

"Huh." Max flopped back against the cushions. "I always assumed I couldn't feel the metal anymore because of the drugs. Why would they bother with all that?"

"I assume to keep you from wielding your power," Micah said.

"No," Max said, shaking his head. "They kept me so weak I couldn't conjure a fart." He went on, detailing how they had kept him immobile until his muscles had atrophied, feeding him only thin liquids until he was so malnourished he could hardly speak.

"They knew it wasn't you!" I burst out. "They sucked away all the metal so that when the true Inheritor did come for you, she'd be trapped!"

"That's…" Max began, then fell silent. He knew I was right, since that's exactly what *had* happened: I had gone to rescue my brother, and they'd almost had me. If not for Micah, I'd have been stuffed in a nice plastic coffin for all eternity. The only flaw in their plan had been that the wrong sister had come a-calling.

I laced my fingers with Micah's, and put voice to the question we were all thinking. "What does Ferra have to do with this?"

"Easy," said Mom. "She wants to be the most powerful Elemental, so she wants to eliminate the true Inheritor. It's why she went after Beau in the first place. The Ravens have always wielded metal."

"I hate her," I grumbled. "I hated her the moment I met her."

"She probably hated you, too," Mom said. Then she downed her eye-wateringly alcoholic beverage in one gulp, stood, and regarded us. "Well? Let's go."

"Go where?" I asked.

"To the Institute," she replied, as if it were obvious. "I'd like to watch Ferra and the bastards who held Max destroy each other. And," she added with a grin that made my blood run cold, "I'll be there to deal with whoever's left."

chapter 21

When we got to the Institute for Elemental Research, the edifice's true purpose was revealed. It really was a stone fortress, equally as able to fend off an invasion as to keep Elementals imprisoned. Guards prowled the battlements, scowling as they brandished their plastic weaponry. I shivered, amazed that I'd managed to enter and leave such a place twice. Hopefully, there wouldn't be a third time.

If Micah's nerves were the least bit shaken by the sight before us, he hid it well. Instead of staring at the Institute in mingled horror and revulsion, as we Corbeaus were, his hand kept finding its way to my bottom.

"Stop," I whispered, indicating the others with my eyes. "What's gotten into you?"

"Your strange attire is growing on me," Micah murmured, a not-unpleasant glint in his eye. True to their promise, the silverkin had managed a few pairs of jeans, all of which fit like gloves. That, coupled with the boots and form-fitting shirt (with a hood!) they'd also provided, and I looked pretty hot, if I did say so myself.

"I thought you didn't like it when I dressed like a man," I teased.

"My Sara, there is nothing manly about you," he replied, punctuating the comment with a gentle squeeze. Since an interlude behind the tree line was out of the question, I hiked his hand up to my waist and turned my attention toward the Institute.

The evil acts committed within those stone walls—which I now saw were topped with plastic razor wire, likely for Max's benefit—had certainly left their mark, the accumulated misery swirling about it in cold, cold waves. I shivered and wished we had a stone Elemental with us, a strong one, one who could reduce this place to rubble in the blink of an eye.

"They have one," Max mumbled. I hadn't realized I was speaking aloud. "They keep her in a special glass cylinder."

"Is she still in there?" I asked.

"Yeah. They pumped the cylinder full of cement, just to see what she'd do." Max fell silent, his anguished eyes telling us exactly what the results had been: slow, painful suffocation. Just because we have an affinity for one element doesn't mean we don't need the rest. I resumed staring at the Institute, trying to glean what the Peacekeepers were up to.

"Still no metal," I murmured, eyeing their plastic weapons. "If Max is gone, why not bust out the real guns?"

"What they wield now has proven quite effective," Micah stated. "Or, perhaps they fear Max's return. And yours."

I doubted that, since they must have figured out that Max wasn't the Inheritor years ago, which meant they were trying to keep metal away from yet another Elemental. I swept my gaze around the perimeter of the vale and found my answer. I made a mental note to tell Mr. Handsy not to distract me during recon.

"Ferra." I nodded toward what was obviously the Iron Queen's encampment. Who else would erect tents of iron, cold and glaring in the midday sun? I saw her warriors milling about the perimeter, some blackened and pitted from the many battles they'd fought, others gleaming as if newly forged. Then the queen herself stepped out of the central tent, and I rolled my eyes in disgust.

"Does she *ever* wear a shirt?" I muttered. In true Iron Queen fashion, Ferra was wearing gleaming steel vambraces and greaves, along with a winged headband that reminded me of a cartoon I'd watched as a kid. Completing her battle gear was a low-slung armored skirt made of half-moon-shaped metal plates that reached the tops of her thighs and the crimson cloak she'd worn when she'd received us in her castle. Oh, and she was completely, totally topless. You could hear Max's jaw unhinge as it thudded against the ground.

"Time was, we all went to battle thusly," Mom murmured, a wistful look in her eye. I reached back in my memories and recalled the stories Dad used to tell us about an Irish queen famous for her cattle raids.

"Weren't you cold?" I ventured.

"At first, but the battle quickly heats you. And," she continued with a wink, "blood washes off healthy flesh much more easily than garments or armor, no matter how fine."

"Huh." I put aside the image of my bare-breasted mother bellowing war cries as she drove her chariot over the hills and concentrated on the situation at hand. "So, Ferra's going to battle the humans?"

"So it would seem," Mom murmured.

"But, why?" All eyes turned to me. "Why would she be against them now? The only thing that's changed is that Max is free. Wouldn't she be happier with Max locked up? I mean, aren't you a threat to her?" Max's brow furrowed, but he nodded. For my older brother to agree with me, things must be truly dire.

"What's more, how does she know you've escaped?" wondered Mom. "You haven't been free two days yet, and surely these gaolers don't broadcast their failures. She must have someone on the inside."

We all murmured in agreement, but no one had any grand ideas of how to proceed. Then, Micah suggested, "Why don't we ask her?" As if that was a good idea.

"Ask her? Why would she tell us anything?" I demanded. "She's not exactly friendly with us."

"No, she isn't." Micah watched Ferra for another moment, his brow furrowed, then he murmured a few words to Mom and handed her his cloak before turning and making his way down the ridge. Not knowing what else to do, I followed him to the edge of the Iron Queen's encampment.

The iron warriors crossed their spears before us, barring our way to the camp. "My consort and I wish to speak with the queen," Micah stated.

The warrior on the left turned toward Micah, his neck creaking. I remembered last night's rain and wondered if he needed oiling. "Name?"

"Lord and Lady Silverstrand," Micah bit off. I threaded my fingers through his, willing him to be calm. It certainly wouldn't do to have an outburst here; I mean, if we were going to freak out and cause some damage, I'd really like to damage Ferra in the process. The iron warrior cocked his head, then after a moment's contemplation both guards simultaneously raised their spears. Micah didn't look at them as we passed, nor did he look around the camp. I did, and I wished I hadn't.

Unsurprisingly, the Iron Queen's retinue was somewhat less than honorable. Granted, there were naked pixies and fauns frolicking around Micah's home at all hours, but that was consensual frolicking. A quick glance around the camp revealed acts of debauchery one didn't usually see committed out in the open, and certainly not in full daylight. Creatures I'd heard of, such as dwarves and centaurs, along with fantastical beings I hadn't met in my worst nightmares, cavorted in varying stages of dress, alone and in groups. I nearly gasped aloud when I saw a female with a long, scaly tail lasso another female— with her tail, mind you—and plunge its barbed tip into her. The victim only laughed.

These foul acts weren't limited to the flesh and blood creatures, either. An iron warrior, obviously male, had been strung between two trees and was being methodically sawed apart by two iron females. His screams grated like unoiled pistons, like that final grunt an engine gives before it seizes up. The females taunted him, claiming it was time he was taken down a size. I shuddered when I realized what they were resizing.

A pathetic whimper wafted toward me, and I turned to see a pixie bolted down by her wings to a splintery wooden plank. Her miserable face betrayed that, unlike the rest, she wasn't a willing participant in this mess. Her captor, a burly Satyr whose furry legs were smeared in blood and gods knew what else, teased her mercilessly with the tip of his riding crop. Suddenly, he ripped off her dress and howled as he turned around and held his trophy aloft before his companions. While they were so distracted, I flicked my wrist and loosened the metal bolts that held her down. Sensing what might be her only chance at freedom, the pixie leapt into the air and didn't look back.

It was hard to ignore the bellowing, infuriated Satyrs, but I managed. I didn't know if Micah had sensed my part in the pixie's freedom, but it was too late to ask. We had reached Ferra's tent, and she emerged to greet us.

"Micah," she drawled, "I hadn't hoped to see you today. Come to offer your assistance?" As she spoke, Ferra gathered her cloak over one shoulder and thrust her torso forward. Yes, I wanted to scream, we can see your naked breasts! But I didn't, though I wondered if I'd bite through my tongue. Micah, wonderful man that he is, never let his eyes leave Ferra's face.

"The silverkin alerted me to a disturbance," Micah said levelly. "My consort and I wondered if we could offer assistance." Ferra's gaze flicked over me for the barest moment.

"Mmm. She's a bit more of a consort now, eh?" *Can she really see the difference, or is she just taunting me?* Micah's impassive face betrayed nothing, but I felt the hot blood spilling up my neck.

"My lady, please advise me as to how we may assist you," Micah repeated. After another look up and down my body, Ferra turned and beckoned us to follow. We left the camp and halted when we reached the crest of the ridge, the Institute situated in the vale beneath.

"The mortals have lost a prisoner," Ferra explained, gesturing to the stone building, "and they seem to think I have him."

"Why would they think that?" Micah wondered. "Surely you have no use for human criminals."

"He's not a criminal. He's the Inheritor of Metal," Ferra informed us. Micah nodded slowly, squeezing my fingers so hard I thought they'd break.

"Then we shall locate him, and keep him out of the mortals' reach," Micah declared. "How difficult can it be to locate a lone man?"

"Oh, but I already have." Ferra's voice was sickly sweet, like molasses, and I followed her gaze across the ridge to where my family waited. "I feel it when the Inheritor is near; his power calls to me, yearns to be with me." Ferra turned to me and looked me in the face for the first time. I wished she hadn't. "Little Sara, I feel your brother."

"Turn around and you can see him."

The three of us turned in time to see Max drop Micah's chameleon skin cloak, which had let Max, along with Mom and Sadie, slip into the Iron Queen's camp with her creaky guards none the wiser.

"Max," Ferra drawled. "Aren't you looking terrible. And aren't you foolish, being that you weren't the Inheritor the mortals thought you were. And, you have, at last, led the true Inheritor to her end." Ferra grinned like a jack-o-lantern left out long after the first frost and flicked her wrist, but nothing happened. No guards responded to their queen's command. None moved, or called out, or did anything. They remained motionless. Panic skated across the Iron Queen's face, but it was quickly replaced with a sneer.

"You can't fight me for long," Ferra purred. "You know that I've always been stronger."

"Not stronger than me," Sadie whispered. I saw her hand where it tightly gripped Max's, her whitened knuckles. Ferra's eyes widened; had she really thought that Sadie, the true Inheritor, wouldn't try to resist her? "You've never been stronger than me."

"That was always the problem," Mom spoke up. "You wanted to be the most powerful, but you're not. You never were more than lowly old iron. That's why you helped the mortals hold Max."

"I have never assisted the mortals in any way!" Ferra shrieked.

"But you have," Micah said calmly. "Who but the Iron Queen could so thoroughly remove all traces of metal from where Max was held without disturbing the soil or rock beneath? Few have such power. The Gold Queen did, once, before you stripped and defiled her. I do, but I was not a party to this plot. That leaves two individuals: you, and the Inheritor. I don't believe Sadie imprisoned her own brother."

"Baudoin could have—" Ferra began.

"Say Beau's name again, and I'll kill you," Mom growled. Fury blazed in Ferra's eyes, but before I could make my own witty comment, my stomach lurched. Sweat broke out across my forehead and neck, and I knew I was about to faint.

"Your mistake, my lady, was in thinking us as foolish as you," Micah corrected, a note of sadness in his voice. I tried to get Micah's attention, but my voice wouldn't obey me. "I thought the Iron Queen was wise enough not to underestimate her foes. Not that we ever should have been enemies."

Ferra's face was red as her cloak, then purple. Her fury radiated out in palpable waves, squeezing my heart and lungs. I felt like I was floating—no, falling. Falling over a cliff... Too late, I realized that that was what she was doing: she was sending every molecule of metal in my body straight to my lungs.

Then, I did fall, my body no longer responding to my commands to get up, to scream, to run away. Hell, if I couldn't breathe, what was the point of all those other acts? I flailed about like a fish washed up on the shore, flopping and gasping while Micah and Mom shouted, until I spied the jewel in the center of my palm. *I didn't know what sort of help she could offer, if any, but a favor is a favor, no?*

I stared at the jewel, having lost the strength to close my hand, and visualized the Bright Lady's face. In the next moment I sputtered, though not because Ferra was crushing my lungs. A wave had just swept across us, the cold water having scrubbed me free of Ferra's influence.

A wave?

I spluttered and coughed as I struggled to rise, only to fall back, frustrated. But at least I was breathing. It was another moment before I noticed a similarly drenched Micah roll to a sitting position. He drew me against him, pushing the soaked hair back from my face while I choked up an entire lake's worth of water.

"Breathe, love," Micah rasped into my ear. I nodded, trying to ask him where all this water had come from, but my words degraded into hacking splutters. He understood me anyway and jerked his chin forward.

Impossibly, or maybe because she was of iron, and therefore much heavier than Micah or me, Ferra still stood, the water swirling in little eddies about her hips. Then, as quickly as it had appeared, the water drained away, and I saw something truly amazing. Ferra had begun to rust.

It was hardly noticeable, and I probably only saw the telltale brownish marks by virtue of my closeness. But they were there, manifesting in dark smudges, slowly spreading around her ankles and knees. Right at her joints, right where she was weakest.

I twisted around to ask Micah if he'd ever seen such a thing and promptly vomited brackish water all over his chest. Furiously embarrassed, I started a babbling apology, only to be drowned out by a familiar, squeaky voice.

"I have favored this one!" I turned toward the shrill chirping and saw the Bright Lady standing in front of the rusty queen, hand on her hip, waggling a finger in Ferra's face. I looked at my palm; the jewel was gone. Talk about cashing in your favor at the right time. "I will not abide those I favor being harmed!"

Ferra opened her mouth, whether to protest or call out a curse we'd never know. Instead of words, a horrible creak issued from Ferra's lips, followed by the sound of metal scraping against metal. Impossibly, the Iron Queen's chin had already rusted through, her lips now swollen and flaking. The rust quickly spread downward to her shoulders, then her weakened ankles collapsed and she fell onto her side.

The water got inside her. I marveled at how quickly Ferra's sleek form had been reduced to so much garbage, but then, that's all she really was. Garbage.

"Are you unharmed?" I looked up and met the Bright Lady's sea-colored eyes, her usually placid features now creased with concern.

"I am," I affirmed. "Thank you. You have saved my family. I do not know how I can ever repay you."

"Lest you forget, I owed *you* the favor," she replied. "However, I would not complain if you sent that one to my pool." She gestured toward Max, and between her suggestive glance, and Max's mingled embarrassment and elation, I laughed so hard I started sputtering again. Micah rubbed my back, and by the time I was done coughing, the Bright Lady was gone.

"Back to her pool, I assume," Micah replied when I asked. He helped me to my feet, and after I assured

Mom I hadn't drowned, we turned to regard Ferra. She'd been reduced to little more than jagged metal, twitching convulsively as her limbs succumbed to the rapid oxidation.

"Will she die?" I asked. Uncharacteristically brave, Sadie prodded Ferra's rusty heel with her toe. The Iron Queen tried to lash out, but her leg was too corroded to do more than twitch.

"I don't know," Micah murmured. "Without aid, most definitely, though I cannot say what could assist her. Our queen has found herself in a rather dire circumstance."

Mom strode forward, planted her foot on Ferra's chest and mercilessly pushed her onto her back. "What can you tell me of Beau?" Mom demanded. Ferra responded with a malicious grin. Mom, not seeing the humor, crouched beside Ferra and spoke quietly, murmuring in her ear like a lover would. Only there was no love between my mother and Ferra.

"You know that I can save you. Of all of us, only I have the power to halt the corrosion that spreads through you. I can make you whole again. Beautiful, even." Suddenly Mom's hand shot out and she grabbed the Iron Queen's chin. Mom's thumb poked through the rusted flesh of Ferra's jaw, dislodging a few teeth.

"But, I do hate you," she seethed. "I'd much rather watch you rot than do anything to preserve your filthy hide. So, unless you can offer me sound information with regard to Beau, I don't care what happens to you."

Ferra's grin widened, creakily stretching her mouth as rust flakes floated to the ground. Then she spat, disgorging a measure of brown liquid, like water that had lain stagnant too long in an iron pipe, onto Mom's foot.

Mom looked pointedly from Ferra's crumbling mouth to the stain on her shoe. Wordlessly, she released Ferra's chin and walked away. The rest of us watched, mesmerized, as the Iron Queen disintegrated into the ground. A few heartbeats later, all that remained of the fearsome ruler was a pool of filthy water.

"She's really gone," Max mumbled. "I thought she'd live forever. Strong as iron, you know?"

"We all thought her stronger than death," Micah agreed, then he launched into a cautionary tale about not underestimating one's enemies. I hardly heard him as I kept my eyes trained on Sadie. The poor kid. Just a few hours ago she'd been studying for her degree in library sciences, a normal college girl with her life laid out before her. Now, not only was she the Inheritor of Metal, she was a fugitive in the Otherworld. No Corbeau could go back to the Mundane realm, not while magic remained outlawed.

Then again, it hadn't been so long ago that I had been an ordinary office worker, spending happy hour at The Room, drowning my sorrows as I pretended that magic didn't affect my life. Though I'd never admitted it, I had been miserable. From the day Dad had left us to join the war mages, my life had stopped, and I'd been holding my breath, just waiting for it to start up again.

Today, I was (almost) Lady Silverstrand. I was happy and loved, and my family was so much closer to whole. I could breathe again.

We were all going to be just fine.

I laced my fingers with Sadie's, but she didn't turn to look at me. When I asked what was up, she jerked her chin toward the object of her gaze. There were Peacekeepers moving around on the roof of the Institute for Elemental Research, and one in particular was staring at me.

Juliana.

Juliana was the best friend I'd ever had. She'd been there for me when I was failing Mr. Belhumer's algebra class, terrified that Mom would ground me if I brought home an F. She'd been there for my first dance, first boyfriend, and when that boyfriend dumped me. When I'd walked into REES to find that Juliana was the office manager, I'd thought it was the best day of my life.

What an idiot I'd been.

Now, I understood that I had never been more than a pawn to her. All those years of friendship had been the worst sort of falsehood. Juliana—if that was even her name—was nothing more than an agent of the government, a two-faced Peacekeeper, whose sole purpose was to make life hell for me and my family.

"I knew it wasn't Max," Juliana called from her perch on the battlements. "Still, I did everything I could to keep him safe."

An image of Max, unconscious and shivering in the plastic coffin, flashed behind my eyes. Yeah. My brother had been real safe in her care.

"If you come after my family, I'll kill you," I said, matter-of-factly. "If you approach us, even step in our direction, I'll kill you." I turned to walk away, assuming we were done. Like I said, I was an idiot.

"Sara, listen—"

"No!" I rounded on her, seeing that she was now flanked by guards armed with their puny plastic guns. "You listen! I trusted you! I confided in you! All for nothing!"

"I was always your friend! That was real!"

"Real?" I spread my hands to encompass the scene: a stone fortress built by humans to house their magical captives in the Otherworld, a military armed with weapons specially modified to capture Elementals, my broken family, and my horribly tortured brother. "Is this what real friendship looks like?"

"Believe what you want," Juliana said. "I know the truth."

I shook my head and looked at the ground. "Whatever." As I started to walk away, she called after me.

"I can't let you leave."

"How exactly will you stop me?" I countered. Juliana gestured, and the militiamen melted out of the trees. Drones rose from behind the stone wall, their harmless cameras replaced by long, sharp weapons, like bayonets.

"Where did they come from?" Sadie squeaked.

"Portal," Max replied. "They're all over the woods." Micah began his rant about the Peacekeepers carelessly using all the magic they'd forbidden to the masses, when Juliana started up again.

"It doesn't have to be this way," Juliana yelled. "We don't need to fight. We can work together."

"This is you working together?" I eyed the drones, still hovering just above the wall. "You want us all in our own plastic prisons?"

"We need to learn how your power works! If we can isolate the part of the brain that generates an Elemental's power, like Max's—"

"No!" The mention of Max's name pushed me over the edge. No one, least of all this traitor, was going to harm my family again. I raised my arms as white-hot pain flashed inside my mind. Again, I was falling.

When the pain subsided, Micah and I were seated on the ground, his arms fast around me as he held me upright, and there was a metal wall between me and Juliana's crew. A metal wall?

On closer inspection, it wasn't just a wall, but a dome. It curved over the Institute, effectively trapping the Peacekeepers in their own house of horrors. Good.

I assumed that Micah, or maybe Max and Sadie, had created the wall to protect us, but that wasn't the case.

"You did it, my Sara," Micah informed me. "You grasped Ferra's tents and warriors and reshaped them into what you see before you. Truly, it was most impressive."

I gazed at the metal wall and saw the remnants of a warrior's leg here, a shield there. There were even a few flattened drones, but I was too exhausted to be amazed by what I'd done. "Do you think it will hold them for long?"

"I don't know," he admitted. "I imagine they have ways to escape, but surely your display will give them pause before any Peacekeeper attempts to harm you and yours."

I realized that my fingers were clutching Micah's in a death grip. I looked up and saw Mom, Max, and Sadie watching the two of us with worried faces. And they should have been worried, since we couldn't go home again. We, the Raven clan, the most powerful Elemental bloodline still in existence, were now outcasts from our own world.

But was that so bad? I thought of my Mundane life, my lame job, my tiny apartment. All of my good memories had happened at the Raven Compound, except for those involving Micah. Every thought or deed that had ever made me smile was a direct result of the four people with me now. I didn't need to return to the mortal realm, not now or ever.

What's more, I thought of all I had now. A man who loved me, a family that was almost complete, and a shiny silver mansion to hang out in, not to mention all the silver servants. Really, my life had never been better.

"Good," I said, as Micah pulled me to my feet. "Let's go home."

acknowledgements

It never ceases to amaze me how many people it takes to produce one little book; editors and publicists and copy editors and cover artists and even more editors. I mean, when you get right down to it, a book is just a heap of paper glued together. Who knew that these heaps of paper entailed so much work.

Now, all of our combined efforts—the editing and the angsty calls and the stressful emails, and yes, a few tears here and there—have been collected and distilled into this bit of paper you're holding. Or maybe to a few blips on your ereader, whatever.

If I thanked each and every one of the people who helped make Copper Girl a reality individually, it would take another book (not to mention more work), so let me personally thank the one person who was there for me through all of it, and saw me through to the end: Robb. Love you, baby.

Call of the Jersey Devil

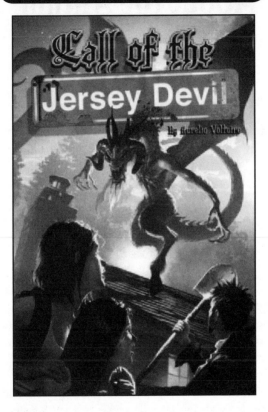

Four Goth teens and a washed up musician get stranded in the Pine Barrens and discover that New Jersey really is a gate to Hell—and if they don't do something, being banned from the mall is the least of their worries.

About the Author

Jennifer Allis Provost writes stories about faeries, orcs, elves, and the occasional zombie. She's a native New Englander who lives in a sprawling colonial along with her beautiful and precocious twins, a dog, two cats, a maroon-bellied conure, and a wonderful husband who never forgets to buy ice cream. As a child, she read anything and everything she could get her hands on, including a set of encyclopedias, but fantasy was always her favorite. She spends her days drinking vast amounts of coffee, arguing with her computer, and avoiding any and all domestic behavior.

Find her on the web at jenniferallisprovost.com.